A HERO BORN

JIN YONG

Legends of the
Condor Heroes I

A HERO BORN

Translated from Chinese by
Anna Holmwood

St. Martin's Press ≈ New York

First published in the United States by St. Martin's Press, an imprint of St. Martin's Publishing Group

A HERO BORN. Copyright © 1957 by Jin Yong (Louis Cha). English translation copyright © 2018 by Anna Holmwood. Illustrations copyright © Jiang Yun Xing. All rights reserved. Printed in the United States of America. For information, address St. Martin's Publishing Group, 120 Broadway, New York, NY 10271.

Jacket endpapers: Chang Jung Shan

www.stmartins.com

Library of Congress Cataloging-in-Publication Data

Names: Jin, Yong, 1924–2018, author. | Holmwood, Anna, translator.
Title: A hero born : a novel / Jin Yong ; translated from the Chinese by Anna Holmwood.
Other titles: She diao ying xiong zhuan English
Description: First U.S. edition. | New York : St. Martin's Press New York, 2019.
Identifiers: LCCN 2019016755 | ISBN 9781250220608 (hardcover) | ISBN 9781250220615 (ebook)
Classification: LCC PL2848.Y8 S513 2019 | DDC 895.13/52—dc23
LC record available at https://lccn.loc.gov/2019016755

Our books may be purchased in bulk for promotional, educational, or business use. Please contact your local bookseller or the Macmillan Corporate and Premium Sales Department at 1-800-221-7945, extension 5442, or by email at MacmillanSpecialMarkets@macmillan.com.

First published in the Chinese language as Shediao Yingxiong Zhuan in 1957.

First published in the English language in Great Britain by MacLehose Press, an imprint of Quercus Publishing Ltd., a Hachette UK company.

First U.S. Edition: September 2019

10 9 8 7 6 5 4 3 2 1

CONTENTS

INTRODUCTION

DEAR READER,

It begins with a storyteller, with news from the north, a tale of crushing defeat and humiliation, a great Chinese Empire in tatters and fleeing south.

It begins with a court corrupt to the core, willing to sacrifice the Chinese people to the invading Jurchen tribes for the chance of gold and escape.

It begins with two patriots, two farmers self-taught in the martial arts, and one Taoist priest determined to avenge their deaths.

It begins with two sons, still in their mothers' bellies when their fathers are slain, divided and taken into enemy hands, brought up far away from their Chinese motherland.

This is the start of an explosive epic of courage, honor, and justice by one of the world's best-loved writers.

You are about to begin a journey that will span the lengths of the Chinese Empire and beyond, traverse centuries, and witness dynasties rise and fall in brutal wars and deceitful invasions, brave men fight and die for their homeland, and traitors exchange honor for personal gain. You will meet young men and women with remarkable kung fu skills, and you will encounter gruff men who, despite appearances, always respect the code of honor that governs the martial arts world. You will be amazed by semi-celestial animals, magic medicinal concoctions, and poison-tipped weapons. You will come face-to-face with princes who manipulate and mothers who are easily manipulated, men whose love is undying and women whose hearts never err.

Jin Yong was the pen name of Louis Cha, born in Zhejiang Province in China in 1924. As Jin Yong, his fictional universe has captured the imagination of generations of Chinese readers ever since his first novel appeared in serialized form in the Hong Kong newspaper *New Evening Post* in 1955. He went on to write fourteen novels, most of which are in fact the length of several novels by modern publishing standards, and one final short story. These epics, of which *Legends of the Condor Heroes* is considered one of his best, quickly cemented Jin Yong's reputation as a master of the *wuxia* genre, which can be roughly translated as "martial heroes" literature. The genre has its antecedents in some of the earliest vernacular writing found in Chinese. Although disparaged by some early commentators, elements now considered fundamental to this literature have been argued to be present in great works of "serious" literature such as Sima Qian's *Records of the Grand Historian* (*Shiji*). *Wuxia* fiction's counterculture credentials have, however, always formed a large part of its appeal. While there are features that feel familiar to us from western chivalric literature, the martial arts fighters who populate Jin Yong's books are often lone figures from the lower levels of society rather than members of court, who burn with a strong sense of justice and righteousness, or sometimes mere ego and greed.

Unashamedly entertaining, even to this day some have wished to write martial arts fiction off as merely the stuff of pulp, but with Jin Yong's writing came a serious challenge. Born into a wealthy landowning family later stripped of their wealth under Maoism, Louis

Cha attended law school before turning to journalism after moving to Hong Kong. Yet this was merely the start of a life of learning, which saw him gain two PhDs in his eighties, one on Tang dynasty history at Cambridge University and one in Chinese literature at Peking University. The depth of his knowledge of Chinese history and the classics of Chinese writing are evident everywhere in his novels. Furthermore, his body of writing has given rise to an area of academic study all of its own, known as Jinology.

Remarkably, you hold in your hands the first edition of *Legends of the Condor Heroes* to have ever been published in English in the United States. Considering that he has sold in the hundreds of millions and his reputation extends over most of East Asia, it is astonishing that it has taken sixty years to get here. Why, may you ask? Many have considered Jin Yong's world too foreign, too Chinese, for an English-speaking readership. Impossible to translate. The fact that it hadn't been done was proof that it could never be done.

I first came across Jin Yong in my first term of reading Modern Chinese Studies at Oxford University. I was still stuck in the rudimentaries, shakily tracing my first characters and trying to sound out the correct tones of *ni hao,* hello. Even then, without a hope of being able to read them, Chinese friends were telling me about their favorite author. "You must read his books! I've loved them since I was a child," I kept hearing. It was to take me another three years of intensive study to even dare to open one and try. And instantly, I was hooked. With a dictionary by my side, I started to wander great emotional landscapes of love, loyalty, honor, and the power of the individual against successive corrupt governments and invading forces.

It was to be some years later, however, that I would actually try to translate Jin Yong's writing. I had published a few translations of contemporary Chinese novels already and was starting out on my career as an agent representing Chinese writers when I got the chance to try pitching and translating *Legends of the Condor Heroes.* I was convinced that it would work in English, that people would fall in love with these stories the way Jin Yong's readers had in China if only they got the chance. The supposed "untranslatability" of it seemed strange to me, as the fundamental emotional worlds of these characters felt as universal as any story could hope to be. And yet ... my first attempt was a disappointment, dry and flat. The action felt dead on the page. I was beginning to understand why it was considered difficult. After months of work, edits, and feedback from the agent I was working with, we had a draft that was ready to be shown to editors. And the reaction was instant. Six publishers were keen, but one of the UK's most eminent editors was determined to have it for his list. Before I knew it, I was embarking on a full-length translation.

It was, and as I continue through the series continues to be, a life-defining challenge to translate these books. Jin Yong's status, his many, many, many adoring fans, and their expectations have worn heavy on my shoulders. But my greatest debt lies to you, the English reader, those of you who cannot pick up an original copy and discover Jin Yong on his terms alone. Perhaps this is always the hardest part of being a translator. To me, the most important thing is to try to re-create the feeling of reading Jin Yong in Chinese, the pace, the excitement, the emotional highs and lows. There will be words and concepts unfamiliar, quotations from ancient verse and philosophical texts alongside amusing set pieces and great humor. These are the things that make Jin Yong a master, my *shifu* if I may presume to call him such, because he can combine the profound and the comical like no other. In 2018, we lost Louis Cha. But we will always have Jin Yong, and his legacy lives on now in ever more languages around the world.

So, dear reader, all that is left is to enter through these pages into a universe at once fantastical and based on real historical events, one both foreign and intimately familiar, a story full of heart and of remarkable physical prowess.

—Anna Holmwood,
TRANSLATOR

CHARACTERS

As they appear in this, the first volume of
Legends of the Condor Heroes: A Hero Born

MAIN CHARACTERS

Guo Jing, son of Skyfury Guo and Lily Li. After his father's death before he was born, he grows up with his mother in Mongolia, where they are looked after by the future Genghis Khan.

Yang Kang, son of Ironheart Yang and Charity Bao, sworn as brother to Guo Jing while both are still in their mothers' bellies.

Lotus Huang is highly skilled in kung fu, but she refuses to reveal the identity of her Master when challenged.

THE SONG PATRIOTS

Ironheart Yang, descendent of Triumph Yang, onetime rebel turned patriot who served under General Yue Fei. Ironheart practices the Yang Family Spear, a technique passed from father to son.

Married to **Charity Bao**, daughter of a country scholar from Red Plum Village.

Skyfury Guo, sworn brother to Ironheart Yang, he is descended from Prosperity Guo, one of the heroes of the Marshes of Mount Liang.

Skyfury fights with the double halberd, in keeping with the Guo family tradition.

Married to **Lily Li**, Guo Jing's mother. She escapes the attack on Ox Village and ends up in Mongolia with Guo Jing.

Qu San, owner of Ox Village's only tavern, he keeps his kung fu skills secret from the rest of the villagers.

Mu Yi travels all across Song- and Jin-controlled lands with his daughter **Mercy Mu**, organizing a martial contest in order to find her a suitable husband.

SONG IMPERIAL TRAITORS

Justice Duan, an army officer to the Song who, in actual fact, works for the Jin.

Wang Daoqian, a military official in the Song court, he is killed by Qiu Chuji for accepting bribes by the Jin.

THE FIVE GREATS

Considered the five greatest martial artists after a contest was held on Mount Hua. Only two are mentioned in this first book in the series:

The Eastern Heretic Apothecary Huang, a loner and radical who practices his unorthodox martial arts on Peach Blossom Island along with his wife and six students. He holds traditions and their accompanying morals in contempt and believes only in true love and honor. His eccentricity and heretical views make others suspicious of him, an image he himself cultivates.

Double Sun Wang Chongyang, founder of the Quanzhen Sect in the Zhongnan Mountains, with the aim of training Taoists in the martial arts so that they might defend the Song against the Jurchen invasion. A real historical figure, he lived from A.D. 1113 to 1170.

THE QUANZHEN TAOIST SECT

A real branch of Taoism, whose name means "Way of Complete Perfection."

THE SEVEN IMMORTALS, STUDENTS OF WANG CHONGYANG

Only three of the Immortals make their appearance in this first book of the series:

Scarlet Sun Ma Yu, the oldest of the Immortals, teaches internal kung fu based on breathing techniques.

Eternal Spring Qiu Chuji befriends Ironheart Yang and Skyfury Guo at the beginning of the series and vows to protect their unborn offspring. To this end, he devises a martial contest with the Seven Freaks of the South. He becomes teacher to Yang Kang.

Jade Sun Wang Chuyi, the Iron Foot Immortal, befriends Guo Jing after hearing of Qiu Chuji's contest with the Seven Freaks of the South.

Harmony Yin, apprentice to Qiu Chuji.

THE SEVEN FREAKS OF THE SOUTH

Also known as the Seven Heroes of the South when being addressed respectfully by other characters. They refer to themselves as a martial family, despite being of no blood relation.

Ke Zhen'e, Suppressor of Evil, also known as **Flying Bat**. The oldest of the Freaks, he is often referred to as Big Brother. Blinded in a fight, his preferred weapon is his flying devilnuts, iron projectiles made in the shape of a kind of water chestnut native to China.

Quick Hands Zhu Cong the Intelligent is known for his quick thinking and even quicker sleight of hand. His dirty scholar's dress and broken oilpaper fan, really made from iron, belie his real martial skill. He is particularly knowledgeable in acupressure points, using them to disable his opponents in a fight. At times, he might also use his skills to steal gold and other items, but only from those he thinks dishonorable and thus deserving of such trickery.

Ryder Han, Protector of the Steeds, only three feet in height but a formidable fighter when sitting astride a horse.

Woodcutter Nan the Merciful, known for his kind, if not shy, nature, teaches Guo Jing saber technique. He fights with an iron-tipped shoulder pole.

Zhang Asheng, also known as the **Laughing Buddha**, is a burly man dressed as a butcher, whose preferred weapon is a butcher's knife. He is secretly in love with Jade Han.

Gilden Quan the Prosperous, Cloaked Master of the Market, is a master of the rules of the marketplace and always looking for a good deal. He fights with a set of scales.

Jade Han, Maiden of the Yue Sword, is the youngest and only female of the group. She is trained in the Yue Sword, a technique particular to the region surrounding Jiaxing and developed when the Kingdom of Yue was at war with the Kingdom of Wu in the fifth century B.C.

THE MONGOLIANS

The Great Khan Temujin, one of the great warlords who will go on to unite the various Mongolian tribes and assume the name Genghis Khan.

Temujin's children:

Jochi, Temujin's eldest son.

Chagatai, the second son.

Ogedai, the third son.

Tolui, the fourth son, and Guo Jing's sworn brother.

Khojin, one of many daughters whose names are mostly lost to history. Temujin betroths her first to Tusakha, son of his rival Senggum, and then to Guo Jing.

Temujin's allies and followers:

Jamuka, Temujin's sworn brother and ally.

Jebe, whose name means "arrow" and "Divine Archer" in Mongolian, is made a commander of Temujin's men after demonstrating his great skill with a bow and arrow, and showing himself to be a loyal fighter of considerable principle.

Temujin's Four Great Generals:

Muqali, **Bogurchi**, **Boroqul**, and **Tchila'un**.

Temujin's rivals:

    Ong Khan, sworn brother of Temujin's father.

    Senggum, son of Ong Khan.

    Tusakha, son of Senggum, is only a few years older than Guo Jing and bullies him and Tolui when they are young.

THE JIN EMPIRE

Wanyan Honglie, Sixth Prince, titled **Prince of Zhao**, has made conquering the Song his own personal mission, in order to secure his reputation and legacy among his own people. He is an astute tactician, using rivalries and jealousies within the Song court and the *wulin* to his own advantage.

Wanyan Hongxi, Third Prince, lacks his younger brother's political sense, especially when dealing with the Mongols.

Wanyan Kang, son of the Sixth Prince Wanyan Honglie, is arrogant and entitled, but possesses considerable martial skill. He fights Guo Jing after refusing to marry Mercy Mu.

Consort to the Sixth Prince, mother of Wanyan Kang.

FOLLOWERS OF THE SIXTH PRINCE WANYAN HONGLIE

Gallant Ouyang, Master of White Camel Mount in the Kunlun Range, nephew to one of the Five Greats, Viper Ouyang, Venom of the West.

The Dragon King Hector Sha controls the Yellow River with his four rather more useless apprentices, whose lack of skill infuriates their Master, despite the fact that it is most likely his foul temper that has prevented them from learning anything more than their rather basic moves.

The Four Daemons of the Yellow River

    Shen Qinggang the Strong, whose weapon is a saber called the Spirit Cleaver.

    Wu Qinglie the Bold fights with a spear called the Dispatcher.

    Ma Qingxiong the Valiant is known for his Soul Snatcher whip.

Qian Qingjian the Hardy is armed with a pair of axes known as the Great Reapers.

Browbeater Hou, the Three-Horned Dragon, so named for the three cysts on his forehead.

Graybeard Liang, also known as **Old Liang**, the **Ginseng Immortal** and, more disparagingly, the **Ginseng Codger**. He comes from the Mountain of Eternal Snow (Changbai Mountain) up in the northeast, close to the current border with Korea, where he has practiced kung fu for many years as a hermit, as well as mixing special medicinal concoctions with the aim of prolonging life and gaining strength.

Lama Supreme Wisdom Lobsang Choden Rinpoche, from Kokonor, now known as Qinghai. He is famed for his Five Finger Blade kung fu.

Tiger Peng the Outlaw, Butcher of a Thousand Hands, has command of much of the mountainous region surrounding the Jin capital, Yanjing, which would later become Peking.

PEACH BLOSSOM ISLAND

Twice Foul Dark Wind were apprentices of Apothecary Huang, who fled Peach Blossom Island and eloped after stealing the Nine Yin Manual. Husband **Hurricane Chen**, known as Copper Corpse, and wife **Cyclone Mei**, known as Iron Corpse, are masters of Nine Yin Skeleton Claw. They killed Ke Zhen'e's brother, Ke Bixie the Talisman.

THE IMMORTAL CLOUD SECT

Abbot Withered Wood, of Cloudy Perch Temple, is uncle to Justice Duan. He hates his treacherous nephew, but is tricked into enlisting the help of Scorched Wood and the Seven Freaks of the South to fight against Qiu Chuji.

Reverend Scorched Wood, of Fahua Temple, is a fellow disciple of Withered Wood's martial Master.

CHAPTER ONE

SUDDENLY
A SNOW STORM

I

THE QIANTANG RIVER STRETCHES FROM THE WEST, WHERE ITS waters swell day and night, past the new imperial capital of Lin'an and the nearby Ox Village, on to the sea in the east. Ten cypresses stand proudly along its banks, their leaves red like fire. A typical August day. The grasses are turning yellow beneath the trees and the setting sun is breaking through their branches, casting long, bleak shadows. Under the shelter of two giant pine trees, men, women, and children have gathered to listen to a traveling storyteller.

The man is around fifty, a pinched figure in robes once black, now faded a blue-gray. He begins by slapping two pieces of pear wood together, and then, using a bamboo stick, he beats a steady rhythm on a small leather drum. He sings:

> *"Untended, the peach blossoms still open,*
> *As misty, fallow fields draw the crows.*
> *In times past, by the village well,*
> *Families once gathered to vent their sorrows."*

The old man strikes the pieces of wood together a few more times and starts his story.

"This poem tells of villages, where ordinary people once lived, razed by Jurchen tribes and turned to rubble. One such story concerns Old Man Ye, who had a wife, a son, and a daughter, but they were separated from one another by the invasion of the Jin. Years passed before they were reunited and could return to their village. After making the perilous journey back to Weizhou, they arrived to discover their home had been burned to the ground by enemy forces, and they had no choice but to make for the old capital at Kaifeng."

He sings:

> "*The heavens unleash unexpected storms,*
> *People suffer unforeseen misfortune.*

"Upon arrival," he continues, "they encountered a troop of Jin soldiers. Their commanding officer spotted the young Miss Ye, by now a beautiful young maiden, and eager to capture such a glorious prize, he jumped down from his horse and seized her. Laughing, he threw her onto his saddle and cried, 'Pretty girl, you are coming home with me.' What could the young Miss Ye do? She struggled with all her might to free herself from the officer's grip. 'If you continue to resist I will have your family killed!' the man shouted. With that, he picked up his wolf-fang club and smashed it down on her brother's head.

"*The netherworld gains a ghost, just as the mortal world loses one more soul.*" He breaks again into song.

"Old Man Ye and his wife threw themselves on top of their son's body, weeping and sobbing. The commanding officer raised his wolf-fang club and once again brought it down on the mother, and then once more on the father. Rather than cry or plead, the young Miss Ye turned to the soldier and said, 'Sir, rest your weapon, I will go with you.' The soldier was delighted to have persuaded her, but just as he let down his guard the young Miss Ye grabbed the saber from his waist, unsheathed it and held the point of the blade to his chest. Was she about to avenge her family's death?

"Alas, it was not to be. Being experienced on the battlefield, the soldier knew that if he took a deep breath, tensed his muscles and pushed against the blade, she would tumble to the ground. Then he spat in her face. 'Whore!'

"But young Miss Ye brought the blade to her neck. That poor, innocent girl.

> *A beauty made of flower and moon,*
> *And so was taken the sweetest soul that night.*"

He alternates between singing and speaking, all the while beating his small drum with the bamboo stick. The crowd is entranced by the old man's words; they snarl with rage at the soldier's cruelty, and sigh at the young girl's sacrifice.

"Dear friends, as the saying goes, 'Keep honest heart and ever gods in mind. For if evil deeds go unpunished, only evil doth one find.' The Jin have conquered half our territories, killing and burning, there is not an evil deed they have not committed. And yet no punishment is forthcoming. The officials of our great Empire are responsible for this. China has plenty of men, healthy and willing to fight, yet every time our army faces the Jin they turn and run, leaving us peasants behind to suffer. There are stories, a great many stories just like this one, north of the Yangtze. The south is a paradise in comparison, but still you live each day in fear of invasion. 'Rather be a dog in times of peace, than a man in times of trouble.' My name is Old Zhang, thank you for listening to the true story of young Miss Ye!"

The storyteller bangs together the two pieces of pear wood and holds out a plate to the crowd. Villagers shuffle forward and drop a few coins onto it. Old Zhang puts the coins into a pocket and starts gathering his belongings.

As the crowd disperses, a young man of about twenty pushes his way up to the storyteller. "Sir, did you just come from the north?"

He is short but strong, with two hairy caterpillar eyebrows stretched across his brow. He is from the north; it can be heard in his accent.

"Yes," the old storyteller answers, surveying him.

"Then may I buy you a drink?"

"I dare not receive such favor from a stranger," comes the old man's reply.

"After a few drinks we will no longer be strangers." The young man smiles. "My name is Skyfury Guo," he says, before pointing to a handsome, smooth-faced man behind him. "And this is Ironheart Yang. We were listening to your story, and we enjoyed it very much, but we would like to talk with you, ask you some questions. You bring news from home."

"Not a problem, young man. Fate has brought us together today."

Skyfury Guo leads the storyteller to the village's only tavern and there they sit down. Qu San, the owner, hobbles to their table on his crutches and sets down two jugs of warmed rice wine, before returning to fetch snacks of broad beans, salted peanuts, dried tofu, and three salted eggs. Afterward, he sits down on a stool by the door and gazes out as the sun dips lower toward the horizon. Out in the yard his young daughter is chasing chickens.

Skyfury Guo toasts the storyteller and pushes the simple snacks toward him. "Here, please eat. Out in the countryside, we are only able to buy meat on the second and sixteenth days of the month, so I'm afraid we have none tonight. Please forgive us."

"The wine is enough for me. From your accents it seems that you are both from the north?"

"We are from Shandong province," Yang replies. "We came here three years ago after the Jin invaded our hometown. We fell in love with the simple life in the south, as well as the people, and stayed. You said before that the south is a paradise, with only fear of invasion to disturb the peace. Do you really think the Jin will cross the Yangtze?"

The old storyteller sighs. "It is as if gold and silver covers the ground, everywhere your eyes are met with beautiful women, such is the richness and enchantment of the south compared to the north. There isn't a day that passes that the Jin do not think about invading. But the final decision lies not with the Jin but with the Song Imperial Court in Lin'an."

This surprises Skyfury Guo and Ironheart Yang. "Why do you say that?"

"We Han Chinese outnumber the Jurchen by more than a hundred to one. If the Imperial Court decided to employ honest and loyal men, our great Empire would prevail. With one hundred of our men against one of their worthless soldiers, how could the Jin army win? The northern half of our country was handed to them by three generations of useless Emperors, Huizong, Qinzong, and Gaozong. Grandfather to grandson, they all entrusted our country to corrupt officials who oppressed the common people, and purged all the mighty generals who wished to fight the Jin. Such a beautiful land and they gave it away! If the Imperial Court continues to fill its grand halls with corrupt officials, then they may as well kneel before the Jin and beg them to invade!"

"Exactly!" Skyfury Guo slams his hand down on the table, rattling the bowls, plates, and chopsticks.

Ironheart Yang notices their jug of wine is empty and orders another. The three men continue cursing and drinking as Qu San goes to fetch them yet more broad beans and tofu.

"Huh!" Qu San snorts, placing the dishes on the table.

"What is it, Qu San? You disagree?"

"Good cursing! Great cursing! Nothing wrong with that. But do you suppose it would have made any difference if the officials had not been corrupt? With such useless Emperors, generations of them no less, it would have made no difference if the officials had been as honest and good-hearted as the Buddha himself." He turns and shuffles to his stool in the corner, from where he goes back to gazing at a sky now filled with stars. Qu San has a young face for his forty years, but his back is hunched and wisps of white are threaded through his black hair. From behind he looks like an old man, much aged since losing his wife. He moved to Ox Village only a year or so ago with his daughter, fleeing painful memories.

The three men look at each other in silence, until presently the storyteller speaks. "Yes, you are right. That is quite true."

Bang! Skyfury Guo slams his hand down on the table once again, this time knocking over a bowl of wine. "Shameful! Disgraceful! How did these sorry excuses for men ever become Emperor?"

"Xiaozong succeeded Gaozong," the storyteller replies with renewed energy, "and Guangzong succeeded him, and all the while the Jin have controlled half of China. Now Emperor Ningzong has succeeded Guangzong. And all he does is take orders from Chancellor Han. What is our future? It's hard to say."

"What do you mean?" cries Skyfury Guo. "We are in the countryside, not Lin'an. No one is going to cut your head off here. There is not a person in the whole of China who does not call Chancellor Han a crook!"

Now that the topic has moved on to current politics, the old storyteller is beginning to feel nervous and dares not speak straight from the heart as before. He downs another bowl of rice wine and says, "Thank you, gentlemen, for the wine. But before I go, may I offer a modest word of advice? I know you are both passionate men, but still, it is best to be cautious in both word and deed. This is the only way to avoid calamity. With things as they are, the best we normal folk can hope to do is muddle along. Ah, it is just like the old song:

> *Surrounded by mountains, dancing in halls,*
> *The shores of West Lake echo in song.*
> *Southern fragrances entice and intoxicate*
> *As drunkenly our noblemen mistake Lin'an for Kaifeng!"*

"What's the story behind that song?" Yang asks.

"There is no story," the old man says, pushing himself to his feet with great effort. "The officials care only for parties and pleasures, and as long as that is the case, they won't be trying to recover the north any time soon."

And so the drunken storyteller takes his leave.

2

IT WAS DURING THE THIRD WATCH LATER THAT NIGHT. SKYfury Guo and Ironheart Yang had been waiting for more than two hours to spear a boar or a muntjac in the woods seven *li* west of the village, but it was looking increasingly unlikely they would catch anything and they were losing patience.

At that moment a loud smack of wood against metal echoed around the woodland from beyond the tree line. Skyfury and Ironheart looked at each other.

Then came the sound of men shouting:

"Where do you think you're going?"

"Stop, now!"

A shadow had entered the woods and was running in their direction. The moonlight caught a man's robes and Guo and Yang were able to make him out. It was Qu San. He was jabbing his wooden crutches into the undergrowth. Knowing that he would struggle to outrun the men following him, Qu San flew straight up into the air and back down behind a nearby tree. Guo and Yang looked at each other in astonishment.

"Qu San practices martial arts?"

By now Qu San's pursuers had reached the edge of the woods. There were three of them, and they stopped, whispered something to each other, and began to walk toward Guo and Yang. They were dressed in military clothing and each carried a saber, their blades flashing a cold green in the moonlight.

"Damned cripple! We can see you. Come out and surrender!"

Qu San stood utterly still behind his tree. The men were waving their weapons like machetes, swinging and chopping through the straggly bushes, slowly edging closer.

Just then: *Thump!* Qu San thrust his right crutch out from behind the tree, hitting one of the men squarely in the chest and sending him lurching backward with a yelp. Startled, the other two men waved their blades in the direction of the tree.

Using his right crutch for leverage, Qu San flew up to the left, dodging the flailing blades and thrusting his other crutch in one man's face. The man tried to block the crutch with his saber, but Qu San pulled back and swung his right crutch at the other man's stomach. Though he needed the crutches to support himself, he wielded them with speed and elegance.

A saber cut into Qu San's bundle, ripping the cloth and spilling its contents all over the forest floor. Taking advantage of the distraction, Qu San smashed his crutch down onto one man's head, knocking him to the ground. Terrified, the last soldier turned to run. Qu San reached between the folds in his robe, and with a sharp flick of his wrist hurled something at him as he fled. It glinted an inky black as it sailed through the air, drawing a curve and landing on the back of the soldier's head with a dull thud. The man howled and dropped his saber, his arms waving wildly. He fell forward as if in slow motion, and landed in a crumpled heap on the ground. His body spasmed twice, and then he was still.

Guo and Yang watched, their hearts thumping, hardly able to catch their breath. "He just killed government officials. That's punishable by death." Guo gasped. "If he sees us he'll kill us too, to keep us quiet."

But they had not hidden themselves as well as they had thought. Qu San turned toward them and called out: "Master Guo, Master Yang, you can come out now!" Reluctantly they rose to their feet, grasping their pitchforks so tightly their knuckles turned white. Yang looked at his friend and then took two steps forward.

"Master Yang," Qu San said with a smile. "Your family's spear technique is famous throughout our land, but in the absence of a spear, a pitchfork will have to do. Your best friend Guo, however, prefers to fight with a double halberd. The pitchfork doesn't fit his skills. Such friendship is rare!"

Yang felt exposed; Qu San had all but read his mind.

"Master Guo," Qu San continued. "Let's imagine you had your double halberd with you. Do you think together you could beat me?"

Guo shook his head. "No, we couldn't. We must have been blind not to have noticed you were a fellow practitioner of the martial arts. A master, even."

"I don't have full use of my legs. How can I be considered a master?" Qu San shook his head and sighed. "Before my injury, I would have defeated those guards effortlessly."

Guo and Yang glanced at each other, not sure how to respond.

"Would you help me bury them?" Qu San continued.

They looked at each other again, and nodded.

The two men did their best to dig a large hole using their pitchforks. As they were burying the last body, Yang noticed the black, round object sticking out of the back of the dead man's head. Yang tugged at it and succeeded in pulling it out. He had seen one of these before. A steel Taoist Eight Trigram disk. He wiped the blood onto the dead man's uniform and handed it back to Qu San.

"My sincerest gratitude." Qu San took the Eight Trigram disk and put it back inside his robe. He then spread his outer robe on the ground and started to gather his belongings. Guo and Yang finished shoveling soil into the makeshift grave, and then turned to look at Qu San's collection, which included three scrolls, as well as several shiny metal trinkets. Qu San put a gold jug and bowl to one side. After tying up his bundle he handed the jug and bowl to the two men. "I stole these from the Royal Palace at Lin'an. The Emperor has done enough harm to the peasants, it's not really a crime to take something back. Consider these a gift from me."

Neither man moved.

"Are you afraid to accept them, or is it that you don't want them?"

"We did nothing to deserve such gifts," Guo replied. "That's why we can't accept them. As for tonight, you don't have to worry about a thing, Brother Qu. Your secret is safe with us."

"Ha!" Qu San scoffed. "Why should I be worried? I know all about you—why else would I let you walk away alive? Master Guo, you are the descendant of Prosperity Guo, one of the heroes of the Marshes of Mount Liang. You are skilled in the use of the halberd, as taught to you in accordance with your family's customs, only your halberd is short rather than long, and has two blades instead of one. Master Yang, your ancestor is Triumph Yang, one of the commanders who served under the beloved General Yue. You are both descended from two of this country's most loved and respected patriots. When the Jin army conquered the north, you began wandering the lakes and rivers of the south, practicing your martial arts. It was then that you became brothers-in-arms. Together you moved here to Ox Village. Am I right so far?"

The two men nodded, astounded by the detail of Qu San's knowledge.

"Your ancestors Prosperity Guo and Triumph Yang were both rebels before they swapped sides to fight for the Song Empire," Qu San continued. "Both stole from the government, which was in turn stealing from its own people. So tell me: are you going to accept my gifts or not?"

"We are most grateful. Thank you," Yang said as he reached out to receive them.

"Back home!" Qu San said, slinging his bundle over his shoulder.

"I got some excellent things tonight," he continued as the three men picked their way between the trees and out of the woods. "Two paintings by Emperor Huizong and a scroll of his calligraphy. He may have been a useless Emperor, but his skills with the brush were quite superb."

Once home, Guo and Yang buried their gold and made no mention of the night's antics to their wives.

AUTUMN SLOWLY gave way to winter. The days were getting colder and the first flakes of snow were beginning to fall. Soon the earth was covered in a veneer of white that shone like polished jade. Ironheart Yang called to his wife, "I'm going to get some food and rice wine before Skyfury and his wife arrive." Slinging two large gourds over his shoulder, he left for Qu San's tavern.

The snow was falling more heavily. As he trudged up toward the tavern, he noticed the door was shut tight and even the sign had been removed. Yang banged on the door a couple of times, shouting: "Qu San, I'm here for some wine."

Silence.

He called out again, but still no response. He walked over to a window and peered inside. Everything was covered in a thick layer of dust. What's happened? Yang thought. I hope it's nothing serious. He spotted Qu San's daughter playing nearby, but she was too young to give him any answers. As Qu's inn was the only place to buy wine in Ox Village, Yang had no choice but to brave the blizzard and walk the two miles to Red Plum Village. At least there he would also be able to purchase a chicken for their meal.

When her husband returned, Yang's wife, Charity Bao, put the freshly slaughtered chicken into a big pot along with some cabbage, tofu, and thin bean noodles. As it boiled, she cut and arranged a plate of cured meat and fish, and then went next door to call on Skyfury Guo and his wife, Lily Li, who had been suffering of late from morning sickness. Lily did not feel able to eat, so Charity stayed to chat and drink tea, sending Guo ahead.

The two women returned to discover the men sitting by the fire, eating and drinking warm wine. Charity added more wood, then sat down beside her husband. The two men looked agitated.

"What's the matter?" Lily asked. "Has something happened?"

"We were just discussing the latest troubles at the Imperial Court in Lin'an," her husband replied. "I was at the Pavilion of Joyful Rain, the teahouse by Tranquility Bridge, yesterday," Guo added, "when I heard some people talking about that criminal Chancellor Han. One man said all reports at court must now be presented to him, as well as the Emperor, or else they won't be read. Such arrogance is scarcely to be credited."

Yang sighed. "Only bad Emperors keep bad Chancellors. Old Huang, who lives outside Lin'an's Golden Gate, told me a story. One day, when he was out collecting firewood on the mountain, he caught sight of a group of soldiers guarding some officials. It turns out the Chancellor had come on a sightseeing trip with his men. Old Huang was minding his own business, cutting wood, when he heard the Chancellor say, 'What a delightful country scene, such charming bamboo fences and thatched cottages. Shame there are no chickens clucking or dogs barking.' Then, at that moment, they heard barking from behind one of the bushes."

Charity smiled. "That little dog certainly knew how to please the Chancellor."

"I'll say! After a couple of barks it jumped out of the bushes. And what kind of dog do you think it was? Turns out it was our honorable friend, the Magistrate of Lin'an, His Excellency Mr. Zhao!"

Charity burst into laughter.

"And that's how he'll earn his promotion," Guo concluded.

They continued drinking as the snow fell outside, the wine warming their bellies. After a while, Guo and Yang decided to step outside to cool down. Suddenly the stillness was broken by the sound of feet swishing across the snow. There, up ahead, was a Taoist monk wearing a conical bamboo hat tied under his chin with a ribbon, and a cape speckled with large flakes of snow. He carried a sword on his back, the yellow tassel swinging from side to side as it dangled from the handle. He was the only person braving the weather, a lonely silhouette making rapid progress across the gray-white fields.

"Look at how he skims across the snow," breathed Guo in admiration. "A master of kung fu."

"Indeed," Yang replied in equal amazement. "Let's invite him in for a drink."

They hurried to the edge of the field in front of Yang's house. In the short time it had taken them to run the hundred-odd meters, the monk had already passed by, and was some distance down the raised path that ran between the fields.

"Your Reverence, please stop!" Yang called out.

The Taoist monk turned and gave them a cursory nod.

"Such terrible weather," Yang continued shouting through the snow. "Why don't you come inside and drink a couple of bowls of wine to warm up?"

Within seconds the Taoist was standing before them. "Why do you want me to stop?" His reply was as cold as the winter air. "Speak!"

Yang was shocked and angered by the Taoist's tone, so he looked down at his feet and gave no reply. Guo clasped his fist as a sign of respect and said, "We were drinking by the fire when we saw you pass by alone in the snow. So we thought you might like to join us. Please forgive us if we have offended you."

The Taoist rolled his eyes. "All right. If you want to drink, let's drink," he said, walking past them and in through Yang's door.

This made Yang even angrier. Without thinking, he grabbed the Taoist's left wrist and tugged. "We don't know how to address you, Your Reverence." But the Taoist's hand slipped through Yang's fingers like a fish. Yang knew he was in trouble and stepped back, but before he could pull away he felt a sharp, hot pain as the Taoist tightened his grip around his wrist. No matter how hard he struggled he could not free himself, and he felt all his strength draining away as his arm went limp.

Guo could see from his friend's crimson cheeks that he was in a lot of pain. "Your Reverence," he said. "Please sit."

The Taoist laughed coldly. He let go of Yang, walked deliberately into the center of the room and sat down in one smooth movement. "You two young men are obviously from the north but pretending to be farmers here in the south. Your accents give you away. And what's more, why would two farmers know kung fu?" He, too, spoke with a Shandong accent.

Yang felt embarrassed and angry, and retreated to the back room.

There he found a small dagger in a drawer, which he tucked into his shirt before returning to the front room. He poured out three bowls of wine, raised his as a toast, and downed its contents without a word.

The Taoist looked past the two men, and out toward the snow falling outside. He neither drank nor spoke. Guo guessed that the monk was suspicious of the wine, so he took the bowl intended for their guest and drank it down in one gulp. "The wine gets cold quickly. Let me pour you another bowl, Your Reverence. A warm one." He filled a clean bowl and handed it to the Taoist, who in turn drank it down in one.

"It wouldn't have mattered if you had drugged the wine," the Taoist replied. "It wouldn't have affected me."

Yang had had about as much as he could take. "We invited you into our home to drink with us, not to try and hurt you. If this is how you are going to behave, please leave now! It's not as if we gave you sour wine or rotten food."

The Taoist ignored him, and grabbed the wine gourd. He poured and drank three more bowls of wine in quick succession, and then untied his bamboo hat and threw it on the floor, along with his cape. For the first time, Guo and Yang could properly examine his face. He was around thirty years of age, with slanted eyebrows and a square jaw, his cheeks flushed red. His eyes had a penetrating quality. Next, he untied the leather bundle from his back and threw it down on the table.

Together, Guo and Yang jumped up in disgust as from out of the bundle rolled a bloody human head.

A scream came from the corner where Charity had been standing, and she ran into the back room, followed by Lily Li. Yang's hand moved to his chest to make sure the dagger was in place. The Taoist gave the leather bundle a shake, and two more bloody lumps of flesh fell out. A heart and a liver.

"You good-for-nothing Taoist!" Yang shouted as he pulled the dagger from his chest and lunged at the monk.

The Taoist was amused. "You want to fight?" He tapped Yang's wrist with his left hand. A numbing pain shot down through Yang's hands to his fingers. Before he realized what was happening, the dagger was gone.

Guo was astounded. His friend's kung fu was much better than his own, but even Yang was powerless against the monk. Guo knew the move was the legendary Bare Hand Seizes Blade, but he had never actually seen anyone perform it. Guo reached for the wooden bench he had been sitting on, just in case he had to block the dagger.

But still the Taoist ignored them. Instead, he turned his attention to the heart and liver, which he began hacking to pieces with Yang's dagger. Then, without warning, he roared. The tiles on the roof rattled, and he chopped down so hard, the objects on the table jumped and the table split in two. The head rolled onto the floor.

Yang was furious. He reached for an iron spear in the corner and marched outside into the snow. "Come. I'll give you a lesson in the art of the Yang Family Spear!"

"A government lackey like you knows the Yang Family Spear?" The Taoist smiled as he followed Yang outside.

Guo ran back to his house to fetch his double halberds. By the time he got back, the Taoist was standing ready, his sleeves flapping in the wind.

"Unsheathe your sword!" Yang cried.

"I'll fight you traitors with my bare hands," was the Taoist's only reply.

Without warning, Yang launched straight into Deadly Dragon Flies the Cave, his spear a smear of red as the tassel spun and the tip swirled toward the Taoist's chest.

"Impressive!" the monk called as his upper body arched backward until it was almost horizontal. He then spun to the left and swung back up again. Once on his feet, his palm flipped upward and knocked the spear away from Yang's hands.

Ironheart Yang had spent years practicing with his spear, ever since his father taught him his first moves as a young boy, a variant of the southern tradition. The northern tradition had been lost many years ago. His ancestor Triumph Yang led an army of three hundred Song soldiers against forty thousand invading Jin at the Battle of Little Merchant Bridge, with his spear his only weapon. They killed over two thousand Jin men that day, including their highest-ranking commander. The Jin's arrows had fallen like rain, but Triumph Yang merely snapped the shafts from the arrowheads lodged in his flesh and carried on fighting. He gave his life for his country on that battlefield. When the Jin army burned his body, over two *jin* of molten metal flowed into the mud beneath him. After this battle the Yang Family Spear became famous all across China's great plains.

Ironheart Yang may not have been a true master of the technique like his forefathers, but those years of training had not been in vain. He thrust, swung, flicked, blocked, the point of his spear glinting silver in the sunlight, the tassel a blur of red.

Yang's moves may have been quick, but the Taoist dodged them with ease. The Yang Family Spear consisted of seventy-two separate moves, and after having used seventy-one without success, Yang was exhausted and desperate. He lowered his spear, turned and walked away. But just as he had anticipated, the Taoist came after him, and drawing together all the strength he had left, Yang pulled his weapon up into both hands, twisted at the waist and thrust it back at the Taoist's face. Known as the Returning Horse, this move was traditionally used to break enemy formations. Triumph Yang had in fact used it to kill General Yue's brother before he left the rebels and joined the Song army.

The Taoist clapped his hands together, clamping hold of the spear's point just before it plunged into his left cheek. "Excellent!" Yang put all his weight behind the spear and pushed, but it did not move. Alarmed, he tried pulling it back instead, but still he could not free his spear from the Taoist's grip. The Taoist chuckled. Suddenly he moved his right hand, and quick as light he struck the handle of the spear with his palm. Yang felt the base of his thumb and index finger go numb, and instantly the weapon fell to the snow at his feet.

"You appear to know some Yang Family Spear after all." The Taoist smiled. "Sorry if I offended you. Will you do me the honor of telling me your name?"

Still in shock, Yang answered without thinking, "My family name is Yang, my given name Ironheart."

"Are you a descendant of General Triumph Yang?"

"Yes, he was my great-grandfather."

The Taoist cupped his fist and nodded his head in respect. "I mistook you for scoundrels, but it turns out that you are descended from patriots. Please forgive me. May I be so bold as to ask this gentleman's name?"

"My name is Skyfury Guo."

"He is my brother-in-arms," Yang said, "the descendant of Prosperity Guo, one of the heroes of the Marshes of Mount Liang."

The Taoist bowed again. "Your humble servant was rude, and quick to make assumptions. Please forgive me."

Guo and Yang bowed in return. "Not at all. Would the Reverend please come in for more rice wine?" Yang said, picking up his spear.

"Of course! I'd be delighted to join you."

Charity and Lily Li had been observing the fight anxiously from the doorway, and at this they scuttled back inside to warm the wine.

They sat at the table and the men asked the Taoist his name. "My name is Qiu Chuji."

Yang jumped up in surprise, and Guo was similarly aghast. "Master Eternal Spring?"

"That is the name my Taoist friends gave me." Qiu Chuji smiled. "I dare not claim such a name myself."

"Master Eternal Spring of the Quanzhen Sect," Guo said, "I am honored to make your acquaintance." The two men cast themselves onto the packed earth floor of the cottage and kowtowed.

Qiu Chuji leaped up from his bench and helped them to their feet. "I killed a traitor today," he began to explain. "The government's men were chasing me, and then you gentlemen suddenly invited me in for a drink. We are close to the capital here and it is clear that you are not ordinary farmers, so I became suspicious."

"My friend here has always had a temper," Guo said with a smile. "And then he tried to fight the Master. You were right to be suspicious."

"Indeed, farmers aren't usually that strong. I thought you were undercover government dogs."

Yang smiled. "You weren't to know."

The men continued to drink and chat until Qiu Chuji pointed at the battered head lying on the floor: "That's Wang Daoqian. He was a traitor. Last year he was sent by our Emperor to convey his respects to the Jin Emperor on the occasion of his birthday, but once there, he agreed to help them invade the south. I pursued him for ten days before at last catching him."

"We are so lucky to have met the Master," Yang said. "Won't you stay a couple of days?"

But just as Qiu Chuji was about to answer, his expression froze and hardened.

"What's wrong?" Guo asked.

"Someone has come for me. Whatever happens, you two must stay inside. Do not come out under any circumstances. Do you understand?" The two men nodded. Qiu Chuji picked up the human head and went outside, where he jumped up into the branches of a tree and hid among its dense crest of leaves.

Guo and Yang had no idea what had just happened. They could hear nothing save for the howling of the wind. They waited, until a few minutes later they could discern from the west the faint sound of hooves beating against frozen ground.

"How did he hear that?" Yang asked in a whisper. The rhythmic thudding of the hooves was growing louder and on the horizon a cloud of snow was making its way toward the village. Before long, ten riders dressed in black appeared and reined in a hundred meters from their door.

"The footprints stop over there. It looks like there's just been a fight." Several of the men jumped down from their horses and inspected the footprints in the snow. "Search the house!" the man who appeared to be their officer barked. Two more men jumped from their horses and hammered on the door.

Suddenly something came flying through the air from a nearby tree, thwacking one of the men on the head with such force that it cracked open his skull. The other men started to yell as they surrounded the tree. One man picked up the object and cried out in shock: "His Excellency Wang's head!"

Their commanding officer pulled out a saber and the remaining men rushed to form a ring around the tree trunk. The leader shouted another order, and five men raised their bows and shot into the dense clump of leaves above them.

Yang reached for his spear, but Guo grabbed at his arm and hissed, "Master Eternal Spring told us not to go outside. Let's wait awhile at least. If he gets into trouble we can help him then." Just then an arrow came hurtling from the branches above and hit one of the men still on his horse. He cried out, dropped from the horse's back and landed in the snow with a dull thud.

Qiu Chuji removed his sword, jumped down from the tree, and sliced through two of the men before the soldiers could react.

"It's the Taoist!"

Qiu Chuji bowed quickly and then *sha, sha, sha!* slashed his sword through the whipping wind, knocking another two men from their horses. Yang watched in awe, trying to follow the movement of the Master's sword. Qiu Chuji had obviously held back during their duel; if he had not, Yang would be dead by now.

Qiu Chuji moved as if he were being carried by the wind as he bounced and hopped between the horses, branches, and the ground. His next opponent was the commanding officer, who continued to bark orders at his men. He had a certain gift for fighting, but Guo and Yang could tell Qiu Chuji was deliberately prolonging the duel so as to use breaks in their fight to outmaneuver the other men. If he killed the leader before he managed to kill his men, they might run.

By now there were only six men left. The officer knew they could never defeat the Taoist, so he turned his horse and tried to escape. Qiu Chuji reached out with his left hand and grabbed the horse's tail. Pulling on it lightly, Qiu Chuji lifted himself from the ground. Before he had landed on the horse's back, he had already sliced his sword straight through the officer's back to the base of his spine. Qiu Chuji threw the body from the horse, grabbed hold of the reins, and started to chase the others, his blade dancing silver against the gray-white of the storm. Screams were swallowed by the wind as one body after another fell to the ground and plumes of blood decorated the snow.

Qiu Chuji stopped and looked around him. The only sound came from the three riderless horses galloping into the distance, their hooves pounding at the softly packed snow. He rode back to where Guo and Yang stood by the door, waved, and called, "How did you like that?"

Guo and Yang opened the front door and stepped slowly out. "Your Reverence, who were they?" Guo asked, still in shock.

"We'll know when we search them."

Guo walked over to the commanding officer's body and leaned down to take a look. His torso was sliced in two, and lay in a pond of blood. Guo reached for a leather pouch still fastened around the man's waist, and removed an official-looking document. It was from Magistrate Zhao, and stated that an order had come from the Jin ambassador that Song government troops were to assist them in capturing Wang Daoqian's murderer. Guo's hands shook with rage as he rose to his feet. He was just about to show the document to the other two men when Yang called out. He had found some tags written in the Jurchen language on some of the bodies. There were Jin soldiers among these men.

"Our government has now given free rein to enemy soldiers to capture and kill patriots within our own borders?" Guo exclaimed. "Song officials now take orders from the Jin?"

"Even our Emperor must refer to himself as an official of the Jin."

Yang sighed. "Our officials and generals are now no more than their slaves."

"We monks are supposed to be merciful and good in heart and action, we are not supposed to harm any living being," Qiu Chuji added bitterly. "But I could no longer withhold my anger, not when faced with traitors and enemies who do nothing but torture our people."

"You were right to kill them!" Yang said.

"They deserved to die!" Guo added.

Ox Village was small, and in a snowstorm like this everyone kept to their homes. If there had been any witnesses it was doubtful they would come out and ask questions. Yang went to fetch two shovels and a hoe, and the three men buried the bodies. Lily Li and Charity fetched brooms and began sweeping the bloodstained snow until the stench began to make Charity retch. A white mist descended in front of her eyes and with a gasp she fell to her knees.

Yang dropped his shovel and ran over to her. "What's the matter?"

But Charity closed her eyes and did not answer. Her face and hands were now as white as the snow that fell upon them.

Qiu Chuji hurried over, took hold of Charity's wrist and felt her pulse. A smile burst across his face. "Congratulations!" Yang looked aghast as Qiu Chuji grabbed his hand.

"What is it? What's happened?"

Charity came to with a faint grunt. The three men were standing above her. Feeling shy, she scrambled to her feet, and with Lily's help went inside, where her friend poured her a cup of tea.

"Your wife is pregnant."

"Are you sure?"

"I am master of nothing and can claim to know a little of only three things. Of these little kung fu tricks I am a mere novice, and as for poetry I am able to write a few couplets, but no more. But I can safely say that if I can lay claim to any expertise, it is in the field of medicine."

"Your Reverence, if yours are only 'little kung fu tricks,' then we are merely children playing."

Having finished burying the bodies, the men collected their tools and went inside to celebrate.

Yang could not stop smiling. If Qiu Chuji wrote poetry, he reasoned, he would be the perfect person to name his child, as well as Guo's. "My brother Skyfury's wife is pregnant as well. Could we trouble Your Reverence to think of two names for our children?"

Qiu Chuji sipped from his bowl of rice wine and thought for a while. "For Master Guo's child I suggest Guo Jing, meaning 'Serenity,' and for Master Yang's child, Yang Kang, meaning 'Vitality.' This will remind them of the humiliation of the year Jingkang, when Kaifeng was sacked and the Emperor captured by the Jin. These names can be used for girls just as well as boys."

He reached into his shirt, removed two daggers, and put them on the table. They were identical in every way, each with a green leather sheath, a gold cross guard, and an ebony handle. He picked up one of the daggers and on the handle swiftly carved the characters for "Serenity Guo" as if writing with brush and ink. Then he carved "Vitality Yang" on the handle of the other. He turned to the two fathers-to-be and said, "I don't have anything else suitable with me, only this pair of daggers. For the children."

The two men received them and thanked him. Yang unsheathed his. The blade was cold in his palm, and sharp.

"I came to possess these daggers quite by accident. They are extremely sharp, but they are too small for me to use. They would be perfect for the children. In ten years' time, if I am still lucky enough to be of this world, I will return to Ox Village and teach them some kung fu."

The two men were delighted and thanked the Reverend repeatedly.

"The Jin are occupying the north and torturing the people there," Qiu Chuji went on as he took his last gulps of rice wine. "The situation cannot continue for long. Gentlemen, please take care of yourselves."

Then he stood up and made for the door. Guo and Yang jumped to their feet and tried to make him stay, but he had already slipped out into the storm.

"Masters like him come and go like the wind." Guo sighed. "We were lucky to meet him today. I was hoping to talk to him some more, but alas it was not to be."

Yang smiled. "Brother, at least we witnessed Master Eternal Spring killing Jin soldiers." He held up the dagger and unsheathed it again. Gently stroking the blade, he suddenly looked up at his friend. "Brother, I've just had a foolish idea. Tell me what you think of it."

"What is it?"

"If our children are boys, they will be sworn brothers. If they are girls, they will be sworn sisters—"

"And if we have one boy and one girl, they shall be married," Guo cut in. The men laughed and embraced.

At that moment, Lily Li and Charity emerged from the back room. "Why are you so happy?" Yang repeated their agreement and they blushed, happy their families would forever be united.

"Let's swap the daggers now as our pledge," Yang suggested. "If they turn out to be sworn brothers or sisters, we can switch back. If they are to be married—"

"Then apologies, but both daggers will belong to my family," Guo interrupted.

Charity laughed. "You never know. Maybe we will be the ones to have a boy."

The men swapped daggers and gave them to their wives for safekeeping.

3

YANG WAS SLUMPED AT THE TABLE, PLAYING WITH THE DAGGER, more drunk than he had realized. Charity helped her husband into bed and collected the dishes. The navy blue sky was dotted with stars, but there was still enough light for her to go outside and collect the chicken cages. Just as she was pulling the back door shut, however, she caught sight of some blood on the snow only a few meters from the house. I must clean it up right away, or else there could be trouble. She hurried to collect her broom and stepped out again into the icy night.

But the blood did not stop there. She followed it with her broom all the way to the pine trees behind the house. The snow had also been disturbed; someone had clearly dragged themselves through it toward the woods. There, by an old grave tucked in between the trees, she spotted a large black mound on the snow.

Charity approached to get a better look. A body! One of the men Qiu Chuji had been fighting earlier. She was about to go and wake her husband to ask him to bury it when it struck her that someone could come past at any moment and see the body. No, it would be better to pull it into a nearby bush and then go and tell her husband. She edged toward it and, summoning all her strength, she took hold of its black clothes and pulled.

Suddenly the body twitched and groaned.

Was it a ghost? Fear paralyzed her. She watched it for a minute or so, but it did not move. Reaching for her broom, she gently poked it. The body groaned again, only this time the sound was much quieter. He was still alive. She approached and peered over the body. There, embedded in the back of his shoulder, was a large wolf-fang arrow. The snow was still falling, albeit much lighter now, and a thin layer of snowflakes had settled on the young man's face. He would soon freeze to death out here.

Charity had always been exceptionally kindhearted, ever since she was a young girl. She was forever bringing home injured sparrows, frogs, and even insects, which she would nurse back to health, and those she could not save she would bury, the tears flowing down her cheeks. Her father, a country scholar from Red Plum Village, had named her for this unusual sensitivity, and her mother was never allowed to slaughter any of their roosters or hens. Any chicken served

25

at the Bao family table for dinner had to be brought home from the market. Indeed, Charity had not changed much as she grew older, and this was one of the things Ironheart Yang loved about her. Their backyard was still a sanctuary for chickens, ducks, and every other sort of small creature that chose to make its home there.

There was no way she could let this man die in the snow. She knew he must be bad, but she could not leave him here. She scrambled to her feet and ran back to the house to discuss it with her husband. But Yang had fallen into a deep sleep, and no matter how she shook him, he would not wake up.

Deciding that she should save the man first and worry about the consequences later, she ran to the herbal medicine cabinet and fetched her husband's blood-clotting powder, and then found a small knife and some pieces of cloth. She grabbed the jug of warm wine that was still on the stove, and ran back outside. He had not moved. Charity helped him sit up and she trickled the leftover wine into his mouth. She knew a bit of basic medicine. The arrow sat deep in his flesh, and pulling it out might cause him to lose a lot of blood. But if she did not remove it, there would be no way of caring for the wound. So she took a breath, cut around the arrowhead, and tugged as hard as she could. The man screamed and instantly passed out. Blood spurted from the wound, covering her shirt in bright red splashes. Her heart was thumping in her chest but, steadying her shaking hands, she sprinkled the blood-clotting powder over the sore and bandaged it as tight as she could with the scraps of cloth. After a short time he began to regain consciousness.

Charity was so frightened her arms could barely muster the strength to hold the man up, let alone move him. But she had an idea. She went to the small barn by the side of the house and found a loose wooden plank. She pushed the plank under the man and shunted him onto it, and then dragged the plank through the snow back to the barn, as if pulling a sled.

Knowing he was safely sheltered, she crept back inside the house to change out of her bloodied shirt and wash her face and hands.

She then ladled a bowl of leftover chicken soup, lit a candle, and went back to the barn. His breathing was now steady, if weak. Charity approached the man and urged him to sit up again so that she could feed him the soup.

She held the bowl to the man's lips with her right hand, and in her left she moved the candle so that the warm glow highlighted his sculpted features and elegant nose. This was the first time she had been able to take a good look at his face and she almost gasped. He was so handsome. The blood rose in her cheeks and her hand began to tremble, splashing a drop of candle wax onto his smooth forehead.

He winced, and for the first time looked up at her. There, before him, was a face as delicate as a flower, two cheeks flushed pink like rose petals, and a pair of kind eyes sparkling like stars reflected in a river.

"Are you feeling any better?" Charity whispered. "Here, drink the rest of the soup." The man tried to take the bowl in his hands, but he was too weak and nearly spilled the hot broth on himself. Charity quickly took the bowl back and continued to feed him, one spoonful at a time.

By the time he finished the bowl, some color had returned to his cheeks. He looked up at the heavenly creature nursing him with such care, but Charity squirmed under his gaze. Hastily she clambered to her feet, and fetched an armful of straw to keep him warm. Taking the candle with her, she slipped out of the barn and back inside the house.

She did not sleep well that night. Her husband was plunging his spear through the man's chest. The man lunged at her husband with his saber. The man chased her between the pine trees. Every few hours she woke from a new nightmare, damp with sweat. As the sun warmed her eyelids, she began to stir, and she turned to discover that the other side of the bed was empty. She sat up. Had her husband found the man? She climbed down, folded the quilt, put on her outer robe and hurried into the front room. He was sitting at the table, sharpening the head of his spear. She nodded, before slipping outside toward the

27

barn and pushing open the door. But she saw no one there, just a messy pile of straw. The man had gone.

There, beyond the barn, a fresh trail in the snow led out toward the pine trees behind the house. For a minute or so she was lost in her thoughts as she stared out in the direction in which the man had left. A gust of icy wind rushed at her cheeks, and as if wakening her to her body, she felt a sharp pain in her stomach and her legs buckled. She stumbled back inside, where her husband greeted her with a proud grin: "I made you and the baby some rice porridge."

She smiled weakly, and sat. He would only get angry and jealous if he knew about the events of the previous night, so, she reasoned, she would have to keep them to herself.

WINTER GASPED its last breath and spring returned. Charity's belly had ballooned, and preparations for the baby's arrival had pushed almost all thoughts of the man in black from her mind.

The Yang family had just finished dinner, and Charity was huddled by the small pool of light cast by their lamp, sewing new clothes for her husband. Yang was hanging up the two pairs of straw sandals he had just finished weaving, ready for the spring.

"I'm going to see Carpenter Zhang tomorrow to see if he can fix the plow I broke this morning." Yang looked over at his wife. "Please don't make me any more clothes. Rest, my dear. Think of the baby."

Charity looked up at her husband and smiled, her fingers still moving the needle swiftly through the cloth. Yang walked over to where she was sitting, and took the sewing from her. Charity stretched, blew out the lamp, and together they went to bed.

At midnight, Charity was suddenly snapped out of her dreams by her husband sitting up in bed. In the distance, to the west, came a faint sound of hooves drumming against the dirt. Before long it could be heard from all directions.

"Why are there so many horses?"

Yang jumped down from the bed and started dressing. The drumming was growing louder; a neighbor's dog started barking. "We're being surrounded."

"What's happening?" Charity's voice was trembling.

"I have no idea," her husband replied, handing her the dagger Qiu Chuji had given them. "Take this, to protect yourself!" He unhooked his spear from the wall.

By now the sound of hooves had subsided into an intermittent clatter, largely drowned out by the horses neighing and their masters shouting. Yang opened one of the shutters at the front of the house and looked outside. A company of soldiers had surrounded the entire village, the light from their torches illuminating his neighbors' cottages. Some of the riders were struggling to still their excited horses as they rode among the houses.

"Find the traitors," the man in charge shouted to his men. "They must not get away!"

Were they here for Qu San? Yang had not seen the tavern keeper since before winter had come and gone. Even he would struggle to fight off so many men.

Suddenly one of the soldiers shouted something that made Yang's heart freeze in his chest. "Skyfury Guo! Ironheart Yang! Come out now and face the consequences of your treacherous actions!"

Charity had joined her husband by the window. These words made the blood drain from her cheeks.

"They come chasing innocent citizens when the traitors are among their own ranks!" Ironheart said. "Skyfury and I can't possibly fight so many men at once. Our only option is to run. Don't worry, I will protect you with my spear." He fetched a bow, slung it across his back and wedged some arrows in his belt. He then reached for his wife's hand and squeezed it tightly.

"I'll pack," she replied.

"Pack? We're leaving everything."

"But . . . our home?" A tear had crept from the corner of her eye and was making its way down her cheek.

"We've got to focus on getting away first. We can start another home elsewhere."

"But what about the chickens? And the cats?"

"Silly girl, thinking about them at a time like this?" He paused and then continued. "What would they do with your chickens and cats?"

"They eat chickens."

Just then a red-orange light came flickering through the window, throwing shadows across their simple furniture. The soldiers had just set fire to two thatched cottages nearby. Two foot soldiers were walking toward them along the main road through the village. "Skyfury Guo! Ironheart Yang! If you don't come out now we'll set fire to the whole village!"

A red rage rose in Yang, and before Charity could stop him, he had opened the door and stepped out. "I am Ironheart Yang. What do you want?"

Two soldiers dropped their torches in fright and backed away.

One of the other men rode his horse up to the front of the Yang family house and stopped. "So you are Ironheart Yang? Come with us to see the magistrate." Turning to the foot soldiers, the man barked, "Take him!"

Four men ran toward him. Yang twirled his spear in a Rainbow Crosses the Sky, and swept three of the soldiers to the ground. He followed this with a Deafening Spring Thunder, picking up one of the soldiers with the shaft of his spear and throwing him into two other men. "First you must tell me what crimes I am being charged with."

"Traitor!" the man on the horse bellowed. "How dare you resist arrest?" He may have sounded brave, but he was noticeably reluctant to come any closer.

Another man on horseback drew level with the first man. "Come without a fight and there will be no new charges to add to your existing crimes. We have the official documents for your arrest here."

"Let me see them!"

"What about the other traitor, Skyfury Guo?"

Skyfury thrust his upper body out of the window of his house, along with a bow and arrow, and called, "Here I am!" He aimed the arrow at the first man on horseback.

"Put down your bow. Only then will I read the document to you."

"Read it now!" Guo pulled the arrow all the way back.

Glancing at the other man on horseback, he rolled out the document and began reading. *"Skyfury Guo and Ironheart Yang of Ox Village, Lin'an Prefecture, are charged with collusion with the intent of wrongdoing. A warrant for their arrest has been issued in accordance with the laws of the Great Song Empire, in the name of the Ningzong Emperor."*

"Which official issued the order?" Guo asked.

"Chancellor Han himself."

Guo and Yang were taken aback. What have we done that could merit the ire of Chancellor Han? Yang thought to himself. Did they find out about Qiu Chuji's visit?

"Who is the accuser?" Guo added. "Based on what evidence?"

"We only have orders to capture you and bring you to the court at Lin'an. If you want to plead your case, you can do so with the judge."

"The court at Lin'an only knows how to harass innocent citizens. Everyone knows that!" Guo called back. "We're not falling for that lie!" He shifted his arrow so it was now pointing at this soldier.

"So you are resisting arrest?" the first man on horseback called back. "Another crime to add to the list."

Yang turned to his wife and whispered, "Quickly, put on some more clothes. I'll get his horse for you. Once I shoot their commanding officer, the rest of the men will panic."

He drew his bow from his bag and shot an arrow, hitting the officer in charge in the chest. *"Aiya!"* The force knocked him from his horse and he fell with a thud into the dirt. The soldiers started shouting in surprise: "Seize them!" The foot soldiers ran forward. Yang and Guo began firing arrows as fast as they could, and within seconds they had killed seven more men between them. But there were still too many soldiers.

Howling, Ironheart Yang swung his spear up above his head and charged forward. The soldiers shrank back in surprise and fear. He made straight for an official sitting astride a white horse, and lunged his spear at him. The man tried to block it with his own lance, but Yang was too quick, plunging his spear deep into the official's thigh. He lifted the man like a piece of meat on the end of a skewer, and flicked him from his horse.

Yang then dug the other end of his spear into the ground and flipped himself onto the back of the horse. Squeezing his calves, he jolted the horse forward. It reared, before leaping straight toward the house. Yang speared another soldier by the door, leaned down and scooped Charity up with one arm. "Brother, follow me!"

Guo was spinning his double halberd at the crowd of men, holding his wife behind him with his other hand. The remaining soldiers were frightened and began shooting arrows in panic.

Yang galloped over to Guo and Lily, and dropped down from the horse's back. "Sister, get on." Against her protests, he threw her up onto the horse. Charity took hold of the reins and started to move the horse forward. The two men followed on foot, spearing and slicing any soldiers brave enough to approach.

Suddenly, a thundering of hooves sounded in the west. Yang and Guo glanced at each other and started looking for an escape route. Just then Charity screamed; the horse had been hit by an arrow. It lurched forward and landed on its front knees, before falling to its side and throwing the two women to the ground.

"Brother, you look after them," Yang said. "I'll get another horse." Clutching his spear, Yang ran straight into the crowd of soldiers ahead. A dozen or so formed a line, raising their bows at Yang.

There were just too many soldiers, Guo reasoned, and their chances of escaping with their wives was not looking good. Perhaps they should give themselves up and argue their case in court? None of the men had survived the fight against Qiu Chuji that winter's afternoon, so there could be no witness to say they had been part of it, let alone killed any of the soldiers themselves. "Ironheart, stop!" Guo called. "Let's go with them!"

Yang halted in surprise and ran back, dragging his spear in the dirt.

The officer in command of this second group of soldiers ordered the men not to shoot and instead surround the traitors. "Throw down your weapons, and you will be spared!"

"Brother, don't fall for their lies," Yang hissed. Guo shook his head, looked his friend straight in the eye and, holding his gaze, threw his double halberd to the dirt. Yang looked across at his wife. Fear seemed to reach out of her eyes and cling to him. He sighed and threw his spear to the ground. Ten spearheads appeared inches from their faces, and eight foot soldiers stepped forward to bind their hands.

Yang held his head high, a sneer spread across his face. The officer in charge walked his horse forward and lashed Yang across the cheek with his whip. "Damned traitor! Are you really not afraid to die?"

"And what's your name?" came Yang's reply, a snarl rather than a question.

This drove the man on the horse even wilder with rage. "Justice Duan—His Excellency Duan to you! And don't forget it. You can tell them about me when you reach the gates of hell!"

Yang stared back at the man without blinking, his eyes fixed on Duan's.

"I've got a scar on my forehead and a birthmark on my right cheek," Duan continued. "Know who I am now?" At this he whipped Yang across the other cheek.

"He's a good man, he's done nothing wrong," Charity called out. "Why are you beating him?"

Yang spat at Duan and a globule of phlegm landed on his birthmark. Furious, Duan pulled out his saber. "I'm going to kill you right now, you disgusting traitor!" He lifted his saber high above his head and brought it down in a clumsy slash. It was not hard for Yang to step out of the way. Two foot soldiers moved their spears to Yang's sides and pushed the metal tips against his taut muscles, pincering him. Duan raised his saber again and swung it down somewhat more elegantly than before. Unable to move sideways, Yang could only pull back. Despite appearances Duan had in fact practiced some martial arts, and immediately he thrust his saber forward. The blade had a saw-toothed edge, and this time he managed to swipe it through Yang's left shoulder. He pulled back again for another chop.

At that moment Guo jumped up and thrust his feet at Duan's face. Duan tried to block Guo's feet with his saber, but despite having his hands tied behind his back, Guo managed to twirl his left leg away and round Duan's sword, while jabbing his right foot into Duan's stomach.

"Spear them!" Duan coughed. "Our orders were to kill them should they resist arrest."

But Guo had kicked two men to the ground. Duan came from behind him and swung his saber down hard, severing Guo's right arm at the shoulder. Yang had been trying to struggle free from the ropes around his wrists, but seeing his oldest friend so badly wounded gave him a new surge of strength. He snapped his bonds, punched the closest soldier, and grabbed his spear. By now he had nothing to lose: he could fight or they would all die. He speared two more in quick succession.

Duan shrank back in fear. He could see renewed and ferocious determination in Yang's eyes, the fear of killing government troops now gone. The remaining soldiers ran.

Rather than give chase, Yang turned to his friend. He crouched down beside Guo. Blood was pumping from the wound in crimson spurts and his cream robe was already drenched down one side. Tears ran like rivulets down his cheeks.

Guo forced a smile. "Ironheart, don't worry about me. Go. Go!"

"I'm going to fetch a horse," Yang said. "Whatever happens, I'm going to save you."

"No, don't worry." Guo passed out.

Ironheart Yang removed his shirt so he could bandage up the wound. But Duan's sword had sliced through Guo's shoulder and into his chest. It would be impossible to stem the bleeding. Guo came round again and called, "Brother, save our wives. I'm not going to make it." Then he gasped and died.

Ever since they were little, the two friends had always thought of each other as flesh and blood. Rage surged in Yang's chest, and he recalled they had once sworn to each other, "Together we will die, same day, same month, same year." Yang looked around him. He had no idea what had happened to their wives amid the chaos.

"Brother, I will avenge your death!" he cried out, grabbing hold of his spear and charging toward the nearest group of soldiers.

By now the soldiers had resumed their formation. Justice Duan issued an order, and a swarm of arrows came flying straight at Yang. But he marched ahead through the storm, knocking the arrows aside. One military officer swung his saber hard at Ironheart's head, but Ironheart ducked and tucked himself underneath the belly of his horse. The saber was left to swipe blindly through the air. The officer was trying to turn his horse when a spear pierced through his back and into his heart. Yang lifted the corpse and flicked it off the end of his spear, before mounting. He waved his spear at the remaining soldiers. None dared fight him, choosing instead to flee.

Yang continued to chase them for a while until he caught sight of one of the officers riding away, with a woman slung over his horse. Ironheart jumped down from his horse and skewered one of the foot soldiers with his spear. Taking the soldier's bow and arrow, he aimed as best he could, with the light from the burning houses as his only guide, pulled back and fired. The arrow speared the horse's behind, sending the animal to its knees and the two riders tumbling to the ground. Ironheart fired another arrow, killing the officer. He then ran over to the woman, who was struggling to sit up.

4

CHARITY THREW HERSELF INTO HER HUSBAND'S ARMS IN RE-
lief.

"Where is our sister Lily Li?" Yang asked.

"Up ahead. She was captured by soldiers."

"Stay here and wait for me. I'm going to find her."

"But there are more soldiers coming!" Charity replied, aghast.

Ironheart turned to watch a cluster of torches approaching.

"Brother Guo is dead," Yang said, turning back to Charity. "I have
to find Lily Li, to save his family line. The heavens will take pity on
us, I will come back for you!"

Charity clung to her husband's neck and would not let go. "We
were never to part," she said, tears gathering. "You said so yourself.
We're going to die together."

Ironheart took her in his arms and kissed her. He then peeled her
arms from around his neck and picked up his spear. He ran a few
dozen meters, then stopped and looked back. There she sat, crouched
in the dust, crying. The soldiers were upon her.

Ironheart turned and wiped the mixture of tears, sweat, and blood
from his cheeks with his sleeve. The Guo family must have descendants.

He carried onward on foot until he spotted a stray horse, and a
man nearby. "Which way did the soldiers go?" he demanded.

"That way." The man pointed. Ironheart belted the horse with his
heel, and spurred onward.

Then, a scream. A woman's scream, in the woods by the road. He
jerked the horse round and charged straight at the trees. Lily Li had
wrestled her hands free from the ropes and was fighting off two foot
soldiers. She was a strong, robust country girl; the foot soldiers
laughed and cursed, but they could not overcome her. Ironheart was
upon them, and with two jabs speared them both. He then pulled

Lily up behind him and together they raced back to where he had left his wife.

But there was no one to be found.

Morning was approaching. Ironheart dismounted his horse and searched for any trace of his wife by the day's first light. There, a trail; someone had been dragged through the dirt. His wife, captured by soldiers.

Ironheart jumped back up onto the horse and booted it in the stomach. The horse was galloping at full speed when a bugle sounded and a group of ten soldiers dressed in black and on horseback charged onto the path. The first man was wielding a wolf-fang club but Ironheart blocked it, parrying with his spear. The man then planed the club toward Ironheart's stomach—an unusual move in these parts.

The wolf-fang club was a heavy weapon, and not generally popular in the *wulin*. The Jin army, however, were known to favor it. The Jurchen had grown up strong in the fight against the freezing climate, east of the Liao River. When the Jin invaded the north, the wolf-fang club had been their weapon of choice.

Ironheart was growing suspicious and recalled his brother's words. Judging by range and quality of the man's skills, he must be of high rank in the Jin army. But what was he doing here? Ironheart quickened his spear and struck the man from his horse. The rest fled in shock.

Ironheart turned to check that Lily Li was unhurt. At that moment, an arrow whistled through the air toward him and buried itself in his back.

"Brother!" Lily Li cried.

It felt like ice piercing his heart. So this is it, Ironheart said to himself. But I must defeat these men first, so Lily can escape.

With the last of his strength he lifted his spear, spurred his horse and rushed at the new crowd of soldiers that had appeared. But the pain was too much. A dark curtain drew across his eyes and he fainted, slumped over his horse.

5

THE MOMENT HER IRONHEART HAD PUSHED HER AWAY, CHARITY felt as if her heart had been sliced in two by her husband's own blade. The soldiers were upon her within seconds. There was no escape.

One of the officers held a torch to her face.

"It's her," he said. "Who'd have guessed those two southerners alone could have caused our men such injury."

"At least we can say we were the ones to complete the job," another said. "They'll have to give us at least ten *taels* of silver for our efforts."

"Huh!" the first officer snorted. "I'll just be happy if the generals leave a few coins for us." He turned to the bugler. "Time to go back."

The bugler brought his instrument to his lips and blew.

❧

THEY KEPT riding. Charity tried to swallow her tears. What had happened to her husband? The sun had now risen. People started to appear on the road, but they slipped away again at the sight of the soldiers. Charity was surprised, however, to find the men polite in both word and deed, so after some time she began to relax.

After several more *li,* they heard shouts coming from up ahead. Another group of men clad in black charged at them from the side of the road.

"Disgusting vermin!" their leader shouted. "Murdering innocent subjects! Get down from your horses!"

The highest-ranking officer was furious. "How dare you bandits show your faces out here on the outskirts of the capital? Get away, now!"

The men in black rushed forward. What they lacked in numbers, they made up for with their superior kung fu.

Charity was quietly excited. Maybe her dear Ironheart's friends had come to rescue her?

In the chaos, an arrow came flying toward Charity from behind and hit her horse in the rump. It jerked and began racing forward. Charity desperately wrapped her arms around the horse's neck for fear of falling. Before long, she heard the beating of hooves against the dirt behind her. A black horse drew level with hers and then edged in front. The man riding it was spinning a rope, and with a *swish!* it flew through the air and looped over the head of Charity's horse. The man pulled on the rope, drawing them level and then slowing them. He whistled, stopping his animal dead. Charity's horse was pulled to a halt, neighing and rearing.

Charity was worn out after such a long and eventful night. Terror and grief had weakened her so she could no longer hold the reins. She fainted, flopping from the horse and to the ground.

CHARITY FELT herself waking gradually. She did not know how long she had been asleep. A cozy feeling cloaked her, and she imagined herself to be lying on a soft bed, wrapped in a thick cotton quilt. As she opened her eyes, the first thing she saw was a fine green canopy decorated with flowers above her, and as she turned, a lamp lit on a bedside table. Was she imagining it? Or was there a man in black sitting by her bed?

Hearing her stir, the man stood up and parted the bed curtains. "Are you awake?" he whispered.

Charity was still half-asleep, but the man seemed familiar.

"You still have a fever," the man murmured, placing his hand on her forehead. "Don't worry, the doctor will be here soon."

Dazed, Charity fell back into the comfort of sleep.

Later, she was dimly aware of a doctor examining her and someone feeding her medicine. She felt almost paralyzed by exhaustion.

Then, suddenly: "Ironheart! My dear Ironheart!" She broke from her dream with a start. Someone stroked her shoulder, consoled her.

The sun was high in the sky by the time she next woke. A groan

39

rose from deep within her. Someone came to the bed and pulled aside the curtain. She looked at him, and shock shot through her. The handsome, friendly-looking man standing before her was none other than the injured soldier she had saved in the snow all those months ago.

"Where am I? Where is my husband?"

The young man gestured for her to be quiet. "There are soldiers everywhere out there looking for us. We're staying with a local farmer. Your humble servant begs your forgiveness, my lady, I had to lie to the farmer and say that I am your husband. Please don't say anything."

Charity blushed and nodded. "Where's my husband?"

"My lady is still weak. I will tell you everything once you feel better."

A jolt went through Charity; the tone of his voice was enough to tell her it was serious. She gripped the corner of her quilt and asked again, her voice shaking, "He . . . What happened?"

"Worrying will accomplish nothing now. Your health is the most important thing."

"Is he dead?" she pressed.

"Was Squire Yang tall, with broad shoulders, around twenty? Did he use a spear?"

"Yes, that's him."

Knowing he had no choice but to tell her now, he nodded. "Squire Yang was unlucky. Those hateful soldiers killed him." He shook his head and sighed.

Pain pulsed in her chest and she fainted. When she came to again she instantly began sobbing. The man tried to soothe her.

"How did he die?" she stuttered between sobs.

"I saw him fighting a group of soldiers earlier today. He killed a few of them. But then . . . one of the soldiers crept up behind him and stabbed him in the back with his spear."

The shock temporarily knocked her out again. For the rest of the day she neither drank nor ate. The man did not force her, and instead attempted to distract her with chatter.

After some time, Charity began to feel guilty for not asking the man any questions. "May I ask sir's name? How did you know we were in trouble and needed help?"

"My surname is Yan, my given name is Lie. I was passing by with my friends when we saw those soldiers harassing you. We decided to help, and as it turns out, the heavens decreed that I should save my own savior. We were destined to meet again."

His words made her blush and she turned away from him. But her mind was working as his story struck her as suspicious. She turned back to face him. "Are you one of them?"

Yan Lie looked surprised.

"Weren't you one of the soldiers who tried to capture the Taoist that day? That's how you got hurt?"

"I was unlucky, that's all. I was coming south and was passing through your village on my way to Lin'an. But then an arrow came out of nowhere and hit me in the back. If it weren't for my lady's benevolence, I would have died out there. But why were they trying to catch the monk? Taoists catch ghosts—why would a soldier want to catch a monk? They've got it all muddled." He looked amused.

"So you were just passing through? You weren't with them? I thought you were also coming after the Taoist. I wasn't sure I should help you that day." She then went on to tell him why the soldiers were there and how Qiu Chuji killed them all.

Charity continued talking, until she caught him staring at her, captivated. She fell silent.

"My apologies." He smiled. "I was just thinking about how we're going to escape without getting caught by the soldiers."

Charity started to cry. "My husband's gone—how can I live on? It is my duty, as his wife. I should do the honorable thing."

"Madam, your husband was murdered by rebel soldiers and his death is yet to be avenged. How can you think of suicide? Squire Yang was a hero in life. He'll never find peace beneath the Nine Springs of the Underworld if he hears you talking like that."

"But I'm just a feeble woman. How can I possibly avenge his death?"

"My lady's burden," Yan Lie said in righteous anger, "I will gladly assume. Do you know who the culprit is?"

Charity thought for a while before answering. "Their leader was called Justice Duan. He has a scar on his forehead and a birthmark on his cheek."

"We have a name and distinguishing features. It doesn't matter if he runs to the ends of the earth or the corners of the sea, we will bring him to justice!" He went outside and came back with a bowl of rice porridge and some peeled salted eggs. "But you won't get your revenge if you don't take care of your health first."

Charity agreed this made sense, took the bowl and started to eat. She then fell back into a fitful sleep.

The next morning, Charity arranged her clothes and got out of bed. She went to the mirror and brushed her hair, found a piece of white cloth and fixed a white flower in her hair, out of respect for her husband. But the sight of the beautiful woman in the mirror, widowed at such a young age, plunged her back into the depths of her grief and she started weeping bitterly.

Just then Yan Lie walked in. He waited for a pause in her sobs. "The soldiers have retreated. Let's be on our way," he said softly.

Charity followed him out. Yan Lie handed the master of the house a piece of silver, and then brought the two horses round. Her horse's wound had been taken care of.

"Where to now?" Charity asked.

Yan Lie hushed her with a look, and helped her up onto her horse. Together they began riding northward, side by side.

"Where are you taking me?" Charity asked again, several *li* thence.

"First we're going to find somewhere to lie low. Once everything has calmed, I will go back and bury your husband. Then I will kill Justice Duan!"

Charity was mild in character and rarely put forward her own suggestions. Furthermore, the events of the previous night had left her all alone in the world, and she was just grateful that Yan Lie had a plan.

"Master Yan, how am I ever to repay you?"

"My lady, you were the one to save me!" he exclaimed. "I will be your humble servant for the rest of my days, through fire and rain, even in the face of the cruellest torture."

"I only hope we can kill that horrible man as soon as possible, so that I can join my husband in the knowledge he has been avenged." Tears tumbled down her cheeks.

They rode for a full day before stopping for the night at an inn in Chang'an. Yan Lie told the innkeeper they were married and got one room. This made Charity extremely nervous, but she remained silent, and instead gripped Qiu Chuji's dagger under her clothes. If he does anything untoward, I'll kill myself, she decided.

Yan Lie instructed one of the men to bring them two bundles of rice straw. Once the man left, he locked the door and arranged the bundles on the floor. He then lay down on one of them and drew a rug over himself. "Sleep well, my lady," he said, and closed his eyes.

Charity's heart was thumping. Thoughts of her dead husband tore at her insides, and she sat staring into the darkness for over an hour before eventually blowing out the candle with a sigh. Clutching the dagger, she climbed onto her bundle of straw and slept in her clothes.

BY THE time Charity woke the next day, Yan Lie had already readied the horses and was requesting breakfast. Charity was grateful he was proving to be such a gentleman, and began to think perhaps she need not be so worried. Breakfast consisted of fried strips of chicken and tofu, ham, sliced sausage, smoked fish, and a small pot of the most deliciously fragrant rice porridge. Charity was from a simple but honest background and had lived off the land since marrying into the Yang family. Breakfast for her usually consisted of pickles and a small piece of tofu. She only got to eat such varied fare at Spring Festival or wedding banquets. She ate, but felt a little uncomfortable.

After they finished, an inn boy came in with a bundle. Yan Lie had already left the room.

"What's this?" Charity asked.

"As soon as the sun was up, Master went out and bought new clothes for Madam. He says you are to wear them." He placed the bundle on the floor and left.

Charity opened the bundle and was surprised to find a mourning dress made from white silk, with a complete set of matching accessories, from stockings, shoes, underwear to a padded jacket, silk scarf, and sash.

"He's thought of everything," she muttered. "What an unusual young man."

She dressed in her new clothes, but just knowing Yan Lie had selected them made her blush. She had left home in a hurry and her own clothes were now torn and dirty after a night on the road. The new outfit did cheer her a little. When Yan Lie returned, she noticed he too was dressed in expensive new clothes.

And so they set off again, riding in single file, or sometimes side by side. Spring was just turning into summer south of the Yangtze. Willows by the side of the road reached out and brushed against their shoulders as they passed, flowers filled the air with their intoxicating scent, and the fields were covered in a green quilt of new shoots.

Yan Lie spent the entire journey idly chatting in order to distract Charity from her grief. Charity's father, a minor scholar, was the most educated man of their small village, and her husband and his sworn brother had both been straightforward, simple men. Never had she met a man as refined and cultured as Yan Lie. His every word revealed a depth and sharpness of thought. But they seemed to be heading farther and farther north, away from Lin'an, and he had not mentioned the subject of avenging her husband's unjust death all day. She could hold back no longer: "Master Yan, do you know the whereabouts of my husband's body?"

"Of course I wish to look for Squire Yang's body and give him a proper burial, it's just that I killed government men while rescuing my lady. Right now it's very dangerous for me to go back there; they would kill me as soon as I set foot in Lin'an. In any case, soldiers are out everywhere looking for my lady. Squire Yang committed treason by killing officials of the Song Empire, after all, and that's a serious crime. When they capture the relatives of a traitor, the men are beheaded and the women forced into prostitution. I'm not so worried about my own safety, but I couldn't leave my lady without protection. They would do terrible things to you."

Charity nodded at his sincerity.

"I have given the matter considerable thought," Yan Lie continued. "The most important thing is to give your husband a proper burial. So we are heading for Jiaxing where I can obtain enough silver to send someone to Lin'an to take care of it. If Madam will only find peace in the knowledge that I have organized it personally, then I will first make sure you are safe in Jiaxing, and then go back myself."

Charity thought it would be expecting too much to ask him to take such a big risk for her, so she replied, "If Master can find someone trustworthy to handle it, then I suppose that will do." She paused, and then continued, "My husband also had a friend—they were sworn brothers—by the name of Skyfury Guo. He died alongside my husband. I'm sorry to trouble you by asking this, but if you could ensure that he too is buried properly . . . Well, I would . . ." She was interrupted by her own tears.

"It's no trouble," Yan Lie replied. "Just leave it to me. As for avenging their deaths, the traitor Justice Duan is a government official, so it's going to be difficult to kill him. Besides, we need to be especially careful right now. We're going to have to be patient and wait for our moment."

Charity knew Yan Lie was right, but she was desperate to see Justice Duan dead so she could join her husband in the next world. But who knew when such an opportunity would arise? She would have to be patient. The tears flowed even faster.

"I don't care about getting revenge," she stuttered between sobs.

"Even a hero like my husband was unable to defeat him. I'm just a wretched woman—how can I wait for him to be brought to justice? Just let me join my husband."

Yan Lie paused to think. "Madam, do you have faith in me?"

Charity nodded.

"Then the only answer," he said, "is to continue north, away from the soldiers. The Song officials can't catch us up in the north, we'll be out of danger as soon as we cross the River Huai. Once things have calmed, we'll come back south to avenge these heroes. Please be assured, my lady, I will see to it that justice is done."

I have no family now, Charity thought to herself, hesitating. If I don't follow him, where is a woman like me to make a life for herself? I saw those soldiers attack my husband and burn our home with my own eyes. Had they captured me, I would have suffered a fate worse than death. Yet this man is neither friend nor relative. Should a widow like me be traveling on her own with a young man like him? But he would no doubt stop me if I tried to commit suicide. All she knew for sure was that the road ahead would be difficult and uncertain, and her guts felt twisted with worry. She had been crying for days now and it felt as if she had no tears left.

"If my lady doesn't agree with any part of my plan, then please tell me. I will do anything Madam asks."

He was so accommodating that it made Charity feel guilty. Other than taking her own life, she could see no other way. "Then let's do as you suggest," she said, unable to look up.

Yan Lie visibly rejoiced, and exclaimed, "I am forever in Madam's debt, for you saved my l—"

"Please don't mention it again," Charity interrupted.

"Of course."

⁂

THAT NIGHT, they stopped at another inn in the town of Wudun, and once again Yan Lie arranged for them to stay in the same room.

He had been noticeably less reserved since Charity had agreed to go with him to the north, and occasionally he would become a little too excited. She was beginning to feel uneasy again, but as he was yet to do anything improper as such, she decided he must just be trying to show his gratitude.

They arrived at Jiaxing around noon the next day. It was one of the biggest cities in western Zhejiang, where the rice and silk trades had thrived for centuries. Known as Drunken Plums in ancient times and Bounteous Grains during the Five Dynasties, it had changed its name to Jiaxing following Emperor Xiaozong's birth in the city.

"Let's find a place to rest," Yan Lie suggested.

Charity, however, was concerned the soldiers might find them. "It's still early, let's press on."

"The markets here are good and Madam's clothes are worn. We should buy you some new ones first."

"But you bought these only yesterday," Charity said. "You call these worn?"

"The roads are dusty; clothes lose their shine after only a couple of days. Besides, Madam is so beautiful, it wouldn't be right for you to wear anything but the finest."

Charity enjoyed his compliment, even if she could not admit it, but she looked away. "I'm in mourning"

"But of course," he replied at once. "I understand."

Charity was quiet. She was indeed a beautiful young woman, but her husband had never once told her so. She stole a glance at Yan Lie. He seemed sincere. A flutter went through her, but it was tinged with anxiety.

Yan Lie asked passersby for a place to stay and was directed to the Elegant Waters Inn, the largest in the city. After freshening up, Yan Lie and Charity ordered some snacks in their room and sat facing each other, eating. Charity had wanted to ask for a separate room, but did not know how to phrase it. Her cheeks alternated between bright crimson and pallid white as they ate, her worries pressing constantly against her chest.

47

"Please make yourself comfortable, my lady. I'm just going to buy a few things. I'll be back soon."

Charity nodded. "Please don't spend too much."

Yan Lie smiled. "It's such a shame Madam is in mourning and cannot wear pearls or gems. Anyhow, I could never spend too much, even if it was my greatest desire."

CHAPTER TWO

THE SEVEN FREAKS
OF THE SOUTH

I

YAN LIE STEPPED OUT INTO THE CORRIDOR. A YAWNING middle-aged man was shuffling toward him, his leather slippers scuffing along the floorboards. He seemed to be half smiling, perhaps even winking at him. His clothes were ragged and spotted with grease, his face grimy as if he had not washed in weeks, and he fanned himself with a broken black oilpaper fan.

His dress showed he was a man of some education, but his filthy appearance disgusted Yan Lie, who scuttled on, pressing himself against the wall so as not to brush up against him. Just as they were passing each other, however, the man broke into a harsh, hollow laugh, flipped his fan shut and tapped it against Yan Lie's shoulder.

"What are you doing?" Yan Lie cried, unable to deflect the fan in time.

Another dry laugh, and the scholar shuffled away, his slippers scuffing against the floorboards. The man then turned to one of the men working at the inn and said, "You there, young man. I may look as if I've fallen on hard times, but I travel with silver in my pocket.

It's not me you should be watchful of, but those men in fancy clothes pretending they are important. They seduce respectable women, eat without paying, take rooms and never settle the bill. Keep an eye out for those types. I would make them pay in advance, just to be sure." He had already disappeared down the corridor before the attendant could reply.

Yan Lie was furious. The attendant glanced at Yan Lie, walked up to him and bowed.

"Please don't take offense, sir," the attendant simpered, "I don't mean to be rude, but . . ."

"Take this, and make sure you put it somewhere safe!" He snorted, reaching beneath his shirt for his silver. But the color drained from his face. He had tucked at least forty or fifty *taels* in there before leaving his room, but they were gone.

The attendant straightened himself and puffed up his chest. So the scholar was right, and not just bitter. "What's that? No money?"

"Wait here," Yan Lie replied. "I have some in my room." I must have forgotten it as I hurried out, he thought. But back in his room, he opened his pouch to discover all his gold and silver had vanished. He had no idea when it could have been taken. Madam Bao and I both went to the lavatory at the same time just now, he said to himself, but we were only away from the room for a matter of moments. Could someone have stolen it in such a short space of time? The thieves of Jiaxing were impressive indeed.

The attendant poked his head through the door. Yan Lie was still puzzled, his hands empty. "Is this woman even your wife?" The attendant was angry now. "If you've kidnapped her, we will be implicated!"

Charity was mortified, her cheeks flushed crimson. Yan Lie took one large stride toward the door and slapped the back of his hand against the attendant's face, knocking out several teeth.

The attendant brought his hands to his bleeding cheeks. "First you don't pay, then you start a fight!" he cried.

Yan Lie kicked the attendant in the behind, sending him crashing out the door.

"Let's go, we can't stay here any longer," Charity said, shaken.

"Not to worry." Yan Lie smiled, grabbing a chair and sitting by the door. "We are going to get our silver back first."

Before long, the attendant came rushing back in with a group of thugs, each armed with a club. Yan Lie smiled. "A fight?"

He leaped up and snatched a club from the hand of one of the men, faked a right, jabbed to the left, and knocked half the men to the ground. They were used to turning up and merely intimidating their opponents, but it was obvious their fighting skills were nothing compared to this wealthy guest's, so the remaining men threw down their clubs and swarmed out of the room. The others scrambled to their feet and followed.

"This is serious," Charity said, her voice shaking. "The authorities might come after us."

"That is exactly my intention," Yan Lie said.

Charity did not know what was going on, so decided to stay quiet. Within the hour, shouting could be heard outside and a dozen government runners burst into the courtyard holding sabers and shorter broadswords.

Over the sound of clanging metal, Yan Lie heard a man say: "Kidnapped her and then assaulted you? How dare he! Where is this crook?"

The men rushed in. Yan Lie was sitting perfectly still in a chair. He cut an intimidating figure in his expensive clothes.

"You, what's your name?" the man in charge demanded. "What are you doing here in Jiaxing?"

"Fetch me Gai Yuncong!" came Yan Lie's reply.

The men were surprised and angered to hear him use the Governor of Jiaxing's name so casually. "Have you lost your mind? How dare you use the Honorable Governor's given name?"

Yan Lie removed a letter from inside his shirt and threw it on the table. "Deliver this to Gai Yuncong and see if he comes."

The man in charge walked over to the table, took the letter and read the characters on the front. He was visibly shocked, but hesitated, unsure if the letter was genuine. "Watch him, make sure he doesn't get away," he hissed as he dashed out of the door.

Charity sat, her heart thumping and her cheeks deathly pale.

It was not long before another dozen government men came crowding into the room, two among them clothed head-to-toe in full ceremonial dress. They ran over to Yan Lie, dropped to their knees and kowtowed at his feet: "Your humble servants Governor Gai Yuncong of Jiaxing and Magistrate Jiang Wentong bow before Your Excellency. Your humble servants were not informed of Your Excellency's arrival; please forgive us such an improper reception."

Yan Lie waved at them and lifted himself from his seat a little. "I was robbed of some silver this morning. May I trouble you two good sirs to investigate?"

"Of course." Gai Yuncong nodded, waving two of his men over. They each carried a tray; one glowed the warm yellow of gold, the other glinted the dazzling white of silver. "Your humble servant is ashamed to admit such brazen and odious villains roam free in our county, and that they have stolen from Your Excellency. The fault is all mine. Will Your Excellency accept this as a small token of our regret?"

Yan Lie smiled and nodded. Gai Yuncong further presented Yan Lie with a letter. "Your humble servant has just had the Governor's residence cleaned, and Your Excellency and His Lady are cordially invited to stay there as long as Your Excellency may wish."

"That won't be necessary. I like it here, it's peaceful. We don't want to be disturbed again," he said, his face darkening.

"Yes, of course! Should Your Excellency require anything, please let me know. Your humble servant will take care of it."

Yan Lie did not reply but waved them away, at which the two men ushered the others out.

The attendant had been cowering in fear, but now the innkeeper dragged him over to Yan Lie and made him kowtow and beg for mercy, declaring they would accept whatever punishment His Excellency might choose to mete out. Yan Lie took an ingot of silver from the plate and threw it on the ground. "There's your payment. Now go." The attendant froze in stunned silence, but the owner judged there to be no malice in Yan Lie's actions, so he grabbed the piece of silver, bowed a few times and pulled the attendant out of the door.

Charity was as uneasy as before. "What was so special about that letter? Why would an official be so frightened after reading it?"

"I don't actually have any authority over them," Yan Lie said, "but these officials are useless. Zhao Kuo likes to surround himself with worthless men. If he doesn't end up losing his land, then there's no justice in this world."

"Zhao Kuo?"

"Emperor Ningzong of Song."

"Shhh!" Charity was horrified. "You can't use His Majesty's given name. Someone will hear."

Yan Lie was pleased that she cared for his safety. "It's fine. That's what we call him in the north."

"The north?"

Yan Lie nodded and was about to explain when they heard the sound of beating hooves outside. Another group of men on horses stopped in front of the inn. A warm flush of red had just returned to Charity's snowy cheeks, but the sound of horses' hooves brought back memories of her capture only days before and once again they faded to ashen white. Yan Lie's brow wrinkled, displeasure clearly etched across his face.

Footsteps echoed around the courtyard outside as the men, dressed in brocade, entered the inn. "Your Royal Highness!" They saluted Yan Lie in unison, dropping to their knees.

"You found me at last," Yan Lie said with a smile.

Charity was now even more surprised. She watched as they stood up, her eyes tracing the muscles beneath their clothing.

"Everyone outside." Yan Lie waved at them. The men barked their assent and filed out. He then turned to Charity. "What do you think of my men? How do they compare to the Song's soldiers?"

"These men don't fight for the Song?"

"I suppose I should be honest with you. These are elite forces fighting on behalf of the Great Jin Empire!"

"Then, you're . . ." There was a tremble in her voice.

"Madam, I cannot lie anymore. My name is not Yan Lie. There are two characters missing. I am in fact Wanyan Honglie, the Sixth Prince of the Jin, titled Prince Zhao."

Charity had been weaned on her father's stories of how the Jin had ravaged Song lands and massacred the peasants of the north, and how the Song Emperors had let themselves be captured. Her husband's hatred for the Jin ran even deeper. Had she really spent the last few days with a Jin prince?

Wanyan Honglie could see the expression on Charity's face change. "I've long heard about the wonders of the south," he continued, "so last year I asked my father, the Emperor of the Jin, to send me to Lin'an to act as envoy for the New Year Celebrations. And in any case, the Song Emperor still had not paid his annual tribute, a few hundred thousand *taels* of silver, so my father wanted me to collect that as well."

"Annual tribute?"

"Indeed, the Song Emperors pay us a tribute of silver and silk so we won't invade. They always claim they cannot collect enough in taxes in order to pay it promptly. But this time I demanded it from Chancellor Han. I told him that if they did not pay within a month, I'd lead Jin soldiers to the south myself to collect in full."

"How did Chancellor Han respond?"

"In the only way he could: the silk and silver were in the north before I even left the city!" He laughed. Charity frowned and did not answer. "Of course, they didn't really need me to chase the tribute," he continued. "A special envoy would have been good enough. But I wanted to see the beauty of the south myself, the scenery, the people, their customs. I never imagined I would meet my lady, and that you would save my life! Luck was shining on me, indeed."

Charity's head swirled and panic was rising within her.

"And now I'm going to buy some more clothes for you."

"That's not necessary," Charity replied without looking up.

"The money the Governor gave me himself from his own pocket would be enough to buy my lady a new outfit every day for a thousand years! Please don't be afraid, Madam; the inn is surrounded by my men, nobody can harm you." With that, he left.

Charity was left with her thoughts of all that had happened since the day she first met him. He, a royal prince, treating a lowly widow with such kindness. His intentions had to be dishonorable. Her husband was dead, leaving her, a poor wretched woman, all on her own, and instead of running away she had ended up she knew not where. Panic pulsed through her again. She hugged her pillow close, her tears running into it.

WANYAN HONGLIE tucked the gold and silver into his shirt and walked in the direction of the market. He watched as the local peasants went about their business. There was something dignified about them despite the simplicity of their situations, and he could not help but admire them.

All of a sudden, drumming hooves. A horse appeared up ahead, galloping toward him. The street was narrow and filled with market stalls and people shopping. Wanyan Honglie jerked to the side just as the sandy-colored mare came sailing through the sea of people. Miraculously the horse drifted through the crowd without knocking against a single person or kicking anything over, each stride light, each jump smooth, as it skimmed over a stall selling ceramics and baskets of vegetables. It was as if the horse was floating across open grasslands, rather than charging through a busy market street.

The horse was handsome, towering and muscular. Wanyan Honglie drew his eyes from the horse up to the rider and was surprised to see a short, beefy man, straddling it as if he were sat astride a lump of meat. His arms and legs were short, as was his almost nonexistent neck, making his enormous head look as if it had been pressed into his shoulders.

Incredible, Wanyan Honglie thought, unable to contain himself.

The man turned toward Wanyan as he floated past, revealing cheeks red and blotchy from too much rice wine, and a nose shiny and round like a persimmon stuck in the middle.

Such a fine horse, I must have it whatever the price, Wanyan Honglie thought to himself. At that moment, two children ran out into the lane from the opposite direction, chasing each other, straight into the horse's path. Surprised, the horse kicked out. Just as the beast's left hoof was about to strike one of the children, the man pulled hard on the reins and lifted out of the saddle, pulling the horse up, its hooves narrowly grazing the tops of the children's heads. Disaster averted, the man sat back in his saddle.

Wanyan Honglie stared in amazement; there were many fine riders among his people, yet this man was surely the finest horseman he had ever seen. If I took him back with me to the capital, my army could conquer the world, he thought. Much better than merely buying the horse. He had been scouting out locations to station troops throughout this trip south, where to cross rivers, even noting the names and competencies of every county official he passed on the way. Such remarkable talent is going to waste here in the south where the government is so corrupt, he said to himself. Why not offer him a position with me? It was decided: he was going to take him back to the Jin capital in the north to cultivate his talents.

He started running after the horse, afraid he would lose them. He was about to call out after them, but the horse halted suddenly at the corner of the main road. The abruptness with which animal and rider stopped was remarkable; this alone would have convinced him of the man's superior capabilities. He watched as the rider jumped down from his saddle and entered a shop.

Wanyan Honglie hurried closer and peered at a large wooden sign inside: LI PO'S LEGACY. He stepped back and looked up at the large gold-lettered sign hanging from the eaves: *Garden of the Eight Drunken Immortals,* written in the finest calligraphy, and beside it, *By the hand of Su Dongpo,* one of the Song's best calligraphers, poets, and statesmen. Such imposing luxury; this must be one of the town's best taverns. I'll treat him to a fine meal and plenty of drink, Wanyan Honglie said to himself. I couldn't have hoped for a better opportunity.

Just then the stocky man came scuttling back down the stairs carrying a large wine jug, and waddled up to his horse. Wanyan Honglie slipped out of view.

The man looked even fatter and uglier up close. He could not have been more than three feet, about the height of his horse's stirrups, with shoulders almost as broad as he was tall. He struck the neck of the jug a few times, swiped the top half off so that it became a basin, and placed it before the animal. The horse reared up onto its hind legs, neighed with delight and started drinking the contents. Wanyan Honglie could smell it from where he was standing. Blushing Maiden, a famous fragrant wine from Shaoxing. Aged for ten years, he deduced from a longer sniff.

The man walked back into the tavern and threw a large *sycee* ingot of silver onto the counter. "Bring us three tables of your best food, two with meat, one vegetarian," he instructed.

"Certainly, Third Brother Han." The innkeeper smiled. "Today we have the finest perch from the River Song, the perfect accompaniment to some of our best rice wine. Take back your silver, eat first."

"What? The wine is free, is it?" he said in a strange voice and with a hint of defiance in his eyes. "Are you suggesting Third Brother Han is a villain who eats without paying?"

The innkeeper chuckled, taking it in good jest, before calling to the waiters, "Boys, get to work and prepare Third Brother Han's food!"

"Yes, sir!" the men responded.

He's not especially well dressed, Wanyan Honglie said to himself, but he spends generously and is treated with respect. He must be important. Looks like it's not going to be easy to persuade him to continue farther north. I'll keep watching to see who he's inviting to dinner.

He slipped upstairs, found a seat by a window and ordered a jug of wine and a few dishes.

2

THE GARDEN OF THE EIGHT DRUNKEN IMMORTALS SAT ON THE banks of South Lake. It was late spring and the water was clear like a sheet of blue-green jade. A light mist clung to the water's surface, which trembled as leisure boats scored ripples across it. The lake too was scattered with the emerald leaves of the water chestnut. South Lake produced the sweetest, most tender water chestnuts for miles around, crisp and refreshing.

Wanyan Honglie's eyes drew in the scene and he felt relaxed and contented. Just then a long, narrow boat came skating across the water, its bow jutting upward. He was not paying particular attention at first, until he noticed that it had overtaken another boat which only moments before had been some way out in front. As it came closer he noted the passenger and someone at the back with a paddle, wearing a cape made from rushes. To his surprise, the oarsman was in fact a woman. She twisted the paddle lightly, slicing the boat through the water like an arrow. The boat alone must have weighed at least one hundred *jin,* Wanyan Honglie reflected, which meant both oarswoman and oar must be exceptionally strong.

With just a few more twists the boat pulled up beside the tavern. Sunlight glinted off the paddle. It must have been made of metal. The woman tied the boat to a wooden post at the foot of the tavern's stone steps and jumped adroitly onto land, taking the paddle with her. The man in the boat picked up a shoulder pole with two bundles of firewood and followed her up the stairs to the first floor of the restaurant.

"Third Brother!" the woman called out to the rider, and sat beside him.

"Fourth Brother, Seventh Sister, you're early!" he replied.

Wanyan Honglie surveyed the two new arrivals. She looked to be around seventeen or eighteen, slim, with large eyes, long eyelashes and skin white like snow. A pretty girl of the local rivers and lakes. She had removed the straw hat to reveal her gorgeous black hair, which hung, like inky clouds from a painting, around her face. She may not be as beautiful as my Madam Bao, but she has a certain charm, he thought to himself.

The man with the firewood looked to be in his late twenties, dressed from head to toe in black, with a coarse rope tied around his waist—into which was tucked a small axe—and straw sandals on his feet. His hands and feet were huge, his expression honest but dull. He put down the shoulder pole and leaned it against the table. Large enough to sit eight, it creaked and shot back a few centimeters under the weight of the pole. The pole did not appear to be remarkable in any way, black and glossy with a slight bend in the middle, each end capped by a small sheath, Wanyan observed. It too must have been cast from metal.

Just as they took their seats, the sound of footsteps echoed on the stairs and two more people emerged.

"Fifth Brother, Sixth Brother, you're here."

The first man was tall and sturdy, and must have weighed some two hundred and fifty *jin*. His shirt was open and he had rolled up his sleeves, revealing a bushy chest and arms covered in thick black hair. Over this he wore a greasy butcher's apron, with a foot-long knife tucked into its strings. Behind him came a shorter man, his skin pearly white, a felt cap perched on his head. He carried a set of scales and a bamboo basket.

At that moment, they heard what sounded like someone beating metal against stone. The sound grew louder. A man appeared, dressed in rags, dragging an iron staff up the stairs. Wanyan Honglie thought he looked to be around thirty, with razor-sharp features and a graying complexion. His eyes were covered in a white film.

The others stood up and announced in unison: "Big Brother."

"Big Brother, sit here," the woman said, patting the seat beside her.

"Thank you," the blind man replied. "Second Brother isn't here yet?"

"Second Brother just arrived in Jiaxing," the butcher replied. "He should be here any moment."

"That's him," the woman said, smiling, as they heard the sound of leather slapping against the steps.

Wanyan Honglie froze. There, at the top of the stairs, appeared a broken black oilpaper fan.

It quaked briefly, and then behind it followed a head. It was him.

"He took my money," Wanyan Honglie growled, anger germinating inside him. The man grinned at him, stuck out his tongue and turned to greet the others. This was Second Brother.

They're clearly important fighters of the *jianghu,* Wanyan Honglie thought. They could do a lot for me. The filthy one may have stolen my money, but it will be of no consequence if I can persuade them to come with me to the north.

Second Brother took a swig of wine and began reciting a poem, his head swaying from side to side as the words dipped and soared:

> "*Ill-gotten gains, let them go,*
> *For the Jade Emperor is about to blow!*"

He reached into his shirt and removed ingot after ingot, laying them out neatly on the table. Eight gold, two silver.

Wanyan Honglie recognized them by their size and lustre—they were his! But caution overcame his anger. I can understand how he took the ones from my room, that was easy, but my shirt? He tapped me with his fan, but otherwise I didn't feel a thing.

It soon became clear the seven martial siblings were the hosts, and they were waiting for guests. The innkeeper had placed only one set of chopsticks and a cup at each of the two remaining tables. Two guests. I wonder if they will be as strange, Wanyan Honglie thought to himself.

One cup of tea later, they heard someone reciting Buddhist scriptures at the bottom of the stairs. *"Amituofo!"*

"Venerable Monk Scorched Wood is here," the blind man said.

"Amituofo!"

At that moment, an emaciated monk, spindly like a twig, appeared at the top of the stairs. He must have been around fifty years of age, dressed in jute robes. In his hand he carried a piece of firewood, one end scorched black. What could it be for? Wanyan Honglie wondered.

The monk greeted his seven friends and the man in rags led him to one of the empty tables. "He came looking for me," the monk said, hovering above his seat before sitting, "but I knew at once that he was too strong. I must thank the Seven Heroes of the South for your kind help and ever solid sense of justice; I am forever in your debt."

"Do not thank us, Venerable Monk Scorched Wood," the blind man replied. "It is we who are indebted to your daily kindness. How could we just look on when Your Reverence was in trouble? Why did this fellow challenge Your Reverence to a fight? He obviously doesn't think much of us masters of the southern *wulin*. There was no need—"

Before he could finish his sentence, the stairs began to creak. Indeed, it was so loud it sounded as though a water buffalo or some other giant creature was coming up the stairs.

"You can't take that up there!"

"You're going to break the floorboards!"

"Quick, stop him! Bring him back down!"

The innkeeper and his men were clamoring, but the creaking continued and only grew louder.

Wanyan Honglie was aghast. There, at the top of the stairs, stood a Taoist carrying a full-sized temple censer made of bronze, usually used for burning large quantities of paper money and sticks of incense. It was Elder Eternal Spring, Qiu Chuji.

The real purpose of Wanyan Honglie's previous trip had been to gain favor with important officials under the Emperor, so that when the Jin invaded the south, they would have secret allies inside the Song court. He was accompanied on his travels by a Song envoy, Wang Daoqian, who had done everything he could to exact the highest bribes from the Jin for his cooperation. Having long been protected by the northern barbarians, he was a symbol of the worst excesses of Song corruption. But as soon as they entered the city, he was happened upon by a Taoist, who had chopped off his head. Fearful his scheme had been uncovered by the Taoist, Wanyan Honglie fled with his aides. With the help of Lin'an's finest soldiers, they returned to track the assassin, chasing him all the way to Ox Village, where they engaged him in battle, only to discover he was an exceptional practitioner of the martial arts. Qiu Chuji caught Wanyan Honglie in the shoulder with an arrow before he had even launched one punch, and then went on to kill the rest of Wanyan's men. Had Wanyan Honglie not fled and chanced upon Charity's kindness, Qiu Chuji would have made Ox Village his grave.

Wanyan Honglie collected himself. Qiu Chuji had barely glanced in his direction and seemed far more concerned with Scorched Wood and the Seven Heroes of the South. Perhaps the Taoist had defeated him so quickly he could not recognize him? He calmed himself and turned his attention to the enormous censer the Taoist was carrying.

At four feet in diameter, it must have weighed more than two hundred *jin* on its own, but a waft of fragrant rice wine told Wanyan Honglie that it was not empty and must be considerably heavier. And yet the Taoist looked perfectly comfortable holding it. The weight continued to make the floorboards groan, and downstairs the innkeeper, his men, and the other guests had pressed through the main door and out onto the street, fearful that the ceiling was about to collapse.

"We thank the esteemed Taoist for gracing us with his presence," Scorched Wood said coldly, "but why has he brought with him the bronze incense burner from my temple?"

Qiu Chuji raised his left hand out of respect. "I went first to the temple, but the Abbot Withered Wood told me the Venerable Monk Scorched Wood had invited me to the Garden of the Eight Drunken Immortals to drink wine with him. I assumed the Venerable Monk Scorched Wood wouldn't be alone, and I was right."

"Let me introduce the Seven Heroes of the South."

"I have long heard spoken the great deeds of the Seven Heroes of the South. Your reputation precedes you, and today I am lucky enough to make your acquaintance myself. It has been my life's great wish."

"This is Elder Eternal Spring, Qiu Chuji, of the Quanzhen Sect," Scorched Wood explained to the Seven Heroes. Turning to Qiu Chuji, he continued. "This," he said, gesturing to the blind man, "is their leader, Flying Bat Master Ke Zhen'e, Suppressor of Evil."

He went on to introduce the others, one by one. Wanyan Honglie listened carefully, committing each name to memory. The second was the dirty man who had stolen his silver, Quick Hands Zhu Cong the Intelligent. Next came the short, rotund man who arrived on a horse, Protector of the Steeds, Ryder Han. The fourth man to be introduced was the farmer carrying firewood, Woodcutter Nan the Merciful. Fifth was the burly man in a butcher's apron, Laughing Buddha Zhang Asheng. The young man who carried the scales was called Gilden Quan the Prosperous, also known as the Masked Haggler. Last came the young oarswoman, Maiden of the Yue Sword, Jade Han. She was the youngest.

Qiu Chuji bowed at each in turn as they were introduced. He was still holding the heavy bronze censer in his right hand but did not appear tired. Meanwhile, the other customers started venturing back inside and some even climbed the stairs, curious to see what was going on.

"We are a martial family, often called the Seven Freaks of the South," Ke Zhen'e began. "We are mere eccentrics, we daren't call ourselves martial arts masters. We have long been great admirers of the Seven Disciples of the Quanzhen Sect, and greatly respect Elder Eternal Spring for using his *wuxia* skills solely in the name of justice.

63

Venerable Monk Scorched Wood is in turn most considerate and warmhearted. How, may I ask, might he have offended Elder Eternal Spring? Please do us the honor of letting us act as peacemakers. While you both may pray to different deities, you have still both chosen a life of the temple, and are great men of the *wulin*. Why not air past grievances and drink together?"

"Venerable Monk Scorched Wood and I are strangers to one another," Qiu Chuji replied. "There is no ill will between us. If he surrenders the women, I will return to Fahua Temple and offer my sincerest apologies."

"Surrender which women?"

"Two of my friends were betrayed by the Song government and died violent deaths at the hands of marauding Jin soldiers," Qiu Chuji replied. "Each left behind a widow without family or friends. Master Ke, do you think I should ignore this injustice?"

The cup in Wanyan Honglie's hand shook, spilling a little wine onto the table.

"They need not be friends of ours for us to feel compelled to act. We would only have to hear of such a story to be moved, it is our duty as members of the *wulin*."

"Indeed! And so I am asking our friend the monk to hand over the two wretched widows. He has assumed the robes of a holy man, so why is he detaining them in his temple? The Seven Heroes live by the *wulin*'s code of honor; can you explain this logic to me?"

Scorched Wood and the Seven Freaks were astonished by Qiu Chuji's words, as was Wanyan Honglie. Does he mean the wives of Ironheart Yang and Skyfury Guo? he asked himself.

Scorched Wood's normally sunken cheeks flushed crimson with anger. It took him a while to gather the words to reply. "How can you make such dishonorable accusations?" he stammered. "They are nonsense."

This angered Qiu Chuji even more. "You are also a great man of the *wulin*. How dare you lie to me!" he cried, and with one hand flung the bronze censer full of wine at Scorched Wood.

The frightened crowd gathered at the top of the stairs now pushed at each other in a scramble back down.

The monk dived out of the way. Laughing Buddha Zhang calculated he would be able to catch it, despite its weight. He strode forward, moved his inner strength to his arms and roared. The censer swooped at Zhang Asheng and stopped in his arms, the muscles in his shoulders and back bulging as his body absorbed its momentum. He lifted the censer above his head, but the weight was too much for the floor beneath him and his left foot tore through the wooden floorboards. A scream went up from downstairs. Zhang Asheng stepped forward, his arms slightly bent, and performed Open the Window and Push Back the Moon, thrusting the censer back at Qiu Chuji.

Qiu Chuji caught the censer with his right hand and held it above his head. "The Seven Heroes of the South are deserving of their reputation!" Then he turned to Scorched Wood. "What about the women? You have captured them and are keeping them in the temple. What do you want with them? If you hurt so much as one strand of their hair, I will grind your treacherous bones to dust and burn your temple to the ground!"

"His Holiness Scorched Wood is a virtuous and eminent monk," Zhu Cong said, flicking his fan and nodding. "How could he possibly do such a terrible thing? Your Reverence must have heard this rumor from some lowly beggar. Who could believe such fabrications!"

"I saw it with my own eyes," Qiu Chuji cried with rage. "How could it be a fabrication?"

The Seven Freaks froze.

"You have come south to establish your name—why ruin mine in the process?" Scorched Wood cried. "Ask the people of Jiaxing, could Scorched Wood the Monk be capable of such an evil deed?"

"Fine." Qiu Chuji smiled coldly. "You have supporters. Without them, defeat would be certain. But I will not let this go. You are hiding two women in a sacred temple, which is sin enough. Why kill their husbands, two such loyal patriots?"

"Elder Eternal Spring claims the Venerable Monk Scorched Wood is hiding the women, and the Venerable Monk insists he is not," Ke Zhen'e summarized. "Why don't we go to Fahua Temple and see who is telling the truth? I may be blind, but the rest of my martial family are perfectly able to see." The others agreed.

"Search the temple?" Qiu Chuji smiled. "I have already searched it several times, but even though I saw them enter, I could not find them inside. I don't understand it. So it is up to our friend the monk to hand the women over!"

"Perhaps they were not women," Ke Zhen'e interrupted.

"What?"

Ke Zhen'e gazed unseeing at Qiu Chuji, his face still with perfect solemnity. "They must be goddesses. Either they have made themselves invisible or else they have disappeared into thin air." The other Freaks tittered.

"I see you are mocking me. The Seven Freaks have allied themselves with the monk."

"Our skills may not seem much to a Master of the Quanzhen Sect. You may laugh at them, perhaps. But here in the south we can claim some fame. People say, 'Those Seven Freaks may be crazy, but they are no cowards.' We may not be masters of the *wulin,* perhaps, but we will not stand by and watch a friend be bullied."

"The Seven Heroes of the South do indeed claim a fine reputation, I have long heard of your skill. But this matter does not concern you, there is no need to be sullied by such murky matters. Let me deal with the Venerable Monk myself. Please forgive me, my friend; come with me." Qiu Chuji reached his left hand to take Scorched Wood by the wrist, but Scorched Wood twisted free of his grip.

The fight was starting.

"Elder Eternal Spring!" Ryder Han cried. "Are you deaf to reason?"

"What is it, Third Brother Han?"

"We believe Venerable Monk Scorched Wood is telling the truth," Ryder Han replied. "If he says he doesn't have them, then he doesn't have them. Such a steadfast and respected member of the *wulin* cannot be lying."

"So if he is not lying, then it is I who is the liar?" Qiu Chuji was furious. "I, Elder Eternal Spring, am to distrust my very own eyes? Seeing as they are so easily deceived, perhaps I should gouge them out and present them as a gift? They are useless to me. So, to confirm, you are allied with the monk?"

"Yes!" the Seven Freaks responded in unison.

"In that case, please everyone take a cup of wine. Let us first drink, then we fight." He lowered his right arm, put the bronze censer to his mouth and took a long gulp. "Here, for you." He flung the bronze censer at Zhang Asheng.

How am I going to drink from it, even if I catch it above my head? Zhang Asheng thought to himself. He retreated back two steps and placed his hands outstretched before him, but as the censer came hurtling toward him he opened his arms and let it crash against his chest. He carried some extra weight in that area, so his flesh absorbed the impact as if it were a soft cushion. With a deep breath, he thrust forward his chest and wrapped his arms around it. Gripping it tightly, he dipped his head and drank from the bowl. "Delicious!"

He pulled his arms away and let the censer balance a few moments, before pushing it away in a move known throughout the *wulin* as Two Hands to Move a Mountain. Wanyan Honglie watched in amazement.

Qiu Chuji caught the censer, drank another large mouthful of wine before propelling it toward Ke Zhen'e. "Master Ke, please!"

He's blind, how will he catch it? Wanyan Honglie thought. But he was unfamiliar with the extent of the Seven Freaks' martial skill, and the fact that Brother Ke was the most accomplished among them. Using his hearing alone, Ke could place a flying object to within a centimeter just by listening for the rush of air around it. He sat calmly, focused, seemingly unconcerned by Qiu Chuji's cry. Then, at the last possible moment, up shot his hand, and he struck the censer with his walking staff. He caught the censer and it spun like a plate on a bamboo stick. Ke Zhen'e then tipped the staff and the censer dipped, spinning a stream of rice wine from the rim. Ke Zhen'e opened his mouth and drank three or four mouthfuls, the spray drenching his clothes. He then jerked the stick with the lightest of touches, righting the censer, before flicking it up in the air. As it fell, he hit the censer one more time, sending it back, ringing, to Qiu Chuji.

"Master Ke must spin plates in his spare time!" Qiu Chuji laughed as he caught the censer with ease.

"We didn't have much money when I was a child; I used to spin plates to help my parents," Ke Zhen'e said, through gritted teeth.

"Honest work makes the man," Qiu Chuji said. "A toast to Fourth Brother Nan!" He took another gulp of wine and sent the censer to Woodcutter Nan.

Clang! Woodcutter Nan said nothing, but stopped the censer with his shoulder pole and scooped a handful of wine as it fell. He then spun his pole horizontally, dropped onto his right knee, placed the pole on his left, caught the censer with the other end of the pole and, pushing downward, flicked it back into the air.

As the censer flew back in the direction of Qiu Chuji, Gilden Quan spoke. "I never turn down a good deal, let me drink." He appeared at Woodcutter Nan's side and waited for the censer's return. Just as it was falling, he too fished out a handful of wine, caught the censer with his feet and then kicked it back at Qiu Chuji. The backward momentum sent him flying into the wall behind, where he slid to the ground.

"Wonderful, simply wonderful!" Zhu Cong declared, flicking his broken fan.

Qiu Chuji caught the censer and drank again. "Wonderful, wonderful. Now a drink for Second Brother."

"*Aiya!* I'm a master of the mind, not of the body. I can't hold my drink. I'll be drunk in seconds." The censer was already making its way back toward him before Zhu Cong could finish. "Help, it's going to squash me!"

He dipped his fan into the wine, drank, then struck the bottom

of the censer, flicking it away. At that point, the floorboards creaked and a large crack appeared. "Help!" he cried as he fell through.

Everyone knew he was playing the fool. Wanyan Honglie, however, was still marveling at Zhu Cong's use of the small fan, which appeared as strong as Woodcutter Nan's shoulder pole.

"What about me?" Jade Han called, and with the tap of her right foot she flew up into the air like a swallow. In an instant she had jumped over the censer, lowered her head and drunk from it, before landing nimbly on the window ledge. She was a master of lightness *qinggong* kung fu and swordsmanship, but she was not the strongest and realized it would have been beyond her to catch the censer and launch it back at the Taoist.

The censer, meanwhile, flew past Jade, through the window and out onto the crowded street. Alarmed, Qiu Chuji raced out to stop it, but with a *whoosh!* and a whistle, Ryder Han swept past the Taoist, calling his horse round onto the street. Everyone gathered upstairs ran to the window to watch Ryder Han career into the censer, knocking them both onto the back of his horse. The horse lurched forward and steadied itself, then turned back toward the tavern and started climbing the steps. The treads creaked and cracked under its weight, but somehow it made it upstairs.

Ryder Han was in fact balanced beneath the horse's belly, his left foot caught in a stirrup and his hands holding the censer on the saddle. The horse was fast and steady on the stairs. Once at the summit, Ryder Han flipped back onto the horse's back, leaned down and drank from the censer, before pushing it off the horse with his left arm. He then snorted, cracked his whip and jumped out of the window, landing the beast with ease on the street outside. Ryder Han then dismounted and walked back up the stairs, arm in arm with Zhu Cong.

"The Seven Heroes of the South are worthy of their reputation indeed," Qiu Chuji responded. "I am humbled by your skills. As long as Venerable Monk Scorched Wood vows to release the women, I will trouble him no further and leave."

"Elder Eternal Spring," Ke Zhen'e replied, "in this matter you are mistaken. Venerable Monk Scorched Wood has spent decades living a life free from bodily temptations, he is a virtuous and devout Buddhist whom we have long admired. Fahua Temple is also one of Jiaxing's most sacred Buddhist sites. How could he be hiding respectable women inside?"

"There are always those who claim good reputations falsely," Qiu Chuji declared.

"Elder Eternal Spring believes us to be lying?" Ryder Han was struggling to control his fury.

"I choose to believe my own eyes."

"So what is Elder Eternal Spring going to do now?" Ryder Han bellowed. The power of his voice more than made up for his short stature.

"This matter did not concern the Seven Heroes to begin with, but as you insist upon getting involved, you must be confident in your skills. I am a mere novice, so I can only suggest we fight it out. If I lose, the Seven Heroes may decide how the matter is to be settled."

"If this is Elder Eternal Spring's desired recourse, please lay out the rules," Ke Zhen'e said.

Qiu Chuji hesitated, then spoke. "There is no feeling of enmity between us and I have always admired the Seven Heroes of the South. To take up weapons or use our fists will only harm our friendship. We will do it like this . . . Innkeeper!" he called out. "Bring us fourteen large bowls!"

The innkeeper had been hiding downstairs, but as all was quiet upstairs he went to fetch the bowls.

Qiu Chuji instructed him to fill them from the censer. "A drinking competition," he said, turning to the Seven Freaks. "For every bowl you drink, I will have one, until we have our winner. How about that?"

Ryder Han and Zhang Asheng were drinkers, so they agreed.

"But this is one against seven," Ke Zhen'e contended. "It could never be an honorable win for us. Could Elder Eternal Spring devise another contest?"

"What makes you so sure you'll win?"

"Fine! Then I'll start!" Jade Han retorted. She was forthright by nature, particularly for a young woman. "I have never known anyone to treat us with such disrespect." She grabbed a bowl of wine and gulped it down in one, her snowy cheeks blooming cherry red.

"Miss Han is quite the brave young squire!" Qiu Chuji exclaimed. "Men, please!"

The other men each picked up a bowl and drank. Qiu Chuji downed bowl after bowl as each was emptied. The innkeeper was now in higher spirits and cheerfully refilled the bowls. Within moments, they had been drained again.

By the third round of drinks, Jade Han's hands were shaking so much she could not lift the bowl to her lips. Zhang Asheng took the bowl from her: "Sister, I will finish for you."

"Elder Qiu, is that acceptable?" she asked.

"Of course, I don't mind who drinks."

They drank another round before Gilden Quan was also forced to stop.

By now Qiu Chuji had downed twenty-eight bowls, and to the surprise of the Seven Freaks, he appeared entirely sober. Wanyan Honglie was still watching and was even more shocked. I hope they get this Taoist drunk and finish him off, he said to himself.

Gilden Quan calculated there were still Five Freaks left, each capable of drinking for two men, and good for at least another three, maybe four, rounds. Could the Taoist really take another twenty bowls of wine in his belly? The volume alone would be too much; victory had to be theirs. But at that moment, he happened to glance down at Qiu Chuji's feet, where a large puddle had formed.

"Second Brother," he whispered in Zhu Cong's ear. "Look!" He pointed down at the floor.

Zhu Cong glanced down. "This isn't good. He's using his inner strength to force the wine out through his feet."

"Amazing. What now?"

Zhu Cong paused to think. "With this little trick, he could drink a hundred more bowls. We need another contest."

He stepped back and without warning dropped through the hole in the floorboards he had created earlier. "I'm so drunk!" he called as he fell. They started another round, but by now the floor beneath Qiu Chuji's feet was soaked through as if a spring had appeared underneath the boards. Woodcutter Nan, Ryder Han, and the others had also noticed, and were applauding such an amazing feat of inner strength, while Zhu Cong climbed back to join them.

Ryder Han placed his bowl back on the table, ready to admit defeat. But Zhu Cong looked at him meaningfully and turned to Qiu Chuji. "Elder Eternal Spring's display of inner strength is quite remarkable, we are indeed much in admiration. But we are still five against one. It does not seem an honorable fight."

This surprised Qiu Chuji. "Then what does Second Brother Zhu suggest?"

"Let me take you on, one on one," Zhu Cong said, smiling.

The others were puzzled. Zhu Cong was clearly the most drunk; why would he take the Taoist on by himself? But they also knew that, while their brother liked to appear the fool, in actual fact he had a belly full of tricks. He always had the best plan in any given situation.

"The Seven Heroes are competitive, that's for certain." Qiu Chuji chuckled. "How about this: if Second Brother Zhu and I can finish what's left of the wine, and neither passes out, then we'll say it is I who has lost."

The censer was still half full; they would have to have bellies like two laughing Buddhas to be able to finish it. But Zhu Cong was unconcerned. "I may not be famed for holding my liquor, but I did once drink a few sturdy men under the table while on my travels," he said, fluttering his fan in his right hand and waving the sleeve of his left. "In one!" he cried, and drank.

Together they drained bowl after bowl. "What a drinker!" Qiu Chuji exclaimed.

"I once went to India, where the king challenged me to a drinking competition with a water buffalo. They never determined who won."

Qiu Chuji knew he was being made fun of, but he didn't care. He did notice, however, that despite the nonsense and the wild gesticulating, Zhu Cong was keeping pace. He did not seem to be expelling the liquid by the use of inner strength, and his belly had swollen in size. Was he able to expand it with just the force of his mind?

"Two years ago I went to Siam," Zhu Cong continued. "That was even crazier. The Chancellor brought out an elephant to see who would win. The idiot drank seven barrels. How many do you think I had?"

Qiu Chuji knew Zhu Cong was making it up, but he could not help himself. "How many?"

Zhu Cong's tone suddenly turned solemn and, lowering his voice, he hissed, "Nine." Then, raising his voice again, he cried, "That's it, drink up!"

Zhu Cong's movements were growing ever wilder as he oscillated between drunk and crazy, but together they finished the wine. The other Freaks had no idea Zhu Cong could drink so much, but they were happy, if a little uneasy.

"Brother, what a feat. I salute you!" Qiu Chuji said, genuflecting in admiration.

Zhu Cong laughed. "Elder Eternal Spring used his inner strength, but I had to resort to external skills. Take a look!" He flipped backward and landed, holding a wooden bucket. A quick swirl released the sweet aroma of Blushing Maiden rice wine. Only Ke Zhen'e knew what his martial brother had been doing, and Zhu Cong's stomach was now perfectly flat. The Seven Freaks of the South convulsed with laughter. Qiu Chuji's cheeks went pale.

He was Quick Hands Zhu Cong, sleight of hand was his forte. This was no new trick, it had been handed down from generation to generation. Always a flourish, always a backflip. One backflip, a gold fish. Another backflip, a bowl of water. It continues—another backflip, another bowl with a fish swimming inside. Audiences in raptures. Zhu Cong had fetched the bucket when he dropped through the hole in the floorboards, of course, and the mad gesticulating was designed to distract Qiu Chuji. A true magician's illusions cannot be deduced even with hundreds of eyes watching, and Qiu Chuji had not the merest notion that Zhu Cong would devise such a scheme.

"You call that drinking?" he said.

"And what about you? My wine is in this bucket, yours is on the floor. What's the difference?"

And he paced up and down, slipping on the puddle of wine at Qiu Chuji's feet. Qiu Chuji caught him. Zhu Cong jumped back and started walking in a circle. "Such a beautiful poem!" he cried out abruptly.

> *"Since ancient times mid-autumn's moon,*
> *Radiant, as icy winds clean the night;*
> *Heavy hangs the Milky Way*
> *As water dragons vault the seas."*

He almost sang the lines, stretching out the words.

Qiu Chuji was speechless. That's the poem I started writing around Mid-Autumn Festival last year but did not finish, he thought to himself. I keep it on me at all times, as I can never think of the next four lines. But I have never shown it to anyone. He reached into his shirt, only to find the poem missing.

Zhu Cong spread the poem out on the table, a smile unfolding across his face. "Elder Eternal Spring is not only a peerless master of the martial arts, but his poetry is quite exquisite. Wondrous!"

I did not feel a thing, Qiu Chuji said to himself. What if he had tried stabbing me instead of merely stealing a poem? He could have killed me. But he showed mercy. This quelled his anxiety. "As Master Zhu finished the censer of wine with me, I will keep my word and admit defeat. Let it be known that, today, here in the Garden of the Eight Drunken Immortals, Qiu Chuji was defeated by the Seven Heroes of the South."

"Please, please," the Seven Freaks exclaimed politely. "It was all just a silly game."

"And Elder Eternal Spring displayed an inner strength none of us could ever hope to equal," Zhu Cong added.

"I may be admitting defeat," Qiu Chuji replied, "but the fact remains, those two widows of my friends must be rescued." He cupped his hands in a sign of respect and picked up the censer. "I'm going to Fahua Temple."

"But you have admitted defeat. How dare you continue to trouble Scorched Wood the Monk?" Ke Zhen'e was furious.

"They are in grave danger. Victory, defeat, it's all irrelevant. Great Hero Ke, if your friend was killed and his widow left to suffer all manner of insults, would you stand back and do nothing?" Suddenly his expression changed. There was a pause. "You called for backup? Even if you bring ten thousand men on ten thousand horses, I won't give in!"

"We are seven, no more," Zhang Asheng said. "Why would we call on anyone else?"

But Ke Zhen'e had also heard it. The clanging of metal. Men were approaching. "Everyone get back!"

They all heard it now and reached for their weapons. Moments later there came a clattering from below.

Men in Jin army regalia appeared at the top of the stairs.

Qiu Chuji respected the way the Seven Freaks of the South conducted themselves and had assumed they were ignorant of Scorched Wood's true nature. He had been careful not to offend them. But Jin soldiers? Rage surged inside him. "Scorched Wood!" he said. "Seven Freaks! Jin soldiers? How dare you claim to be righteous members of the *wulin*?"

"Who called on the Jin?" Ryder Han cried back.

These men formed part of Wanyan Honglie's personal retinue. Rumors were spreading of a violent confrontation at the Garden of the Eight Drunken Immortals, and Wanyan Honglie had not returned.

"Excuse me if I don't stay any longer! But this is not over." Still carrying the censer, Qiu Chuji went toward the stairs.

"Reverend Qiu, there's been a misunderstanding!" Ke Zhen'e said, rising from his seat.

Qiu Chuji did not stop. "A misunderstanding? You're the heroes, you tell me why you called on Jin soldiers to help you."

"We didn't," Ke Zhen'e replied.

"I'm not blind," Qiu Chuji retorted.

If there was one thing Ke Zhen'e could not abide, it was being laughed at for his impairment. "But I am, it's true," he snarled, planting his iron staff on the floor.

Qiu Chuji said nothing, raised his left hand and struck his palm against the forehead of one of the Jin soldiers, killing him instantly. "That's what I can do!" And with a flick of his wrist, he pushed him down the stairs.

Horrified, the soldiers lunged at Qiu Chuji with their lances, but he flicked each one away without turning. The men were ready to charge when Wanyan Honglie called for them to stop.

"This loathsome Taoist is beyond belief," he said, turning to Ke Zhen'e. "Why don't you all join me for a drink and we can discuss how to deal with him?"

Ke Zhen'e was furious. "Get the hell out of here!"

Wanyan Honglie was visibly taken aback.

"Brother said, 'Get the hell out'!" Ryder Han cried, shunting Wanyan Honglie in the left hip with his right shoulder. Wanyan Honglie stumbled a few steps backward, as the Seven Freaks and Scorched Wood fled.

Zhu Cong was last. He tapped Wanyan Honglie on the shoulder as he passed. "Have you sold the girl you kidnapped? Why not sell her to me?" Zhu Cong had not known who Wanyan Honglie was when they first met, but he had realized instantly Wanyan Honglie and Charity were not husband and wife. He had heard Wanyan boast of his wealth and decided to teach him a lesson. Now it transpired he was of some rank in the Jin army. Justice done then, surely?

Wanyan Honglie reached into his shirt and, as expected, his gold was gone. He was relieved he had not approached Ryder Han about joining him in the north. Given their fighting skills, he had no desire to reveal to the Seven Freaks that Madam Bao was with him. He rushed back to the inn. They would leave for the Jin capital that night.

3

THE NIGHT QIU CHUJI CHANCED UPON SKYFURY GUO AND IRON-heart Yang, he had traveled back to Lin'an in some distress. He spent the next few days resting by West Lake. At its north end towers Ge Peak, where the Taoist Ge Hong made his renowned immortality pills. Qiu Chuji's mornings were spent sightseeing and his afternoons in the temple practicing martial arts and reading from the Taoist canon.

As he was strolling along Qinghefang Lane one day, he noticed a small group of soldiers staggering toward him, swinging their helmets and dragging their armor and broken weapons behind them. They had just been defeated in battle. We are not at war with the Jin at the moment, Qiu Chuji thought, and I have not heard talk of bandits lately. What battle have they been fighting? He asked people on the street but no one knew. His curiosity piqued, he followed the soldiers back to their camp at Command Post Six.

Late that night, Qiu Chuji crept into the camp. There he found a soldier and dragged him outside into a nearby alley for interrogation. The soldier, fast asleep only moments before, now had a blade at his throat. He told Qiu Chuji everything he knew about the events in Ox Village, including Skyfury Guo's death and Ironheart Yang's injuries. It was unlikely Ironheart had survived, but no one knew of his whereabouts. The wives were captured, but their captors had been ambushed by another group of men while riding back. A bloody fight ensued and they lost many of their number.

Qiu Chuji grew ever more furious as the story went on, but the soldier had just been following orders. There was no use getting angry with him. "Who is your commander?"

"Justice Duan."

Early the next morning, a pole was erected in front of the camp, bearing a severed head. A warning. Qiu Chuji recognized it at once; it was Skyfury Guo. These men were descended from loyal patriots, he said to himself. They invited you to drink with them and yet you repaid their kindness by bringing death upon them and destroying their families. Picking up a stone, he flung it at the flagpole, splintering it.

He waited until darkness, climbed the pole and took down Guo's head. He then went to the shores of West Lake, where he buried it. Placing his palms together, he bowed, and with tears spilling down his cheeks he made a promise: "Brother Guo, Brother Yang, I swore I would pass my kung fu skills on to your children. When I make a promise, I keep it. If I don't make martial arts heroes of them, I will not be fit to face you both in the afterlife."

First, he would find Justice Duan and kill him. Then he would rescue the widows and settle them somewhere safe so they could give birth and continue the Guo and Yang family lines.

For two nights he searched Command Post Six, but Justice Duan was nowhere to be found. Perhaps he lived in luxury, rather than alongside his soldiers? On the third night, he made his way to the commander's residence: "Justice Duan, I know you're in there! Come out at once!"

Duan was inside and happened to be questioning Lily Li over the disappearance of her husband's head—which bandits did Guo count among his friends?—when he was interrupted by the disturbance outside. He poked his head through the window and saw a Taoist breaking through a crowd of his men, a soldier in each hand.

"Loose your arrows!" those of rank were shouting, but the men either had no bows or else no arrows.

Justice Duan was furious, drew the saber from his belt and ran out. "Is this a rebellion?"

He brandished the weapon at Qiu Chuji, but the Taoist stopped, cast aside the soldiers and grabbed Duan's wrist. "Tell me, where is that foul dog, Justice Duan?"

A searing pain shot through Duan's wrist and body. "Is Your Reverence looking for Commander Duan? He . . . You'll find him on a pleasure boat on the West Lake. I'm not sure if he plans to return this evening."

Taking this stranger at his word, Qiu Chuji released him. Duan then turned to two nearby soldiers. "Take the Reverend to the lake. He's looking for Commander Duan."

The soldiers hesitated.

"Hurry!" Duan growled. "Or the commander will be angry!"

The two men understood, turned and left. Qiu Chuji followed.

Justice Duan was too frightened to remain at the camp, so he gathered some men and Lily Li, and hurried to Command Post Eight. The commanders frequently enjoyed an evening drink together. Duan's friend was furious when he heard what had happened to him. But just as the eighth commander was about to order some of his men to track down this vile Taoist and have him killed, an altercation was heard outside. The Taoist had come to them. The soldiers must have cracked under Qiu Chuji's questioning.

Justice Duan ran, taking his men and Lily Li. This time they made for Command Post Two at Quanjie, outside the city. It was more remote and therefore less easy to find. Duan was frightened; the image of the Taoist fighting his way through a whole crowd of soldiers would not leave him. His wrist was also throbbing and beginning to swell. The army doctor examined it and determined he had broken two bones. After being treated with ointment and fitted with a splint, Duan decided he could not return to his encampment, but would have to stay at Command Post Two for the night.

Duan slept soundly until midnight, when he was awoken by more shouting outside. Reports came that one of the sentries had vanished.

He leaped out of bed, sensing that the guards must have been captured by Qiu Chuji. As long as he stayed in army camps the Taoist was going to find him. And he was too skilled a fighter for Duan. So what now? The Taoist seemed determined to catch him. Duan's men might not be able to protect him. As panic started to take hold of him, he remembered his uncle, a monk of exceptional martial skill now residing in Cloudy Perch Temple. The Taoist's arrival had to have something to do with Skyfury Guo's death, so he would take Lily Li with him for security. He forced the widow to disguise herself as a soldier and dragged her out into the night.

HIS UNCLE had assumed holy robes many years before, taking the name Withered Wood. He was now Abbot of Cloudy Perch Temple, but had once been an officer in the army and received his martial arts training from the Masters of the Immortal Cloud Sect, a branch of the Shaolin school dominant in the areas of the *jianghu* straddling southern Zhejiang and Fujian.

Withered Wood had always despised his nephew and did as much as he could to avoid any association with him, so when Duan arrived at the temple door in the middle of the night, his response was less than welcoming. "What are you doing here?"

Duan knew the extent of his uncle's hatred for the Jin, so he could not possibly tell him the truth: that he had helped the enemy kill two patriots. Uncle would have him killed there and then. But Duan had spent the journey concocting a story. He knelt before his uncle, and under the monk's cold gaze, kowtowed. "Uncle, I beg for your help. I am being threatened."

"You're an officer in the army, people thank the heavens above for every day that you're not bullying them. Who would trouble you?"

"Indeed, I deserve it," Duan replied, putting on his best performance. "Uncle is right. Some friends and I went to Blushing Cherry Lodge by Lingqing Bridge the day before yesterday to enjoy the atmosphere."

Withered Wood snorted. The story had not started well. The ladies of Blushing Cherry Lodge did not provide the kind of atmosphere respectable men enjoyed.

"I usually visit one girl in particular, my mistress I suppose. She was drinking and singing with me, when without warning a Taoist came bursting in. As soon as he heard my girl singing, he demanded she join him instead . . ."

"Ha! Nonsense. Men of holy robes do not frequent such obscene places."

"Exactly. I made some comment to that effect and ordered him to leave. But the Taoist turned nasty and started cursing me. Then he said I shouldn't bother picking fights when I'd be losing my head soon anyway."

"What did he mean by that?"

"He said the Jin will be crossing the Yangtze within days and are going to kill the entire Song army."

"He said that?"

"Yes. I got angry and started arguing with him. Even if the Jin did come south, I said, we would fight to defend this great country. And there was nothing to say we would be defeated."

Justice Duan's words were calculated to rouse emotion in his uncle, and the Abbot nodded as his nephew spoke. These were the only sensible words to have come out of his nephew's mouth since the day he emerged from his mother's womb.

Duan saw they were having the desired effect, so continued. "We then got into a fight, but as you know, I'm no match for a Taoist trained in the martial arts. He pursued me and I had nowhere to go. Uncle, you're my only hope."

"I am a monk," Withered Wood said, shaking his head. "I cannot understand these petty fights over a woman's attentions."

"I ask for Uncle's help just this once. It will never happen again."

Withered Wood could not help but think of his brothers in the army and fury rose within him. "Fine, you can hide here in the temple for a few days. But no trouble."

Justice Duan nodded.

"You're an army officer." Withered Wood sighed before continuing. "Such debauched behavior. What will we do if the Jin really do decide to cross into the south? Back when I was a soldier . . ."

Duan may have threatened Lily Li into silence, but she was listening to every word.

4

THE FOLLOWING AFTERNOON AN ATTENDING MONK RAN IN TO speak with the Abbot.

"There's a Taoist in a rage outside. He says Commander Duan must come out at once."

Withered Wood sent for Justice Duan.

"It's him, the Taoist," Duan said, trembling.

"What a despicable excuse for a monk. To which sect does he belong?"

"I have no idea where this crook is from. I don't think his martial arts are anything special. But he's strong, to be sure. Stronger than me."

"Then I shall speak to him," Withered Wood said, and made for the Great Hall.

Qiu Chuji was just then engaged in a tussle with the guards, trying to push his way into the Inner Hall. Withered Wood walked up to him and, using his *neigong* inner strength, tried to push Qiu out with minimal pressure to the shoulder. To his surprise, however, the Taoist's upper arm felt like fresh cotton. He tried to pull back but it was too late; he was stumbling backward, and with a *peng!* his back smacked against the altar table, which collapsed, the incense burner and candles crashing down around him.

"What brings Your Reverence to my humble temple, may I ask?" Withered Wood said from where he sat, smarting.

"I am looking for a beggar by the name of Duan."

Withered Wood understood the extent of the Taoist's kung fu, so tried another tactic. "We spiritual men must show mercy and benevolence. Why is the monk behaving as if he were no more enlightened than a mere farmer?"

Qiu Chuji ignored him and strode into the Inner Hall. Justice Duan had already escaped into a secret chamber with Lily Li. Cloudy Perch Temple was fogged with plumes of incense as worshippers crowded the halls for spring pilgrimage season. He would struggle to find the commander in there. Qiu Chuji snorted and left.

Justice Duan emerged from his hiding place.

"Who is he?" Withered Wood said. "He could have killed me if he'd wanted to."

"He's an agent working on behalf of the Jin. Why else would he be picking a fight with an officer of the Song?" Duan replied.

At that moment, the attendant monk came back in to confirm that the Taoist had left.

"Did he say anything as he went?" Withered Wood said.

"He said he would not rest until the temple had surrendered Commander Duan."

Withered Wood glared at his nephew. "You're not telling me the whole truth. The Taoist is accomplished in the martial arts; you would never come out of an encounter with him alive." He paused briefly before continuing. "You can't stay here. I only know of one person who could fight this Taoist: a fellow disciple of my Master. His name is Scorched Wood. I think you should seek shelter with him for a while."

Withered Wood provided Duan with a letter and hired a boat to take him through the night to Jiaxing to seek refuge with Scorched Wood of Fahua Temple.

5

SCORCHED WOOD COULD BARELY COMPREHEND WHAT HAD just happened. He left the Garden of the Eight Drunken Immortals with the Seven Freaks and together they made their way back to his temple.

"My martial brother Withered Wood sent his nephew Justice Duan and another young man to me with a letter and asked me to protect them," he explained. "Elder Qiu is one of the Seven Masters of the Quanzhen Sect, who all trained under the great *shifu* Double Sun. Among them Elder Qiu is said to be the best. He may be a bit coarse, but he doesn't seem the type of man to stir up trouble without good cause. He can bear no grudge against an old monk like me. There must have been some grave misunderstanding."

"Let us speak with the two young men and ask them what's going on," Gilden Quan suggested.

"Good idea. They haven't told me their story yet," Scorched Wood said.

He was just about to send for Justice Duan when Ke Zhen'e spoke. "Qiu Chuji has quite the temper. He clearly doesn't think much of us wanderers of the southern *wulin*. The Quanzhen Sect may command a great reputation in the north, but they can't behave like that down here. A martial challenge, that's the answer. We take him on, one at a time. Only the honorable need apply."

"We should fight him together," Zhu Cong said.

"Eight against one? Doesn't sound very honorable to me," Ryder Han said.

"We're not going to kill him, only calm him enough so that he will listen to what the Venerable Monk has to say," Gilden Quan said.

"Won't it damage our reputation if word gets out among our friends in the *wulin* that Scorched Wood the Monk and the Seven Freaks fought Qiu Chuji together, eight against one?" Jade Han said.

Just then came a terrible clanging, a bell in the Great Hall.

"He's here," Ke Zhen'e said, jumping to his feet.

They ran toward the sound. Another clang, and then the sound of metal tearing. It was him, slamming the bronze censer against the large bell which hung from the center of the ceiling. Qiu Chuji's whiskers stood spiky like a porcupine, his eyes fixed and round. The Seven Freaks weren't to know this was extreme behavior for the otherwise mild Taoist. Days had passed with no sign of the traitor Justice Duan and anger had been smoldering inside him.

Qiu Chuji's frustration was erupting.

The Seven Quanzhen Masters' reputations only made the Seven Freaks even more determined to fight. Had Qiu Chuji been just another unknown wanderer of the *wulin* they might have been content to resolve the dispute by other means.

"Sister, we'll go first!" Ryder Han cried to Jade, who was in fact his cousin on his father's side. Ryder Han was the most impatient of the Seven Freaks. He pulled the Golden Dragon whip from his belt and performed a move known as Wind Disperses Swirling Clouds at Qiu Chuji's hand. Jade Han drew a long sword and lunged at Qiu Chuji's back. But the Taoist's reactions were quick, twisting his wrist so that the whip struck the censer instead, and dipping his body to let Jade Han's sword pass by him.

In ancient times, the two southern kingdoms of Yue and Wu were long at war. The King of Yue, Gou Qian, kept himself ready for combat at all times by sleeping on a bed of straw and drinking from a gall bladder. But the Wu army was universally acknowledged to be superior, mainly due to General Wu Zixu's strategic prowess, learned under the master tactician Sun Tzu. One day, however, a beautiful young woman, accomplished in the art of the sword, arrived in Jiaxing, then located just inside the Yue border. One of the kingdom's highest-ranking ministers, Fan Li, asked if she would teach them her skills so they might defeat the Wu. So it happened that Jiaxing came to be the home of this particular sword technique, passed from master to disciple, generation to generation. It was, however, designed for battle, for slicing generals and puncturing horses. When used against the masters of the *wulin,* it lacked the necessary agility and forcefulness. It was not until the dying years of the Tang dynasty that the repertoire came to be expanded by a swordsman familiar with the martial arts of ancient times, who added his own moves and made it faster and more complex.

Jade Han had studied the technique to such a level as to earn her the nickname Maiden of the Yue Sword.

It took no more than a few moves, however, for Qiu Chuji to assess the extent of her skills. All he needed to defeat her was speed; she was fast, but he could be faster. With the censer in his right hand, he blocked Ryder Han's Golden Dragon whip and with his left palm he struck Jade Han, seizing her sword. Within seconds she had been beaten back, taking shelter behind a statue of the Buddha.

Woodcutter Nan and Zhang Asheng rushed forward. Qiu Chuji's left palm shot out at Zhang Asheng's face. Zhang bent backward, but the move was a diversion. Qiu Chuji's foot struck Zhang's wrist, sending a sharp pain up his arm and forcing him to drop his knife. Zhang was better with his bare fists, however. Balancing on his left foot, he faked a right, roared, and punched with his left with all his strength.

"Beautiful!" Qiu Chuji said as he dodged to the side. "Such a shame!"

"What do you mean?"

"You are so accomplished and yet insist upon associating with that evil monk and living in thrall to the Jin."

"You are the most brazen of traitors," Zhang cried. "You're the thrall!" He struck three times at Qiu Chuji, each blow dodged or blocked with use of the censer. Two of Zhang's punches clanged squarely against the bronze vessel.

The Seven Freaks were losing, despite their four-to-one advantage. Zhu Cong gestured at Gilden Quan and together they launched themselves at the Taoist. Gilden Quan always carried a large steel balance, the arm of which could be used as a spear or club, the hook as a flying claw, and the weight as a hammer on a chain. One scale, therefore, became three weapons. Zhu Cong, in turn, preferred to strike the metal frame of his broken oilpaper fan against his opponent's pressure points, while dodging dancing weapons.

Qiu Chuji spun the censer, angling it in front of him like a shield. Using his free hand, he chopped and grabbed, slipping punches through the weaknesses in the Freaks' defenses. The weight of the vessel may have slowed his movements, but it also made it almost impossible for the Seven Freaks to land a blow, which gradually drained their strength.

Scorched Wood looked on, growing ever more anxious his friends might get hurt. "Stop, everyone!" he cried. "Listen to me, please!"

But men of the *wulin* do not stop midfight.

"You good-for-nothing!" Qiu Chuji shouted back. "No one wants to listen to your prattle. Watch this instead!" Alternating at speed between punches and slaps, in a move known as the Flying Mountain, Qiu Chuji chopped at Zhang Asheng.

"Your Reverence, please stop!" Scorched Wood cried.

But with two more fighters yet to join in, Qiu Chuji was in fact growing tired and afraid; he had no desire to die in this crumbling temple deep in the swampy south. Yet now he understood his opponents' weaknesses he had to push on.

Zhang Asheng was specially trained in Iron Shirt kung fu, by which he had toughened his skin to withstand the sharpest weapons. He was used to wrestling bulls bare-chested in the slaughterhouse, so his muscles were as hard as if covered in a thick layer of hide. Gathering the *qi* to his shoulders, he prepared himself for Qiu Chuji's attack. "Go on!"

Qiu Chuji's palm struck his shoulder, and with a *crack!* the bone in Zhang's upper arm snapped.

Zhu Cong tapped his metal fan at Qiu Chuji's Jade Pivot pressure point just below the collarbone, trying to break the flow of the attack.

But Qiu Chuji was energized by his small victory and made a grab at the weapons aimed at him.

"*Hai!*" Gilden Quan cried as Qiu Chuji seized one end of his scales. With a tug, Qiu Chuji pulled him closer. Blocking Woodcutter Nan and Zhu Cong with the spinning censer, he then struck Gilden Quan on the crown of the head.

At this point Ryder Han and Jade leaped in, aiming at Qiu Chuji's chest with their weapons. Qiu Chuji was forced to dodge to the side, letting go of Quan. Quan was dripping with sweat, but before he could get clear he felt a sharp kick to his side. He fell to the ground and was unable to get up again.

Scorched Wood the Monk had not wished to fight the Taoist and somehow had hoped to calm him with words. But he could not stand by as his friends were being hurt, not when they had come to his aid. Rolling up his sleeves, he picked up a piece of charred firewood and sprang at Qiu Chuji's armpit.

But Qiu Chuji sensed the move. He's going for my vital points, he realized, focusing.

Judging from the cries and moans, Ke Zhen'e, meanwhile, understood that two of his martial brothers had been badly hurt. He took up his metal staff and was about to join the fray when Gilden Quan called out, "Brother, your iron devilnuts, one in the direction of the Prospering and another toward the Small Surpassing!" Before he could finish, Ke had already fired the two metal projectiles, one between Qiu Chuji's eyebrows and the other at his right hip bone.

Qiu Chuji deflected them with the spinning censer, but he was surprised by their weight and the accuracy of Ke Zhen'e's aim. These weapons were unique to Ke Zhen'e, with points shaped like bat wings, only sharper, and quite unlike the round water chestnuts that grew in his hometown around South Lake. Ke had learned to use them before he was blinded.

The other Freaks had cleared the way. Gilden Quan continued shouting instructions, using points of the wheel from the I'Ching to denote directions. "Toward the Inner Truth, and the Radiance. Good. Now he's at the Darkening Light." After so many years of practice, it was as if the martial brothers were seeing with the same pair of eyes. Gilden Quan was the only one of the Freaks who could guide him in this way.

Within seconds Ke Zhen'e had fired a dozen iron devilnuts, forcing Qiu Chuji back as he fended them off. But still the Taoist was unharmed.

He can hear Brother Quan's instructions as well as I can and can prepare, it suddenly occurred to Ke Zhen'e. No wonder I'm not hitting him. Gilden Quan's voice was fading, and in between calls Ke could hear his brother moaning from the pain. He had not heard anything from Brother Zhang in a while. He could not even be sure he was still alive.

"The Fellowship . . . Aim . . ."

But instead Ke Zhen'e threw four devilnuts at once, two at the Self-Restraint and the Diminishing to the right of the Fellowship, and the other two at the Abundance and Radiance positions on the left.

Qiu Chuji stepped to the left in anticipation of Gilden Quan's instructions.

At that moment, two yelps.

One of the devilnuts struck Qiu Chuji's right shoulder. Ke Zhen'e fired another in the direction of the Diminishing and instead hit Jade Han in the back.

The blow did not hurt exactly, but Qiu Chuji started to feel numb in his upper arm. Poison! he realized in surprise. A chill spread to Qiu Chuji's heart, but rather than surrender, he drew all his last strength and launched himself at Woodcutter Nan.

Woodcutter Nan saw the attack coming, planted his feet firmly, and taking up his carrying pole blocked the Taoist with a Lock Across the River. But rather than withdraw his attack, Qiu Chuji struck the center of the pole with a *hai!* Vibrations shot through Nan, tearing the skin between his thumb and forefinger on both hands. Blood spurted everywhere and the pole fell to the ground with a loud clatter. The punch caused Nan serious internal injuries, his legs shook and spots flickered before his eyes. A sweet, metallic taste gurgled in his throat, and scarlet spit stained his clothes as he coughed.

Qiu Chuji was losing sensation in his shoulder and was struggling to keep the censer aloft. Once again gathering his *qi,* he performed a sweeping kick, which Ryder Han jumped.

"Where are you going?" Qiu Chuji cried, tipping the censer over. Ryder Han tried to backflip in midair, but it came straight for him.

He wrapped his head in his arms and curled into a ball. The censer crashed onto the floor, trapping him inside.

Qiu Chuji drew his sword. With a tap of the foot, he shot straight up and sliced through the rope attaching the giant bell to the ceiling. It must have weighed over one thousand *jin,* but Qiu Chuji guided it with the gentlest of pushes. The room shook as it landed on top of the censer. There was no way Ryder Han could escape now.

Qiu Chuji was a little sore after these exertions, and beads of sweat the size of soybeans clung to his forehead.

"Throw down your sword!" Ke Zhen'e cried. "Or you won't leave here alive."

But the evil monk Scorched Wood was colluding with the Jin and keeping women hidden in his temple, and Qiu Chuji was inclined to believe the Seven Freaks were not much better. Not everyone could be deserving of their reputation. Qiu Chuji would rather die than bow before these traitors and surrender. He held his sword high.

Only Ke Zhen'e and Zhu Cong were still capable of fighting. Using his staff, Ke Zhen'e blocked the exit.

Qiu Chuji was determined to get out. He thrust his sword at Ke Zhen'e's face, but Flying Bat Ke sensed the *whoosh!* of air as the sword approached. Sword and staff interlocked, and to his surprise, Qiu Chuji nearly lost his weapon. Is the blind man's inner strength more powerful than mine? He withdrew his sword and tried once more, and was met yet again with the staff. Only now did he realize how much power he had lost in his right shoulder; it was not that Ke was particularly strong, but rather that he, Qiu Chuji, was growing weaker. He swapped his sword to his left hand and performed a move he had learned as a young student but had never before used in combat: the Sword of Mutual Demise. With a flash of the blade, he struck simultaneously at Ke Zhen'e, Zhu Cong, and Scorched Wood's vital points.

The move was a tacit acknowledgment of relative weakness, and involved aiming at an enemy's acupressure points. It took great skill, but nevertheless utilized the same essential techniques as common street scraps between bandits and hooligans. Many years previously, the Quanzhen Sect faced a particularly fierce adversary who had lived many years in the untamed west. Only their *shifu* could have defeated him, but he had long since passed away. The Seven Masters knew this man alone could destroy their sect and they feared his return to the Middle Kingdom. They did have one move against him, the Plow Formation, but it required all seven Masters at once to be effective. The Sword of Mutual Demise was designed for lone combat against precisely this great master of kung fu. The strategy was to ensure his death through one's own, as a sacrifice to protect one's brothers. Qiu Chuji would not normally need to use such an extreme move on the Seven Freaks, but he was growing weaker from the poison. It was time to make use of his Master's greatest lesson.

Ten moves into the sequence, Ke Zhen'e was hit in the leg.

"Brother Ke, Brother Zhu, why not let the Taoist go?" Scorched Wood cried, distracting Ke Zhen'e long enough for Qiu to strike him in the ribs. Ke fell, screaming in pain.

Qiu Chuji was struggling to keep his balance. The whites of Zhu Cong's eyes were shot through with blood, but he continued to fight, shouting and insulting Qiu Chuji as he circled him. Ke Zhen'e could not place the sound made by the Taoist's sword, and he was caught again, this time in the right leg. Ke Zhen'e toppled forward with a thud.

"You dog, you dirty Taoist!" Zhu Cong shouted. "The poison will soon reach your heart. You'll see."

Qiu Chuji's brow scrunched with rage and he stumbled at Zhu Cong, clutching his sword in his left hand. But Zhu Cong was trained in lightness kung fu. He took off, flying around the Great Hall, bouncing off the many statues of the Buddha dotted around it.

Qiu Chuji stopped, panting. His strength was waning, his vision becoming blurred. His focus turned to finding an escape route.

Then, a thud.

One of Zhu Cong's cloth shoes hit him with considerable force in the back.

Qiu Chuji swayed, and a blanket of mist clouded his eyes. He was losing consciousness.

Thud!

This time it hit him against the back of the head: a wooden fish, one of the percussive instruments the monks used while chanting the scriptures. Zhu Cong had found it by one of the Buddhas. Such a powerful blow to the head would have killed most people, but Qiu Chuji had spent years training his inner strength. But this time his vision went black. This is it, he said to himself. Master Eternal Spring has today met his fate at the hands of these shameless villains! His legs buckled, and he collapsed to the floor.

Zhu Cong approached Qiu Chuji and stretched his fan to tap the pressure point in the center of his chest. At that moment, Qiu Chuji's left hand twitched. Zhu Cong knew he was in trouble. He blocked his heart with his right arm, but felt a force in his abdomen that sent him backward, blood spraying from his mouth. He landed with a crash.

Qiu Chuji could barely move.

THE OTHER monks of Fahua Temple were not practiced in kung fu and had been ignorant of their Abbot's skills, choosing to flee rather than take part. But since silence had descended upon the Great Hall, the bravest among them ventured to peek inside, only to see the floor strewn with bodies and the hall painted in blood. Horrified, they ran to find Justice Duan.

Justice Duan was still hiding in the cellar. That the fight had turned out to be so bloody only pleased him, and he sent one of the monks back to check if the Taoist was among the injured, or perhaps even dead. Only once the monk had returned to report that Qiu Chuji was lying motionless, his eyes shut, did Duan feel safe enough to emerge with Lily Li.

He approached Qiu Chuji and prodded him with his foot. The Taoist replied with an almost imperceptible moan. He was still alive. Duan pulled the dagger from his belt and leaned in. "You filthy Taoist!" he snarled. "You've chased and harassed me. Today I take my revenge. Prepare to join your friends in the next world."

"You mustn't hurt him," Scorched Wood called from where he lay.

"Why not?"

"He's a good man. Just a little short-tempered," Scorched Wood said. "There was a misunderstanding."

Justice Duan scoffed and aimed his dagger at Qiu Chuji's face. Qiu Chuji's eyes remained closed, but unbeknownst to Duan, he was gathering his *qi*. With a sudden movement he struck at Duan's shoulder, cracking the bones with a deafening crunch. Duan's dagger spun across the floor.

Scorched Wood summoned the last of his strength and threw the piece of burned wood in his hand at Duan. Duan tried to duck, but he was too slow, and the lump of wood struck him in the corner of the mouth, knocking three teeth clean out of his gums. The pain was intense and Duan was furious. He snatched the dagger from the floor, and ran at the Abbot, aiming the blade at his head. One of the younger monks grabbed him by the arm and another around the neck. Enraged, Duan turned the knife on them.

Qiu Chuji, Scorched Wood, and the Seven Freaks were too badly injured to do anything other than watch.

Just then, a howl.

"You filthy villain!" It was Lily Li. "Stop!" She had been waiting all this time to get her revenge. Now her captor was about to kill yet more righteous men, she could wait no longer. She ran and jumped up onto his back and wrestled with all her strength. With one broken arm, Duan could not put up much of a fight.

She was dressed in an army uniform, so the others had assumed her to be part of Duan's retinue. Her attack took them all by surprise.

But it was Ke Zhen'e who first realized this young man was in fact a woman, just from her voice. "Venerable Monk Scorched Wood," he said, turning to the Abbot, "you've misled us and put us in grave danger. You had a woman hiding in your temple all along!"

Scorched Wood realized at once what had happened. This one small oversight had not only caused injury to himself, but also great harm to his friends. He planted his fist on the floor and, pushing himself to his feet, spread his hands and rushed at Justice Duan. Again Duan managed to dive out of the way, but Scorched Wood's approach was clumsy and he ran headfirst into one of the temple columns and was killed instantly.

Justice Duan was terror-stricken. He could stay not a moment longer. Grabbing Lily Li, he ran.

"Help! No! He's kidnapping me!"

Lily Li's shouts faded into the distance.

CHAPTER THREE

SWIRLING
SANDS

I

THE MONKS SOBBED BITTERLY AT THEIR ABBOT'S DEATH, BUT
quickly turned to bandaging the wounded and carrying them to the
temple guesthouse.

A knocking from inside the bell in the hall suddenly interrupted
their work. The monks looked at each other: was it a monster? They
began chanting "The King's Sutra," accompanied by the mysterious
banging. Eventually some among them pulled the bell aside and
together lifted the censer. To their horror, out rolled a ball of flesh.
The monks jumped back in fright. The ball then slowly uncurled and
stood up; it was Ryder Han. He was unaware of how the fight had
ended, but immediately spotted that Scorched Wood was at eternal
rest and his martial family gravely injured. Taking up his Golden
Dragon whip he marched toward where Qiu Chuji was lying and
raised it above the Taoist's head.

"Third Brother, no!" Gilden Quan cried.

"Why not?"

"You mustn't," was all his brother could manage through the pulsing pain in his stomach.

Ke Zhen'e had been struck in both legs, but he was not badly hurt and was as alert as ever. He removed a vial of antidote from inside his shirt and instructed one of the monks to administer it to Qiu Chuji and Jade Han. He then explained all that had happened to his third martial brother.

"Where is Duan?" Ryder Han demanded.

"We'll find the scoundrel soon enough," Ke Zhen'e replied. "First you must help your brothers, they are badly wounded."

Zhu Cong and Woodcutter Nan's injuries were the most serious, and the kick to Gilden Quan's stomach had done its damage too. Zhang Asheng's arm was broken and his chest thumped with pain, but at least he was conscious once again.

The monks sent runners to report the day's events to Withered Wood at Cloudy Perch Temple, and to start making arrangements for Abbot Scorched Wood's funeral.

IT TOOK a few days for the poison to dissipate. Qiu Chuji was in fact well versed in the medicinal arts and spent his time mixing herbal recipes and giving massages to the Freaks. Before long they were able to sit up in bed. Together they gathered in the monks' sleeping quarters.

Eventually Jade Han broke the silence. "Elder Qiu is wise and capable, and the Seven Freaks are not exactly amateurs. And yet this dog tricked us into turning on each other. If word gets out, we'll be laughed out of the *wulin*. Your Reverence," she said, turning to Qiu Chuji, "what do you think we should do?"

Qiu Chuji held himself very much responsible. If only he had spoken calmly with Scorched Wood, surely the truth would have come out. "What do you think, Brother Ke?"

Ke Zhen'e was short-tempered by nature, and had only become more so following the events which led to his being blinded. He considered the defeat of his martial family at the hands of the Taoist an event of unparalleled humiliation, and his leg was spasming with pain. His answer, therefore, was rather short. "Elder Qiu has no respect for anyone, so long as he carries his sword. Why ask us our opinion?"

Qiu Chuji was stunned by this response, but understood Ke Zhen'e's anger. He got to his feet and bowed to each in turn. "Please forgive my ill manners. I have wronged each one of you. I beg for your forgiveness."

Zhu Cong and the Seven Freaks bowed too, all except Ke Zhen'e, who pretended not to notice. "My martial brothers and I are no longer worthy of involving ourselves in matters of the martial world. We shall take to fishing or collecting firewood. As long as Your Reverence would be so good as to allow us a horse and leave us alone, we will live out the rest of our days in peace."

Qiu Chuji blushed at Ke Zhen'e's reproof. He sat stiffly, saying nothing, and then took to his feet. "It was I who was at fault. I will not insult you further by wasting your time with my chatter. As for Abbot Scorched Wood's death, the responsibility is mine and I will ensure that the villain Duan meets my blade. Now I must go." Qiu Chuji bowed once more and turned to leave.

"Wait!" Ke Zhen'e called after him.

Qiu Chuji turned. "Was there anything else, Brother Ke?"

"You have caused each of us great injury," Ke Zhen'e said. "Is that all you have to say?"

"What was Brother Ke hoping for? I will do everything in my power to please you."

"Your tone is most rude. You can't just expect us to swallow it," Ke Zhen'e answered, his voice quiet.

The Seven Freaks could be generous and just, but they were also afflicted by an exaggerated pride, bordering on arrogance. It was not for nothing they were named the Seven Freaks, after all. As individuals they were accomplished, but together they were formidable. This was their first taste of defeat. Some years previously, they triumphed over the Huaiyang Gang on the shores of the Yangtze River, defeating more than a hundred men. Jade Han was only a child at the time, but she had killed two. From that day on, their fame spread throughout the *jianghu*. To be defeated by a lone Taoist was intolerable; all the more so that they were responsible for the death of their good friend Scorched Wood, and for no just cause. No, Qiu Chuji was to blame: he had been impetuous. Never mind that he had been right about a woman hiding in the temple. Skyfury Guo's wife, no less.

"I was gravely injured," Qiu Chuji said, "and would have died, had it not been for Brother Ke's antidote. So I must admit defeat this time."

"If that is so," Ke Zhen'e replied, "then leave us the sword on your back as proof, so there can be no more fighting."

Only Ryder Han and Jade Han were fit for combat, and there was no way they could prevail alone. Ke would rather his martial brothers die by his own hand than by the Taoist's blade.

I have saved them face by admitting defeat, Qiu Chuji said to himself. What else do they want? "The sword is my protection, just like Brother Ke's staff."

"Are you ridiculing my condition?" Ke Zhen'e raised his voice.

"I wouldn't dare."

"Everyone is injured; we cannot fight again," Ke Zhen'e growled. "But I invite Your Reverence to meet us back in the Garden of the Eight Drunken Immortals this very day one year from now."

Qiu Chuji frowned. Suddenly an idea hit him. "Of course we can arrange another fight, but I should set the rules. Although perhaps we needn't go another round as I already lost the drinking contest to Brother Zhu and have lost again in the temple."

Ryder Han, Jade Han, and Zhang Asheng took to their feet and the others straightened themselves as much as their injuries allowed. "We are happy to fight one more round. Our opponent may choose the time, the place, and the rules."

Qiu Chuji smiled. They were indeed competitive. "So you will agree to my suggestion, no matter what?"

Zhu Cong and Gilden Quan were confident they stood a chance at victory, whatever perverse or clever trick the Taoist came up with. "You decide!"

"The word of a gentleman . . ." Qiu Chuji said.

". . . is as true as a horseman's whip!" Jade Han finished.

Ke Zhen'e made no reply.

"If my terms are deemed unsuitable, I will of course admit defeat," Qiu Chuji continued. It was an obvious tactic, playing to their vanity.

"Just give us the rules," Ke Zhen'e said.

Qiu Chuji sat back down. "The method I have devised may seem protracted, but it is a true test of skill rather than brute force or momentary bravery. Every martial artist is trained to fight with fist and blade, there is nothing special about that. And besides, we have our good reputations to protect. We are not mere thugs."

If we're not going to fight, then what? the Seven Freaks wondered. Another drinking contest?

"This challenge, seven against one, will not only determine who has more skill, but also determination and stamina, as well as tactical intelligence. By the end, we will know who is worthy of the name 'hero.'"

The Seven Freaks were boiling over with anticipation.

"Tell us!" Jade Han said.

"If the challenge involves mixing together elixirs of immortality or charms to drive away ghosts we must accept defeat now," Zhu Cong said, smiling.

Qiu Chuji smiled back. "And I wouldn't want to compete with Brother Zhu in a contest of pickpocketing and filching."

"Tell us!" Jade Han was growing ever more impatient.

"At the heart of our dispute lay a misunderstanding. All because the lives of two descendants of loyal patriots are in danger. It is to this matter we must return."

Qiu Chuji began relating the story of how he met Skyfury Guo and Ironheart Yang, the fight in the snow and his pursuit of Justice Duan to this very temple. The Seven Freaks were just as disgusted with the corrupt Song court as with the brutal Jin, and vowed their allegiance to the brothers Guo and Yang.

"The woman Commander Duan kidnapped was Skyfury Guo's widow, Madam Li. You saw her, I am sure."

"I remember her voice—I could never forget it," Ke Zhen'e said.

"Good," Qiu Chuji continued. "I know not where Ironheart Yang's widow is to be found, however. But I have met her, and you have not. So, my suggestion is—"

"We find Madam Li and you find Madam Bao, and whoever succeeds first will be determined the winner. Am I right?" Jade Han interrupted.

"Finding them may not be easy, but it is hardly a test worthy of determining a hero. No, my proposal is more complicated."

"What is it?" Impatience was now getting the better of Ke Zhen'e.

"Both women are pregnant. We will find them, make sure they are safe and help them with the birth. As the children grow and mature . . ."

The Seven Freaks were astonished at where this was going.

"Then what?" Ryder Han urged.

"We will train them. Once they have reached the age of eighteen, we and other invited masters of the *wulin* will gather at the Garden of the Eight Drunken Immortals. First we will feast, and then our disciples will fight each other."

The Seven Freaks looked at each other.

"Were we to fight and the Seven Heroes defeat me, the glory of the victory would be tainted by the fact that you outnumber me. But in passing our skills on to one disciple each, we will better see whose skills are worthy of earning them the title 'Master.'"

"So it shall be!" Ke Zhen'e cried, thumping his staff against the temple floor.

"But what if Madam Li has already been killed by Commander Duan?" said Gilden Quan.

"That is a matter for fate," Qiu Chuji replied. "If the heavens have favored me, then so be it."

"Fine," Ryder Han rejoined. "We will have helped those poor

widows and their unborn children even if we lose, which is the noblest course of action."

"Exactly, Brother Han," Qiu Chuji said, gesturing his approval. "I would be most grateful if the Seven Heroes took care of my dead brother Guo's child and raised him to adulthood." He turned and bowed to each one in turn.

"You have been exceedingly clever with this plan," Zhu Cong said, "as it will involve eighteen years of hard work."

Qiu Chuji's countenance changed and he started laughing.

"What's so funny?" Jade Han challenged.

"The Seven Heroes have a reputation for generosity and a willingness to help others in need," Qiu Chuji said. "Heroes with a strong sense of justice, they say."

"And?" Ryder Han and Zhang Asheng demanded in unison.

"But I see now this was a gross exaggeration."

The Freaks were incensed and Ryder Han slammed his fist on the bench. But Qiu Chuji continued before he could interrupt.

"Since time immemorial, martial heroes have sworn allegiance to one another. They have been prepared to die for friendship. 'In times of peril, who cares for mine own flesh.' Justice was the only honorable consideration, for who could balk at giving their life for such a noble cause? Could you imagine Jing Ke or Nie Zheng hestitating over such a matter? The Yang and Guo families are in grave distress and in need of our assistance, and you quibble over the details of our contest?"

Zhu Cong's cheeks were hot with shame. He was an educated man and knew well the righteous conduct of ancient men described in the biographies from Sima Qian's *Records of the Grand Historian*. "Yes, Your Reverence is correct to point this out. I was mistaken. We will do just as you suggest."

"Today is the twenty-fourth day of the third lunar month," Qiu Chuji began, standing up. "We shall meet again on this very same day, eighteen years from now, at noon, at the Garden of the Eight Drunken Immortals. With the other heroes of the *wulin* as our witness,

we will see who among us is truly deserving of the title 'Master.'"
And with a flick of his sleeve, he left.

"I'm going to look for Justice Duan," Ryder Han announced. "We can't let him go to ground, or we'll never track him down."

As the only one not to have sustained any injury, he marched out of the door, swung himself up onto his famous golden steed, Wind Chaser, and went in pursuit of Commander Duan and Lily Li.

"Brother, brother!" Zhu Cong called after him. "You've never laid eyes on them before!"

But it was too late; Ryder Han was impatient by nature and his horse true to its name.

2

JUSTICE DUAN GRABBED AT LILY LI, SLIPPED OUT OF THE TEMPLE and began running. Some distance thence, he looked back, and was relieved to see no one following them. He slowed the pace and made for the river. There he spotted a small boat, jumped down onto the bow and, brandishing his sword, ordered the ferryman to start moving. The land south of the Yangtze was crisscrossed with a spider's web of rivers. Canals and boats were the usual mode of transportation, just as northerners traveled the plains by horse and carriage. No boatman would dare disobey an official, so the man unfastened the moorings and pushed the boat out away from the city.

What a mess! Duan's thoughts were an internal tussle. If I go back to Lin'an, my uncle will surely have me killed. I'd better go north. With any luck the Taoist and the Seven Freaks will have perished from their injuries and my uncle from his anger. Then I will be able to return and resume my post.

He instructed the boatman to follow the river northward. Duan changed out of his official's clothes and forced Lily Li to do the same.

They swapped boats several times on their way north. After ten days they arrived in Yangzhou, where Duan stopped at an inn. But just as they had settled in, he heard someone outside asking the innkeeper if a Commander Duan had come this way. He peered through a crack in the door. There stood an extraordinarily ugly, stumpy man accompanied by a pretty young girl. They spoke with heavy Jiaxing dialects. The Seven Freaks, he deduced. As luck would have it, the Yangzhou innkeeper was struggling to understand them, giving Duan enough time to grab Lily Li and slip out the back door. She tried to call out, but Duan silenced her, boxing her around the ear despite the searing pain in his arm. He then dragged her back to the water.

They were back on the Grand Canal within minutes and on their way north again. This time, they did not stop until they arrived at the garrison post of Liguo on the shores of Lake Mount Wei, just inside the borders of Shandong province.

Lily Li spent every waking hour wailing and cursing her captor. Duan was no gentleman, to be sure, but he never had any improper intentions, as far as she could discern; she was a somewhat plain country girl with unbound feet, who was by now much swollen with child. Instead, they bickered and scuffled, and never had a moment's peace. He may have been a commanding officer in the Song army, but his martial arts were poor, and fighting Lily Li with only one arm was taking all his strength.

Within days, however, the short man and the pretty girl had caught up with them. Duan wanted to hide in their room, but knowing her rescuers had come, Lily Li started screaming. Duan seized a cotton quilt and stuffed it into her mouth, hitting her as he did so.

Lily Li was proving to be a liability. He would be better off killing her, he reflected. After they heard Ryder Han and Jade Han leave, Duan drew his saber.

Lily Li had been waiting for a chance to avenge her husband, but Duan tied her hands and legs every night before bed. She saw a murderous glimmer in his eyes, and whispered to herself, "Dear husband, please protect me and help me kill this villain. I will be with you soon."

She reached into her shirt and removed the dagger Qiu Chuji had given her. She had hidden it so well that Duan was unaware of its existence.

Duan sneered and raised his saber. Lily Li was prepared. She summoned her strength and ran at Duan, dagger first. A gust of cold air skimmed Duan's cheeks. He twisted his weapon, hoping to knock the dagger from her grasp. Yet its blade was so sharp that it sliced crisply through the saber's blade. The tip of Lily's dagger chipped off and ricocheted in the direction of Duan's rib cage. He stumbled backward as it slashed open the front of his shirt, and scored his flesh with a bloody stripe. Had Lily used just a little more force, the blade would have eviscerated him. He grabbed a chair and held it in front of him. "Put the dagger down and I won't hurt you!"

Too exhausted to fight anymore, and with the baby kicking inside her, Lily crumpled in a heap on the floor, panting. But she held the dagger firm.

Duan manhandled her onto another boat and together they headed farther northward to Linqing, Dezhou, and on to Hebei province.

Lily Li was not making escape any easier. She screamed and shouted nonsense when they stopped at inns or traveled in boats, attracting considerable attention. She would tear at her clothes and pull strange faces. Had she gone mad? At first Duan believed it must be so. But after a few days he realized she was leaving a trail of clues for her rescuers. Summer had passed and an autumn chill cooled the air. They were by now far into the Jin-controlled north, but Duan was running out of silver and his enemies were still close behind.

They traveled until they reached the Jin Empire's capital, Yanjing. There they would find a quiet place to hide, and Duan would get rid of her. The Seven Freaks would never find them in such a large city.

But before they reached the city gates, a group of Jin soldiers stopped them and commanded them to carry supplies. The soldiers were traveling north with an emissary, charged with presenting the northern Mongolian tribes with Jin imperial ordinances. Ordinary Han Chinese citizens were being forced to act as porters. Lily was dressed in men's clothing, but as she was so short was given a lighter pole. Duan was left to stagger under his one-hundred-*jin* load.

Duan tried protesting their treatment, but reply came in the form of several lashes across the head. This was not an alien situation to Duan, it was just that previously he had been the one holding the whip. A crucial difference.

Octobers in the north were bitter, the sky swirled with snow and sand, and shelter was hard to come by. They lined up alongside the three hundred Jin soldiers, and together they trudged through open country. One by one they caught the faint sound of shouting carried on the wind from up ahead, and in the distance they could make out a cloud of sand kicked up by a throng of horses.

They fast approached: a defeated tribe from beyond the Gobi, swathed in furs. The Jin ranks dispersed, throwing their weapons behind them. Those without horses escaped on foot, but were soon crushed in the stampede.

Lily Li dropped her pole and ran in the opposite direction to the others. She could not see where Duan had gone, but no one was taking any notice of her.

She ran and ran, until after some distance she felt a stabbing pain in her stomach. She collapsed behind a sand dune and fainted. There she remained until long after nightfall, when she woke to what in her confusion sounded like the cries of a baby. Her mind a fog, she wondered if she might in fact have passed into the afterlife, but the wails were getting louder. With a sudden jerk, she felt something warm between her legs. There was a break in the snow and a bright round moon peered from behind the clouds. She was awake now, and her chest was heaving with heavy sobs. Her baby was born.

She sat up and took the baby into her arms. A boy. Still crying, she bit through the umbilical cord and wrapped him tight to her bosom. His eyes shone in the moonlight, beneath two thick eyebrows. His cries were strong and carried far. These were no conditions for giving birth, but the sight of her baby gave Lily Li a strength she had never before known. She rolled over onto her knees, and pulled them both into a small ditch nearby to take shelter. There she cried for her baby's father, lost forever.

They made the ditch their home for the night. The next day, when the sun was high in the sky, Lily Li summoned the courage to move. She looked out across the steppe at the dead men and horses scattered everywhere. Not a survivor to be seen.

She found some food in the knapsack of a dead soldier, as well as a knife and flint. She sliced some flesh from a horse and cooked it over a fire. Then she skinned another, wrapping one hide around the baby and another around herself. She and the baby lived like this for ten days, eating horse meat preserved in the snow, until she had regained enough strength to take her child and make her way east in the direction of the rising sun. The hate and anger she had been carrying with her was now transformed into love, and on she walked, doing her best to protect her son from the cutting desert winds.

She walked for days, the ground around her gradually turning ever greener. As the sun began to set, she saw two horses approaching on the horizon. The riders pulled on their reins and stopped to ask if she needed assistance. They were Mongolian shepherds, and did not know Chinese, but instinctively they understood the young mother's story. They brought her back to their *gers* and gave her food and a place to rest. They were moving camp the next morning in search of fresh pasture, but before departing they gave her four lambs for her new family.

And so it came to pass that Guo's son was born and raised on the Mongolian steppe.

3

YEARS PASSED. LILY LI NAMED THE BOY GUO JING AS QIU
Chuji had suggested. He was a slow developer, speaking his first
words only at the age of four, but he was strong and able to herd
cattle and sheep all by himself. Mother and son depended on each
other for survival, living a simple yet backbreaking existence. They
learned Mongolian, but when together, still spoke in the Lin'an dialect of Chinese. The boy's soft voice saddened his mother. "You
should also be able to speak your father's Shandong tongue, but I
never learned it in the short time we had together," she would say.

It was October, the air was growing colder. Guo Jing, now six
years old, rode each day out to pasture, accompanied by his sheepdog.
Just as the sun was at its highest, a large black bird appeared in the
sky. It hovered above the herd briefly, then swooped. One of the
young sheep broke free and ran.

Guo Jing jumped onto his pony and galloped seven or eight *li*
before at last catching it. Just as he was about to turn back with the
sheep, a deep rumble came echoing across the steppe. Was it thunder?
He was not sure what it was, but it frightened him. It grew louder,
until a horse's neigh rose above it, followed by more horses and men
shouting.

He had never heard anything like it. He hurried the sheep up a
small hill and into a nearby clump of bushes. Safely hidden, he
ventured a glimpse out.

Through the plumes of dust an army was racing toward him. Guo
Jing watched as the commanding general barked an order, and the
army broke into two and within seconds assumed formation. They
wore splendid white turbans, into which they had stuck colored
feathers.

A brief silence, then a blast of horns from the left. Another army.
Three rows charged forward. The young man leading them, an elon-
gated figure in a red cape, held his sword high. The two armies clashed

and a bloody battle commenced. The advancing army had fewer men and were beaten back before long, but support was quick to arrive and the fighting grew ever more fierce. And just as the battle appeared to be waning, a blast of horns came again from the east, shaking the remaining men into new life.

"The Great Khan Temujin has arrived! The Great Khan has arrived!"

The fighting continued, but now the soldiers kept looking over in the direction of the horns.

Guo Jing followed their gazes eastward. A cloud of sand swelled, until through it broke a group of riders, holding high a pole from which hung white hair. Their cheers grew louder, bolstering the riders' allies and scattering the hitherto tight formations of their foe. Guo Jing watched from deeper under cover as the banner approached the very hill upon which he was standing.

A tall, middle-aged man was prominent among the riders. He wore a helmet made of shiny metal and his chin laid growth to a brown tuft of beard. Guo Jing did not know this was the leader of the Mongolians, the Great Khan Temujin, later to be known throughout history as the mighty Genghis Khan; he did not even know what the word "khan" meant. But he understood the man's power, and it frightened him.

Temujin and a few of his men sat astride their horses, watching the battle below. Presently they were joined by the young man dressed in the red cape, who called to the Khan.

"Father, we are outnumbered. Should we retreat?"

"Yes, take your men to the east."

He turned back to the battlefield. "Muqali, accompany the Second Prince and his men back to the west. Bogurchi, you and Tchila'un go north. Kublai, you and Subotai, south. When my banner is raised and the bugle sounds, turn back and attack."

The men rode down the hill and within moments the Mongolian army was on the retreat.

"Capture Temujin, capture Temujin!" The enemy forces, meanwhile, were trying to fight their way up the hill.

Temujin stood firm at the top, protected from coming arrows by a wall of shields. Three thousand men, led by Temujin's brother-in-arms Kutuku and his bravest general Jelme, were mounting a valiant defense at the foot of the hill.

The ground shook with the clash of swords and roar of battle. Guo Jing watched, now just as excited as he was frightened.

The fighting continued for an hour or so, as thousands of enemy soldiers mounted charge after charge. Temujin's elite guard lost some four hundred men, but killed at least ten thousand. And yet arrow-fire remained intense. Combat was especially savage on the northeastern side, where the Khan's ranks looked as if they might collapse at any moment.

"Father, isn't it time to raise the banner?" Ogedai, Temujin's third son, implored.

Temujin's eyes were sharply focused like an eagle's, never moving from the battlefield. "But their men are not yet spent," he answered gruffly.

The enemy soldiers mounted a renewed attack on the northeastern side under the command of three of their best generals, each with his own black banner. The Mongol forces were steadily losing ground. Jelme came riding up the hill.

"Khan, our men can't hold on much longer!"

"Can't hold on? Call yourself a man fit to lead men?"

Jelme's cheeks flushed. He grabbed a sword from one of Temujin's guard, turned and howled as he charged forward, hacking a bloody path through the enemy, right up to the black banners. The generals pulled back hard. Jelme stabbed all three bannermen in quick succession, then threw down his weapon, grabbed the flags and returned to Temujin, planting them upside down at the Khan's feet.

Fighting continued. An enemy commander dressed in black appeared from the southwest. Within seconds, he had shot a quiver's worth of arrows, each taking one Mongol soldier. Two Mongol commanders charged at him with their spears. Both commanders were shot from their horses.

"Lovely!" Temujin said, just as an arrow lodged in his neck. Another followed close behind, heading straight for his stomach.

Temujin reared his horse. The arrow sank deep into the steed's chest, so only the feathers remained visible. The horse fell to the ground. Temujin's men watched in shock. The enemy were pouring up the hill, howling as loudly as their lungs would allow. Ogedai pulled the arrow from his father's neck, tore the shirt from his back and began bandaging the wound.

"Don't worry about me, son," Temujin said. "Defend the pass!"

Ogedai turned and shot down two enemy soldiers.

Kutuku had been leading an attack from the west, but his men were forced to retreat after using up all of their arrows.

"Kutuku," Jelme said, his eyes red. "You run like a scared rabbit?"

"Run?" Kutuku replied. "We have no more arrows."

Temujin threw Kutuku a handful of arrows from where he lay in the mud. Kutuku loaded his bow and shot the closest general, then ran down the hill and retrieved his horse.

"Excellent, my brother!" Temujin said as Kutuku returned.

"Why not raise the banner and sound the horns?" Kutuku suggested, his cheeks smeared with blood.

Temujin pressed against the wound in his neck. Blood pulsed through his fingers and down his wrist. "Not yet. The enemy still have life left in them."

"We are not afraid to die here on the field," Kutuku said, dropping to his knees, "but the Khan is in grave danger."

Temujin took the reins and struggled up onto the saddle. "We must defend the pass!" he said as he spurred his horse. Raising his saber, he sliced through three enemy soldiers charging up the hill toward them.

Temujin's reappearance took the enemy by surprise. Now was the time.

"Raise the banners! Sound the horns!"

A howl went up. One of the guardsmen stood on his horse and raised the white horsehair banner. The horns sounded. The deafening blast was instantly drowned out by the roar of battle, as line after line of soldiers thundered forward.

The enemy outnumbered the Mongols, but they were now facing an attack from all sides. The outer forces broke within moments, and the fighting engulfed the central guard. The general in black was barking orders, but morale was crumbling.

It took the Mongol army less than an hour to obliterate their opponents. Those left alive fled, including the general in black, who galloped off toward the horizon.

"Three *jin* of gold to whoever catches him!" Temujin called.

A dozen of Temujin's best men sped after the fleeing general.

The general turned and fired back at his pursuers, knocking man after man from his horse, until they dropped back and let him go.

Temujin's men had claimed a resolute victory over their long-standing enemy, the Tayichi'ud. Temujin was flooded with memories of his capture at their hands, their beatings and insults, the torture and the yoke. Today's victory had gone some way to redressing that humiliation. His heart quickened, and a laugh bubbled up from within. The earth shook with the shouts of his men as they withdrew from the bloody field.

4

GUO JING WAITED UNTIL DARKNESS HAD FALLEN AND THE soldiers charged with clearing the battlefield had left, before emerging from his bush and starting back.

It was well past midnight by the time he arrived home, where Lily Li had been waiting with ever increasing alarm. Guo Jing was met by a relieved mother's arms. He described to her all he had seen. Lily Li listened to her son's stammering, clumsy account, and was reminded of her late husband—his twitching caterpillar eyebrows, his fascination with battle—and it felt like the thrust of a blade to her heart.

A few days later, Lily Li left for the nearest market, some thirty *li* hence, with two wool blankets. Guo Jing, meanwhile, took the sheep out to pasture as usual. Out in the grassland, his mind galloped back to the fight. He spurred his horse, raised his whip and shouted, herding his flock, imagining himself to be a general leading his men.

Just then the beating of hooves could be heard in the east. A horse was approaching. At first it appeared to be riderless, but Guo Jing realized as it drew close that its master was resting his head on the mane. It stopped and the rider looked up.

It was the black general from the battle, his face soiled with blood and dirt. In his left hand he held what remained of his saber, not more than a hilt—it, too, covered in blood. This was his only weapon. His left cheek had been slashed, with blood pouring from the wound, as had his horse's legs. The man shuddered, locking his bloodshot eyes on Guo Jing.

"Water . . . Some water please?" the man managed to gasp.

Guo Jing ran the short distance back home and emerged with a bowl of water. The man grabbed it and drank it all down at once. "Another bowl!"

Guo Jing fetched another. Blood turned the water red as he drank. The man laughed, then his face twitched and he fell from his horse.

Guo Jing did not know what to do. But before long the man regained consciousness. "Some water for my horse. And how about something to eat?" he said.

Guo Jing reemerged with some chunks of cooked lamb and more water.

Food seemed to energize the man, and once finished he struggled to his feet. "Thank you, brother!" He then slipped a thick gold bracelet from his wrist and handed it to Guo Jing. "Here—for you."

Guo Jing shook his head. "Mother says you should never expect anything in return for common kindness."

"You're a good boy!" the man said, replacing the bracelet. He then tore a section from his sleeve and began bandaging the horse's wounds as well as his own.

Then, from the east, came the sound of more horses.

"Won't they let me go?" the man growled.

On the horizon, rolling waves of dust were already visible. They were coming this way.

"Boy, do you keep a bow and arrows in the house?"

"Yes!" Guo Jing replied, and ran back inside.

The man was visibly relieved, but relief quickly turned to disappointment when he saw Guo Jing reappear with the small bow and arrow he used for playing. "I meant the kind for fighting—a big one!"

Guo Jing shook his head.

The riders were getting closer, their banners now visible in the distance. The black general realized he would not be able to outrun them on an injured horse.

"I can't fight them by myself, so I'm going to hide," he said to Guo Jing. But there was nowhere suitable in or around the small thatched cottage. He was desperate. The only place he could think of was the large pile of drying hay nearby.

"I'm going to hide in there," he said, pointing. "Chase my horse away as far as you can. Then find somewhere to hide and don't let them see you." With that, he scrambled into the haystack.

Guo Jing whipped the man's horse and it cantered far into the distance before stopping to munch on some fresh grass. Guo Jing mounted his colt and took off in the opposite direction.

The riders had spotted people ahead, and sent two men on before them. They soon caught up.

"Boy, have you seen a man on a black horse come past this way?"

Guo Jing was no good at lying, so he did not answer. The men asked again, and again, but still the boy refused to speak.

"Let's take him to see the Prince," one of the men suggested. They took hold of Guo Jing's reins and rode with him back to the cottage.

I won't tell them anything, Guo Jing decided as they approached his home.

There stood a tall, thin man draped in a red cape, encircled by a crowd of soldiers. Guo Jing recognized the man: he had taken part in the battle on the hill only two days before.

"What did the boy say?" the Prince barked.

"He's frightened and won't speak."

The Prince cast his eyes around him until they fell upon a black horse grazing in the distance. "Is that his horse? Bring it here," he said.

Ten soldiers split into pairs, surrounded the horse and led it back.

"This is Jebe's horse, is it not?"

"Yes, sir!"

The Prince approached Guo Jing and struck him lightly across the head with his whip. "Where is he? Tell me. You can't fool me."

Jebe gripped his broken saber even tighter, his heart thudding. He knew this was Temujin's eldest son, Jochi, famed for his brutality. The boy was going to give him away; he had to be prepared to fight.

Guo Jing was in pain but fought back his tears. "Why did you hit me?" he asked, holding his head high. "I haven't done anything wrong!"

"You're a stubborn boy," Jochi growled as he whipped Guo Jing once more. This time tears gathered in Guo Jing's eyes.

Jochi's soldiers had been searching the house, and two men even poked at the haystack with their spears, but as luck would have it, they did not hit Jebe.

"He can't have got far without his horse. Boy, are you going to tell me where he is?" Jochi struck Guo Jing across the head three more times, each time a little harder. Guo Jing made a vain attempt to grab the Prince's whip.

Then came the sound of horns in the distance.

"The Great Khan is coming!"

Jochi lowered his whip. The soldiers rushed to gather around the Khan as he stopped in front of them. "Father!"

Temujin's injuries were grave. The Khan had summoned his last reserves of energy to fight out the battle, but fainted several times after

Jebe fled. His general Jelme and third son Ogedai took turns sucking the blood clots from his wounds, and together his four sons and best generals waited by his bed through the night until he was out of danger. Early the next morning, the Khan's men rode in search of Jebe, swearing they would catch and quarter him. One small group found him around dawn that morning and a fight ensued, but the black general had prevailed.

"Father, we found his horse!" Jochi announced, pointing it out for the Khan.

"The horse is no good to me. I want the man!" Temujin replied.

"Of course, Father, we'll find him," Jochi said. He went back to Guo Jing, unsheathed his saber and swung it menacingly above the boy's head. "Well? Are you going to tell me now?"

The earlier beating had emboldened the boy. "No!"

Temujin noted the boy did not claim ignorance. "Trick it out of him," Temujin whispered to his third son.

Ogedai approached Guo Jing with a smile and plucked two resplendent peacock feathers from his helmet. "These are yours if you tell me."

"No!" Guo Jing insisted.

"Release the dogs!" An order from Temujin's second son, Chagatai. The soldiers brought forth six of Chagatai's beloved mastiffs, led them to where Jebe's horse was grazing to catch his scent, and then let them loose. They ran straight for the cottage and out again, roaring and barking.

Guo Jing was no friend to Jebe, but he had admired the general's bravery on the battlefield, and Jochi's whipping had only strengthened his resolve. Guo Jing whistled to his sheepdog. Chagatai's mastiffs were circling in on the haystack, but Guo Jing commanded his dog to block them. Chagatai shouted and the mastiffs pounced. Howls, barks, teeth clashing. Though outnumbered, Guo Jing's sheepdog fought back bravely, but within moments he was covered in large gashes. Guo Jing cheered between his tears.

Temujin, Ogedai, and the rest of their men knew Jebe must be in

the haystack, but as there was no escape for the black general they decided to enjoy the dogfight first.

But Jochi could not wait and took his whip to Guo Jing. The boy rolled on the grass in pain, close to where Jochi was standing. Then suddenly he jumped up and grabbed hold of Jochi's right leg. Jochi tried to shake him off, but Guo Jing was surprisingly strong. Jochi's brothers started laughing and even the Great Khan had to hide a smile. Jochi's cheeks flashed scarlet. He pulled out his saber and swung at Guo Jing's head. Just as the blade was about to slice the boy's head clean from his neck, out from the haystack popped a broken saber to block his swing. Jochi felt his fingers shake and he nearly dropped his weapon.

Jebe scrambled out from under the hay and pulled Guo Jing behind him. "Taken to bullying children now? Have you no shame?"

The soldiers surrounded Jebe, spears at the ready. He had nowhere to go. Jebe threw down his broken saber. Jochi made to punch Jebe in the chest.

"Go on, kill me!" the black general shouted back, instead of defending himself. "Shame I won't be granted the honor of dying at the hands of a true hero."

"What did you say?" Temujin cried.

"Were I to die on the battlefield, defeated by a hero, I would have no regrets. But today an eagle has fallen and is about to be eaten by ants."

Jebe then howled. Chagatai's hunting dogs had pinned Guo Jing's sheepdog to the ground and were chomping and snarling at it, but Jebe's call stopped them, and they retreated, tails between their legs.

"Great Khan, such arrogance is not to be tolerated," one of Temujin's men cried, stepping out from the crowd. "Let me fight him!"

"Fine! You show him," Temujin replied. It was one of his best generals, Bogurchi. "If there's one thing we have plenty of, it's heroes."

"I'll kill you. So you may die with no regrets," Bogurchi cried, as he stepped forward.

"And who are you?" Jebe replied, eyeing the sturdy man opposing him.

"My name is Bogurchi! Maybe you've heard of me?"

Jebe felt a shiver go through him. So this is the famous Bogurchi? Jebe said to himself. His fame precedes him; he is a hero among the Mongols. But he rolled his eyes and snorted, feigning indifference.

"You are named for your great skills with the bow and arrow," Temujin said to Jebe. "Why not see who is more skilled: you, or my sworn brother here?"

"You are a sworn brother to the Great Khan?" Jebe turned to Bogurchi. "In that case, I'll take pleasure in killing you first."

The Mongol soldiers burst into laughter. Bogurchi's unparalleled fighting skills had made him famous across the steppe. Jebe may well be a talented archer, but was he a match for the great Bogurchi?

As a boy, Temujin had been taken prisoner by his father's former allies, the Tayichi'ud, and taken to the banks of the Onon River, where they thrust his head through the flat wooden panel of a cangue. There they drank, and lashed him with their whips. Temujin waited until his captors were incapacitated with drink before knocking the guard over the head with the cangue, still locked around his neck, and escaping into the forest.

The Tayichi'uds called a search across the steppe. A young man by the name of Tchila'un took pity on Temujin, and, risking the wrath of the Tayichi'ud, broke the cangue from Temujin's neck, burned it, and sheltered the fugitive in a cart of fleeces. Presently the Tayichi'ud men came and searched Tchila'un's home. The men spotted the cart and began removing the fleeces, one layer at a time. Just as they were about to uncover the future Khan, Tchila'un's father interrupted the soldiers.

"The weather is so hot, how could he be hiding in the fleeces? He would be dead by now."

The summer solstice was upon them, and sweat poured from their bodies like storm rains. The old man spoke sense, so the soldiers left.

Temujin had fled home, and now, along with his mother and younger brother, was forced to keep moving across the steppe, surviving on wild rats and his horsemanship to keep them ahead of their pursuers.

One day, eight of Temujin's white horses were stolen by a rival tribe. Temujin was giving chase when he encountered a young man, milking his horse. Had he seen where the thieves had fled? This was Bogurchi. "We both know the hardships a man faces in these grasslands. Let us be friends," he said.

They rode together for three days before at last catching up with the thieves. They fought side by side. Their arrows slayed hundreds of men, and together they recovered the horses. Temujin offered to give Bogurchi four, but Bogurchi refused. "This I did for friendship, nothing more."

In one another they found a bond deeper than any other.

Temujin now gave his bow to Bogurchi and jumped down from his steed. "Ride my horse, use my bow and arrows. It will be as if I killed him myself."

"As you command." Bogurchi took the bow in his left hand, the arrows in his right, and jumped up onto Temujin's beloved white horse.

"Give your horse to Jebe," Temujin said to Ogedai.

"He is most fortunate indeed," Ogedai said, dismounting. One of the bodyguards led the horse to Jebe.

"I am surrounded," Jebe said to Temujin, once seated on Ogedai's horse. "You could have killed me easier than a sheep. I dare not ask for more favors. Just give me a bow—no arrows are necessary."

"No arrows?" Bogurchi said.

"That's right. I can kill you with just a bow."

Again the Mongolian soldiers guffawed.

"How he boasts!"

"What a braggart!"

Temujin ordered them to give Jebe one of their best bows.

Bogurchi knew Jebe's shot was precise. But to fight without

arrows? Bogurchi realized Jebe must be planning to send his arrows back at him. He squeezed his thighs and Temujin's horse sprang forward.

Jebe pulled on his reins. Bogurchi nocked an arrow, pulled back and shot. Jebe reached out. The arrow was in his hand.

Impressive, Bogurchi said to himself.

Another arrow.

Jebe listened as it cut through the air. This one he couldn't catch. He pressed his body flat against the horse's back. The arrow passed above, ruffling the hairs on his head. He spurred, turned his horse, hauled himself upright. But Bogurchi fed his bow quickly, and two more arrows came whistling toward him. He slipped down from his saddle, his right foot still hooked into the stirrup, and held himself inches from the ground slipping by below. There he fluttered at the horse's feet, like a trapped kite. He turned, loaded the arrow he had caught, fired it, and flipped back into the saddle.

"Amazing," Bogurchi breathed. He shot at the approaching arrow. The arrowheads clashed, twisted and sank into the sand. Cheers rose from Temujin and his men.

Bogurchi nocked an arrow, aimed left, waited for Jebe to react, and shot right. Jebe knocked the arrow away with his bow into the dirt. Bogurchi fired three more arrows in a rapid flurry, all of which Jebe dodged with ease. Jebe spurred his horse, leaned down, picked three arrows from the dirt, bent his bow and shot.

Bogurchi leaped up and stood on his saddle in an extravagant display. Balancing on his left foot, he kicked the flying arrows away with his right, before pulling back his bow with all his power and letting fly. Jebe jerked to one side and shot an arrow at Bogurchi's, splitting it along the shaft.

Bogurchi was growing uneasy and increasingly impatient. He fired a blur of arrows. Unable to catch so many in succession, Jebe contrived to avoid them. But still the arrows kept coming, thick and fast, until he was struck in the left shoulder. The crowd cheered.

Smiling, Bogurchi reached for another arrow, intending to kill

Jebe. His hand felt into his quiver's deepest corners. There were none left. He always took sufficient supplies with him into battle: two quivers around his waist and six on the horse. But he was not using his own mount now; he was riding the Khan's. He pulled the horse round, stooped, and swept at the moving grass.

Jebe knew this was his chance, and fired an arrow square into Bogurchi's back. A gasp rose from the crowd. It was a painful blow, but despite the force of the shot, the arrow failed to penetrate Bogurchi's clothing and fell to the ground. Bogurchi reached down and inspected the arrow. Jebe had removed the arrowhead.

"I avenge the Great Khan! You needn't show me any mercy!" Bogurchi cried, sitting back in the saddle.

"Jebe shows no mercy to his enemies. I have killed you, in all but deed."

Temujin had been watching in distress, but his fears were allayed when he realized Bogurchi was unhurt. He would have exchanged ten thousand sheep, oxen, and horses to keep his best general and friend from being killed. "Enough!" Temujin called. "You have proven your prowess. We no longer seek vengeance upon you."

"I am not asking the Khan to spare my life."

"Then what do you want?"

"It is him I wish to be spared!" Jebe answered, pointing at Guo Jing standing by the door. "All I ask is that the Khan troubles the child no more. As for myself," he continued, "I wounded the Khan and deserve punishment. Come, Bogurchi!" He pulled the arrow from his shoulder and loaded his bow, the blood still dripping from the tip.

"Fine! Let's fight!"

A deluge of arrows rushed from Bogurchi's bow, forming a chain through the air.

Jebe hooked his foot through the stirrup, tucked himself under his horse's belly, and aimed. Bogurchi's white colt pulled left without his master's command, but Jebe had been swift, and the arrow hit the horse in the forehead, bringing it crashing to the ground.

Bogurchi fired as he rolled, splitting the bow in Jebe's hand. Jebe cursed, and steered his horse away from Bogurchi's arrows. Cheers rose from the spectators.

He's an impressive archer, Bogurchi had to admit. He bent his bow, aimed at Jebe's back and let go.

The arrow hit Jebe in the back of the head. Jebe convulsed and fell from his horse, the arrow landing in the grass beside him. But Bogurchi too had removed the arrowhead. He loaded another arrow and held it aimed at Jebe. "Great Khan!" he cried, turning to Temujin. "Have mercy and let him go!"

"Will you not surrender?" Temujin responded.

Jebe's stubborn defiance was overcome. He ran over to Temujin and knelt at his feet.

Temujin smiled. "From this day forward, you fight with me!"

Mongolians often turn to song to express their feelings. Kneeling before the Khan, Jebe began to sing:

> "The Great Khan is merciful, as befits his name,
> Which I will repay with my protection,
> With contempt of fire and water,
> And rebel against dark seas and rupturing cliffs.
> Take our enemies, gouge out their hearts!
> I will go wherever I am needed.
> For the Khan I am always willing,
> Ten thousand miles by sun or moon!"

Temujin produced two gold ingots and gave one each to Bogurchi and Jebe.

"Great Khan, may I give this to the boy?"

"You may do with your gold as you please," Temujin replied.

Jebe approached Guo Jing and held out the ingot, but Guo Jing shook his head: "Mother says you should never expect anything in return for common kindness."

Temujin admired the boy's bravery, but liked him even more after hearing this. "What an impressive young man!" Then, turning to Jebe:

"Bring him to me later." He then left, instructing a squad to mount the dead horse on the backs of two others, and to follow behind.

Jebe was exhausted, but pleased with the outcome. He lay in the grass to rest and wait for the boy's mother to return.

"You're a good boy, you did the right thing," Lily Li said to Guo Jing after Jebe told her of her son's fearless conduct, even if the wounds on his face did trouble her. But how would the boy avenge his father's death if he remained a shepherd his whole life? No, it would be better to let him train with the Great Khan's men. So mother and son agreed to go with Jebe, and join Temujin's tribe.

Jebe was put in command of a team of ten under Temujin's third son, Ogedai. Jebe and Bogurchi held each other in great esteem, and became loyal friends. Nor did Jebe forget his debt to Guo Jing. He took good care of mother and son, and decided he would teach Guo Jing all his skills with the bow and arrow, as soon as the boy was old enough.

5

ONE DAY, GUO JING WAS PLAYING WITH SOME OF THE OTHER children when two riders came galloping into the encampment with urgent news for the Khan. They rushed to Temujin's *ger* and within moments the horns were sounded and soldiers ran from their tents. The men were organized into squads of ten, each with its own commander. These were then organized into companies made up of ten squads, battalions of one thousand men and, finally, divisions of ten thousand, each with their own commander. Temujin kept close control of his army through this chain of command.

Guo Jing and the other children watched as the men took up their weapons and mounted their horses. Another horn blast sounded, and the ground shook as the horses gathered into formation. By the end of the third blast, silence had descended as all fifty thousand men were lined up before the encampment's main gate. Only the occasional horse's snort broke the quiet; no one spoke, no clanging of weapons was heard.

"Of our many victories the Jin Empire knows," Temujin cried as he walked through the main gate with his three sons. "The Jin Emperor sent his Third and Sixth Princes here today to appoint your Khan an officer of the Jin!"

The soldiers raised their weapons and hailed their Khan. The Jin controlled all of northern China by the force of a strong and disciplined army; their influence stretched east to the seas and west to the deserts. The Mongols, in contrast, were just one of many nomadic tribes on the steppe. To be named an official of the Jin Empire was an honor for Temujin.

The Khan ordered his eldest son, Jochi, to lead his ten-thousand-strong corps to welcome their guests. The remaining forty thousand men would wait in formation.

News of the growing power of northern tribes such as Temujin's worried the Jin Emperor Wanyan Jing, titled Ming Chang. In reality, the Princes were not here just to secure an alliance between the Mongols and the Jin Empire, but to ascertain at firsthand their capabilities in case of future conflict. The Sixth Prince, Wanyan Honglie, was the very same Prince who had traveled to Lin'an, where he was wounded by Qiu Chuji, and on to Jiaxing, where he encountered the Seven Freaks of the South.

After some wait, a blot of dust appeared on the horizon, announcing Jochi's return with the two Princes, Wanyan Hongxi and Wanyan Honglie, and their force of ten thousand elite soldiers, dressed in the finest brocade and armor. Those on the left of the formation were armed with spears and those on the right with wolf-fang clubs. The clanking of their armor was audible for miles. Sunlight glinted on their uniforms of silk and metal, and they shone ever more resplendent as they came into view. The brothers rode side by side, while Temujin and his men stood by the road, waiting.

As they drew near, Wanyan Hongxi caught sight of the children watching, and laughed. He puffed himself up, reached into his shirt for a handful of gold coins and threw them at them. "A gift!"

But, to Mongolians, throwing coins like this was the height of disrespect. These children were descended from soldiers and generals. Not one of them moved to pick up the coins.

"Come on, you little devils!" Wanyan Hongxi cried, throwing another handful of coins in frustration.

This angered Temujin and his men even more. They may not have had the grand outward trappings of other great civilizations, but the Mongolians were a refined people. They did not swear, even against their gravest enemies or in jest. To step inside a *ger* was to be treated with utmost hospitality, whether friend or foe, and a guest was to return this favor with decorum. They may not have understood Wanyan Hongxi's heavily accented Mongolian, but they understood his attitude all too well.

Guo Jing had grown up on stories of Jin scorn, and of how they had invaded his motherland China, corrupted its officials and killed its greatest general, Yue Fei. He stepped forward now. "We don't want your money!" he cried, picking some coins from the dirt. He ran and hurled them as hard as he could at the Third Prince.

Wanyan Hongxi ducked, but one struck him on the cheekbone. Temujin's men cheered.

It did not especially hurt, but such humiliation at the hands of a six-year-old boy was too much. He swiped a spear from one of his guards. "I've got you, you little devil!"

"Brother!" Wanyan Honglie said, realizing the situation was getting out of control. But it was too late: the Third Prince had already thrown the weapon. Guo Jing turned, rather than stepped aside. At the last possible moment, an arrow came from the left, like a meteor shooting for the moon, and hit the spear on the head, deflecting it. Guo Jing ran back to the other children, the cheers of Temujin's men shaking the ground beneath him.

The arrow belonged to Jebe.

"Third Brother, forget about him!" Wanyan Honglie hissed.

The cheers of Temujin's men left Wanyan Hongxi shaken. He glared at Guo Jing. "Little bastard," he muttered.

Temujin and his sons stepped forward and led the Princes to the Khan's *ger,* where they served their guests *koumiss* and plates of lamb and beef. With the help of interpreters, Wanyan Hongxi read the royal decree, conferring upon Temujin the title of "Queller of Northern Uprisings." Temujin knelt before Wanyan Hongxi and accepted the title and a golden belt, a symbol of his allegiance to the Jin Empire.

THAT NIGHT the Mongolians honored their guests with a lavish feast.

"Tomorrow, my brother and I will bestow Ong Khan with a title," Wanyan Hongxi stuttered, drunk on *koumiss.* "Will our Queller of Uprisings join us?"

Temujin was delighted and agreed at once. Ong Khan, a Kerait, was recognized as leader of the northern tribes of the steppe. He was the richest, and commanded the most men, but was known to be fair and magnanimous in his treatment of others. He was universally liked and respected. Ong Khan was sworn brother of Temujin's father. After Temujin's father was poisoned and Temujin fled, it was Ong Khan who took him in as his own son. Not long after Temujin was married, his wife was captured by the Merkits. It was only after receiving help from Ong Khan and Jamuka, Temujin's sworn brother, that Temujin managed to defeat the Merkits and reclaim his wife.

"Is the Jin Empire granting titles on anyone else?" Temujin asked.

"No," Wanyan Hongxi said. "There are only two men of note in the northern steppe: Ong Khan and the Great Khan Temujin."

"No one else would be worthy of a title," Wanyan Honglie added.

"I disagree. There is one man the Princes are perhaps unfamiliar with," Temujin said.

"Is that so? Who?" Wanyan Honglie said.

"My sworn brother, Jamuka. He is most righteous and commands his men with a just hand. May I ask the Princes to bestow an official title on him as well?"

Temujin and Jamuka had grown up together, cementing their friendship with a bond of brotherhood when Temujin was just eleven, a custom known among the Mongolians as *anda,* sealed with an exchange of gifts. Jamuka and Temujin swapped hunting stones made from deer bone. After the boys became *anda,* they went to the Onon River while it was still frozen over and threw them out across it. When spring came the boys swore their brotherhood again, Jamuka giving Temujin a whistling arrow he had carved himself from two ox horns, while Temujin presented his friend with a cedar arrowhead.

When they reached manhood, they lived with Ong Khan. They would compete every day to see who could rise first and drink a cup of yoghurt from Ong Khan's own jade cup. After Jamuka and Ong Khan helped recover Temujin's wife, the sworn brothers exchanged gifts once more, this time gold belts and horses. By day the men drank wine from the same cup and at night slept under the same blanket.

Their tribes, however, were eventually forced to take different directions in the search for fresh pasture, and the two men were separated. But both tribes flourished and their loyalty endured. It was natural that he should wish for his *anda* to be honored as well.

"We don't have titles to give to all you Mongolians. How many do you think we have?" Wanyan Hongxi stammered, by now half drunk. Wanyan Honglie cast his brother a meaningful look, but was ignored.

"Fine, give him my title instead."

"Does a title mean so little you would give it away?" Wanyan Hongxi cried.

Temujin stood up. Without uttering another word, he downed the contents of his cup and left. Wanyan Honglie was left to diffuse the situation with some hasty and not particularly amusing jokes.

THE NEXT morning, just as the sun was climbing above the horizon, Temujin mounted his horse and went to inspect the five thousand mounted horses already lined up in formation. The Jurchen Princes and their men were still sleeping.

Temujin had at first been impressed by the Jurchen army; they appeared strong and well equipped. But still sleeping? Temujin snorted. Now he saw they were undisciplined and libertine. "What do you think of the Jin?" he asked Muqali.

"A thousand of our men could defeat five thousand of theirs," was Muqali's reply.

"Just what I thought," Temujin said with a smile. "But they say the Jin has more than a million men at its command. We have only fifty thousand."

"But you can't lead one million men into battle at once. If we were to fight them, we could take ten thousand today and another ten thousand tomorrow."

"We always agree when it comes to military strategy." Temujin patted him on the shoulder. "A man weighing one hundred *jin* can eat ten oxen, each weighing ten thousand *jin*. He just needs time." They laughed.

Temujin pulled at his reins. Then he caught sight of his fourth son Tolui's horse without its rider. "Where is Tolui?"

Tolui was only nine years old, but Temujin treated his sons in the same way he did his troops, with an iron discipline. Anyone breaking his rules was punished.

Temujin's men were uneasy. General Boroqul, Tolui's mentor, was overly concerned. "The boy never sleeps late. Let me see."

Just as he turned his horse, he saw two children running toward him holding hands. The boy with a strip of brocade tied around his forehead was Tolui, the other was Guo Jing.

"Father!" Tolui was excited.

"Where have you been?" Temujin demanded.

"Guo Jing and I swore an oath of brotherhood down by the river. Look, he gave me this," Tolui said, waving an embroidered red handkerchief Lily Li had made for her son.

Temujin recalled with fondness the time he and Jamuka became sworn *anda,* two innocent children just like those standing before him now. "And what did you give him?"

"This!" Guo Jing said, pointing to his neck, to the gold necklace Temujin's son usually wore.

"From now on, you must love and look after each other," Temujin said.

They nodded.

"Now, mount your horses," Temujin said. "Guo Jing is coming with us."

The boys climbed into their saddles in excitement.

After yet another hour's waiting, the Jin Princes emerged from their *gers,* washed and dressed at last. Wanyan Honglie caught sight of the Mongolian soldiers waiting in formation and sent a hurried order to his men to get ready. But Wanyan Hongxi believed in making the Mongolians wait, to let them know who had the power. He ate at a leisurely pace, accompanying the snacks with a few cups of wine, and then mounted his horse. It took another hour for the ten-thousand-strong Jin army to muster before setting off.

They marched northward for six days until they were met with a delegation sent by Ong Khan consisting of the Khan's son Senggum and his adopted son Jamuka. When word reached Temujin that his sworn brother was up ahead, he galloped on. The two men jumped from their horses and embraced. Temujin's sons followed close behind to greet their uncle.

Jamuka was tall and spindly, Wanyan Honglie observed, his upper lip decorated with the finest threads of gold. His eyes were quick. Senggum, in contrast, was pale and flabby, no doubt from having lived a life of opulence. He looked nothing like the men hewn by the harsh climate of the steppe. He was haughty and showed a noticeable disregard for the Great Khan.

Together they rode on again for another day. Then, just as they were approaching Ong Khan's camp, two of Temujin's advance guards came riding back. "The Naiman are blocking the way ahead. Some thirty thousand of them."

"What do they want?" Wanyan Hongxi was anxious after hearing the translation.

"To fight, it would seem."

"They've really brought thirty thousand men?" Wanyan Hongxi stuttered. "Isn't . . . Aren't we outnumbered?"

Temujin did not wait for Wanyan Hongxi to finish. Turning to Muqali he said, "Find out what's going on."

Muqali rode on with ten bodyguards while the rest of the entourage waited. He was back before long. "The Naiman say that since the Great Jin Empire granted a title to our Khan, the Princes should bestow one on them too. If Your Excellencies don't, they will take you hostage until such a title is forthcoming. Not only that, they want a rank of higher status than that given to our Great Khan Temujin."

"Demanding a title?" Wanyan Hongxi's cheeks had gone pale. "That's sedition. What should we do?"

Wanyan Honglie started organizing his troops into their fighting positions as a precaution.

"Brother," Jamuka said, turning to Temujin, "the Naiman frequently steal our livestock and harass our people. Are we really going to let them get away with this? What do Your Excellencies want us to do?"

Temujin had by now surveyed the terrain and concocted a plan. "Let's show the Princes how we do things here on the steppe." Temujin let out a cry and cracked his whip twice. Five thousand Mongolians howled in response, startling the Jin Princes.

Up ahead, the Naiman were approaching.

"Brother," Wanyan Hongxi said, "order our men to charge. These Mongols don't know how to fight."

"Let them go first," Wanyan Honglie whispered.

Realizing his brother's intentions, Wanyan Hongxi nodded. The Mongolian soldiers howled again, but still they did not move.

"Why are they howling like animals?" Wanyan Hongxi said. "Shouting alone isn't going to make them turn back."

Boroqul was positioned on the left flank. He turned to Tolui, who along with his sworn brother Guo Jing had joined his voice with the other men. "Follow me and don't fall behind. Watch and learn."

Just then enemy soldiers appeared through the dust up ahead. Still the Mongols howled, still they did not move.

Wanyan Honglie was growing more and more anxious. The Naiman were fierce and might attack at any moment.

"Fire!"

The first row of Jin men released several rounds of arrows, but the Naiman were still beyond reach. They were charging at speed toward them. Wanyan Hongxi began to panic, his heart thudding. "Why don't we just give them what they want?" he said to his brother. "We can make up some title, something high ranking, it doesn't matter. It wouldn't cost us anything."

With two cracks of Temujin's whip, the Mongols fell silent and split into two flanks. Temujin and Jamuka each took one. Leaning low in their saddles, they galloped toward higher ground on either side, calling orders to their men as they rode. The riders split off into small groups as they ascended, covering all positions. Now they had the height to their advantage, they loaded their bows and held them high.

The commander of the Naiman too looked for higher ground. But the Mongolians had erected walls made from layers of sheep's fleece to shield them from incoming arrows. The Naiman shot up at the Mongolians, but their arrows fell short, or were caught up in the fleece barricades.

The Mongolians returned fire, and the Naiman fell back in chaos and confusion.

Temujin watched the tumult from his position high on the left. "Jelme, attack the rear!"

Armed with his saber, Jelme charged, one thousand men behind him, and blocked the Naiman retreat.

Jebe took up his spear and pressed to the front of the charge. His target was the Naiman commander in chief; he would kill him as an expression of gratitude to Temujin.

Within moments the Naiman rear guard fell apart and the foremost ranks were in chaos. The Naiman commander hesitated, giving Jamuka and Senggum time to join the charge. Facing attack on all sides, the Naiman fell into disarray. Abandoned by their commander, the remaining men threw down their bows, dismounted and surrendered.

The Mongols had killed over a thousand Naiman men, captured two thousand more and gained almost as many horses before the rest of the army fled. They had lost no more than a hundred of their own.

Temujin ordered the captives be stripped of their armor and split into four groups, one for the Wanyan brothers, one for his adoptive father Ong Khan, one for his sworn brother Jamuka and one for himself. Mongolians whose relatives had died in battle received compensation: five horses and five slaves.

The battle now over, Wanyan Hongxi burst into nervous laughter. "They want a title?" he said, turning to his brother. "How about 'Conqueror of the Northern Queller of Uprisings'?"

For all his brother's jokes, Wanyan Honglie was feeling decidedly nervous. The Empire would be in trouble if Temujin or Jamuka ever united the northern tribes and took command of the steppe.

The Mongols were a genuine threat.

He was still mulling this over when yet more dust appeared on the horizon. Another army approaching.

CHAPTER FOUR

A DARK WIND BLOWS

I

"TAKE UP YOUR WEAPONS, ANOTHER ARMY IS COMING!" WANYAN Hongxi cried.

Moments later, the scouts returned. "Ong Khan is here to welcome the Princes in person."

Temujin, Jamuka, and Senggum rode out ahead.

From the clouds of dust an army emerged, led by Ong Khan. He drew close, rolled down from his horse and knelt before the Princes, flanked by his adopted sons Temujin and Jamuka. He was a heavyset man with a head of glittering silver hair. His robe was made from the finest black panther furs fastened with a gold belt.

Wanyan Honglie too dismounted and returned the gesture of respect, but Wanyan Hongxi remained in his saddle, deigning only to cup his fists in the most perfunctory manner.

"Your humble servant received advice of your treatment at the hands of the Naiman," Ong Khan began. "I hope Your Excellencies were not too affronted. I sent my men as fast as I could. Thankfully, with Your Excellencies' grace upon them, my three boys were able to prevail without my men."

Ong Khan then led the Wanyan brothers back to his *ger*. The inside walls were lined with leopard and fox furs and decorated with the most elegant furniture money could buy. Even his personal guards were better dressed than Temujin Khan himself. Horns were regularly sounded and could be heard for miles around. The Jin Princes had never witnessed such grandeur beyond the bounds of the Great Wall.

Once Ong Khan's new title had been bestowed, they settled down to a banquet of spectacular proportions. Female slaves danced late into the night and the celebrations became ever more raucous. Quite a contrast to the simple and somewhat rustic welcome provided by Temujin. Wanyan Hongxi in particular was enjoying the feast and had spotted two girls that took his fancy. Ideas began forming, but it did not occur to him to ask Ong Khan's permission.

The *koumiss* skins were now half empty. Wanyan Honglie turned to Ong Khan. "Your heroism is known across the steppe and even those of us from within the Great Wall have long admired your prowess. But I would like to meet some younger Mongolians of distinction."

"My adopted sons are the two greatest heroes we Mongols can claim," was Ong Khan's response. He smiled.

Senggum, a son born of Ong Khan's own loins, was sitting nearby and did not take kindly to this remark. He downed yet another cup of *koumiss*.

"What about your own son?" Wanyan Honglie asked, noticing Senggum's displeasure.

"He will succeed me upon my death, of course," Ong Khan said. "But in comparison to his adopted brothers? Jamuka is quick-witted. Temujin is even more courageous. He rose to his current position with only the help of his own fortitude and valor. I ask you, who wouldn't want to serve such a fine man?"

"Is that to say Ong Khan's generals are not as impressive as Temujin's?" Wanyan Honglie continued.

Temujin noticed the Sixth Prince was trying to stir resentment among them. He prepared himself for the response.

Ong Khan stroked his beard and at first did not reply. He took another long swig from his *koumiss* skin.

"Not so long ago the Naiman came past this way and stole several thousand of my livestock. Had it not been for Temujin and his Four Great Generals, we would never have recovered them. He may not have many men under his command, but they are without exception all of singular bravery and skill. Your Excellency must have noticed this today."

Senggum's cheeks turned a deeper shade of scarlet and he slammed his golden cup down on the table.

"My current fortune has nothing to do with skill, but is merely a reflection of my adoptive father's generosity and attention," Temujin added hastily.

"Temujin's Four Great Generals? Who are they? I would like to meet them," Wanyan Honglie said, changing the subject.

"Why not summon them to our party?" Ong Khan asked Temujin. Temujin clapped his hands and, within moments, four men marched into the *ger*.

The first man was gentle-looking and pale in complexion, more of a scholar than a fighter. This was the master strategist Muqali. The second was of sturdy build, his eyes intense like a bird of prey. He was Temujin's good friend Bogurchi. The third, Tolui's teacher Boroqul, was short but quick in movement. The last man was covered in scars from battle, his face a bloody red. This was the man who had saved Temujin's life all those years ago, Tchila'un. These were the founding commanders of the rising Mongol Empire, Temujin's Four Great Generals.

Wanyan Honglie could not help but admire them and toasted each in turn.

"Today there was a commander dressed in black who led the

charge through the Naiman ranks. What is his name?" Wanyan Honglie said once the generals had finished their *koumiss*.

"I just recruited him, he is our newest squad leader," Temujin answered. "Everyone calls him Jebe."

"Then why not invite him to drink with us as well?"

Temujin obliged and issued the command.

Jebe entered the *ger* and performed the gestures of gratitude appropriate to his rank and invitation. But just as he was about to drink, Senggum interrupted him.

"How dare you, a mere squad leader, drink from my golden cup?"

Jebe held the cup against his lips, shaking with rage at such an insult. He glanced at Temujin.

For the sake of my adoptive father, I will overlook Senggum's rudeness, Temujin decided. "Bring it to me," he announced. "I am thirsty, I will drink it!" He took the cup from Jebe's hands and emptied it. Jebe gave Senggum a dirty look, turned and made for the door.

"Come back!" Senggum said, but Jebe ignored him and left.

"Brother Temujin may have his Four Great Generals, but I have something capable of besting them all, should I choose to use it." Senggum was growing ever more enraged that things were not turning out as he wished. Senggum and Temujin were no *anda*; they were brothers only in the loosest sense.

"Really? And what is that? What force could be so potent?" Wanyan Hongxi's interest had been piqued.

"Come outside and I will show you," Senggum said.

"We are drinking, why stir up trouble?" Ong Khan said.

"I'm bored—let's go and take a look." Wanyan Hongxi stood up and walked out. He liked the idea of trouble. The others had no choice but to follow.

The soldiers had lit hundreds of fires and were gathered around them, celebrating. Seeing the Khans emerge, those on the western flank scrambled to their feet, sending a rumble echoing around the camp. Within moments they were lined up and had settled into perfect silence. These were Temujin's men. In contrast, Ong Khan's troops to the east were slow and disorganized. Titters could be heard as they joked among themselves.

Ong Khan's men may outnumber Temujin's, but they are far less disciplined, Wanyan Honglie concluded.

"More drink!" Temujin cried. He had noticed Jebe's pained expression in the glow of the fire. A large jug was brought to him. "Today's victory over the Naiman was the result of collective bravery," he announced.

"Because we are led by Ong Khan, Temujin Khan, and Jamuka!" the men replied.

"But today, I saw one man whose bravery deserves special mention. He charged the enemy rear no less than three times. Dozens of men were felled by his bow. Who do I mean?"

"Squad Leader Jebe!" the soldiers answered again.

"No, not Squad Leader Jebe . . . *Commander* Jebe!"

For a moment there was silence, then the men began to cheer.

"Jebe is a great fighter! He deserves to be commander!"

"Bring me my helmet," Temujin said to Jelme. Jelme returned moments later and presented it to him.

"This is the helmet I wear into battle. This is the helmet I wear when I slay our enemies." Temujin lifted it high above his head for everyone to see. "Now, this warrior will drink from it."

He poured the jug's contents into the helmet. Bringing it up to his lips, he drank from it and then offered it to Jebe.

Jebe lowered his head in gratitude and knelt on one knee to receive the honor. He finished the remaining *koumiss*.

"Even the world's most precious diamond-studded golden cup could never compare to my Khan's helmet," he said quietly. Temujin smiled as Jebe passed it back to him and he put it back on his head.

Cheering erupted. Everyone in the camp already knew of Jebe's humiliation and even Ong Khan's retinue believed Senggum to have behaved badly.

Temujin is greatly revered, Wanyan Honglie said to himself as he watched events unfold. Jebe would gladly die a thousand times for him. Jin officials believe the north to be populated by ignorant barbarians, but it is obvious we have grossly underestimated these people.

"And what about this thing you possess that is capable of defeating Temujin's Four Great Generals?" Wanyan Hongxi said, leaning back in the tiger-pelt chair his servants had carried out for him.

"Your Excellency, are you prepared to see something very special?" Senggum replied. Ha! These Generals are nothing compared to my secret weapons, Senggum said to himself with a smile. "Where are my brother Temujin's Generals?"

The Generals came forward and bowed before their superiors. Senggum turned and whispered something to his most trusted servant, who nodded and then ran off. Soon after, two loud roars reverberated around the camp and a pair of giant golden, spotted leopards appeared from behind the *ger*. They stalked toward them in the darkness, their eyes glowing like jade lanterns. Terrified, Wanyan Hongxi gripped the handle of his saber. Only when they came closer to the fires did he see that they were, in fact, being restrained by ropes held by two burly men. These men were solely charged with caring for Senggum's most prized possessions. The animals snarled and clawed, their muscles taut and ready. Wanyan Hongxi's heart convulsed and he wriggled in his seat. The men hardly seemed capable of holding back two such powerful beasts.

"Brother, if your Four Great Generals can subdue my leopards barehanded, then I will stand forever corrected," Senggum said, turning to Temujin.

Temujin's Generals were incensed. First you humiliate Jebe, now you degrade us? Are we mere wolves to be prodded and played with? Is it our duty to fight leopards?

Temujin could barely hide his displeasure. "I love these men as I love myself—why should I let them fight with leopards?"

"Is that so?" Senggum laughed. "Then why call them your Four Great Generals, or whatever their names are? Clearly they are cowards."

Tchila'un was particularly short of temper and could withstand these insults no longer. He stepped forward. "My Great Khan, they may laugh at us, but we cannot allow them to humiliate you. I will fight these beasts."

Wanyan Hongxi was delighted, so much so that he pulled a ruby ring from his finger and threw it on the ground. "Yours, if you win."

Tchila'un did not even look at the ring and instead prepared to charge. But Muqali pulled him back just in time. "We are famous across the steppe for having defeated so many of our enemies. But can a leopard command an army? Can a leopard ambush or surround a whole company of men?"

"Brother Senggum, this is yours. You win," Temujin said as he bent down, picked up the ring and gave it to Senggum. Senggum put the ring on one of his fingers, held it high and laughed. Ong Khan's men roared.

Jamuka said nothing, a frown carved across his brow. Temujin looked calm. The Four Great Generals returned to their men, bitterly embarrassed.

Wanyan Hongxi felt cheated. He asked for two female slaves and retired to his *ger* for the night.

2

THE NEXT MORNING TOLUI AND GUO JING WERE PLAYING IN the grasslands far from the main camp when they spotted a white rabbit up ahead. Tolui raised his small bow and arrow, aimed and hit it in the belly. The shot lacked power, however, and the rabbit ran away with the arrow still embedded in its fur. Howling, the two boys ran after it.

Before too long, the rabbit collapsed. The boys cried out in delight and were just about to retrieve the animal when a group of children emerged from a wooded area nearby. One boy of around twelve years of age made a grab for the creature, pulling out the arrow and throwing it to the ground. He then gave the boys a fierce look and ran away.

"Hey, I shot that rabbit. It's mine," Tolui shouted after him.

The boy turned around and came back. "Says who?"

"It's my arrow, isn't it?"

The older boy's eyebrows shot up and his eyes bulged. "This rabbit was my pet, you're lucky I'm not asking you to pay me back for killing it."

"You're lying, it's obviously wild," Tolui said.

The boy was furious. He stomped up to Tolui and shoved him. "Watch what you're saying. My grandpa is Ong Khan and my papa is Senggum. Do you know who they are? It's mine now, even if you did shoot it. What are you going to do?"

"And my father is Temujin!" Tolui said.

"Ha! So what? Your father is a coward. He's scared of both my grandpa and my papa!" This was Tusakha, Senggum's only son. Senggum had waited years and sired several daughters before at last fathering the long-awaited boy. Tusakha was the youngest and therefore most spoiled, and Senggum let him bully the other children. It had been years since Temujin, Ong Khan, and Senggum had met, and the last time their sons played together they were but small children. As far as they were concerned, this was their first encounter.

"Says who? My father isn't scared of anyone!"

"When your mother was kidnapped, it was my grandpa and papa who retrieved her and gave her back to your father. Did you think I didn't know that? I'm taking your precious little rabbit. What are you going to do about it?"

Senggum had long been envious of Temujin's fame and he had been sure to let everyone know the part he had played in the recovery of Temujin's wife. His son had heard the story many times. Temujin, on the other hand, had always considered it an immense embarrassment and had never spoken of it to Tolui.

Tolui was so angry his cheeks turned purple. "You're a liar! I'm going to tell my father!" He turned and started walking away.

"So what?" Tusakha laughed. "Your father's Four Great Generals were so scared of my father's leopards last night that they couldn't move."

This only made Tolui even more furious and he could barely form the words to respond. "My father isn't scared of tigers, so why should he be scared of leopards? But there is no dignity in fighting wild animals."

Tusakha stepped up to the boy and slapped him across the face. "How dare you talk back to me? Don't you know who I am?"

Tolui was startled and his cheek throbbed. Tears collected in his eyes but he did not let the other boy see.

Guo Jing had been watching from the sidelines, silently boiling up inside with anger. He could stand it no longer. He lunged and rammed his head squarely into Tusakha's stomach, knocking him flat on his back.

Tolui clapped and then grabbed Guo Jing's hand. The boys ran.

"Kill them!" Tusakha screamed. Tusakha's friends ran after the two young boys and Tusakha followed close behind. They were older and Tolui and Guo Jing were quickly outmuscled. Within moments they had been pinned to the ground.

"Ready to surrender?" Tusakha spat, punching Guo Jing in the back. Guo Jing tried to wrestle the boy off him but Tusakha was too heavy. Tolui had two on top of him.

Just then the sound of horse bells was heard coming from beyond a sand dune and a small group of riders appeared. The first, a short, plump man on a golden steed, caught sight of the fight in the distance. "Excellent. A brawl."

As he rode closer for a better look he realized that it was two children being bullied by a gang of older boys. They were trapped, the punches came hard and their faces were swollen and bruised blue.

"Shame on you! Let them go!" he shouted.

"Mind your own business!" Tusakha yelled back. "Don't you know who my father is? I can do what I want and there's nothing you can do about it!"

"What a spoiled child. Let go of them!" The rest of the group rode up to join the first man.

"Third Brother," the woman in the group said. "Don't stick your nose in where it doesn't belong. Let's go."

"But look at them! What kind of fighting is this?"

It was the Seven Freaks of the South. They had followed Justice Duan's trail all the way up here to the northern steppe before losing him, and for six years now they had been roaming the grasslands in search of Skyfury Guo's wife, Lily Li, and the child she was assumed to have borne. Despite having learned Mongolian, they were no closer to finding them. The Seven Freaks were stubborn and competitive and they would never think to concede to Qiu Chuji before the eighteen years were up.

"Two against one, we can't allow that." Jade Han hopped down from her horse and pulled the two children sitting on Tolui from his back.

Thus freed, Tolui struggled to his feet. Tusakha hesitated for a moment and Guo Jing seized his chance, flipping over and crawling out from between Tusakha's legs. The two boys then started to run.

"Get them!" Tusakha yelled, leading the rest of his gang in pursuit.

Smiles spread across their faces as the Seven Freaks watched the little Mongolian children fighting and they were reminded of their own youthful misadventures.

"We have to go," Ke Zhen'e said. "The market will close soon and we must ask around today before everyone goes home."

Tusakha's gang of bullies had, by then, caught up with Tolui and Guo Jing.

"Now do you surrender?" Tusakha demanded. Tolui, still furious, shook his head fiercely.

"You asked for it!" The boys pounced on them again.

Suddenly, a flash of cold, silver light caught Zhu Cong's eye just as he was turning away. A small dagger had appeared in Guo Jing's hand.

"Now who's the coward?"

Lily Li had given Guo Jing the dagger Qiu Chuji had left them to protect him from evil spirits. Now he could put it to use against these bullies.

Tusakha's gang shrank back.

What an unusually bright blade, Zhu Cong thought, I should take a closer look. Zhu Cong had spent his entire life stealing from government treasuries and the vaults of the rich, so he was quite the expert in spotting objects of value. He pulled sharply at his horse's reins and turned back. There stood the young boy, dagger in hand. It flashed blue again in the sun. There could be no doubt, this was a weapon of rare quality. But how did it end up in the hands of a little boy? He looked at the children more closely and only then did he notice they were all wearing expensive shirts made from leopard skins, all except for the boy with the dagger. What Guo Jing lacked in fancy clothing he made up for with a golden crown nestled on top of his head. These children were clearly all members of influential, wealthy Mongol families. The boy must have stolen his father's favorite knife, Zhu Cong thought. No harm in taking from kings and aristocrats. Having made up his mind, he jumped down from his horse and approached the children, a sweet smile on his face.

"Come on now, stop fighting. Play nice." At that moment, he darted into the circle of children and grabbed the knife. Many years of training meant he could seize a blade with his bare hands. Only the best martial arts masters would be able to stop him; a small child like Guo Jing had no chance.

Having secured the dagger, Zhu Cong ran out and jumped back onto his horse. Laughing, he then jerked the reins and galloped off to catch up with the rest of the Seven Freaks.

"Well, today wasn't a total loss, I managed to snatch myself this little gem." He was still laughing.

"Second Brother, you're never going to grow out of that childish habit of yours, are you?" Laughing Buddha Zhang Asheng said.

"What little gem? Let me see." Gilden Quan was always curious. Zhu Cong threw the dagger at him.

A shard of blue light shot across the sky, breaking into a rainbow of colors. The Seven Freaks gasped in wonder.

"How beautiful!" Gilden Quan cried as the dagger flew toward him, a shiver shooting down his spine. He reached out and caught the dagger by the handle. He examined it more closely. There on the grip were carved two characters: *Yang Kang*. This is a Han name, he said to himself. How did a Han dagger end up here in Mongolia? Yang Kang? Yang Kang? I don't think I've ever heard of a martial arts master named Yang Kang. But why would this Yang Kang possess such an exceptional weapon if he was not a hero of the *wulin*?

"Big Brother! Do you know anyone by the name of Yang Kang?"

"Yang Kang?" Ke Zhen'e searched his memory before shaking his head. "I've never heard the name before."

Yang "Vitality" Kang was the name Qiu Chuji had given the baby in Charity Bao's belly. Charity's husband Ironheart Yang and Skyfury Guo had swapped the daggers as a testimony to their brotherly bond and so it ended up here, in the hands of a small boy of the Mongolian steppes. Of course, the Seven Freaks were not to know all this.

"Qiu Chuji is looking for Ironheart Yang's widow. Could this Yang Kang have something to do with him?" Gilden Quan said.

"If we find Ironheart Yang's widow and take her to the Garden of the Eight Drunken Immortals, we've at least won half a victory over that old monk, I suppose." Zhu Cong smiled. After six years of searching, even such a far-fetched connection was too much to ignore.

"Let's go back and ask the boy," Jade Han suggested.

Ryder Han's horse was the fastest so he rode first, only to discover the boys still fighting. Once again, Tolui and Guo Jing were pinned to the ground. Ryder Han ordered the children to stop, but they ignored him. Growing impatient, he grabbed two and threw them to one side.

Now feeling intimidated, Tusakha pointed at Tolui and said, "You dogs come back tomorrow and we'll finish this then!"

"Fine. Tomorrow it is!" Tolui said as Tusakha led his gang away.

As soon as he got home he would ask his brother Ogedai for help. Ogedai was his favorite sibling, as well as the strongest.

"Give it back!" Guo Jing reached out to Zhu Cong. His face was covered in blood.

"Fine." Zhu Cong waved the blade back and forth in front of Guo Jing's face. "But first you have to tell me where you got it."

"My mother gave it to me," Guo Jing said, wiping the blood from his nose with his sleeve. It was still bleeding.

"And who is your father?"

Guo Jing had never known his father and the question rendered him speechless. He could only shake his head in reply.

"Is your surname Yang?" Gilden Quan asked. Once again, Guo Jing shook his head. The child did not appear to be too sharp, the Seven Freaks reflected.

"Who is Yang Kang?" Zhu Cong probed further. Guo Jing shook his head.

Zhu Cong handed the dagger back to Guo Jing. Whatever anyone might say, the Seven Freaks were always true to their word.

"You can go home now." Jade Han fished out a handkerchief and gently wiped the blood from Guo Jing's face. "Don't go getting into any more fights. You're too small, you're no match for them yet."

The Seven Freaks then climbed back onto their horses. Guo Jing watched as they rode off to the east.

"Guo Jing, let's go home," Tolui said.

The Seven Freaks had already ridden some distance, but Ke Zhen'e caught the two magic words, faint though they were: *Guo Jing*. The name made his entire body shake. He jerked his horse around and galloped back to the children.

"Boy, is your last name Guo? You are Han Chinese, not Mongolian, is that right?"

"Yes," came Guo Jing's reply.

"What is your mother's name?"

"Ma," Guo Jing answered, which made Ke Zhen'e scratch his head.

"Can you take me to see her?"

"Ma isn't here."

"Sister, you ask him," Ke Zhen'e suggested, sensing hostility in Guo Jing's replies.

Jade Han hopped down from her horse. "What about your father?" Her voice was warm.

"My father was killed by bad people. When I grow up, I'm going to kill them and avenge him."

"What was your father's name?" Jade Han was so excited that her voice was trembling. But Guo Jing just shook his head.

"Who killed your father?" Ke Zhen'e cut in again.

"His . . . his name is Justice Duan."

Lily Li had lived these last years in the shadow of her fear, even out here on the steppe, and she had realized that her chances of ever returning to the south were remote at best. If something were to happen to her with her son still ignorant of who had killed his father, she would never forgive herself. So as soon as he was old enough to understand, she told him all about the bad man who had come riding into their village. But why had she not told Guo Jing Skyfury's name? Lily Li was an illiterate country girl and she had only ever referred to her husband by the traditional "Brother" as a sign of respect. She had never thought to ask his given name. Guo Jing, therefore, had only ever known his father as "Papa."

Justice Duan: the name stunned the Seven Freaks into silence, even when whispered so softly. Not even three bolts of lightning striking the ground at their feet could have shocked them more, and the sky was a most beautiful clear blue that day. It felt as if the earth were shaking and the wind had turned. After a brief pause, Jade Han cried out and grabbed at Zhang Asheng's shoulder in order to stop herself from collapsing. Zhang Asheng in turn started beating wildly at his chest. Gilden Quan threw his arms around Nan the Merciful's neck and Ryder Han did a backflip on his horse. Ke Zhen'e threw his head back and laughed, while Zhu Cong spun on the spot. Tolui and Guo Jing watched them, puzzled by such a funny sight.

It took some time for the Seven Freaks to settle.

"Merciful Bodhisattva, thank you, thank you!" Zhang Asheng dropped to his knees and prayed.

"Boy, let's sit down," Jade Han said to Guo Jing. But Tolui tugged at Guo Jing's sleeve. He was in a hurry to get home and speak to Ogedai, and he had a bad feeling about the seven strangers with their strange accents and even stranger behavior. Yes, they had helped them scare off Tusakha and his friends, but now he wanted to leave.

"I have to go," Guo Jing said. He took hold of Tolui's hand and together they began to walk away.

"Hey! Hey! You can't go now. Your friend can go home by himself," Ryder Han said, a note of desperation in his voice.

Ryder Han's pockmarked face scared the two little children, and they started to run. He chased after them and was about to wrap his chubby fingers around the back of Guo Jing's neck when Zhu Cong stopped him.

"Brother, your manners!" Zhu Cong lightly slapped Ryder Han's hand. Zhu Cong then ran round in front of the two little children, picking up three stones from the ground. "I'm going to do some magic, do you boys want to see?"

Guo Jing and Tolui were curious enough to stop and watch.

Zhu Cong held out his right hand, placed the stones in the middle of his palm and clenched his hand into a fist. "Gone!" he said, opening it again. Indeed, it was empty. The boys were amazed. Zhu Cong then pointed at the hat perched on top of his head. "In there!" He then removed it, revealing the pebbles inside. Guo Jing and Tolui clapped their hands and squealed in delight.

Just then they heard the cries of a flock of wild geese making their way toward them in an arrow formation. This gave Zhu Cong an idea.

"Now my brother will show you a trick." He fished out a handkerchief, handed it to Tolui and pointed at Ke Zhen'e. "Blindfold him."

"Are we playing hide-and-seek?" Tolui asked hopefully, as he put the blindfold on Ke Zhen'e.

"No, better than that. He is going to shoot a wild goose out of the sky," Zhu Cong answered, producing a bow and an arrow.

"That's impossible. I don't believe you," Tolui said.

As they were talking, the wild geese flew straight overhead. Zhu Cong flicked his wrist and tossed the three stones in his hand into the sky. The stones shot straight upward, startling the birds. The lead goose squawked and began turning the formation in another direction. Ke Zhen'e drew his bow as far back as it would go and released, hitting a goose square in the belly. The bird whistled to the ground and landed with a thud, the arrow still in its stomach.

Tolui and Guo Jing exploded into whoops and cheers. They ran over to retrieve the goose and brought it back to Ke Zhen'e.

"Remember those boys who ganged up on you? If you learn some martial arts you won't ever have to worry about them again," Zhu Cong said.

"We're going to fight them again tomorrow and I'm going to get my big brother to help," Tolui said.

"Get your big brother to help?" Zhu Cong scoffed. "Only weak children do that. I'll teach you some moves and I guarantee you will beat those boys tomorrow."

"Two against seven?"

"Yes."

"Teach me." Tolui was excited by the thought of beating Tusakha all by himself.

"How about you? Don't you want to learn too?" Zhu Cong asked Guo Jing, who was standing farther away, looking hesitant.

"Ma told me I shouldn't fight. I don't want to make her angry."

"Little coward." Ryder Han smiled.

"If that's true, then why did you fight those boys just now?" Zhu Cong pressed.

"Because they started it."

"So what are you going to do when you come face-to-face with Justice Duan?" Ke Zhen'e said.

"I'm going to kill him!" Guo Jing's eyes flashed a fiery red.

"Your father was an expert in martial arts and yet Justice Duan still managed to kill him. How are you going to avenge your father if you don't learn?"

Ke Zhen'e's question silenced the young boy.

"You're going to have to," Jade Han concluded.

"See that mountain over there?" Zhu Cong pointed at a solitary peak to his left. "If you want to learn martial arts, then meet us up at the top tonight at midnight. But you must come by yourself. No one else can know about this, apart from your little friend here. Do you think you're brave enough? Are you scared of ghosts?"

Guo Jing could not take his eyes away from Zhu Cong, but Tolui was growing impatient. "Teach me instead, I want to learn!"

Zhu Cong grabbed Tolui's wrist, hooked his left foot behind the boy, and moments later Tolui was on the ground.

"Why did you do that?" Tolui demanded as he climbed back to his feet.

"That was kung fu. Can you do it?" Zhu Cong smiled.

Tolui was a clever child and understood. Copying Zhu Cong, he pretended to trip an imaginary foe. "Teach me something else."

Zhu Cong faked a punch at Tolui's face. Tolui dodged to the left, but Zhu Cong had his right hand in position, waiting. There was no force behind the punch however, and it barely nudged Tolui's nose.

"Teach me something else!" Tolui was enjoying himself. Zhu Cong bent down and pushed his shoulder upward into the little boy's stomach, sending him flying into the air. Gilden Quan jumped up, caught him and gently put him back on safe ground.

"Mister, teach me something else!"

"You'll be able to fight off most adults with just those three moves." Zhu Cong smiled. "That's enough." He turned to Guo Jing. "Can you do them?"

Guo Jing shook his head. The Seven Freaks were even more disappointed. Compared to his friend, Guo Jing seemed very slow indeed. Jade Han sighed, and rubbed at her reddened eyes.

"I say we stop wasting our energy," Gilden Quan said in their southern dialect, so Guo Jing and Tolui could not understand. "Why don't we take the mother and son back south and hand them over to Qiu Chuji? We may as well admit defeat."

"The boy doesn't have it in him, he has no natural understanding of kung fu," Zhu Cong agreed.

"He doesn't have an ounce of fight in him. I don't see how we could win," Ryder Han added.

"You can go home now," Jade Han said to the two children, waving them away. Tolui grabbed hold of Guo Jing's hand and they skipped happily off.

The Seven Freaks had spent six long, hard years searching the steppe for Guo Jing. Their joy at finding him had been fleeting in the extreme. Perhaps it would have been better if they had never found him.

Ryder Han beat the ground in frustration, whipping the sand into a whirlwind. The other Freaks tried to calm him, but he would not stop. Only Woodcutter Nan the Merciful was yet to speak.

"What are you thinking, Fourth Brother?" Ke Zhen'e asked.

"A fine boy," Woodcutter Nan replied.

"What do you mean?" Zhu Cong said.

"The boy. I wasn't so bright when I was young." Woodcutter Nan smiled.

Nan's words brought the others a glimmer of hope and their mood lifted.

"Yes, you're right! When has anyone ever called me smart?" Zhang Asheng added, looking across at Jade Han.

"Let's see if he comes tonight," Zhu Cong said.

"Not likely," Gilden Quan said. "I'm going to find out where he lives first."

He mounted his horse and trailed the boys, keeping his distance. He watched from afar and made note of which *ger* Guo Jing entered.

THAT NIGHT the Seven Freaks waited for Guo Jing on the deserted hilltop, watching the stars move through the sky. By quarter to ten, there was still no sign of the boy.

"Our reputation reaches from east to west." Ryder Han sighed. "But today we must concede defeat to that stinking Taoist."

"The Quanzhen Sect is resisting the Jurchen in the north, protecting the Chinese there," Zhu Cong said. "They are patriotic and virtuous. The Seven Masters are exceptional in all aspects of the martial arts, everyone in the *wulin* admires them, and Qiu Chuji is considered the foremost among them. Losing to him will not destroy our reputation. And in any case, we are saving an honorable patriot's line of descent. There will be praise once our friends in the south find out."

Zhu Cong's words brought comfort and the other Freaks nodded in agreement.

In the west, layer upon layer of thick black cloud was building. Above them the sky was still a clear, deep blue. An anxious gust of wind blew its way from the northwest and the moon hovered high above, ringed by a yellow halo.

"It looks like rain," Jade Han remarked. "He's not coming."

"Then we will go to him, tomorrow morning," Zhang Asheng said.

"The boy is allowed to be a bit dull, but we have problems if he's afraid of the dark. *Aiya!*" Ke Zhen'e shook his head.

"Look! What's that?" Ryder Han said, pointing deep into the bush. There, illuminated by the moonlight, were three strange-looking white objects.

Gilden Quan went to investigate. Three piles of neatly stacked human skulls!

"It must have been the children who arranged them like this . . . Wait, what's that? . . . Second Brother, come quick!"

His sudden change in tone unsettled the others. The Seven Freaks rushed over, all except Ke Zhen'e.

"Look at this!" Gilden Quan picked up one of the skulls and handed it to Zhu Cong. Zhu Cong inspected it and observed five holes in the cranium, into which he slotted his fingers and thumb. Almost a perfect fit. The gap for the thumb was too big and the one for his little finger a bit tight.

This was no child's toy.

Zhu Cong's face fell. He bent over and picked up two more skulls. These too had the same holes punched into them. Could someone have made these holes with their fingers? he asked himself. But surely no one could break through bone with their fingers? The thought was terrifying.

"Were they made by some kind of man-eating mountain monster?" Jade Han asked.

"Yes, definitely a monster of sorts," Ryder Han said.

"But what monster would arrange the skulls in such neat piles?" Gilden Quan muttered to himself.

"How have they been arranged?" Ke Zhen'e joined them.

"In three pyramids, each consisting of nine skulls," Gilden Quan said.

"In three layers, am I right? Five on the bottom, then three, then one on top?"

"Yes," Gilden Quan said in surprise. "How did you know, Big Brother?"

"Two of you, take one hundred steps to the northeast and northwest. Quickly! What do you see?"

Master Ke was rarely rattled, but now he seemed acutely alarmed. The other Freaks did not waste a second. Splitting into two groups, they began counting steps in both directions. Before long Jade Han called out from the northeast, just as Gilden Quan shouted from the northwest.

"Skulls!"

"There are skulls here too!"

Ke Zhen'e flew over to Gilden Quan and hissed, "No one make a sound. Our lives depend on it." He then rushed over to where Jade Han was standing and repeated his instructions. The Freaks were astounded.

"What is it? Monsters or human foes?" Zhang Asheng whispered.

"Two of the most violent beings that ever existed. They killed my brother."

The other Freaks rushed to join them, just in time to hear Ke Zhen'e's explanation. This elder brother, Ke Bixie the Talisman, was considered even more skilled than Ke Zhen'e, as the Freaks all knew. His killer must have been terrible in the extreme. The Seven Freaks kept no secrets from each other, but though they had learned of Ke Bixie's death before, this was the first time they had heard their brother mention any details of the circumstances behind it. Ke Zhen'e picked up a skull and felt for the holes. He slotted the fingers of his right hand into them.

"They managed it. They finally managed it," he mumbled, before turning to the others. "Are there three piles here too?"

"Yes," Jade Han said.

"Nine skulls in every pile?"

"One pile has nine, the other two eight." Jade Han again.

"Count the ones over there too."

Jade Han ran over, before returning moments later. "Seven in each pile. All newly decapitated. There's still flesh on the bone."

"Then they'll be back soon," Ke Zhen'e said quietly, handing the skull to Gilden Quan. "Replace this. Don't leave any sign that we were here."

Gilden Quan arranged everything as it had been and returned to Ke Zhen'e's side. Everyone was looking to their Big Brother, waiting for an explanation.

Ke Zhen'e turned his face up to the sky and the others watched as it twitched. "Copper and Iron Corpse."

"But aren't they dead?" Zhu Cong said in disbelief. "How can they still be alive?"

"I thought so too. But it looks as if they have been hiding here, practicing their Nine Yin Skeleton Claw," Ke Zhen'e said. "Mount your horses and head south, as fast as you can. Don't come back for me. Keep riding for one thousand *li* and then wait for ten days. If I do not join you by the eleventh day, there is no need to wait any longer."

"Brother, what are you saying?" said Jade Han. "We have sworn an oath in blood to live and die together. How can you tell us to leave?"

"Go, go now." Ke Zhen'e waved them away. "We don't have time for this."

"What must you think of us? Are we such cowards that we'd leave you here alone?" Ryder Han was furious.

"The Seven Freaks fight and die together," Zhang Asheng cut in. "That's the way it has always been. What reason do we have to run?"

"These two possess incredible martial skill. Now that they've mastered the Nine Yin Skeleton Claw, we cannot prevail. To stay would be pointless."

Ke Zhen'e was a proud man who did not admit defeat easily, not even in the face of a great master such as Qiu Chuji. He always chose to fight. Copper and Iron Corpse must be endowed with a power beyond their comprehension.

"In that case, we'll all go," Gilden Quan said.

"They condemned me to a life of daily mourning," Ke Zhen'e said, his voice raw. "I must avenge my brother."

"Share your blessings and your hardships too will be shared," Woodcutter Nan replied.

Ke Zhen'e paused. His martial family valued loyalty above all else; to even suggest they leave without him must have offended them greatly, he realized. But they were putting themselves in great danger. "Fine. But you must be careful," he said. "They are married; Copper Corpse is the husband, Iron Corpse the wife. Together they are known as Twice Foul Dark Wind. They started practicing the Nine Yin Skeleton Claw about two years ago, and, in doing so, killed many a fine warrior of the *jianghu*. My brother was invited to help stop them and he sent someone to ask me to join them. But we were looking for Lily Li. I didn't want to abandon our search, especially as we had just received new clues as to her whereabouts, and as they already had many great fighters for their cause, I decided that I was not needed. I never expected it to take us so long to find Guo Jing. I was told about my brother's fate at the hands of Twice Foul Dark Wind last spring and only then did I hear their story and learn of the real extent of their kung fu. I knew I would not be able to avenge my brother's death for some time, and fearing the consequences for my martial family, I decided not to tell you."

Ke Zhen'e paused. "Sixth Brother, take one hundred steps to the south and check if there is a coffin."

Gilden Quan counted his steps . . . Ninety-nine, one hundred. No coffin. He looked more carefully. There, poking through the dirt, was the corner of a stone slab. He tried pulling at it, but it would not budge. He turned and waved at the others, who rushed to join him. Zhang Asheng and Ryder Han stooped down and together they pulled and panted and at last loosened the lid. The Seven Freaks peered into the grave beneath. By the moonlight they could make out two bodies, dressed in Mongolian robes.

"Those demons will be back soon to use these bodies for practice. I'll lie in here and take them by surprise. You find places to hide nearby. Whatever you do, do not let them know you're here. Come out only when I'm in trouble and show them no mercy. It might not be the honorable way to fight, but they are too ruthless, too skilled. We will all be killed otherwise."

The Freaks nodded as he spoke, his voice quiet and steady.

"They notice everything, even the slightest disturbance or sign of something unusual. They can sense things from great distances."

Ke Zhen'e lay down in the grave. "Replace the cover, but leave a slit so I can breathe."

The Freaks gently shifted the slab back into place. Taking their weapons, they slid in among the trees and bushes and hid.

Jade Han had never seen her Big Brother like this before. She was as much intrigued as scared and made sure to hide close to Zhu Cong.

"Who are these people? Copper Corpse and Iron Corpse I mean," she whispered across to him.

"Two years ago, Ke Bixie sent a messenger to Master Ke, but he didn't want you all to find out so he asked me to go with him. He wasn't sure if the messenger was who he said he was. The man told us that Copper Corpse and his wife, Iron Corpse, were disciples of the Lord of Peach Blossom Island, out in the Eastern Sea."

"Peach Blossom Island? Then that means they're from Zhejiang, just like us?"

Zhu Cong nodded. "That's right. People say the Lord expelled them. They are skilled to be sure, but also cruel in the extreme. They come and go like ghosts. Our friends in the *jianghu* said they disappeared after killing Master Ke's brother. We all thought they must be dead. But they were hiding here in Mongolia all along."

"What are their real names?"

"Copper Corpse is otherwise known as Hurricane Chen. His cheeks are scorched brown, hence the name, his expression always deathly still."

"And Iron Corpse?"

"Her name is Cyclone Mei."

"Big Brother mentioned something called Nine Yin Skeleton Claw. What kind of kung fu is that?"

"I don't know, I've never heard of it either."

Jade Han glanced across at one of the skulls close by. Its black cavernous eye sockets were staring out at her. A shiver went through her and she turned. "Why didn't Big Brother tell us? Maybe . . ."

Before she could finish, Zhu Cong's hand clapped over her mouth and he pointed down the hill. Jade Han poked her head up from the bushes and saw a long shadow in the distance skimming across the sand.

I should have been keeping watch, not chatting, Jade Han said to herself.

Within moments the shadow had reached the foot of the hill. It belonged in fact to two figures moving at great speed, as if glued together.

"Such monstrous kung fu," Ryder Han said to himself.

The Freaks held their breath and waited for the smudge of black to climb toward them. Zhu Cong gripped his broken fan and Jade clutched her weapon, pushing the blade into the dirt so the moonlight would not catch it. The swishing sound of their feet reached them first. Their hearts were pounding and each second seemed to last forever. A northwesterly wind was picking up and the black clouds on the horizon rolled like mountains on the move, edging ever closer.

Moments later, all was silent. The footsteps had stopped. In the distance before them stood two silhouettes. One wore a leather cap as if in Mongol dress. Beside him, long ribbons of black hair fluttered in the wind.

There they are, Jade Han whispered to herself. Now let's see their skills.

The woman circled the man, slowly at first, her joints cracking as she moved. She began picking up speed and the crackle became an ever-quickening rhythmic accompaniment.

Her inner strength is quite something, Jade Han said to herself. No wonder Big Brother was so frightened.

Cyclone Mei thrust her palms out and back at rapid speed. Her elbows snapped and her hair stuck out like the bristles of a brush.

A chill ran to Jade Han's heart and the hairs on her body stood on end.

Then, without warning, Cyclone Mei's hand struck at the Mongol man's chest.

He can withstand such force? The Freaks watched in amazement as he fell backward. But she had already spun behind him and hit him in the back. So she circled him, whipping up a wind around them, faster and harder. He made no sound. On the ninth strike, she leaped straight into the air and came down, headfirst, swiped his cap and plunged her hand through the top of his head.

Jade Han tried to scream but the terror silenced her.

The woman planted her feet and cackled. The man had collapsed into a heap on the dirt and did not move. Her fingers were smeared with blood and spots of brain. She stretched them out before her, examining them in the moonlight. She was still laughing. She turned and Jade Han caught sight of her face: gruesome but rather beautiful. It was a hideous smile.

This was not her husband, they realized. He was just for practice.

All was silent. She reached down and tore the clothes from the dead man's back. In the north, men wore thick leather coats against the cold, but she ripped it as if it were made of paper. She then pulled open the skin across his torso and removed his organs one by one, surveying them in the moonlight. The Freaks watched as she threw down the pulpy remains. In nine strikes of her hand she had turned his insides into a squelchy mess without breaking a single bone.

Jade Han drew her sword, inch by inch, and prepared to attack, but Zhu Cong stopped her. Iron Corpse is alone, he thought to himself, we might be able to overcome her, seven against one. But we have to fight them separately, Iron Corpse first. Her husband might be hiding somewhere close. Big Brother should take the lead.

A quick inspection of her progress; a smile: Cyclone Mei was satisfied. She sat down with her back to Jade Han and Zhu Cong, her face raised to the moon, and started breathing in long and steady breaths. They watched her body rise and fall.

If I were to use Lightning Ignites the Sky now, I could probably spike my sword right through her, Jade Han said to herself. But if I missed, I would ruin our whole plan. She trembled with indecision.

Zhu Cong was barely breathing. He became aware of a chill as sweat ran down his back. He looked up and noticed the black clouds in the west had spread out above them. The sky was a sheet of imperial green paper splashed with black ink. Lightning flashed a spotlight on them and fear caught in their hearts. Thunder echoed and the air was hot and sticky, as if the clouds had formed a heavy blanket over them.

After some time, Cyclone Mei rose to her feet and pulled the corpse to the grave where Ke Zhen'e was hiding. She reached for the stone cover.

The Freaks held tighter to their weapons, ready for what was to come.

Mei turned. A rustle of leaves. But the air was still. She looked up into the branches of a nearby tree and saw the shape of a human silhouetted against the moonlight.

A piercing howl, and she was up in the branches.

It was Ryder Han. His short stature allowed him to shelter among the foliage. Just the slightest shift of his feet had given away his hiding place. He pulled out his Golden Dragon whip and performed a move known as Black Dragon Fetches Water, directing all his force at Mei's wrist. But, to his surprise, she did not move to avoid it and instead grabbed hold of the other end. Ryder Han yanked with all his strength but this only pulled her closer. She struck out with a bolt of lightning energy. But a gust of wind buffeted her, and Ryder Han had released his weapon and flipped from the branch.

Mei followed close behind, her hand held like a claw aimed at his back.

A cold gust of air rushed at the back of his neck and he pushed forward. Woodcutter Nan was waiting beneath with Gilden Quan. Nan threw a bone-piercing awl and Gilden Quan shot a concealed arrow from his sleeve.

Mei deflected both projectiles with a flick of her middle finger and, with a loud tearing noise, ripped a piece of Ryder Han's shirt. He tapped his foot, intent on shooting up into the air. But Mei had already landed in front of him.

"Who are you?" she cried. "Why are you here?" Her clawed fingers dug into his shoulders and he felt a searing pain as if ten iron spikes had been implanted into his flesh. He aimed a flying kick at Mei's abdomen. She blocked him with a chop, snapping a bone in his foot. He threw himself to the ground and rolled to safety.

Mei went to stamp on his lower back but a shoulder pole came gliding toward her and smashed against her ankle.

Mei lurched back, but within moments was surrounded. From the right came a scholar holding a metal fan and a young girl clutching a sword. From the left, two men, one sturdy with a butcher's knife and another gaunt and carrying some strange military weapon. Before her, a muscular peasant wielding the shoulder pole. And yet more footsteps. The man with the whip. She had no idea who they were, but there was no doubt they were of the *wulin*.

There are too many of them, Mei thought, I'd better kill them quickly. As long as that bastard of a husband of mine is safe. I'll start with the girl.

She leaped at Jade Han, her claws aimed straight at the young girl's face. Zhu Cong launched his iron fan at the Arching Pool vital point on the inside of Mei's elbow, but she was unaffected. She went again for Jade Han, who met the attack with a Mist Hangs Over the River, slicing her sword at Mei's arm. Mei flipped her wrist and reached for Jade Han's blade. Jade shrunk back, just as Zhu Cong struck once again at Mei's elbow. The move should have paralyzed Mei's arm instantaneously, but instead Zhu Cong watched it extend toward him as she grabbed at his head.

Zhu Cong avoided her talons only at the last moment.

Doesn't she have any vital points? he asked himself, shaking.

Ryder Han found his whip and, brandishing their weapons, the Freaks closed in from all sides. But Mei's hands were as if made of steel and she countered each move with a scratch of her nails. The Freaks recalled the holes in the tops of the skulls and shrank back with fear. And it wasn't just her hands; the rest of her body seemed to be equally resistant to their attacks. Gilden Quan struck her twice in the back with his weights, but to no effect. She seemed only to fear Zhang Asheng's knife and Jade Han's sword. Gilden Quan was too slow and she tore a bloody piece of flesh from his arm.

As Zhu Cong was well aware, all practitioners of kung fu have at least one weak point, a spot so tender that all you have to do is touch it to kill them. But what about this witch? Where is hers?

His fan danced around her pressure points, first the Hundred

Convergences on the crown of her head and the Ridge Spring on her throat, then the Spirit Gate on her abdomen and the Central Pivot in the middle of her back. Within seconds, he had tapped at least twelve, trying to ascertain which part of her body she was most protective of. That would be his answer.

Mei realized what he was doing. "You lowdown beggar," she shouted. "This old hag has been training for years. I have no weak point!"

She snatched Zhu's wrist, but he was quick, and before she could dig her nails into his arm he flipped his wrist over and placed his fan into her palm. "There's poison on that fan."

Mei froze and then dropped it. Zhu Cong pulled away. He examined the back of his hand. It was scored with five bloody stripes. A cold sweat crept across his body. This was going to be a long fight, he realized. Three Freaks were already injured. They would never overcome Copper and Iron Corpse together. He looked across at his martial brothers. Zhang Asheng, Ryder Han, and Gilden Quan were sweaty and exhausted. Woodcutter Nan was more practiced in *neigong* inner strength, however, and Jade Han looked as if she still had some energy.

But Cyclone Mei was just getting started.

Then, in the cold light of the moon, Zhu Cong spotted three piles of skulls to his left. A shiver traveled through him as an idea took hold. "Run! Save yourselves!" he shouted, as he rushed over to the grave where Ke Zhen'e was hiding. The Freaks began retreating toward him as they fought.

"You little bastards," Mei snarled. "I don't know which stinking hole you've crawled from. Kill me, just you try! But it's too late to get away now." She charged forward. Nan, Gilden Quan, and Jade Han tried to engage her in combat, while the others tugged and heaved, at last managing to pull the stone aside.

Meanwhile, Mei had wrapped her arm around Nan's shoulder pole and was trying to scratch out his eyes.

Zhu Cong pointed at the sky and beckoned with his hand: "Come, we need you!" He seemed to be calling for help from the spirit world.

Mei's eyes followed the direction of Zhu Cong's fingers. But all she could see was a thick blanket of cloud covering half the moon. Was there anyone up there?

Nan ducked away.

"Seven paces ahead!" Zhu Cong shouted. Ke Zhen'e threw six poisoned devilnuts, two at head height, two toward her middle and two below the waist. Then, with a loud cry, he jumped out of the hole and the other Freaks charged. Mei screamed as two of the projectiles hit her in the eyes. She threw her head back so that they would not penetrate her skull and enter the brain. But within moments she was descended into a darkness from which she would never return.

She thrust her palms down, but Ke Zhen'e had dodged to one side and her hands thudded into the stone slab. Now even more enraged, she kicked at it, sending it flying. The Freaks watched on, keeping their distance.

Mei scrabbled around in her blindness, grabbing and scratching. Zhu Cong gestured to the others to keep back. She was a crazed tiger, a she-devil, pulling at trees, breaking branches, kicking up sand. The Freaks held their breath. She began to feel a tingling in her eyes. The poison. "Who are you?" she cried. "Tell me, so I know before I die."

Zhu Cong gestured at Ke Zhen'e to stay silent, but realized his brother would not be able to see.

"Cyclone Mei." Ke Zhen'e's voice was sharp like a shard of ice. "Do you remember a fellow kung fu master by the name of Flying Divine Dragon, Ke Bixie the Talisman? I am his brother, Ke Zhen'e, Suppressor of Evil."

A long cackle burst from Mei's throat. "I've never seen you before, old fellow! You come to avenge Flying Divine Dragon's death? With poisoned devilnuts?"

"That is correct."

Mei sighed and did not reply.

The moon had almost disappeared behind the clouds and the light that remained was dim and almost cold to the touch. They all felt it.

Mei was still, as if turned to stone, whip in one hand, the other limp by her side. A gray light glinted from her long, sharp nails. A long, silver Python whip was coiled up like a snake on the ground before her. It was a powerful weapon, but she was yet to master it. It was her Nine Yin Skeleton Claw they feared. The wind beat at her hair so that it stood like spikes from her forehead.

Jade Han was positioned in front of her and watched as two streams of blood flowed from her eyes and down her neck.

"Brother!"

Zhu Cong and Gilden Quan shouted together. But Ke Zhen'e had already sensed the rush of air at his chest. He drove his staff into the dirt and flew up, landing in the top branches of a nearby tree. Mei's whip had not met its target and she was propelled forward. She wrapped herself around Ke Zhen'e's tree, lodging her nails into the bark.

The move had taken them all by surprise. Had their eldest martial brother reacted a moment later, he would have been skewered on her talons.

Mei responded with a strange and piercing howl that carried far on the wind.

She was calling her husband Copper Corpse for help, Zhu Cong realized. "Kill her!"

Summoning all his energy, he aimed at Mei's back. Zhang Asheng took a nearby stone and launched himself at her head.

Unlike Brother Ke, she was not used to relying on her hearing alone for defense. She heard a low-pitched rush of air as the stone came toward her, but she could not tell where it was coming from.

Zhu Cong's punch landed with a heavy thud and she screamed in pain. Zhu Cong continued, but Mei slashed her claws at him, forcing him back.

Just as the other Freaks closed in, a long howl, much like the one Mei had used only minutes before, arrived on the wind, and it cleaved through them. Another followed in quick succession, this time much closer.

"Copper Corpse!"

Jade ran to look down toward the plain below. A shadow was speeding toward them, screeching as it drew nearer.

Mei was now on the defensive, concentrating her internal energy on halting the spread of the poison through her body, while she waited for her husband.

Zhu Cong indicated to Gilden Quan that they should hide themselves in the bushes. Judging by his speed, Copper Corpse's skills were even more impressive than his wife's.

Just then Jade Han cried out. There, climbing the hill, was a smaller figure, moving much more slowly. It was a child.

Guo Jing.

She ran to fetch him.

Guo Jing was not very far away now, but Copper Corpse was gaining ground. Jade Han hesitated. She could not possibly take Copper Corpse on by herself. But nor could she leave the child. She ran faster and called down to Guo Jing, "Quickly, boy!"

Guo Jing looked up and yelped in delight, unaware of the danger coming from behind.

Zhang Asheng watched Jade Han as she ran farther into danger. His heart convulsed and he could barely catch his breath. He had to protect her.

The other Freaks paused and watched the events unfolding farther down the hill, weapons at the ready.

Jade Han reached Guo Jing and grabbed hold of his little hand. She turned back up the hill, but after only a few meters she felt his hand slip from hers. Guo Jing cried out. She swung round. Copper Corpse Hurricane Chen had seized him.

Jade Han tapped her foot and spun into a Nodding Phoenix, feigning a right at his armpit. She then moved sidewards, raised the tip of her sword and aimed at his eyes: the very height of Yue Maiden Sword technique.

Chen tucked the boy under his left arm and deflected the blade with his right elbow. He then thrust his palm in a Drive the Boat

Downstream. Jade spun her weapon round, moved back and sliced it at him. But his arm seemed to grow by half a foot and, although she should have been far enough out of reach, his palm somehow struck her on the shoulder and she fell.

It was all over in seconds.

Copper Corpse moved closer, intent on clawing at Jade's head with his nails, strong enough to penetrate bone. Zhang Asheng was by now only a few meters away and he threw himself on top of her. Down came Copper Corpse's claw and ripped through Zhang Asheng's back.

Zhang Asheng howled and thrust his broadsword up at Chen, but Copper Corpse blocked it with his hand, knocking the weapon out of Zhang's grip. He then beat Zhang back down with his palm.

More Freaks charged forward. Only Ke Zhen'e held back.

"My dear harpy, are you all right?" Hurricane Chen called over.

"They blinded me!" Cyclone Mei growled back from where she was slumped against a tree. "Bastard husband of mine, if you let even one of these scoundrels go, I will kill you myself."

"Don't worry, old crone," Chen called back, "they won't get away from me alive. Are you in pain? Don't move." He made for Jade Han's head again; she escaped in a Lazy Donkey Roll. "You won't get away from me!" he shouted.

Zhang Asheng was flat on the ground, badly hurt and confused, but he sensed that his beloved Jade was yet again in danger. Gathering the last of his energy, he kicked out at Chen's hand. Chen plunged his fingers into Zhang's leg. The pain shot through him, but he straightened and flung his arms around Chen's waist. Copper Corpse grabbed hold of Zhang's neck and tried to throw him off. Fearing he would attack Jade again, Zhang refused to let go. Chen punched him in the head. Zhang fainted and his arms flopped.

Meanwhile Jade had clambered to her feet and now launched herself at Hurricane Chen in a twirling display of *qinggong* lightness kung fu.

"Fifth Brother, are you hurt?" she shouted as she spun.

The other Freaks were now close. Zhu Cong and Gilden Quan were first to lunge at Copper Corpse with their weapons.

Chen was surprised to see so many accomplished practitioners of the martial arts so far out here on the steppe. "Old hag!" he shouted. "Who are they?"

"They follow Flying Bat Ke Zhen'e, brother of Flying Divine Dragon."

"We've never met these dogs before, but they will die today." But Copper Corpse could not conceal his concern for his wife's injuries. "Dearest crone, is it serious? Will you make it?"

"Kill them quick," Mei snarled back. "I'm not dead yet."

But Chen could tell it was bad; the fact that she was not coming to his aid was sign enough.

Still, Ke Zhen'e held back.

Hurricane Chen threw Guo Jing aside and launched himself at Gilden Quan. But Gilden Quan ducked, grabbed Guo Jing and somersaulted out of Chen's way in a move known across the *wulin* as the Mischievous Cat Catches the Mouse. He executed the move perfectly, impressing even Chen.

Copper Corpse was cruel by his very nature, and the stronger his opponent, the more he wanted to make them suffer a painful death. Moreover, an attack on his wife was an attack on him. Twice Foul Dark Wind had trained in two of the *wulin*'s most dangerous techniques, the Nine Yin Skeleton Claw and Heartbreaker Palm, and Chen had mastered almost the full repertoire of both.

He howled and propelled himself into attack.

But Ryder Han too charged forward and at the very last moment rolled onto the ground, where he began striking at Chen's legs in a move known as Rolling Whip. Thus distracted, Chen felt a blow to his back from Nan's shoulder pole. He yelped, spun around, and scratched back.

Nan did not have time to pull back his weapon, so he bent backward into an Iron Bridge. He heard a cracking sound and watched in amazement as Hurricane Chen's arm extended at the elbow, his bony hands grazing the top of his brow. Near misses were common in fights among masters of the *wulin*. But just as he thought it had extended to its limit, Chen's arm reached for his forehead. How was he going to get out of this? Chen's palm was now just above Nan's face, his finger poised to puncture his skull.

Nan grabbed hold of Chen's wrist, just as Zhu Cong jumped up onto Copper Corpse's back, hooking his arm around Chen's neck and pulling tight.

Just then thunder reverberated around them and darkness unfolded across the desolate mountaintop as the last of the moon was blocked out by the clouds. Raindrops as big as soybeans started falling from the sky.

A terrible crunching sound and a rush of air followed the thunder; Nan's arm was broken in two and Zhu Cong had received a blow to the chest, sending him tumbling backward. Copper Corpse panted, catching his breath.

"Everyone get back!" Ryder Han called through the darkness. "Seventh Sister, are you all right?"

"Shh," Jade silenced her brother as she moved closer.

"Second Brother, are you all right?" Ke Zhen'e was concerned by what he was hearing.

"We can't see anything," Gilden Quan replied. "It's pitch-black."

The heavens are smiling on us! Ke Zhen'e said to himself, knowing this only played into his hands.

Three of the Freaks were injured. The situation had looked hopeless. But now, as the heavens cracked open, they held their breath and kept utterly still. Ke Zhen'e listened. He could hear a man gasping not ten steps away from him and he knew it was not one of his martial brothers. He reached for his poisoned devilnuts and raised his hand.

Six devilnuts flew in quick succession.

But Hurricane Chen sensed them coming and jumped, narrowly dodging all six. Now he knew where they were coming from. Silently he lunged forward, his claws ready. But Ke Zhen'e had leaped to the side and, from his new position, thrust his staff outward. Fighting by night and day were all the same for him. Chen struck out in all directions. He could not tell if his aim was true.

Ryder Han, Jade Han, and Gilden Quan, meanwhile, were fumbling in the dark, trying to help their brothers. Elder Brother Ke was in the most danger, of course, but they were no good to him. Through the pelting rain, they heard the swooshing of Chen's hands and Ke Zhen'e's iron staff. It felt like they had been fighting for hours. Then came two loud blows and a piercing howl; Copper Corpse had been hit.

A flash of lightning illuminated the scene.

"Brother, lightning, watch out!" Gilden Quan cried a warning.

But Hurricane Chen had orientated himself in that moment of clarity. He gathered his *qi* to his left shoulder, strode straight at Ke's staff and grasped hold of it, scratching at Ke with his other hand. Flying Bat Ke released his weapon and leaped backward. Copper Corpse clenched his fist, reached and punched Ke's chest with the force of all his internal energy. Ke Zhen'e was blasted backward and Chen threw the staff like a spear, roaring with pride. The thunder sounded a booming accompaniment.

Another double flash lit up the sky. Ryder Han saw the staff heading for his brother. He flicked his Golden Dragon whip and caught it.

"Now you, you dog!" Hurricane Chen cried, about to launch a flying kick. But Copper Corpse stumbled over something at his feet. He reached down with his claws and grabbed it: Guo Jing.

"Let me go!" the child shouted.

Chen snorted. Another flash of cold light.

Guo Jing looked up at the sallow face staring down at him, its eyes like hollow caverns. He pulled the dagger from his belt and plunged it through the man's belly button until the blade was fully engulfed by his flesh.

A cry cut through the thick air and Hurricane Chen fell backward. Guo Jing had found Copper Corpse's chosen vulnerable spot, the point he always tried to protect in a fight. A plain fruit knife would have been enough to kill him, let alone Guo Jing's dagger. He had not thought to protect himself against a child. Their encounter at the foot of the hill had told him the boy was no expert in the martial arts. But it is as they say: the swimmer is the one to drown, the cart always breaks on flat ground. No one could have foreseen that a master of the *wulin* such as Copper Corpse would die at the hands of a boy with no training whatsoever.

Guo Jing was still just as terrified and now stood to one side, his mind a muddle. He opened his mouth to cry, but no sound came out.

Mei had started running at the sound of her husband's pained cry. She stumbled, scrabbled, and crawled to get to him. "My loving bastard, big brother, what happened?"

"I can't . . . Run, little sister." His voice was faint.

"I will avenge you." She spoke through clenched teeth.

"I don't want to leave you, little sister, dear wife. I . . . I can't look after you anymore. From now on, you must fight alone. Take care . . ."

And so Hurricane Chen rasped his last breaths and died.

Despite her distress, no tears fell down Mei's cheeks. She took her husband in her arms. "Dearest filthy dog, I don't want to leave you either. Don't go!"

Morning's first light was painting the sky a blue-gray. Now able to make out the faintest outlines around them, Ryder Han, Jade Han, and Gilden Quan rushed in to attack.

Mei was blind and dizzy from the poison. Ke Zhen'e's iron devilnuts would have killed her long ago, were it not for the years Mei and her husband had spent learning Nine Yin Skeleton Claw, ingesting small quantities of arsenic to increase their internal strength, neutralizing the more toxic elements through regularized breathing techniques. It was a ridiculous method to be sure, but it had at least given her a certain level of immunity, which served her well now.

Thus agitated, she put up her last defense, swift and fierce. The Freaks could not get near her.

Ryder Han was becoming increasingly impatient. Our reputation will be good only for sweeping the floor if anyone finds out the Freaks cannot overcome Cyclone Mei, blind and injured, he thought to himself. He kept changing the speed and direction of his whip and cracked it three times against her back. Jade Han noticed her stumble. She and Gilden Quan moved in.

Just as they thought they had her, an angry gale rose, thrashing up the dirt and gravel into a wild dance. The black clouds above once again cut out all remaining light.

The Freaks dropped to the ground and waited for the storm to pass.

IT TOOK hours for the rain to grow lighter and for cracks of sunlight to break through the clouds. Ryder Han scrambled to his feet and howled. Mei had disappeared, along with her husband's body. He looked around him; there, lying on the ground, his fellow Freaks were soaked through. He caught sight of Guo Jing's face peeping out from behind a nearby rock.

Three of the Freaks were unhurt and they started tending to their brothers. Nan the Merciful had broken an arm, but thankfully that was the extent of his injuries. Ke Zhen'e and Zhu Cong had managed to fight off Copper Corpse's attack with their inner strength, so they too were not too badly affected. But Zhang Asheng had been caught twice by the Nine Yin Skeleton Claw, as well as receiving a punch to the head. He was just about conscious, but his prospects looked bleak.

The Freaks were distraught, especially Jade Han. She had long known Zhang Asheng was in love with her. But she was a bold young woman more concerned with martial arts than immediate affairs of the heart and he had always laughed off his feelings. Thinking time was on their side, they had never admitted to each how they really felt. But now he was dying, and all because he had tried to protect her. Jade Han took Zhang Asheng into her arms and wept.

Zhang Asheng, normally so jovial, looked up at her and managed a smile. He opened his butcher's hands, large like fans, and stroked Jade Han's hair. "Don't cry," he said. "Sister, I'm fine."

"Fifth Brother," she said, choking on her tears, "let me be your wife."

Zhang Asheng laughed, overcome by a moment of the purest joy, but the pain was turning his vision hazy.

"Fifth Brother, don't worry, in my heart I am already wedded to you. I'll never marry anyone else, as long as I live. And once I die we will be together, forever."

"Sister, I have not taken care of you as I should have." Zhang was struggling to speak. "I don't deserve you."

"You took the very best care of me, I've always known that. I've always loved you."

Zhang Asheng smiled as if he had never smiled before.

With his eyes full of tears, Zhu Cong turned to Guo Jing. "Did you come to learn martial arts from us?"

"Yes."

"Then from now on you must do as we say."

Guo Jing nodded.

"We will be your *shifus*," Zhu Cong said through his tears. "But your Fifth *Shifu* is about to return to the heavens, so go to him and pay your respects."

Guo Jing did not understand what Zhu Cong meant, but nevertheless he approached the injured man and kowtowed before him, making sure to tap his forehead against the ground several times.

Zhang Asheng forced a smile. "That's enough." He grimaced. "You're a good boy. I won't be able to teach you my skills, but that's just as well. They would have been no use to you. I'm big and clumsy and too lazy to practice. I relied on my strength. If only I'd put in more effort, I wouldn't be lying here today . . ." He was losing consciousness.

Jade Han put her ear to his lips and heard him whisper. "Teach him well. Don't let that stinking Taoist win."

"Don't you worry, the Seven Freaks never lose," she whispered.

Zhang Asheng chuckled one last time, closed his eyes and departed.

The Freaks were overcome with sadness. They had spent the last few years in each other's company, day in, day out, searching for Lily Li and her son. Now one of their brothers was lost, here, in a strange and cruel land. After the tears had run dry, they dug a grave and buried him. The sun was already high in the sky by the time they had covered his final resting place with a large rock to mark the site.

Gilden Quan and Ryder Han went looking for Cyclone Mei, but any footprints she might have left had been wiped away by the storm. They traveled for miles without finding any trace before returning to the hill.

"She can't have got far in the desert without being able to see," Zhu Cong said. "Big Brother hit her with his poisoned devilnuts; she's probably dead by now. Let's take the child home first and treat our wounds. Then those who were not hurt last night can take up the search."

The Freaks nodded, shed their last tears on their brother's grave, and left.

CHAPTER FIVE

DRAW THE BOW,
SHOOT THE CONDOR

I

THE FREAKS WERE DESCENDING THE HILLSIDE BY SIDE WHEN
they heard the roars of a wild beast up ahead.

Ryder Han snatched up his reins, jumped onto Wind Chaser and
spurred him on. He peered into the distance and spotted a crowd
gathered together. He pushed on a bit farther until he could make
out what had drawn their attention: two leopards clawing at a dead
body.

Ryder Han edged ever closer. It was Hurricane Chen. Zhu Cong
drew up level with him. He looked as fierce in death as he had done
in life. Had it not been for Guo Jing and his dagger, they might not
have been standing there to witness this spectacle.

The leopards began eating the corpse. A small boy on a horse
called to the leopard handlers to pull them away. He then turned and
on seeing Guo Jing called out, "So this is where you've been hiding!
Too scared to help Tolui fight? You call yourself his friend?"

Guo Jing recognized him—Senggum's son, Tusakha.

"Have you been beating Tolui again? Where is he?" Guo Jing said.

"I'm taking the leopards to feed on him now. Surrender, or else I'll set them on you too."

But the sight of Guo Jing's companions was enough to hold Tusakha back for now.

"What about Tolui?" Guo Jing asked again.

"Let the leopards eat him!" Tusakha spurred his horse and led the leopard handlers away.

But one of the men spoke up. "Master, that boy is Temujin Khan's son."

"Why should that frighten me?" Tusakha replied with a crack of his whip. "I can do what I want. Come now."

The leopard handler dared not disobey his master and followed. But the other handler knew this could bring him trouble. "I'm going to tell Temujin Khan!" he called, and ran.

Tusakha did not stop him. "Fine," he muttered, "but I'm releasing the leopards on Tolui all the same. By the time Uncle Temujin comes, it'll be too late. What's he going to do then?" He whipped his horse and forced them on.

Guo Jing's concern for his friend's safety eclipsed even his fear of these awesome beasts. "*Shifu*," he said, turning to Jade Han, "Tusakha is going to release the leopards on my sworn brother. I've got to warn him, so he can get away."

"But if you follow, the leopards might get you too. Aren't you scared?"

"Yes."

"And you still want to go?"

Guo Jing hesitated for only a moment before answering. "Yes!"

He then turned and began running as fast as his legs would allow.

Zhu Cong was still in pain and draped over his horse's back. He looked across at Guo Jing and said, "The boy is not the most intelligent, but he's brave all the same."

"You're right, Second Brother. We must save them," Jade Han replied.

"If that little boy keeps leopards, he is surely the son of someone very important," Gilden Quan began, trying to sound a word of caution. "We'd best not cause trouble, especially as three among us are injured."

But Ryder Han was on his way and, using the best of his lightness kung fu, had already swiped Guo Jing up and onto his shoulders. Guo Jing felt as if he were flying. Ryder Han ran back toward Wind Chaser and, in one move, jumped up and into his saddle. Moments later, they were level with Tusakha and the leopard handler.

Up ahead, they caught sight of Tolui, surrounded by a gang of a dozen or so older boys. Tusakha had ordered them not to let Tolui escape.

Tolui had spent the night practicing the three moves Zhu Cong taught him the day before, but when in the morning he had been unable to locate his sworn brother, Guo Jing, nor persuade his brother Ogedai to help, he had gone to face Tusakha alone. Tusakha, in contrast, had backup in the form of eight loyal friends. He had been surprised to see Tolui come on his own, and when the boy had asked that they not attack all at once, Tusakha had agreed out of pity. The boy could not possibly win, after all. But Tolui's moves beat each of Tusakha's gang one by one. They were classics of the Empty Palms boxing and Tolui was quick to learn. Now he needn't fear any of the other Mongolian boys on the steppe. Tusakha was knocked down twice, once from a punch square on the nose. Furious, Tusakha had gone to fetch his father's leopards. Tolui, meanwhile, stood proudly, glaring at the boys he had just beaten.

There he had remained, unaware of the imminent danger.

Then, in the distance, he heard Guo Jing's calls. "Tolui, Tolui, run! Tusakha is coming with his leopards!"

Fear shot through Tolui and he tried to escape the circle, but the boys would not let him out. The rest of the Freaks of the South had followed behind and they came thundering toward them, followed by Tusakha and the leopards. They had decided not to stop Tusakha, preferring first to assess if Guo Jing and Tolui were in danger.

At that moment, the drumming of hooves echoed around them.

"Don't release the leopards!" A shout broke through the noise. It was Temujin's Four Great Generals.

The rogue leopard handler had reached them and told them of the news. They had ridden straight over while the handler continued in search of the Great Khan.

Temujin, Ong Khan, Jamuka, Senggum, and the others had been conversing with the Wanyan Princes back at the camp. They rushed to their horses at once.

"Send word—Tusakha must stop. That is my order," Ong Khan said. "Temujin Khan's son must not be hurt."

Wanyan Hongxi was much excited by these latest developments, particuarly after the disappointments of the night before. "Let's see what's going on," he cried, getting to his feet.

If Senggum's leopards kill Temujin's son, his brother the Sixth Prince of the Jin mused to himself, then a rift will grow between their families and they will probably end up at war. Fortune smiles upon the Jin Empire, if not upon the Mongols!

The Jin Princes followed the others to the scene of the dispute, only to find the leopards already unchained. The beasts were crouched and ready, their throaty growls reverberating around the crowd. And there, standing before them, were Tolui and his sworn *anda,* Guo Jing.

Temujin and his Four Generals aimed their bows at the leopards, their gazes fixed. Temujin knew his son was in danger, but these leopards were Senggum's most precious possessions. He had caught them as cubs and raised them into the fearsome animals they were today. As long as they did not attack Tolui, Temujin would do his best not to have them killed.

Tusakha looked over at the crowd, which now included his doting father and grandfather, and grew in courage. He ordered the leopards to attack.

But his grandfather was most displeased. "Stop this at once!" Ong Khan cried.

Once again they heard horses' hooves, and a beautiful chestnut horse came galloping into the camp. It was ridden by an older woman draped in fur. In her arms she carried a young girl. She jumped down.

This was Temujin's wife, Tolui's mother.

She had been chatting with Senggum's wife in the camp, but came at once upon hearing of the scene unfolding on the grasslands. "Shoot!" she cried, placing her daughter on the ground and forgetting about her.

Khojin was only four years of age and had no conception of the danger up ahead. Giggling, she ran to her brother. The leopards' fur was so pretty, just like her eldest brother Ogedai's hunting dogs, and she reached out to pat one of the animals on the head.

A gasp rose from the crowd.

But it was too late.

The leopards roared.

The crowd cried out.

Temujin had his bow and arrow ready, but the speed at which it all happened caught even him off guard, and before he knew it the leopard was in the air. Khojin's chubby body was blocking the spot on the leopard's head at which Temujin would have aimed. A shot to the body would only injure it, aggravating it further and putting Khojin in even greater danger. Temujin's Four Great Generals threw down their bows and drew their blades.

But Guo Jing was quicker, rolling forward and grabbing Khojin, just as a paw ripped at his shoulder.

The Generals ran toward the leopards, but they heard only a rapid *whoosh!* of air as the beasts fell backward, growled, rolled onto their backs and lay still.

Temujin's wife ran to her children, fished the crying Khojin from Guo Jing's arms and pulled Tolui to her bosom.

"Who killed my leopards?"

No one answered.

Ke Zhen'e, upon hearing the leopards' growling, had launched four iron devilnuts tipped with poison. Everyone had been too focused on the scene unfolding before them to notice.

"Brother Senggum," Temujin said, smiling, "I will buy you four of the best leopards to make up for it, as well as eight pairs of black condors."

Senggum was furious, but gave no reply. Ong Khan, meanwhile, was roaring at Tusakha. Humiliated, the boy threw himself to the ground, where he unleashed a tantrum born of mortification. Ong Khan ordered him to stop, but the boy took no notice.

Temujin was still grateful for all that Ong Khan had done for him in the past and he felt it would be a great shame to sever ties between the families over such a trivial matter. He smiled, bent down, and picked up Tusakha. Tusakha was still clamorous and tried to struggle free, but was held fast.

"Dear Ong Khan, sir, the children were only playing," Temujin said, still smiling. "Let's not get upset. He is a good boy. I am thinking of betrothing my daughter Khojin to him. What do you say?"

Ong Khan looked at Khojin, her eyes filled with tears, clear like a winter's lake, her skin soft as a lamb's. "Why not indeed? Let our families be tied in ever closer bonds; why not unite my eldest grand-daughter with your son Jochi?"

"Thank you, Father," Temujin said, and turned to Senggum. "Brother, we are a proper family now."

Senggum felt that by birth he was of a higher station than Temujin, but he had always been jealous and resentful. He was not pleased that their relationship would be further cemented with these marriages, but he could hardly go against his own father, so he forced a smile.

Wanyan Honglie looked around and noticed the Six Freaks of the South standing in the crowd and a shock rippled through him. What are *they* doing here? he said to himself. They're chasing me. I wonder if that evil Taoist is with them? But this time he had a whole army of soldiers to protect him; all he had to do was give the order. The Freaks, however, seemed not to have even seen him. He slipped behind a group of bodyguards. He was so consumed in thinking of how to deal with the Freaks that he barely noticed the alliance being forged between the two Khans.

Temujin was quick to assess the situation and realized the leopards had been poisoned by the group of strange southerners who had appeared in their midst. They had saved his daughter's life. He waited for Ong Khan and the others to leave before instructing Boroqul to reward them with furs and gold. He ruffled Guo Jing's hair and told him how brave he had been. Most adults would be too scared to risk their lives like that, let alone a child. How could he have been so brave? Temujin asked.

Guo Jing just smiled dumbly. "They were going to eat Tolui and Khojin," was all he could come up with.

Temujin laughed. Tolui then told his father about their fight with Tusakha. Temujin was secretly furious to hear that Senggum's son was bringing up stories of his past humiliation, but he did not let on. "Ignore him in the future," was his only reply. He was silent for a moment, then turned to Gilden Quan.

"How much would you want to stay and teach my son your skills?"

Gilden Quan thought to himself for a moment. They had thought of retreating somewhere remote to teach Guo Jing, but staying here would be even better. "We would never have dared ask the Khan to let us stay and serve you. Pay us what you think we are worth. We are in no position to make demands."

This response pleased the Khan and he instructed Boroqul to make the arrangements. Then he left to organize the farewell for the Jin Princes.

"CYCLONE MEI must have buried Chen here," Ryder Han said when they had a moment to themselves. "So she came this way."

"Our first priority is to find Iron Corpse—dead or alive," Ke Zhen'e said.

"Indeed, if we don't get rid of her, there will only be further trouble," Zhu Cong said. "I fear she did not die from the poison."

"We must avenge Fifth Brother," Jade Han added, her eyes moist.

For the next few days, Ryder Han, Gilden Quan, and Jade Han rode around the steppe looking for Iron Corpse, but they could find no trace of her.

"Brother Ke used poison on his devilnuts," Ryder Han said. "She must have perished in some mountain cave."

The others hoped he was right, but Ke Zhen'e knew just how ruthless Twice Foul Dark Wind were. He was anxious, very anxious, but now was not the time to share his feelings. He knew they would not pass until the day he could touch her corpse for himself.

ONCE SETTLED on the steppe they asked Guo Jing to take them to see his mother, Lily Li, so they could ask after Justice Duan's whereabouts. It was the first time Lily Li had heard her home dialect in years and she burst into tears. She had scarcely met another Han Chinese, let alone someone from Lin'an. She and Jade Han found in each other's hearts shared sorrows—loves lost and dreams of home—and their tears flowed just like their stories.

That night, Lily Li made them a feast of mutton—soy-braised, sliced and made into meatballs, a reminder of the fresh and delicate flavors they had left behind in the south. The Freaks ate greedily and together they reminisced.

"The Khan asked us to stay here to teach his son kung fu, so we will be here a few months at least," Gilden Quan told her.

As evening turned to night, the Freaks took their leave and returned to their *ger* to discuss their plans.

"I don't think we should go back south," said Nan the Merciful.

"Brother," Jade Han replied, "we've spent so many years traveling up here in the bitter cold. Now we've finally found the boy, why not take him back south and teach him our kung fu there?"

"I, too, am homesick. But Sister, what will Guo Jing do in the south?"

"The same as his father: plant rice, grow vegetables, chop wood, and hunt! We will take care of him, but he won't be idle."

"Farming is a full-time job, will he have time to train?"

"That's right, he will have to plow the fields, sow the seeds, transplant the seedlings, weed, water, reap, thresh, separate the hay, look after the oxen. He'll have an hour at most to spare from morning till night."

"That's not enough! He's no natural, let's not forget."

"Boys from the south are only free of the fields if their family has money, in which case they spend their days singing, flirting, and gambling. Or else they study, write poetry, and play chess. No one respects us masters of the *wulin*. If the Mongolians ever invaded, we'd be the only ones able to defend our homeland!"

"It's better he trains here, life in the south is too comfortable."

The Freaks agreed; Guo Jing would be better off training here among the fighters of the steppe. And they had a contest to win.

The next day, Jade Han went to tell Lily Li of their decision. She too missed home, but if the Freaks had decided not to go home, neither would she. So, together, they stayed in the north, where the Freaks could continue teaching their fighting skills to Guo Jing and Tolui.

Temujin knew the Han Chinese were unsurpassed when it came to close combat, but he insisted the boys also learn Mongolian horsemanship and archery. The Freaks were not qualified to teach them this, so this part of their education was left to Jebe and Boroqul.

Evenings were reserved for Guo Jing alone, when the Freaks concentrated on boxing, swordsmanship, concealed weapon techniques, and elements of lightness *qinggong* kung fu. Guo Jing worked hard and without complaint, motivated as ever to avenge his father.

Zhu Cong, Gilden Quan, and Jade Han's skills were still too advanced and Ke Zhen'e's throwing and staff techniques were even more out of his reach, so the burden of teaching fell mostly on Ryder Han and Woodcutter Nan. Guo Jing studied each move with a methodical thoroughness, building a solid foundation. But they were only good for improving strength, not preparing him to meet someone also trained in the martial arts.

"You fight like a camel, boy," Ryder Han often found himself saying. "They may be strong, but can they defeat a leopard?"

Guo Jing responded with a foolish smile.

The Freaks were tireless in their efforts, but could not help but feel discouraged when they saw how difficult it was for the boy to master these basic moves. But they could not give up, even if they knew he had little chance of matching Qiu Chuji's student.

Gilden Quan decided to calculate their odds, using the skills in arithmetic he had honed in the marketplace: "I'd say Qiu Chuji has at most an eighty percent chance of finding Ironheart Yang's widow. That means we've got a twenty percent advantage already. Furthermore, it's fifty-fifty that Yang's widow gave birth to a girl, so that gives us another forty percent. If it was a boy, he might be weaker than even our Guo Jing, so that's another ten percent. Say he's tall and strong, he could be just as stupid as our boy. So, all in all, that adds up to an eighty percent chance of us winning."

The other Freaks paused and then nodded their agreement, even if they knew in their hearts that to imagine that Yang's son would be worse at kung fu than Guo Jing was but a vain attempt at self-reassurance. But the boy was honest and obedient and they liked him very much.

2

TEN YEARS PASSED QUICKLY OUT IN THE STEPPES OF OUTER Mongolia, where the vibrant summer grass was covered year after year by winter's thick blanket of snow. Guo Jing had grown into a burly young man of sixteen. With only two years left before the contest, the Freaks were stepping up their efforts. They had halted his riding and archery practice in order to concentrate solely on boxing and swordsmanship.

Over the years, Temujin's tribe had grown as he defeated his rivals. He was a strict commander, collecting the best men around him, and his force only grew in skill and discipline. His bravery was matched by a deep understanding of strategy, and ever more territory, livestock, and people of the north gradually came under his control. He could now stand as equal to Ong Khan.

The north winds abated, the snow stopped falling, but the desert was still icy cold.

It was Tomb-Sweeping Day and the Six Freaks of the South woke early. They prepared the cows and sheep as sacrifices and took Guo Jing with them to visit Zhang Asheng's grave. The Khan's camp at this point had moved some distance away, so that even on horseback it took half a day to get there. They climbed the hill where they had done battle all those years before and swept away the snow covering their brother's last resting place. They lit candles, burned incense, and said their prayers.

"Brother," Jade Han began, whispering quietly. "These last ten years we have given all our efforts over to teaching the boy. He is not naturally gifted—in fact, he struggles. But we hope you are watching over us and will help him in the contest in two years' time. The boy must not ruin the good reputation of the Seven Freaks of the South."

The raw winds of the north had sculpted faces with sharper angles, bodies with harder edges. White hairs speckled the sides of their faces like stars in the night sky. Jade Han had lost none of her charms, but by now she was a beautiful woman rather than the blushing maid of yesteryear.

Zhu Cong surveyed the skulls piled beside the grave. Despite years of beating winds and snow, they were still perfectly intact. A feeling he could not give words to rose within him. He and Gilden Quan had searched for Iron Corpse all over this harsh landscape, in every valley and cave, yet they could find no trace of her, no skeleton, no sign she had ever existed. How could a blind woman live for so long in seclusion without leaving the slightest clue to her where-abouts? She had blown past like a noxious wind. The only evidence of all that had happened was this grave and the piles of skulls.

The Freaks ate and then started back home to get some rest before practice was due to begin again.

Woodcutter Nan was teaching Guo Jing Split Mountain Palm technique, as it involved many of his most accomplished moves. After some eighty contortions with his hand, Nan suddenly struck at Guo Jing's back and flipped the young man in a move known as the Hawk Fights the Rabbit. Guo Jing ducked and spun his leg in an Autumn Wind Blows the Fallen Leaves. Nan jabbed and thrust his palms in an Iron Ox Plows the Field.

Guo Jing was edging back when Nan shouted: "Pay attention!"

He made to hit Guo Jing in the chest with his left hand, Guo Jing blocked, Nan slapped his palms together, and Guo tumbled to the ground. Guo Jing met the packed earth and sand with both hands and rebounded back to his feet. His cheeks were hot with shame.

Woodcutter Nan was just about to explain the move when laughter burst through a nearby thicket. Out came a young girl. "Guo Jing, did your *shifu* get you again?"

"I'm practicing, leave me alone!"

"I like it when you get beaten up."

It was Khojin. Not much younger than her brother Tolui and Guo Jing, she had grown up with the boys, and this, together with her parents' coddling, had turned her into a know-it-all. They often fought, but Khojin was at least able to admit when she had gone too far.

"I'm busy with my lessons, go away!" Guo Jing replied.

"Being trounced, more like."

Just then a group of Mongolian soldiers came riding up to them. One of the squad commanders jumped down from his horse, and bowed: "Khojin, the Khan has sent for you."

Mongolians did not bother with fancy titles, so his use of the Khan's daughter's given name caused no offense.

"What is it?"

"Ong Khan has sent messengers."

"I'm not going," she said, her brow wrinkled.

"The Khan will be angry if you don't."

Khojin's betrothal to Ong Khan's grandson Tusakha had been decided all those years ago, but her heart had not obeyed and her affections were firmly focused elsewhere. They were too young for it to be called love, but the thought of leaving Guo Jing and marrying the domineering Tusakha was too much to bear. Her lips puckered and she said nothing. But she could not defy her father, so she reluctantly followed the soldiers back to the camp.

THAT NIGHT, Guo Jing was woken by the sound of clapping outside his *ger*. He sat up.

"Guo Jing, come out."

Guo Jing did not recognize the voice—it was speaking Chinese. He lifted a corner of the flap of material that covered the entrance. He could just about make out in the moonlight the shape of a person standing by the tree.

Guo Jing stepped out into the night and approached the figure. It was dressed in long, fluttering robes, hair swept up in a bun.

"Who are you? What do you want?"

"Are you Guo Jing?"

"Yes."

"Where's your dagger? The one that can slice through metal as if it were mud? Show me!" The figure twitched, then suddenly leaped toward him, a palm aimed at his chest.

Guo Jing dodged out of the way. "What was that for?"

"I was just trying to assess the extent of your abilities," he replied, throwing another punch, quick and hard.

Anger exploded in Guo Jing as he leaned back to avoid the blow. He grabbed at the man's wrist and with his other hand seized his elbow in a move known across the *wulin* as the Brave Soldier Breaks Wrist, part of the Split Muscles Lock Bones technique, as taught to him by Zhu Cong. Once you have hold of the wrist and elbow, a push and twist will pop the bones out of place. Zhu Cong had been perfecting the ancient technique over the last ten years in preparation for Cyclone Mei's return.

This was the first time Guo Jing had fought someone other than his *shifus* and his intelligent choice of a Split Muscles Lock Bones move had taken his opponent by surprise. The hours of practice had proved worthwhile. Guo Jing was about to burst the man's wrist out of joint when he saw another palm coming at his face. Guo Jing let go and jumped back. He turned as the force of the move sent a rush of air that burned his cheeks. It had only just missed.

Guo Jing turned back. The man was young and handsome, not much older than himself, it seemed, with long eyelashes and fine features.

"Not bad. Ten years at the hands of the Six Freaks of the South haven't been a waste after all," the man said.

Guo Jing was cautious. "Who are you? What do you want?"

"Let's practice some more." His palms were raised and ready.

Guo Jing did not move. He waited for another rush of air, then tilted, grabbed the man's arm and pinched his cheek with his free hand. Guo Jing tugged at the mystery assailant's jaw. Zhu Cong called this move Laugh the Jaw Out of Joint. But this time, the young man defended with his right and struck with his left. Guo Jing used further maneuvers from the Split Muscles Lock Bones technique, one after another. But the young Taoist was of nimble physique and his hands were quick. He turned and twisted so Guo Jing could not tell what was coming next.

Guo Jing was growing increasingly alarmed. The man's foot flew up and struck his hip. Thankfully he had not put his entire strength behind the kick. Guo Jing's hands flew around his body, defending his vulnerable spots as best he could, but the young man kept increasing the pressure. Just as he was beginning to think he would not be able to hold off the attack for much longer, a voice called from behind him: "Go for his stomach!"

Ryder Han. Guo Jing turned around and saw all six of his *shifus*. He had not realized they were all behind him. His spirit renewed, he did as his Third *Shifu* instructed. Ryder Han was right, the young Taoist's lower body was not as strong. Before long, Guo Jing had forced his opponent back. Victory felt close, so he pressed on. The young man stumbled and Guo Jing performed a Mandarin Duck kick, one foot following the other like a pair of mating birds.

But the young man had laid the perfect trap.

"Watch out!" Ryder Han and Jade called out together.

But Guo Jing did not know what he should be looking out for. Before he knew it, the young man had grabbed hold of his right foot and hit him with his palm. Guo Jing could only somersault out of the hold and land on his back with a thump. Despite the pain, he flipped to his feet in a Flying Carp. He was about to attack again when he saw the Freaks had surrounded his opponent.

The young Taoist cupped his hands and spoke in a slow and clear voice. "Disciple Harmony Yin of the Quanzhen Sect," he said, kneeling down. "I am here on instructions from my revered Master, Elder Eternal Spring Qiu Chuji. He sends his warmest greetings to the Heroes of the South."

The Freaks were surprised and also a little fearful that the young man was here as part of some devious plan.

Harmony Yin rose to his feet, took a letter from inside his shirt and passed it to Zhu Cong.

Just then Ke Zhen'e heard the sounds of Mongolian soldiers on patrol. "Let's move inside and talk."

The young man followed the Freaks into their *ger*. Gilden Quan lit a sheep-fat candle. The Freaks lived here together, except for Jade Han, who lived with the other unmarried Mongolian women of the tribe.

Harmony Yin looked around at the simple surroundings and realized life was not easy out here on the steppe. "Sirs, you have been working hard all these years," he said, bowing again. "My Master has sent me to express his eternal gratitude."

"Huh," Ke Zhen'e snorted. "If that's really why you're here, why did you attack Guo Jing? Were you trying to intimidate us before the contest?"

Zhu Cong opened the letter and began reading out loud:

"*Qiu Chuji, disciple of the Quanzhen Sect, sends his sincerest greetings to the Heroes of the South, Master Ke, Master Zhu, Master Han, Master Nan, Master Quan, Mistress Han, and the late Master Zhang. Once Seven, always Seven. It has been sixteen years now since we left the south and the moons have come and gone so quickly. The Seven Heroes are honorable fighters and people of their word, your righteousness and integrity are awe-inspiring. Your benevolence and chivalry is matched only by the ancients of old.*"

Ke Zhen'e's frown softened. Zhu Cong continued:

"*I was deeply saddened to hear of Master Zhang's passing in Mongolia. He was a loyal and dedicated patriot and he will never be forgotten. I have been blessed with your good fortune, having found Ironheart Yang's wife and child nine years ago without bloodshed.*"

Hearing that the child had been found gave them a momentary shock. They were still yet to tell Guo Jing and his mother about the whole affair.

Zhu Cong looked over at Guo Jing, but he appeared unaffected, so he read on:

"*In another two years, when the flowers are blooming and the grasses of the south are swaying in the wind, we will meet and drink at the Garden of the Eight Drunken Immortals. Life passes like the drying morning dew and these sixteen years have been like a dream. Do the brave heroes of the* wulin *laugh at my foolishness?*"

Zhu Cong stopped.

"And?" Ryder Han asked.

"There is no more. It's definitely his calligraphy."

"The child was also a boy?" Ke Zhen'e said, turning to Harmony Yin. "Is his name Yang 'Vitality' Kang?"

"Yes."

"So you study with him? He is your younger martial brother?"

"He is my senior. I am older than him by one year, but he started his training with the Quanzhen Sect two years before me."

Guo Jing's kung fu was a trifle compared to this young man's, which meant that Yang Kang's skills must be even more impressive. Their mood sank even lower. And Qiu Chuji seemed to know about all that had happened to them in quite some detail, including the death of their brother Zhang Asheng.

"Were you testing him earlier?" Ke Zhen'e pressed.

Harmony Yin sensed the cold edge in his voice and it made him feel anxious. "I wouldn't dare!"

"Go back to your *shifu* and tell him not to worry, we will be there at the Garden of the Eight Drunken Immortals. We send no letter in reply."

Harmony Yin hesitated, unsure what to say. Qiu Chuji had indeed told him to find a way to assess Guo Jing's character and the extent of his kung fu. But Harmony Yin was young, and the only way he could think of to complete the instruction was to fight Guo Jing under the veil of darkness—a crude method, he realized now. Ke Zhen'e's reaction frightened him.

"I'll be going then," was all he could manage in response.

Ke Zhen'e accompanied him out and Harmony Yin bowed.

"How about a somersault too?" Ke replied, and caught hold of the young man's collar. Harmony Yin tried to push Ke's hand away, but Ke's grip was firm and he ended up tumbling back in a somersault after all. This made Ke even more furious. He lifted the boy up, howled and threw him to the ground, where he landed on his back, sending a jolt of pain up his spine.

He managed to scramble to his feet and limped away without another word.

"What terrible manners! At least you taught him a lesson, Brother," Ryder Han said.

Ke did not reply. After a long pause, he gave a deep sigh. The other Freaks understood their brother's mood.

"We have to fight, even if we lose!" Nan said, breaking the silence.

"Fourth Brother is right," Jade Han said. "We wandered the south together for so long before coming north, ever since we swore our oath of martial loyalty all those years ago. We have been through many dangers, but the Seven Freaks of the South have never been cowed."

Ke Zhen'e nodded and turned to Guo Jing. "Go back to sleep. Tomorrow the real work begins."

3

THE FREAKS GREW STRICTER IN THEIR TRAINING. BUT JUST AS in the study of music or chess, demanding fast results can choke initial promise, and Guo Jing was not naturally gifted to begin with. The pressure frightened him and he was easily flustered. In the three months that followed Harmony Yin's visit, he appeared to regress. It had taken many years of bitter toil for the Freaks to gain their individual skills, so for Guo Jing to acquire all of them in the course of just a few short summers and winters would have required a special talent indeed. How could they expect a boy of average capabilities to achieve such a feat? The Freaks knew that it was only realistic to expect the boy to learn Ryder Han or Woodcutter Nan's skills alone, and perhaps after thirty years of persistent effort, he might come to acquire half of their skills put together. Laughing Buddha Zhang Asheng would have made the most suitable *shifu,* if only he had not departed so young. But the Freaks were single-minded in their desire to defeat the Taoist Qiu Chuji, and even though they knew it would be better to concentrate on a few techniques rather than try to teach him everything, they could not help themselves.

For the last sixteen years, Zhu Cong had been going over in his head their encounter with Qiu Chuji in the Garden of the Eight Drunken Immortals, reliving the Taoist's every move and thrust. His memory was uncommonly clear. But try as he might, he could not find any weaknesses to exploit. Only Twice Foul Dark Wind would be capable of defeating that stinky old cow muzzle, he concluded at last.

That morning, as the sun was rising, Jade Han was already busy teaching the young man two moves from the Yue Maiden Sword repertoire. The first, Branch Beats the White Chimpanzee, involved leaping and making two turns in the air before pulling the sword back to attack. Guo Jing had worked hard on his core stability, but his jumps lacked agility and speed. At first he could only manage a half-turn and after at least eight tries he was still half a turn short. Jade Han was becoming more and more frustrated, but she forced herself to stay calm, focusing on teaching him how to concentrate his energy in the tips of his toes, and turn with his waist and legs. He flew up high, but forgot to spin. This continued for several more attempts.

After all these years spent in the deserts of the north, after burying Fifth Brother in these strange lands, after all their efforts, the boy was hopeless. It was all hopeless. The tears poured down Jade Han's cheeks. She cast her sword into the dirt, covered her face and ran away.

Guo Jing ran after her, but she was too quick for him. He stopped, watched her go, his heart pounding. The kindness of his *shifus* had been steady like the mountains; all he wanted was to practice their art well, to show them his gratitude. But he could not do it, no matter how hard he tried.

"Guo Jing, come here!" It was Khojin.

He turned and saw her approach on the back of a horse, her face a mixture of anxiety and excitement.

"What is it?" he replied.

"Come quick and see for yourself," said Khojin. "Condors fighting. Lots of them."

"I'm in the middle of training."

"I just saw your *shifu* leave."

Guo Jing looked up at her.

"The condors are really going for each other, come and take a look."

Guo Jing's heart beat faster. He did want to see it, but he still felt his Seventh *Shifu*'s disappointment. "I can't," he said.

"I came all this way to tell you instead of going to see it myself," Khojin responded hotly. "Don't expect me to go with you later."

"Go now. You can tell me all about it once I'm home. It's all the same to me."

Khojin jumped down from her horse. "If you're not going, I'm not going either," she said, pouting. "I wonder who's going to win—the black condors or the white."

"The pair of white condors that live on the cliff?"

"Yes. The place is surrounded by black ones, but the white ones are much stronger. They've pecked three black ones to death already."

Guo Jing could stand it no longer. He grabbed Khojin's hand, jumped up onto her horse, and together they rode to the bottom of the cliff. Almost twenty huge black birds had surrounded one pair of white condors. They screeched and pecked; feathers flew.

The white condors had made their nest at the top of the cliff. This pair were unusually large specimens of what was an extremely rare breed. The Mongolian elders called them divine and some foolish local women even came to pray to them.

One of the white condors stalked forward and pecked one of the black condors, and it fell, dead, just before Khojin's horse. The remaining black condors scattered but regrouped quickly and surrounded the pair again. Another fight ensued, drawing an ever bigger crowd of locals until there were at least several hundred gathered at the foot of the cliff, discussing every move and attack. Temujin himself arrived, bringing with him Ogedai and Tolui. Everyone was enthralled by the spectacle.

Being regulars at the cliff, Guo Jing, Tolui, and Khojin saw the white condors nearly every day, flying to and from their nest. Sometimes they would throw them chunks of mutton. The children considered the birds their friends.

"Go get them! On the left! Turn! That's it, kill him!"

Two more black birds fell. The white condors' feathers looked as if they had been dipped in red ink.

At that moment, one of the largest black birds squawked and ten or so more beat their wings and took off, disappearing into the clouds above. Four black condors remained. The fight looked to be coming to an end and the crowd whooped and called out in excitement. Soon three more birds took flight, followed by one of the white condors, leaving just one black and one white in a standoff. The last black condor started flapping its wings, about to take flight, when the white condor attacked.

Then, a scream from above.

Ten condors swooped out from the clouds together.

"Excellent tactics!" Temujin laughed.

The white condor dropped to the foot of the cliff and the black condors followed, scratching and clawing at its corpse. The children were shocked and Khojin burst into tears. "Papa, kill them!"

But Temujin turned to his sons. "We must learn from those clever birds, my sons. A most useful military lesson."

The young men nodded.

The black condors flew up and into a cave near the top of the cliff, where two small white heads had been poking out only moments earlier.

"Papa! Why won't you do something?" Khojin then turned. "Guo Jing, look, the white condors have babies. How come we didn't know? Oh, Papa, kill them, please!"

With a smile, Temujin raised his bow and with a *twang!* his arrow took down one of the birds. The crowd clapped. Temujin then gave the bow to Ogedai. "Here, your turn."

Ogedai shot and killed one too. By the time a third fell to Tolui's arrow, the black condors were scattering in all directions.

Temujin's other men also began firing until they had flown up high and out of reach.

"A reward for whoever can bring one down!" Temujin cried.

Jebe wanted his student to show off his skills, so he gave his bow to Guo Jing and whispered, "Kneel down and aim for the neck."

Guo Jing obeyed. He held the weighty bow in his left hand and drew back the arrow. Two black condors were flying wing to wing. He took aim and shot.

The bow bent like the moon, the arrow flashed like a meteor.

It pierced through the first condor's neck and lodged itself into the abdomen of the second. Together, the birds fell to the ground. A roar came from the crowd and, frightened, the remaining birds dispersed.

"Present them to my father," Khojin whispered in his ear.

He fetched the birds and ran over to the Khan's horse, where he kneeled in the dirt, lifting them up before him.

The boy's trick delighted Temujin. The birds had a wingspan of more than three meters and their feathers were hard like shards of metal. They were capable of seizing and making off with large sheep and even ponies. Tigers were known to keep their distance. To kill two with one arrow was a mighty feat indeed.

Temujin ordered one of his men to take the birds. "Good boy, you are most accomplished with the bow."

"My *shifu* Jebe taught me."

"A master known as God of the Bow, and a student to match." Temujin smiled.

"Father," Tolui said, "you promised a reward to whoever could shoot down a condor. My *anda* shot two! What will you give him?"

"He may have whatever his heart desires. What would you like, Guo Jing?"

"Anything?" Tolui asked in excitement. "Anything he wants?"

"Am I known for lying to children?"

Guo Jing had lived all these years under the Khan's protection. He was liked by the whole tribe, especially for his pureness of heart.

They had never treated him differently just because he was Chinese. They turned to the boy and waited for his reply.

"The Khan has always been good to me and my mother has everything she needs," Guo Jing began. "No other reward is necessary."

"You are filial indeed, thinking of your mother first. But what is it you want? There's no need to be frightened—speak from your heart."

Guo Jing paused and looked up at Temujin from where he was still kneeling. "I want for nothing, but I do ask the Khan for one thing, on behalf of another."

"Yes?"

"The Khan's grandson Tusakha is mean and cruel. Khojin will live a bitter life if she marries him. I beg the Khan not to betroth her to him."

Temujin was surprised, but then burst into laughter. "Those are indeed the words of a child! How could I possibly go back on such an agreement? It was decided many years ago, I cannot renege on a promise. Come, come. I shall give you a reward."

Temujin took a small knife from his belt and gave it to Guo Jing. His men clapped and gasped, jealous at such a gift. They knew this weapon had slain countless enemies and was very precious to the Khan. He did not part with it lightly.

Guo Jing thanked Temujin. He had seen it tucked into the Khan's belt many a time, but now he could examine it up close. The scabbard was inlaid with gold and the handle was crowned with a tiger's head cast in the same precious metal, fierce and lifelike.

"This, my boy, is my golden dagger. Take it and use it to kill our enemies."

"I will do my best for the Khan!" Guo Jing replied.

Khojin suddenly began sobbing. She jumped onto her horse and galloped away. Temujin's heart was hard like iron, but even he had noticed his daughter's displeasure at the agreement. He sighed, turned his horse and left for camp. The others followed behind.

Once the crowd had dispersed, Guo Jing removed the dagger from its sheath and held the cold metal in his hand. The blade was tainted with the faintest shadow of blood. Who knew how many had died from a thrust of this weapon? It was short, but thick and heavy.

He put it back in its scabbard and attached it to his belt. Then he drew his sword and began performing some moves from Yue Maiden Sword. Despite the hours he had spent practicing, he just could not get Branch Beats the White Chimpanzee right. He either didn't get enough height, or else he couldn't complete the spins. He was becoming increasingly frustrated and was losing control of his movements. Sweat poured down his forehead.

Guo Jing turned. He could hear the beating of horses' hooves.

He stopped his practice. It was Khojin.

She rode close and dismounted. She then lay down in the grass, her hand propping up her head, and watched Guo Jing.

"Take a break," she called, noticing he seemed out of sorts.

"Leave me be, I don't have time for this."

Khojin did not reply, but continued watching him, a smile lightly drawn on her face. After a while, she removed a small handkerchief from her breast, tied two knots in it and threw it at Guo Jing. "Dry the sweat."

Guo Jing mumbled in response, but continued his practice.

A while later, she spoke again. "Why did you beg my father not to force me to marry Tusakha?"

"Tusakha is a bad man. He once set a pair of leopards on your brother Tolui. If you marry him, he will beat you."

"But you will defend me!"

"How will I do that?" Guo Jing said with surprise.

"Who will marry me if I don't marry him?" Khojin's tone was softer now.

"How should I know?" Guo Jing replied with a shake of his head.

"Huh!" Khojin's gentle blush turned an angry crimson. "What do you know?"

But her anger did not last long and soon the silence between them was interrupted by the cries of the condors' young, high up on the cliff. Then came screeches above; the other white condor had returned. It had been circling all this time, reluctant to return after having witnessed from afar the death of its companion.

Guo Jing stopped and looked up. The bird was howling in pain.

"That poor bird," Khojin said.

"Yes, it must be so sad."

The condor let out one last long scream and flew up into the clouds.

"Why is it flying so high?" Khojin asked.

Just then it came shooting through the clouds and flew straight into the cliff face. Khojin and Guo Jing both yelped and jumped up in shock. They stood beside each other, taking in the scene in silence.

"Impressive, very impressive!" A loud voice came from behind.

They turned and saw an old Chinese man with a white beard and red cheeks. He looked kind and carried a horsetail whip. His dress was strange and he wore his hair in three buns. He stood proudly, his clothes neat and clean, without the slightest trace of dust, which out in this desert landscape was unusual indeed. His robes reminded Guo Jing of those worn by Harmony Yin, who he had later discovered was a Taoist from China's Central Plains.

This man also spoke Chinese, but as Khojin could not understand she soon lost interest and turned back to the cliff. "Those baby condors have lost their mother and father. What are they going to do now?" Khojin continued.

The cliff face was smooth and reached up to touch the clouds. The young condors had not learned to fly yet; they were stuck. They were going to starve up there.

Guo Jing looked up. "Their only hope is that someone grows wings and flies up there to save them."

He glanced at the old man, took up his sword again and went back to his training.

He still was not making any progress and was now starting to despair. Just then the voice came again, loud and clear. "Keep doing it like that and it won't matter if you train for a hundred years, you'll never get it."

Guo Jing turned back to the Taoist. "What did you say?"

He smiled, but did not answer. The man then took two steps forward. Just then Guo Jing felt his arm go numb, and with a flash of green, his sword was suddenly in the man's hand. Zhu Cong had taught him Seize the Blade Barehanded, and though he was yet to perfect the technique, he understood the principle. But the Taoist had done something else and Guo Jing was not sure how. Fear gripped him. He retreated to Khojin's side and drew the dagger Temujin had given him.

"Watch carefully," the Taoist called.

He jumped up, with a swishing sound made six or seven turns with the sword, and softly landed back down. Guo Jing was amazed.

The Taoist threw away the sword and smiled. "That white condor is an impressive bird. We must indeed save its young."

He began running toward the cliff and then, quick like a monkey and light like a bird, he scrambled up the rock face.

Guo Jing and Khojin watched from below, even more astounded than before. Just one slip would kill him. He continued, higher and higher, smaller and smaller, up into the clouds.

Khojin covered her eyes. "What's happening?"

"He's almost at the top. He's there, he made it!"

She lowered her hands and continued to peer up. It really looked as if the Taoist might fall. His sleeves flapped, she screamed, but he was on solid ground. From below, he looked just like one of the condors.

He slipped his hand into the cave where the condors had made their nest, grabbed hold of the two chicks and tucked them into the front of his robes. Then, with his hand against the cliff, he slid back down, slowed every now and again by a bump in the rock or a crevice that caught his foot. He was at the bottom in moments.

They ran to him. The Taoist passed the birds to Khojin and spoke in Mongolian. "Will you look after them?"

"Yes, yes!" she said, reaching out to take them.

"Watch out for their beaks, they may be small, but their peck is painful."

Khojin fastened her belt around their tiny feet and took them in her arms, a smile conquering her face. "I'm going to catch some insects to feed them."

"Wait," the man said. "If you take them, you must promise me one thing."

"What's that?"

"You mustn't tell anyone I climbed the cliff."

"That's fine, I won't tell," Khojin said.

"And another thing. The condors will grow to be very aggressive," he continued. "Feed them insects first, then meat. And be careful."

"We will have one each," she said to Guo Jing, "but I will look after them both to begin with."

Guo Jing nodded mutely as Khojin mounted her horse and galloped away.

In fact, Guo Jing had not really been paying attention to the birds, as he was still confounded by the Taoist's demonstration of Branch Beats the White Chimpanzee. The Taoist picked up Guo Jing's sword, gave it to him and started to leave.

"Wait . . . Please don't go," Guo Jing said.

"And why ever not?"

Guo Jing scratched his head, unsure how to reply. Then, without warning, he dropped to his knees and began touching the ground with his forehead.

"Why are you kowtowing?" the Taoist said.

The Taoist had a kindly air, like an old uncle with whom one could talk freely. A rush of familiarity overcame Guo Jing and two fat tears rolled down his cheeks.

"I'm not smart, I'm always making mistakes in my training. It frustrates my mentors. I have six."

"What are you going to do about it?" The Taoist smiled.

"I practice day and night and still I can't do it . . . I just can't."

"Do you want me to show you a trick?"

"Yes!" said Guo Jing, kowtowing again.

"You are a sincere young man. In three days, it will be the fifteenth day of the month when the moon is at its fullest. I will be waiting for you at the top of the cliff," he said, pointing. "But you mustn't tell a soul!" And then he left.

"Wait, I can't get up there!" Guo Jing cried. But the Taoist was already far, far away, his feet barely skimming the ground.

"He made it impossible on purpose," Guo Jing said to himself. "He never wanted to help me." He paused, and then continued muttering. "I already have a teacher, six of them, all making such an effort. It's my own fault; what could this man say that will fix that? He seems skilled, that's for sure, but what good does that do me? I'll never be able to do what he does." He looked up again at the top of the cliff and decided to forget about the encounter.

He took up his sword and began once again practicing Branch Beats the White Chimpanzee, jumping, turning, until the sun disappeared behind the mountains and his belly began to rumble. It was time to return home.

THREE DAYS sped past. Guo Jing spent the afternoon taking instruction from Ryder Han in the use of his Golden Dragon whip. This weapon was like no other—if it were not mastered it could prove more dangerous to the bearer than to his enemy.

Guo Jing cracked the whip with all his might and ended up slashing himself on the head, bringing up an egg-like bump. Ryder Han, not known to be a gentle teacher, slapped him across the cheek. Guo Jing made no reply, but kept practicing. Ryder Han regretted having been so rough with the boy; he was trying, that much was clear. He decided not to hit him again, despite the constant string of mistakes. He taught the boy five moves in total, loaded him up with words of encouragement, and then mounted his horse and rode off.

The Golden Dragon whip was no easy weapon, and after ten or so attempts Guo Jing was covered in bruises from his head to his arms to his thighs. He was exhausted and in pain, so he decided to lie down on the grass and take a short nap. But time passed faster than his body sensed it, and when he awoke again, the moon had appeared from behind the mountains. His body was throbbing and his cheek was still red from his Third *Shifu*'s slap.

He looked up at the cliff. Somehow sleep had given him new courage. "If Uncle can climb up there, why can't I?" He ran to the bottom of the rock face, grabbed hold of some low snaking vines and roots and began hoisting himself up. But after twenty meters or so the vegetation stopped. He looked up to see a smooth wall above him. How was he going to get up there?

He clenched his teeth and tried to find his next foothold, but he kept slipping. If he fell, he would be nothing more than a pile of bones. There was no way he could go any farther, so he sighed and started making his way back down again. But it soon became apparent the descent would be just as difficult; he could no longer see the places he had put his feet and hands and it was too high to jump.

His Fourth *Shifu*'s words echoed in his ears: *Nothing eludes a man of sound heart and good will.* Since it would be death to stay put, he had no choice but to continue upward. He removed his dagger and chipped away two small holes. In the first he placed one foot, tested to see if it could take his weight and then climbed to the next. So he rose, a few inches at a time, carving hand- and footholds into the rock. The effort made his head spin and his limbs ache.

Some way up, he stopped and clung to the rock to compose himself. Trying to control his breath, he stole a glace upward. How many clefts would he have to chisel away to get to the top? And how many before his knife broke? But there was no turning back. After a short rest, he steeled himself for a renewed ascent.

Just then he heard laughter from above.

He was too scared to lean back to look, so he kept his nose tight against the rock. The laughter continued and then stopped abruptly. Then a thick rope came down toward him and stopped just in front of his eyes.

"Tie the rope around your waist and I'll pull you up."

It was the Taoist with the three buns.

Relieved, Guo Jing put away his dagger and grabbed the rope with his right hand. He wrapped it around his waist twice and tied two knots.

"Is it secure?"

"Yes."

"Is it secure?" He had not heard Guo Jing's reply.

"Yes," Guo Jing called, this time louder.

But he still had not heard. "Ah, I forgot, you haven't trained your breathing enough. Your voice doesn't carry. If you've secured it, tug three times on the rope."

Guo Jing pulled sharply three times and the rope instantly went taut. His body then started soaring up to the sky. The speed of it took him by surprise and in a trice he had landed on his feet.

There he was: the old Taoist.

He had saved Guo Jing's life. The young man dropped to his knees to kowtow again, but the Taoist pulled him up. "Enough, enough. You kowtowed more than enough times last time we met. You certainly know how to behave with your elders."

Guo Jing looked out across the flat expanse of snow. The Taoist pointed to two rocks shaped like drums. "Sit."

"Your student will remain standing, out of respect."

"You are not of my school and I am not your *shifu*, so you are not my student. Sit."

Guo Jing was confused, but sat as instructed.

"Your *shifus* are well respected in the *wulin*. I cannot claim an acquaintance, but I have heard many speak of their prowess. You need only learn the skills of one of them to gain a reputation in the martial world. You are working hard. Do you know why you have made so little progress over the last ten years?"

"I'm too stupid. My *shifus* are doing all they can."

"It needn't be so. It can only be because they do not know how to teach you."

"Please . . . sir . . . I don't understand."

"You already have a solid grasp of the basics. If we look only to the core martial arts, your current skills are far from inconsequential. But you lost your first real fight to the young Taoist Harmony Yin, and this made you question yourself. On this point, however, you are mistaken."

How does he know about that? Guo Jing wondered.

"He performed a somersault, yes, but he used tricks, not skill. Indeed, his mastery of the essentials does not necessarily exceed yours. With such accomplished *shifus,* I cannot teach you any more than they can."

"Yes." Excellent, he thought, my *shifus* are masters of the martial arts. Then the problem does indeed lie with me.

"As your *shifus* have a bet going, they would be most displeased if I were to teach you. They care about honor above all else and would not dream of profiting from any kind of unfair advantage."

"What bet?" asked Guo Jing.

"You don't know? Then if your *shifus* haven't told you, you mustn't ask me. At some point over the next two years, they will explain. You are an honest young man; we were fated to meet. Let me teach you some breathing techniques at least. How to sit, walk, and sleep, that sort of thing."

Sitting, walking, sleeping? Guo Jing thought to himself. I know how to do that already! But he decided not to say so, in case it made him look even more stupid.

"Brush away the snow from this rock and go to sleep."

This was certainly odd, Guo Jing thought, but he did as he was told.

"Why I am teaching you this, you don't need to know. Focus on remembering these words instead:

> *"Clear heart, emotions departed,*
> *In empty body* qi *can spread.*
> *A dead mind, yet the spirit lives,*
> *For Yin thrives but the Yang is shed."*

Guo Jing repeated and memorized it, but he had no idea what it meant.

"You must clear your mind before sleep. Don't leave a single thought. Then settle your body in the correct position, on your side, that's right. Make your breath smooth and even. Release your spirit but don't let your mind wander."

Guo Jing did as he was told. At first his mind was overrun by uncontrollable thoughts, but the Taoist's explanations were slow and thorough and gradually he managed to focus on what he was being told. A warm feeling spread through his abdomen. The air at the top of the cliff was cold enough to cut bone, but he no longer felt it. After two hours, he opened his eyes. He had been lying in meditation like this without feeling the slightest prickling of the hands or feet.

The Taoist was sitting with his legs crossed in front of him. Noticing that Guo Jing was moving, he said, "Now you will be able to sleep."

Guo Jing dozed off. By the time he awoke, the sun was beginning to rise in the east. The Taoist tied a rope around his waist and lowered him back down the cliff with instructions not to tell anyone about what had happened that night.

That evening, Guo Jing returned to the cliff and was once again hoisted up. His mother did not think to ask why he was not returning at night, as the Freaks frequently kept him out late, training. And so he spent his nights learning meditation with the mysterious Taoist. The Six Freaks were none the wiser.

4

IT WAS STRANGE, HE HAD TO ADMIT. THE TAOIST HAD NOT taught him even one martial arts move, but he was noticeably quicker and lighter during his daily practices. Six months on, he was performing moves with a skill and agility that had previously eluded him. "He has finally matured," the Six Freaks could only exclaim.

The Taoist taught him to climb the rock face by himself by moving the *qi* around his body, and only when Guo Jing was exhausted and could climb no more would he rush to the top and lower the rope. Before long, Guo Jing could manage all but the most difficult parts of the ascent.

So the earth circled once more around the sun and there were just a few months left before the day of the contest. It was going to cause a sensation in the *wulin* and the Freaks of the South could talk of nothing else. They felt sure Guo Jing was going to win, given his recent progress, and their excitement at the thought of finally returning to their home in the south grew with each passing day. But they still had not explained to Guo Jing what exactly was going on.

One morning, Gilden Quan turned to the boy: "Young man, you've been practicing with weapons a lot these last few months. I think we should concentrate on your boxing for a while."

Guo Jing nodded.

They arrived at their usual training ground and Gilden Quan had just assumed his usual stance when a storm of dust suddenly rose before them, accompanied by the sounds of horses and someone shouting. A group of horses broke through the sand cloud and their herders followed behind, struggling to retain control.

Just as they had managed to get their animals to settle, a colt, dark red like blood, broke through, kicking and biting. This sent the rest of the horses into a frenzy, until it galloped away again. They watched as it returned and stirred up another uproar. The men were furious and tried desperately to capture it, but it evaded them, stopped and began to proudly shake its mane. The herders could not help smiling. But as it approached for its third attack, one of the herders raised his bow and shot. Just as the arrow approached, the horse spun out of its path.

The Freaks and their disciple watched with growing fascination. Ryder Han, who loved horses like life itself, had never seen such a magnificent steed. It surpassed even his own dear Wind Chaser. He ran over to the herders to ask if they knew anything about it.

"He appeared a few days ago from deep in the mountains. We wanted to catch him, he's such a beauty, but it has proved impossible. We just ended up making him angry, so he's been chasing our animals ever since."

"That's no horse," an older herder among them said solemnly.

Ryder Han looked at the old man in puzzlement. "Then what is it?"

"A dragon sent from the heavens, that's what it is. Don't touch him."

"A dragon? Nonsense," another herder replied.

"And what would you know? I've been herding horses since before you were born and I've never seen anything like it." At that moment, the horse reappeared and started charging at the herd once again.

Ryder Han wasn't known as Protector of the Steeds for nothing. He selected his spot and waited. There wasn't a horse in all his days that he had not managed to tame. Then, as it approached, he jumped. Just as he was about to land perfectly on its back, however, the colt shot forward like an arrow and Ryder Han fell to the ground. Furious, he started running after it, but his short legs could not carry him fast enough.

Just then a figure leaped through the air and caught hold of the young horse's mane. The animal accelerated in surprise, pulling the man with him.

The crowd roared with applause.

To the delight of the Freaks, it was Guo Jing.

"Where did he learn such impressive lightness kung fu?" Zhu Cong asked.

"He's been making such progress recently," Jade Han replied. "Maybe his dead father's spirit is helping him? Or Fifth Brother Zhang?"

They still did not know anything about Guo Jing's secret nightly training in the art of breathing. While the Taoist had not taught him any moves, he had effectively been imparting the great art of *neigong* inner strength without Guo Jing even realizing it. Every evening, the young boy climbed up and down the cliff, itself a lesson in Golden Goose kung fu, one of the foremost branches of lightness technique. The boy was still as muddleheaded as ever, but he slept as per Uncle's instructions. The results of all of this were only ever made clear during Zhu Cong, Gilden Quan, and Jade Han's lessons. But the boy did not realize it himself and the Six Freaks were merely delighted he was finally getting better. They did not imagine there might be a clandestine reason for his progress.

But this move . . . This made the Freaks look at each other. They had not taught him that. The thought that he might have another *shifu* was beginning, ever so slowly, to plant itself in their minds.

Guo Jing had by now somersaulted onto the back of the horse and galloped away. Not long afterward they returned, the horse rearing wildly and bucking. It was all Guo Jing could do to squeeze his thighs and hold on.

Ryder Han began calling out instructions.

The onlookers were astonished. The old herder knelt and began praying, begging the spirits not to punish them for offending the dragon horse. He then called to Guo Jing to jump off. But Guo Jing was concentrating too hard to hear him. It was as if he had tied himself to the animal. No matter how the horse bucked and cried, Guo Jing clung fast.

Guo Jing was thus stuck, clasping on to the back of the horse for over two hours.

"Guo Jing, get down and let your Third *Shifu* take over," Jade Han called.

"No chance," Ryder Han cried. "All his hard work will have been for nothing if I take over!"

This was a strong-willed young colt indeed, but whoever broke him would be his master for life. If Ryder Han stepped in, the horse would never be tamed.

Guo Jing was just as stubborn, but he was beginning to tire. His skin glistened with sweat. He slipped one arm around the horse's neck and embraced it tight. He then began to gather his inner strength to his arms and pulled tighter. The horse bucked and leaped with even greater force, but still the young man held on, his grip suffocating the steed. It had met his master.

The animal stopped.

"You've done it!" Ryder Han called out in delight.

Guo Jing was still scared to jump down in case the animal ran off.

"Come, boy," Ryder Han coaxed. "You've tamed him. He's yours for good now."

Quietly, Guo Jing slipped back onto solid ground.

The auburn horse stuck out its tongue and tenderly licked Guo Jing's hand. The crowd laughed. One of the herders tried to approach, but the horse kicked, sending him sprawling. Guo Jing led his proud colt to a nearby trough and cleaned him.

"From now on, you will be called Ulaan," Guo Jing whispered.

The Freaks decided that Guo Jing had earned himself a rest for the day, but they could not help feeling suspicious about their student's newfound skills.

CHAPTER SIX

COMBAT
AT THE CLIFF

I

AFTER LUNCH, GUO JING WENT TO THE FREAKS' *GER*.

"Guo Jing, show me your Split Mountain Palm," Gilden Quan said.

"In here?"

"Indeed. Potential enemies are everywhere; you have to practice fighting in confined spaces." Gilden Quan feigned a left and struck with his right. Ke Zhen'e sat and listened.

As custom dictated, Guo Jing was waiting until his *shifu*'s fourth move before launching his riposte. Gilden Quan was swift and relentless and suddenly struck at the vital point on Guo Jing's chest with both palms in an Enter the Tiger's Lair. They were no longer practicing; his *shifu* was trying to hurt him! Guo Jing retreated in shock and within moments had his back against the *ger*'s felt walls. Instinct now took over. He hooked his left arm and blocked Gilden Quan's attack. Gilden Quan's fists were still placed on Guo Jing's torso, but the young man was soft as cotton, and before Quan realized what was happening, he had been propelled backward. His arms tingled and he stumbled.

Guo Jing stared at his Master and then knelt on both knees. "I have been foolish, I will accept my Sixth *Shifu's* punishment." Flustered, he could not think what he had done to make his Master try to hurt him in such a way.

The Freaks stood around him with grave expressions on their faces.

"You have been training with someone else in secret. Why didn't you tell us? If your Sixth *Shifu* had not confronted you, how long would you have continued to lie to us?"

"Master Jebe teaches me to use the bow and arrow—that's all."

"Still you lie to us?" Zhu Cong was furious.

"I . . . I wouldn't dare lie to my *shifus*." Tears shone in his eyes.

"Then who taught you this *neigong* inner strength? Now you are supported by this powerful master, you disrespect us?"

"*Neigong*? I don't know any *neigong*."

"Pah!" Zhu Cong spat. He jabbed his finger two inches below the boy's ribs, at the Turtledove Tail acupressure point, which if hit results in an immediate loss of consciousness. Guo Jing was too scared to dodge it, so he stood stiff like a tree. But two years of training with the Taoist with three buns had produced results, even if he did not realize it. His muscles contracted and then pushed away his Master's finger. It hurt, but he felt no other effect. Zhu Cong had not used all his strength, but there was no doubt that Guo Jing had used *neigong* to rebuff the move.

"Are you still trying to tell me you don't know *neigong*?" Zhu Cong snarled.

Could the Taoist have been teaching me *neigong*? Guo Jing asked himself.

"For two years, someone has been instructing me in breathing techniques to aid my sleep, but he never taught me any martial arts. I thought it was just for fun. He told me never to tell anyone. It didn't seem to be doing any harm to my training." Guo Jing began to kowtow. "But I know now I was wrong. I will never meet with him again."

The Freaks looked at each other.

"You didn't realize this was *neigong*?" Jade Han asked.

"I don't really know what *neigong* is. He just told me to sit, breathe and empty my mind. To think of how the *qi* travels around my body. It was hard at first, until recently when it began to feel like there was a warm little mouse running around in there. It feels so strange!"

In one respect, the Six Freaks of the South were delighted, and rather surprised, that he had achieved such proficiency in just two years. But he was a simple young boy with few thoughts to distract him; it was no doubt easier for him to clear his mind than someone of intelligence and wit. Zhu Cong had long given up on their reading lessons.

"Who is this teacher?" Zhu Cong asked.

"He didn't want me to tell you. He said that my *shifus'* kung fu is as accomplished as his, so he has nothing to teach me. He says I am not his student and he is not my Master. He made me promise not to describe what he looks like to anyone."

This only made the Freaks more curious. At first they had assumed Guo Jing had run into a fellow wanderer of the *wulin* by chance, but there seemed to be something else going on.

Zhu Cong gestured for Guo Jing to leave.

"I promise I won't meet him again. I won't go tonight."

"No, listen to me. You will keep practicing *neigong* with him. We aren't angry with you. You go tonight. But don't tell him we know."

Guo Jing nodded and left, happy that his Masters did not blame him. He pulled open the door to the *ger* and saw Khojin standing outside with the two condors by her side. They were fully grown, majestic birds by now, almost as tall as her.

"Come, I've been waiting for you for ages."

One of the birds flew up and hovered on Guo Jing's shoulder.

"I just tamed a horse. It can really run! I'm not sure if he'll let you ride him."

"Then I'll kill him!" Khojin replied.

"I won't let you."

They joined hands and ran to play with the birds and their horses. The Six Freaks, meanwhile, were deliberating their next move.

"He has taught Guo Jing well. There can be no malicious intent, surely?" Jade Han said.

"Then why doesn't he want us to know? And why didn't he explain to the boy what he was teaching him?" Gilden Quan contended.

"I'm afraid we may know him," Zhu Cong said.

"Know him? If he's not a friend, then he must be an enemy," Jade Han said.

"None of our friends possesses such superior *neigong* kung fu," Gilden Quan muttered.

"If he is our enemy, then why teach Guo Jing his skills?" Jade Han said.

"Maybe it is all part of some devilish plan." Ke Zhen'e's words sent a shiver through the other Freaks.

"Sixth Brother and I will follow Guo Jing tonight and find out who he is," Zhu Cong said. The others nodded their approval.

THAT NIGHT, Zhu Cong and Gilden Quan hid themselves outside Guo Jing's mother's *ger,* where they waited for over an hour. Then it came.

"Ma, I'm leaving!" Guo Jing appeared in the doorway and left. He was moving quickly, and within moments he was far ahead. With no trees to block their view out on the grasslands, they could follow at a safe distance.

He arrived at the bottom of the cliff and, without stopping, began to climb. Guo Jing was now able to ascend to the top without help from the Taoist.

Zhu Cong and Gilden Quan watched in astonishment, not knowing what to say. Before long, the other Freaks arrived. They had brought their weapons with them. Zhu Cong told them Guo Jing was already at the top.

"We can't get up there," Jade Han said, gazing up at the clouds which had since swallowed up the summit.

"Let's hide in the bushes and wait for them to descend," Ke Zhen'e said.

Jade Han recalled their fight twelve years previously with Twice Foul Dark Wind. They had hidden in the bushes then as now. A cutting wind had been blowing that night too; the moon's cold light, the large expanse of desert sand, the lonely hill, the occasional neighing of distant horses—it was all so familiar. And by the next morning, her beloved Zhang Asheng was dead, his smiling face still for eternity. A deep sadness came over her.

Time passed, minutes gave way to hours. The morning sun began to burn off the clouds and still there was no Guo Jing. They waited a few more hours, but all was quiet.

"Sixth Brother," Zhu Cong said, turning to Gilden Quan, "why don't we take a look?"

"Can we even get up there?" Ryder Han replied.

"We can only try."

He ran back to their *ger* and returned some time later with two ropes, axes, and a bundle of nails. Together, Gilden Quan and Zhu Cong began to climb, hammering nails, using their lightness kung fu and pulling each other up. It was a long and sweaty process.

But what they saw once they reached the top surprised them both. In fact, it drained the blood from their cheeks.

There, beside the rock where Guo Jing was used to practicing his *neigong,* lay a neat pile of nine skulls: five, three, and then one balancing on top. Closer inspection revealed five perfect, clean-cut holes in each, as if carved with a knife.

Their hearts were thumping as they moved around, scanning their surroundings. Apart from the deep scar that scored the rock, they saw nothing unusual, and so lowered themselves back down the cliff face.

Ryder Han was waiting, shaking with anxiety.

"It's her—Cyclone Mei," Zhu Cong declared. The others froze.

"What about Guo Jing?" Jade Han asked.

"They descended on the other side, as far as we can tell," Gilden Quan replied. He went on to describe what they had seen.

"Eighteen years of hardship, and twelve of them were spent raising a fox," Ke Zhen'e said.

"The boy is loyal and honest, he wouldn't behave in such an ungrateful manner," Jade Han cried.

"Loyal and honest? If so, how could he spend two years training with that witch without saying anything?" Ke Zhen'e's voice was as hard as ice.

Jade Han did not know what to say, her thoughts were so tangled.

"Is that blind hag using Guo Jing to hurt us?" Ryder Han said.

"It looks that way," Zhu Cong said.

"But Guo Jing isn't capable of acting like that. We've known him since he was a child," Jade Han said.

"So she has kept him in the dark as to her true intentions," Gilden Quan said.

"His lightness technique has improved and his *neigong* inner strength is considerable, to be sure," Ryder Han said. "But his martial skills are still lacking. Why hasn't she worked on that?"

"She's using him, she doesn't want him to be truly competent," Ke Zhen'e said. "Guo Jing killed her husband, after all."

"Indeed," Zhu Cong said. "She wants him to kill us all, one by one. Then she will finish Guo Jing herself, her revenge complete."

Their brother's logic sent shivers through them.

Ke Zhen'e jabbed his staff into the ground. "We will go back and pretend we know nothing of this," he said. "When Guo Jing arrives, we will kill him. Then, when the witch comes to find him, we will fight her. Her martial arts may have improved, but she is still blind. It is not beyond us."

"Kill him? What about our bet with Qiu Chuji?" Jade Han said.

"Which is more important—our lives or a bet?"

No one replied.

"We can't!" Woodcutter Nan broke the silence.

"We can't do what, exactly?" Ryder Han asked.

"We can't kill him," Nan said, shaking his head.

"I agree with Fourth Brother," Jade Han said. "We must first investigate the truth before jumping to conclusions."

"This is serious," Gilden Quan said. "If we hesitate, if we let him know we know, who can say what will happen to us!"

"There will be terrible consequences unless we act now. This is Cyclone Mei we are dealing with."

"Third Brother, what do you think we should do?" Ke Zhen'e turned to Ryder Han.

Ryder Han was undecided, but the sight of his sister's tears moved him. "I have to agree with Fourth Brother. I cannot kill Guo Jing."

They had reached a deadlock: three favored killing their disciple, three preferred a more cautious approach.

"If Fifth Brother were here, he would agree with us," Zhu Cong said sadly.

This sent a stabbing pain through Jade Han's heart, and the tears poured down her cheeks in earnest. "We must avenge Fifth Brother. Let us do as Big Brother says!"

"Then let's go back."

The Freaks returned to their *ger* in silence, each nearly drowning in the swell of their own thoughts.

2

WHEN GUO JING CLIMBED TO THE TOP OF THE CLIFF, HE FOUND the Taoist waiting for him as usual. "Look!" the Taoist said, pointing at the rock.

Guo Jing approached and saw nine skulls gleaming in the moonlight.

"Twice Foul Dark Wind are back?" he said, a quiver in his voice.

"You know about Twice Foul Dark Wind?"

Guo Jing told the story of their fight on that bleak mountain top, the battle in which he lost his Fifth *Shifu* and killed Hurricane Chen. The memory made his body shake and he could barely talk. He was just a child back then and he only learned who the two ghastly figures were many years later from his *shifus*.

"Copper Corpse stopped at no evil, but he died by your hand!"

"My *shifus* frequently talk of Twice Foul Dark Wind. My Third and Seventh *Shifus* tell me Cyclone Mei must be dead, but Master Ke always says, 'Not necessarily!' But look! Iron Corpse is still alive." The Taoist saw another shiver go through the boy. "Did you see her?" Guo Jing asked.

"I arrived not long ago, but I spotted the skulls at once. She must have returned for you and your *shifus*."

"Master Ke blinded her. We aren't supposed to be so scared of her."

The Taoist took a skull and examined it. "Her kung fu is impressive indeed," he said, shaking his head. "I fear your *shifus* are no match for her. Not even if I were to help."

The man's words frightened Guo Jing. "Twelve years ago, when she still had her sight, she was unable to overcome my Masters. There were only seven of them then. Now we are eight. You will help us, won't you?"

The Taoist paused before answering. "I cannot understand how her fingers have come to be so strong and terrible. As they say, the good cometh not and those who cometh are not good. She must be confident that she can defeat you."

"Why did she arrange the skulls here? A warning? This way, we have time to take precautions."

"I imagine it is part of the practice of the Nine Yin Skeleton Claw. She probably assumed no one ever comes up here as it's so difficult to reach. We are lucky to have come across them."

"I must warn my *shifus*. At once!"

"Good idea. Tell them a good friend has asked you to pass on this message: They must not fight her; it's not worth it. Instead, you must all hide and think of a solution."

Guo Jing nodded and made his way to the edge of the cliff. But seconds later, the Taoist grabbed him around the waist and jumped, landing lightly behind the rock, where they hid. Guo Jing was about to ask what was happening when a hand cupped his mouth and he was pulled to the ground.

But he could not resist looking, so he raised his head back up above the rock.

A dark silhouette was rising up from behind the other side of the cliff, her long hair fluttering in the moonlight. She had in fact ascended by the more difficult side, but as she was blind, she most likely could not tell. The Six Freaks of the South had been lucky.

Cyclone Mei began spinning quickly and Guo Jing ducked back down. Then he remembered she was blind. By now she was sitting cross-legged on the rock he used for training, breathing slowly and deeply.

Some time passed, and then a cracking sound started echoing around them. First slow, then faster, like beans popping in hot oil. The noise was coming from her joints, but she was sitting perfectly still. Guo Jing had no idea what kind of *neigong* this was, but he became acutely aware of his own limitations in comparison.

The cracking went on for some time before gradually slowing again and coming to a halt. She then rose to her feet and pulled something from her waist. A silver snake? Guo Jing watched in amazement as he realized it was a very long whip.

His Third *Shifu* Ryder Han's Golden Dragon whip barely reached six feet, whereas Mei's must have been more than thirty feet long.

She turned slowly. The light from the moon caught her extraordinary features, but she was a gruesome sight. She had her eyes closed and her hair drooped across her face.

"Dear husband . . ." Her breathy whisper carried through the silence. "Do you miss me down there in the underworld?"

She held the whip with both hands. A deep laugh rose from within her and the whip began to dance.

It was a strange sight. She moved the whip slowly and he could hear no sound. A roll to one side, a flip to the other. Then she struck at a rock, shattering it. The rocks around her soon bore the scars. What was not clear in the dim light of the moon was that it was made from fishing-net rope plaited with copper and silver. Just then she struck at a stone and lifted it as if she had taken it in her palm. Guo Jing watched in astonishment. The whip then sailed through the air toward him, the dozen hooks fastened to it glinting in the moonlight.

Guo Jing clutched at his dagger. As the hooks came closer, he instinctively raised his blade to meet them. But just as quickly, he felt a tingle in his arm and he was on the ground just as a flash of silver passed above him.

It nearly went through my skull! Guo Jing thought to himself, cold with sweat. But the Taoist's movements had been quick and Mei was unaware that they were hiding so close.

She continued to practice a little longer before replacing the whip in her belt, performing some stretches and then making her way back down the cliff.

Guo Jing clambered to his feet.

"We'll follow her and see what she's up to," the Taoist hissed. He caught Guo Jing by the belt and together they too slid down.

Once at the bottom, they caught sight of Iron Corpse already some distance to the north. The Taoist hooked his arm around Guo Jing, who felt himself instantly a lot lighter, and they raced off at great speed across the steppe.

THEY STALKED her across the desert until day's first light started to appear in the east. The faint outlines of a camp made up of a dozen large *gers* appeared on the horizon. Mei disappeared into one of them.

They accelerated, avoiding the lookouts on patrol, and stopped close to a large beige *ger* that blended into the desert sands. They crept in the dirt, lifted a small corner of the tent, and peered in. Inside, they saw a man draw a blade. Just then he sliced it down on another man, who collapsed and, as he fell, he turned, so that he was facing Guo Jing and the Taoist.

"It's him! How come?" Guo Jing whispered, lifting the edge a little further. It was one of Temujin's personal guards. The man with the saber turned, and Guo Jing looked up at his face: Senggum, son of Ong Khan.

Senggum wiped the blood from his blade on the sole of his shoe and spoke. "No more doubts now, huh?"

"My brother Temujin is brave and resourceful," answered another man, hidden from view. "I fear your plan will not be easy to execute."

Jamuka, Temujin's sworn brother. Guo Jing recognized his voice.

"If you love him, why not warn him?" Senggum sneered.

"You too are my sworn brother," Jamuka replied. "Your father has always treated me with kindness; I won't betray you. What is more, Temujin hopes to swallow my army into his, I know this. Our oath of brotherhood is the only thing keeping me from breaking our alliance."

Are they plotting against Temujin? Guo Jing asked himself. How is this possible?

"Who moves first, wins," another man added. "If you let him attack, you'll both be in trouble. If you triumph, all Temujin's livestock, women, and stores of treasure will go to Senggum. His men will be incorporated into Jamuka's army and I will give Jamuka the title of 'Queller of the North.'"

This man had his back to Guo Jing, so he shuffled a little to one side in order to get a better look. He was swathed in expensively embroidered yellow brocade. The Sixth Prince of the Jin Empire.

Jamuka seemed moved. "I will obey, as long as my adoptive father, Ong Khan, gives me the order."

"If my father doesn't give the order, he will have offended the Jin Empire," Senggum replied in obvious delight. "I will ask him. He would never refuse the Sixth Prince."

"Soon our soldiers will move south against the Song," Wanyan

Honglie said. "If each of you bring twenty thousand men and help with the invasion, there will be yet further rewards."

"People say the south is beautiful, the streets are paved with gold and the women are delicate like flowers," Senggum said. "We would be delighted to go with the Prince and see for ourselves."

"That can certainly be arranged," Wanyan Honglie said with a smile. "I only worry there will be too many beautiful women to choose between."

The *ger* erupted with laughter.

"Tell me, how do you plan to deal with Temujin?" Wanyan Honglie paused, and then continued. "I initially asked him to help us invade the Song, but he refused me. He is clever, we mustn't raise his suspicions. You must be especially careful."

Just then the Taoist tugged at Guo Jing's sleeve. He turned and saw Cyclone Mei in the distance, her claws grasped around the figure of a man, as if interrogating him. Whatever she's doing here, for now my *shifus* are not in harm's way, Guo Jing thought to himself. First I must listen and find out what they are planning against the Khan.

He crept back into position.

"My son is betrothed to his daughter," Senggum was saying, "and he sent this man to settle on a date for the union." He pointed at the dead man. "I'll send one of my men at once and invite him to speak with my father tomorrow. He will come alone. I will position my men along the road. That way, no matter if he has heads and legs for three men, he won't get away."

"It is settled. Once we are rid of Temujin, we will raid his camp and kill them all."

Guo Jing was shaking with fury: how could anyone be so heartless as to plot against his own sworn brother? He leaned in to listen further, but felt the Taoist pull at his belt. He turned, and felt a rush of air at his ear as Iron Corpse swept past and on into the distance, a man dangling in her grasp.

The Taoist took Guo Jing by the hand and together they left the camp.

"She wanted to know where your *shifus* are," the Taoist hissed. "We've got to move quickly."

They sped across the desert sand, using the best of their lightness technique. By the time they arrived at the camp, the sun was already reaching its highest point in the sky.

The Taoist spoke. "I wanted to remain discreet, that is why I told you not to tell your *shifus* about me. But this is an emergency, such details are not important anymore. Go in and tell them that Ma 'Treasure' Yu of the Quanzhen Sect seeks an audience with the Six Heroes of the South."

This was the first time in two years of nightly meetings that Guo Jing had heard his name. He did not know who the man standing before him was, that his was a name revered all across the *wulin,* so he merely nodded. He ran to the *ger,* pulled back the cloth covering the doorway and called, "Master!"

Suddenly something grabbed hold of both his wrists. He felt a sharp pain at the back of his knees and he fell to the floor. "Haaaaa!" He looked up and saw above him an iron club making its way toward his head. He turned and saw his First *Shifu* Ke Zhen'e. Terror chased all sense from his body and he was left unable to defend himself. He scrunched into a ball, closed his eyes and waited for the deadly blow. Just then weapons clashed above his head and a body landed on top of him.

"Brother, no!"

He opened his eyes and realized it was his Seventh *Shifu* Jade Han. She was protecting him, but her sword had been knocked away by Ke Zhen'e's staff.

"Sister, you have always been too softhearted," Ke sighed, his staff clattering as it dropped to the ground.

Only then did Guo Jing see that it was Zhu Cong and Gilden Quan clutching his hands. His mind was a muddle.

"And your *neigong* master?" Ke Zhen'e sneered.

"Outside," Guo Jing stammered. "We've come to talk with you, my *shifus*. Cyclone Mei has come back. And she's looking for you. We followed her to Senggum's *ger*."

The Freaks were astonished to hear that Cyclone Mei had come to confront them during the hours of daylight. They took their weapons and rushed outside.

There, bowing before them, a Taoist with a long, wispy beard.

Still clutching Guo Jing's wrist, Zhu Cong turned to the boy. "What about the witch?" he spat.

"We just saw her," Guo Jing said.

The Six Freaks looked at Ma Yu with suspicion.

He took a step forward. "I have long heard of the valiant deeds of the Six Heroes of the South, and today I finally have the honor of making your acquaintance."

Zhu Cong nodded, his grip still tight on the boy. "Might I dare ask the Taoist's name?"

Realizing he had not introduced him properly, Guo Jing cut in. "His name is Ma Yu, of the Quanzhen Sect."

The Six Freaks were taken aback. They knew of Ma Yu, of course, also known by his monastic name Scarlet Sun, the first disciple of Wang Chongyang who had assumed leadership of the Quanzhen Sect upon their Master's death. Elder Eternal Spring Qiu Chuji was his younger martial brother. Ma Yu rarely made an appearance in the martial world, preferring to dedicate himself to meditation, so his brother Qiu was perhaps more famous. No one had ever seen Ma Yu fight, so the level of his kung fu skills was unknown.

"Elder Scarlet Sun of the Quanzhen Sect, please forgive us our impertinence. We did not know to whom he owed the honor," Ke Zhen'e said. "What brings the Master so far north? Is it related to the contest your martial brother challenged us to in Jiaxing?"

"My younger martial should be devoting himself to the Tao, but instead he likes to make bets and enter into duels," Ma Yu replied. "This is a violation of the principle of *wu wei,* action through non-action, and it is not behavior that behooves a monk. I have told him as much many times, but he will not listen. I have no intention of interfering in your contest, I make no inquiries in this regard as it has nothing to do with me. At most, I can acknowledge that you have entered into this arrangement in good faith, in the name of aiding patriots. No, I come not because of that. Two years ago I came across this young boy, and seeing that he was pure of heart I decided to teach him some techniques to strengthen his body and cultivate his mind, techniques by which followers of the Tao prolong life. This I did without asking permission from his *shifus,* the Six Heroes, and for that I wish to express regret and request forgiveness. I have taught him no kung fu and never claimed him as my disciple. He is my young friend, that is all. I wish to make it clear that I have not broken any code of the *wulin.*"

The Freaks were surprised, but had no reason to doubt his explanation. Zhu Cong and Gilden Quan let go of the boy's wrists.

"Boy, you were being taught by His Reverence Ma Yu?" Jade Han said, smiling and patting Guo Jing on the shoulder. "Why didn't you tell us? We accused you without cause."

"He . . . he told me not to say," Guo Jing stammered.

"Boy, do not speak of His Reverence so casually, that is most disrespectful," Jade Han said. Yet her expression told him she was not angry.

"Yes, His Reverence Scarlet Sun," Guo Jing said. For two years they had treated each other as equals, never using titles or formalities in word or conduct. Guo Jing had thought of him as his uncle, and Ma Yu had never been offended.

"I am a cloud with no fixed plan or destination," Ma Yu said. "I do not like to inform people of my wanderings. Please forgive my rudeness at having never visited, despite knowing the Six Heroes were close by." He bowed.

Ma Yu had held the Freaks in great esteem after learning the story of their journey north, but he also heard from Harmony Yin that Guo Jing was lacking in the foundations of *neigong* inner strength. He understood better than anyone else that adherence to the Tao demands selfless service to others and he was displeased in the extreme that his martial brother Qiu Chuji should leave such an important task as teaching a great patriot's son to the Freaks of the South. But no matter how he tried to convince him of the inappropriateness of his methods, Qiu Chuji would not relent. So, without telling anyone, Ma Yu made the journey north to teach Guo Jing and help the Freaks prevail. Could he really have come across the boy just by chance out here on the vast expanse of the northern steppe? Why else would he dedicate two years to the task? Had it not been for Mei's sudden appearance, he would have continued until satisfied that the boy possessed an adequate foundation in *neigong,* and then disappeared back south without anyone ever finding out, neither the Freaks of the South nor Qiu Chuji.

The Freaks bowed, impressed by Ma Yu's modest attitude. They saw in him a learned and virtuous man. The contrast with his rash and arrogant martial brother was plain to see.

Just as they were about to inquire about Cyclone Mei, they were interrupted by the sound of hooves, followed by a group of horses clattering past on their way toward Temujin's camp. Guo Jing knew them to be the messengers Senggum had sent to entrap the Khan and panic rose in him.

"Eldest Master," he said, turning to Ke Zhen'e, "I must go. I will be back soon."

Ke Zhen'e was still feeling guilty at having almost killed him minutes previously and his regard and love for the boy had only grown stronger. He did not want Guo Jing to encounter Mei out on the steppe by himself. "No, you must stay with us. You cannot leave."

Guo Jing wanted to explain his reasons, but Ke Zhen'e had already turned to Ma Yu and begun discussing their encounter all those years ago with Twice Foul Dark Wind, high up on the desolate mountain top. He was agitated—an unusual sight indeed. Master Ke was usually so composed. Yet Guo Jing decided not to interrupt. He would wait for a pause in the conversation to report what was happening over at Temujin's *ger.*

Just then a horse came galloping toward them. The rider was dressed in a short black fox-fur coat. Khojin. She stopped ten paces away and waved at Guo Jing. Guo Jing was afraid of incurring his Master's wrath, so instead he motioned for her to come closer.

Khojin's eyes were red and swollen as if she had been crying. She approached, sniffling. "Pa wants me to marry that man . . . Tusakha." Saying it out loud brought forth another round of tears.

"You have to go back and tell the Khan that it's a trap. Senggum and Jamuka are going to kill him!"

"Are you sure?" Khojin replied in shock.

"Absolutely sure. I heard them talking about it with the Sixth Prince. Go, quickly."

"I will!" Excited, she turned and sped back to the camp.

How can she be happy that they want to kill her father? Guo Jing said to himself. She hopes she won't have to marry Tusakha, he realized. He wanted to protect her, so the possibility that she might escape such a fate was to be welcomed. A smile spread across his face.

Ma Yu's words brought his attention back to more urgent matters.

"It's not that I wish to demean our collective capabilities," he was saying, "but Cyclone Mei is the true successor to the Lord of Peach Blossom Island. She has studied the techniques of the Nine Yin Skeleton Claw to perfection, and her use of the whip is subtle and creative; I fear it may even be the White Python, which has not been popular in the *wulin* for more than a hundred years. Of course, I am not saying that with eight of us defeat is inevitable, but I fear we will have to suffer greivous losses if we are to be rid of her."

"Her kung fu is deadly indeed," Jade Han said, "but the Seven Freaks of the South bear her a hate as deep as any ocean."

"I have heard it spoken in the *wulin* that your Fifth Brother Zhang and Flying Divine Dragon Ke Bixie were both killed by Copper Corpse. But as the Freaks in turn defeated him, it could be said that you have had your revenge. As the ancients said, it is easier to untie an enemy than to put him in knots. Mei is a widow now, blind and alone. Indeed, more than anything she deserves our pity."

The Freaks made no reply.

After a pause of some time, Ryder Han spoke. "We don't know how many die every year thanks to her sinister arts. Your Reverence, your compassion is admirable, but you cannot absolve evil or allow it to go unchallenged."

"She has come to us this time, we did not seek her out," Zhu Cong said.

"Even if we choose not to fight, we will never be safe so long as she wants revenge," Gilden Quan added.

"I do have a plan, but it requires forgiving hearts," Ma Yu said. "A show of mercy. A chance for her to redeem her sins."

Zhu Cong decided to let his eldest brother Ke Zhen'e speak for them.

"We, the Seven Freaks of the South, are coarse by nature and know only the power of physical force," Ke Zhen'e said. "We would be eternally grateful if His Reverence could show us a more enlightened path. Please explain."

Ke Zhen'e had understood from the Taoist's words that Mei's kung fu had advanced over the last twelve years and he was trying to save them from humiliation as much as from her poisoned grip. The other Freaks, having yet to understand this, were astonished by what they thought was a change of heart from their Master, an inclination toward benevolence above all else.

"Your charity will be rewarded by the heavens, valiant Brother Ke. Firstly, I would like to point out that Twice Foul Dark Wind were disciples of the Lord of Peach Blossom Island, Apothecary Huang the Alchemist. If he finds out we have killed Iron Corpse he will be most displeased and our problems will be manifold."

Apothecary Huang's kung fu was often spoken of in such absurdly exaggerated tones that Ke Zhen'e and Zhu Cong found it hard to believe he could be as formidable as people said. Yet Ma Yu was the most senior living Taoist of the *wulin*'s greatest orthodox sect. If he feared him, then there must be truth to the rumors.

"Master Ma is most cautious, and my brothers hold Your Reverence in the highest esteem. Please direct us to the correct path," Zhu Cong said.

"My plan may seem ambitious, arrogant even. All I ask is that the Six Heroes of the South do not laugh at it."

"The Master is too modest. The Seven Quanzhen Disciples of Wang Chongyang are admired throughout our lands." Zhu Cong's respect was indeed genuine, though he felt that Qiu Chuji had done little to deserve it.

"Our reputations rely entirely on the virtues of our late teacher," Ma Yu replied. "But it seems unlikely that Iron Corpse would attack the Quanzhen alone. Therefore, I would like to use our much-exaggerated reputation to scare her away. It is a dishonorable plan, to be sure, but the intention is noble and it will do no damage to the good name of the Heroes."

He began to explain the plan, but the Freaks could not hide the fact that they were insulted by Ma Yu's suggestion. What if Cyclone Mei had made progress in her dark arts? Or if Apothecary Huang came to her aid? They might perish like their brother Zhang, but that would do them no discredit. Yet Ma Yu was steadfast in his efforts to persuade them. An unequal contest brings no honor to the victor, he argued.

Ke Zhen'e listened with displeasure, but even he had to recognize the Taoist's prestige and the care he had taken of their student Guo Jing. It was clear he was trying to help them.

Together they ate and talked, and then made their way to the cliff. Ma Yu and Guo Jing were the first to ascend. The others watched Ma Yu's steady, secure steps as he followed behind the boy. His *neigong* inner strength kung fu was evident. He's certainly as accomplished as Qiu Chuji, they were thinking, only Elder Eternal Spring has found more fame throughout the south. More a question of personality than ability, they concluded. Once at the top, Ma Yu and Guo Jing released the end of a long rope and pulled the Six Freaks up behind them.

There, the Freaks laid eyes on the rock covered in the half-inch gashes Mei had scored across it. It looked more like the work of an axe than a whip. Ma Yu was not exaggerating, after all.

They sat down on the ground and crossed their legs. Dusk began to obscure the landscape around them and there they waited until close to midnight, by which time Ryder Han could take it no longer: "Why isn't she coming?"

"Shh, I think I hear her," Ke Zhen'e hissed.

They strained to listen against the silence, but only Ke Zhen'e could make out the sound of her footsteps several *li* in the distance.

They looked out into the darkness and there, caught in the moonlight, they saw what looked like a wisp of black smoke racing across the sand toward them. Within moments she was climbing. Zhu Cong glanced at Gilden Quan and Jade Han. Their faces were ashen and his must have looked the same.

At that moment she appeared. They could make out the shape of a figure strapped to her back. It wasn't moving. Was it dead? Guo Jing thought he might recognize Khojin's black fox-fur coat. He peered harder. If it wasn't Khojin, then who was it? His mouth was dry and he could not speak. Zhu Cong quickly placed his hand over Guo Jing's mouth and then called out: "Cyclone Mei is an evil demon-witch. Once I, Qiu Chuji, get my hands on her, she will be finished!"

Mei froze in surprise, and then ducked behind a rock, waiting for more. Ma Yu and the Freaks could not help finding the scene amusing, despite the gravity of what was unfolding. Guo Jing, however, was burning with fear for Khojin's safety.

"Cyclone Mei stacked these skulls, so she's been here before." It was Ryder Han who spoke. "All we have to do is wait."

Mei remained where she was, uncertain as to how many kung fu masters Qiu Chuji had brought with him.

"She has done us much evil," Jade Han replied, "but the Quanzhen Sect emphasizes compassion above all else. She must be given another chance."

"The Sage of Tranquility is tender of heart." Zhu Cong chuckled.

"No wonder our Master always said you came to the Way so effortlessly."

Central Divinity Wang Chongyang, founder of the Quanzhen Sect, was Master to seven of the greatest fighters of the *wulin*. Ma Yu, known by his Taoist name Scarlet Sun, was considered his first and best disciple. Then came Eternal Truth Tan Chuduan, Eternal Life Liu Chuxuan, Eternal Spring Qiu Chuji, Jade Sun Wang Chuyi, Infinite Peace Hao Datong, and finally the Sage of Tranquility, Sun Bu'er, who had been married to Ma Yu before he turned to a life of celibacy and meditation.

"Brother Tan, what do you say?" Jade Han said, turning to Nan the Merciful.

"She is deserving of the harshest punishment!"

"Brother Tan, you have made great progress of late in your Finger Brush technique," Zhu Cong continued. "Will you give us a demonstration when the witch arrives?"

"I rather think Brother Wang's Iron Foot would be more appropriate," Nan said. "He could kick her off the cliff and reduce her to a pile of bones."

Jade Sun Wang Chuyi was one of the most renowned of the Seven Disciples, close behind Qiu Chuji. He once stood for hours on the edge of a high ravine on one foot, as a bet, the wind beating against him and his fluttering sleeves. A crowd of martial artists who had traveled from the north watched in astonishment, giving him the name Immortal of the Iron Foot. He spent nine years living as a recluse in a mountain cave, practicing his arts. Qiu Chuji wrote a poem in honor of his skill, including the now famous couplet:

> *Nine summers he stood, greeting the sun,*
> *Three winters he embraced the snow as he slept.*

The exchange had been discussed in advance. Only Ke Zhen'e had ever spoken to Mei, so they were sure she would not recognize the others' voices.

Iron Corpse grew more alarmed as she listened. All seven Masters of the Quanzhen here, on the steppe? One noxious Taoist would be no problem . . . but seven?

The moon was still high in the sky, bathing the summit in its cold light. But it was not going to last for long.

"A bank of black clouds is coming in," Zhu Cong said quietly. "Soon we won't be able to see our own hands. We must be careful not to let the witch escape."

Mei knew that night's cloak would work to her advantage.

Guo Jing's gaze was still fixed on Khojin. Just then he saw her slowly open her eyes. She was still alive! He tried to wave at her not to move.

Khojin caught sight of her friend. "Help! Save me!"

"Shhh!" Guo Jing hissed back.

Mei froze. She then quickly pressed a finger against one of Khojin's pressure points and the girl went limp. Now she was suspicious.

"Harmony Yin, did you say something?" Zhu Cong said.

"I . . . Yes . . ." Guo Jing stuttered.

"I think I heard the voice of a young girl," Zhu Cong continued.

"Yes, I think you're right," Guo Jing replied.

What are the chances of me meeting all seven Masters of the Quanzhen Sect here, on this particular summit, so far out in the wilds of the north? Mei began to ask herself. It could be a trick. I cannot see them, after all.

Ma Yu watched as she slowly rose to her feet from behind the rock, and understood that her suspicions were aroused. If she realized it was all a lie and attacked, he would no doubt escape unscathed, but Khojin would certainly be sacrificed, as would some of the Freaks. Quick thinking was not his strong point, and, at this moment, he had not the slightest idea what to do.

Zhu Cong caught sight of Mei's long silver whip. She raised it slowly above her head. "Brother, you have been practicing the Twenty-Four Secrets of the Golden Gate and Jade Lock, as passed down by our Great Master, for years now. You must be quite the expert. Will you show us? Perhaps we could learn a few tricks."

"While I may be the eldest among us," Ma Yu replied, understanding Zhu Cong's plan, "I have been slow to absorb our Master's deepest teachings—I can replicate only a fraction of the full repertoire. What do I have to show you, my brothers?" His breathing was deliberate as he used it to carry his words loud and clear to where Mei was standing. Though modest in content, each word shook the valley walls and echoed against the rocks, carried on the cliff winds like a dragon's roar and eagle's cry.

Mei recognized his powerful *neigong* inner strength and lowered herself back behind the rock.

"I heard that she is blind in both eyes and deserves our pity," Ma Yu continued. "If she would promise to never again attack the innocent or cause trouble for the Six Freaks of the South, then we could let her go. Our Master was after all a good friend of the Lord of Peach Blossom Island. They held each other in great esteem. Brother Qiu, you are acquainted with the Freaks, why don't you try to negotiate. Tell them to abandon their hopes of revenge. If everyone decides to forgive what is in the past, the feud will be over." This time he spoke without the aid of his internal strength so as not to expose the Freaks as having lesser kung fu.

"Of course. But the real issue is whether Cyclone Mei will agree to a reconciliation," Zhu Cong replied.

Just then a voice sharp and cold like ice came from behind the rock. "May I thank the Seven Masters of the Quanzhen Sect for their kindness. I am Cyclone Mei." There she was.

Ma Yu had planned to frighten her away so that she could reflect on the matter by herself. But Iron Corpse was braver than he had given her credit for.

"As a lowly woman, I dare not seek advice from the Masters," she continued. "But I have long heard that the Sage of Tranquility is of consummate skill. May I ask that she shows me some of her moves?" She lifted her whip and waited for Jade Han's reply.

Guo Jing, meanwhile, was still concerned about Khojin, who was now lying motionless on the ground. Unable to stand it any longer, he rushed over to her and swooped her up into his arms. But Mei heard him and hooked her claws around his wrist. Using the inner strength he had been cultivating under Ma Yu's instructions, Guo Jing flicked Khojin toward Jade Han and, with a twist of his left hand, wrestled free. Mei responded quickly, seizing him again and pressing on his artery, paralyzing him.

"Who are you?" she hissed.

"Harmony, be careful!" Zhu Cong called out.

Zhu Cong's words had come just in time, as in his panic Guo Jing was about to give away his real identity.

"I . . . am Harmony Yin," he stuttered. "Disciple of . . . Eternal Spring." He had practiced the phrase at least forty times, but still he could not get the words out smoothly.

A young follower, but his *neigong* is of note, Mei said to herself. He managed to save the girl and free himself from my grip. I'd better keep my distance. She snorted and let him go.

Guo Jing ran back to the others and examined the five indentations she had left in his flesh. She had not used all her strength—that much he understood. She could have snapped his hand off if she so desired.

Mei was now no longer so keen to fight with the Sage of Tranquility. A thought came to her. "Elder Ma, could you explain to me what is meant by Conserve the Lead and Mercury of Immortality?"

"Lead is solid like the kidneys," Ma Yu began, "and mercury flows like water, like the body's internal heat. The principle of storing mercury and lead in the body in order to achieve immortality essentially means consolidating the kidneys and extinguishing the fires of the heart-mind, that is to say pent-up anger or worry. This can be achieved through breathing exercises."

"And what about Three Splendors Gather at the Crown, Five Forces to the Origin? My Master, Lord of Peach Blossom Island, gave the most beautiful explanations. I am wondering what the Quanzhen Sect says."

Ma Yu realized that she was asking him to explain the secrets of *neigong* inner strength kung fu. "Ask your own Master! Go, get out of here!"

Mei cackled. "Thank you, Elder Ma, for your wise reply."

She lurched upward, whipped the rock one last time and sailed off down the mountainside. It was a marvelous, terrifying sight.

They watched in relief as the cloud of black smoke sped across the desert sands. The witch was far away now, but they could not shake their fear quite so fast.

Ma Yu pressed on Khojin's pressure points and she came to life. They then laid her out on the rock so that she could recover.

"I never imagined she would be able to make such progress in just ten years," Zhu Cong said. "We Freaks would have encountered a terrible fate indeed had it not been for Elder Ma's generous help."

Ma Yu made a humble reply but his brow was furrowed and he could not hide his worry.

"While we may not have the greatest skills," Zhu Cong continued, "if there is anything Elder Ma would like us to do, please do not hesitate to ask."

"That witch caught me in a moment of inattention," Ma Yu replied.

"Did she injure you? Did she use some secret weapon?"

"No, no, nothing like that. It is that I fear the answer I gave to her questions will bring great trouble."

The Freaks were confused.

"Iron Corpse has achieved great heights in her external kung fu techniques. Even if my martial brothers Qiu Chuji and Jade Sun Wang Chuyi had been here to help, I doubt we could have defeated her. This only proves the exceptional talents of her Master, Lord of Peach Blossom Island. But it is her *neigong* inner kung fu that is lacking. I don't know where she managed to find the secret formulas of Taoist *neigong* practice, but she will be unable to comprehend them without the instructions of a *shifu*. Her lack of understanding has kept her progress to date in check, but I fear that my explanation will allow her to make considerable advancements."

"Or perhaps she will realize her mistake and stop this evil," Jade Han said.

"Let us hope so, or else it will prove even more difficult to stop her. It is all my fault for letting down my guard." He paused for a moment and continued. "But the skills taught on Peach Blossom Island are very different to those of the Quanzhen. How did she know to ask those questions?"

The others stopped and noticed as Khojin began to stir. She sat up and spoke. "Guo Jing, Papa didn't believe me. He's gone to visit Ong Khan."

"How could he not believe you?" Guo Jing cried.

"I told him that Uncle Senggum and Uncle Jamuka were plotting against him, but he laughed and said that I was just trying to get out of marrying Tusakha, and that I was lying. I said that you were the one who heard them and that made him even more suspicious. He said he would punish you on his return. He took three of my brothers and some of his men. I came to find you but that blind woman captured me. Did she bring me to you?"

You are lucky we were here, the Freaks thought to themselves, otherwise you would have five holes in your head by now.

"When did the Great Khan leave?" Guo Jing demanded.

"Hours ago. Papa wanted to get there as soon as possible. He didn't want to wait for morning, so they took their fastest horses. They must be very far away by now. Does Uncle Senggum really want to hurt Papa? What are we going to do?" She started crying. Guo Jing did not know what to say; it was the first time he had ever had to deal with a crisis of this magnitude.

"Guo, go back down the cliff, get your horse and ride out after the Khan," Zhu Cong said, taking charge. "We will send someone to determine what is going on. Khojin, you go and ask your remaining brothers to gather their men and go after your father."

Guo Jing was already making his way down the cliff face. Ma Yu lowered Khojin on a rope.

Guo Jing hurried back to his mother's *ger*, mounted his little auburn horse, Ulaan, and set off northward. The morning sun's first rays were drowning out the moon. His heart was racing as fast as his steed's hooves against the dirt. What if the Great Khan has already fallen prey to Senggum's trap? he thought to himself. What if I'm too late?

Guo Jing's horse loved to gallop, to feel its hooves pounding through the dust. Guo Jing tried to stop for a rest, fearing that it might stumble from fatigue, but as soon as he loosened the reins, it neighed and picked up speed again. The colt kept a steady breath and ran with no apparent effort.

Guo Jing was able to ride like this for hours due to his inner strength kung fu training. Three hours had passed when he spotted three ranks lined up farther ahead. There must have been at least three thousand men.

He rode closer. Ong Khan's banner. The men stood with arrows drawn, swords ready. They are blocking the road, Guo Jing said to himself. The Khan must be up ahead.

He squeezed his thighs and the horse shot on. He heard shouts and the drumming of hooves, but Guo Jing was already past them and gone.

Up ahead he could see another three companies of men lying in ambush. Farther on in the distance, the white hairs of Temujin's banner were edging on northward, accompanied by several hundred men on horses. Guo Jing pushed onward and drew up beside the Khan himself.

"Great Khan, you must turn around!"

Temujin stopped in surprise. "Why?"

Guo Jing repeated to the Khan all that he had overheard in Senggum's *ger* the previous evening, adding that the road behind him had been blocked. Temujin surveyed the boy with skepticism, trying to work out if it was a trick. Senggum had always been hostile, it was true, but his adoptive father Ong Khan put great trust in him. And how could his *anda* Jamuka plot against him? Unless this was the work of the Sixth Prince of the Jin Empire, sowing discord among the Mongols?

"Great Khan, if you send someone back, you will know I am telling the truth."

Temujin had survived incalculable battles; he was raised on plot and intrigue. The chances that Ong Khan and Jamuka were betraying him were slim, but something nevertheless told him he should be careful. It never hurt anyone to be too cautious . . . He turned to his second son, Chagatai, and ordered that he and Tchila'un should turn back to survey the situation. "Find out if the boy is right!"

They swung their horses around and sped away.

Temujin looked out across the land. "Take that hill and prepare!" He may have only had a few hundred men with him, but they were his best fighters. They galloped up to high ground and started moving stones and digging trenches.

Before long, clouds of dust rose in the south, quickly followed by thousands of men on horses chasing Chagatai and Tchila'un; Jebe could just make out the banners behind them.

"Ong Khan's men," he shouted.

They were divided into several teams and were trying to outflank Temujin's scouts. But Chagatai and Tchila'un were lying flat in their saddles, spurring their horses as hard as they could.

"Guo Jing, we will help them!" Jebe cried.

The two men galloped down the hill. Guo Jing's steed rushed in excitement to join the other horses and within moments he was close to Tchila'un. He felt a rush of air. Guo Jing released three arrows, hitting the first three of Ong Khan's men. He then drove his horse behind Chagatai and Tchila'un and continued firing. Another man fell. Jebe drew up beside Guo Jing and he too shot and killed several men. But with a continuous swell of soldiers crashing toward them, how could they possibly triumph?

Chagatai, Tchila'un, Jebe, and Guo Jing drew close to the hill where Temujin and the others were standing guard. Arrows rained down from higher ground, forcing Ong Khan's men to hold back.

Temujin kept watch from where he stood. Ong Khan's army was closing in from all sides. It would be near impossible to break their formation, so the best they could do, Temujin realized, was to employ their best delaying tactics. "Invite Senggum to come and speak with me," he roared.

Senggum ascended under an umbrella of a dozen shields. He was in high spirits and called out, "Temujin, time to surrender!"

"Please tell me first how it is I came to offend my adopted father Ong Khan so that he attacks me?"

"We Mongolians have lived in our separate tribes for generations, dividing our flocks between us," Senggum replied. "You tell me, Temujin, why it is you insist on violating the ways of our ancestors by mixing the clans. My father frequently tells us that, in this, you do wrong."

"We Mongolians live in subjugation to the Jin Empire which demands of us a tribute of tens of thousands of our cattle and horses each year," came Temujin's reply. "Do you think this is proper? We will starve if it continues. Why should we fear the Jin? They are a threat only when we fight each other. I have always had a good relationship with my adoptive father. There is no hatred between our families. This is the work of the Jin, they sow discord between us!"

Temujin's words moved Senggum's soldiers, who found he spoke with reason.

"We Mongolians are warriors, all of us," Temujin continued. "Why shouldn't *we* take gold and silver from the Jin, rather than giving away our best fleeces? Why should we be the ones to pay tribute? There are idle men among us, to be sure, but there are many who work hard to herd our cattle. Why should they toil and provide for the ones who refuse to do their part? Why not give them more reward? May the lazy be left to starve—they bring it on themselves!"

Mongolians were organized around a clan principle that held their cattle for all. Herds had been growing and the tribes had learned from the Chinese to use iron tools and weapons. But in reality, as Temujin knew, most herders wished to keep the fruits of their own labor, just as soldiers are reluctant to share the spoils of war with those who did not go to fight.

Senggum was disturbed by the effect Temujin's words were having on his men. "Lay down your weapons and surrender! All I have to do is give one signal with my whip and ten thousand arrows will come raining down upon you!"

The situation was becoming critical and Guo Jing did not know what to do. Just then his eye was caught by a young officer draped in a silvery gray sable coat at the foot of the hill. His horse was pacing and in his hand he carried a long broadsword. Tusakha, Senggum's son! The bully from his childhood, the boy who had tried to release leopards on Tolui. Guo Jing could not pretend to understand why Ong Khan, Senggum, and Jamuka were turning on Temujin. They had always lived side by side in peace. The only explanation he could come up with was a plot by Tusakha and his father, under the influence of the Sixth Prince of the Jin. Vicious lies. Maybe if I capture Tusakha and force him to admit it, then everyone can be reconciled? Guo Jing spurred his horse and sped down the hill.

Before anyone could stop him, he drew up to the young man.

Tusakha was startled by Guo Jing's approach and sliced his blade in defense. Guo Jing ducked into his saddle just in time, grabbed at Tusakha's left wrist and pressed on the artery in one of Zhu Cong's Split Muscles Lock Bones moves. Tusakha was rendered powerless and Guo Jing tugged him from his saddle.

Just then Guo Jing heard the whistle of something speeding through the air toward him. He squeezed his thighs, and with a lurch, his small horse leaped back up the hill.

"Fire!"

Guo Jing hauled Tusakha onto his saddle behind him. Senggum's men could not shoot at him for fear of hurting their commander's son.

Once at the summit, Guo Jing threw Tusakha on the ground at Temujin's feet. "Great Khan, it's all the fault of this beggar. He can tell you himself!"

Guo Jing's actions delighted Temujin and he placed the point of his lance on the young man's chest. Looking down at Senggum, he called, "Tell your men to retreat three hundred paces!"

Senggum had no choice but to comply. He ordered his soldiers to retreat back to their positions around the hill, forming a perimeter so that Temujin's horses could not break through.

Temujin praised Guo Jing for his bravery and told him to tie the captive's hands behind his back with his belt.

Senggum sent three messengers in succession to negotiate. The Khan would be spared if he released Tusakha. But each time Temujin sent the messenger back with his ears sliced off.

Deadlock. The sun edged down below the horizon. Fearing an attack once the light had faded, Temujin urged his men not to lose their focus.

As midnight drew near, a man dressed in white approached the foot of the hill.

"It's me, Jamuka. I wish to speak with my sworn brother Temujin."

"Come up!" the Great Khan replied.

His pace was slow at first, but once he caught sight of Temujin's commanding figure at the top he started to run as if to embrace him. But Temujin drew his sword from his belt and called, "You consider me your sworn brother, still?"

Jamuka sighed and sat down cross-legged on the grass. "Brother," he said, "you are already a tribal chief. Why do you insist on uniting the Mongols?"

"What is your opinion?" Temujin replied.

"The clan chiefs all say our ancestors have lived this way for hundreds of years. Why does Temujin want to change our traditions? The heavens will not allow it!"

"Do you remember the story of our ancestor Lady Alan Qo'a? Her five sons could not live in peace, so she invited them to come and dine with her. She gave them each an arrow and asked them to break it. This they did with ease. Then she tied together another five arrows and asked them to break them. Each son tried, but none was able to do it. Do you remember what she said to them?"

"If each of you stands alone, you will be broken as easily as an arrow," Jamuka said quietly. "But if united, no one and nothing can break you."

"And then what happened?"

"They joined together and conquered the steppe for future generations. They were the founders of our tribes."

"Exactly that! We too are heroes fit to stand beside Lady Alan Qo'a's sons, so why fight among ourselves? Why not unite and destroy the Jin?"

"But the Jin command a powerful army, their lands are scattered with gold and they live among mountains of rice. How can the Mongols defeat them?"

"So you prefer to live under their yoke?" Temujin snorted.

"We are not oppressed by them. Their Emperor made you Queller of Northern Uprisings!"

"I trusted them at first, that is true. But then I came to understand their greed. Every year they demand more. First they were satisfied with sheep and cows, then they wanted horses and now they want our men. What do we care for their war with the Song? Even if we help the Jin conquer the south, the land will belong to them alone. We lose soldiers, and for what? Are we going to feed our cattle on the sand on the other side of these mountains? If we fight, we fight the Jin!"

"But Ong Khan and Senggum don't want to betray them."

"Betray them? Ha! What about you?"

"Brother, I beg you, don't let your anger cloud your thoughts. Let Tusakha go. I guarantee personally that Senggum will release you."

"Senggum? I don't trust him and now I don't trust you."

"Senggum said himself: if a son dies, a man may produce more sons. But there can only be one Temujin! If you don't let Tusakha go, you will not live to see the sun rise tomorrow."

Temujin knew the two men well; they would certainly have him killed. If Ong Khan had been leading the attack, he might have had a chance. He drew his sword again and flashed it above him. "Temujin never surrenders, Temujin dies only in battle!"

Jamuka rose to his feet. "You surrendered in the past, when you were weaker than you are now. You give the spoils of war to your soldiers, telling them it belongs to them, not to the whole tribe. In this, again the clan leaders say you do wrong. It's against our traditions."

"But it pleases my young fighters! The clan leaders claim they cannot keep it because they want it for themselves. Such traditions make the fighters angry. Who do we need more? Brave soldiers or greedy, stupid clan leaders?"

"Brother, you have always acted alone, as if you didn't need the help or advice of the other clan leaders. You have also been sending messengers to persuade my soldiers to surrender and join you, promising them riches, that the livestock won't be shared among all the people of the tribe. Did you think I was blind to what you have been doing?"

Now you know that, we can never be reconciled, Temujin thought to himself. He removed a small pouch from inside his shirt and threw it at Jamuka. "The gifts you gave me on the three separate occasions we swore our loyalty to each other. Have them back. That way, when you cut your blade here," he said, drawing his finger across his neck, "you will be killing your enemy and not your brother." He paused, sighed and continued. "I am a hero, you are a hero. The steppe may be vast, but it's not big enough for two such as us."

Jamuka picked up the bag, reached for his own and placed it in silence at Temujin's feet. He then turned and walked back down the hill.

Temujin watched as he left. He stood for a long time without saying anything. He then took up Jamuka's bag and tipped out the stones and arrowheads of their childhood. He still remembered the games they had played. He then scratched a hole in the dirt with a dagger and buried his brother's gifts.

Guo Jing stood beside him. He understood the significance of the moment. Temujin was burying his most precious friendship.

The Great Khan stood up and looked out at the scene below. As far as the eye could see, Senggum and Jamuka's men had lit fires. It was as if the stars in the sky were being reflected across the grass-lands. He turned to Guo Jing. "Are you afraid?"

"I was thinking about my ma," Guo Jing answered.

"You are a brave fighter. An excellent fighter." He pointed to the fires. "And so are they! We Mongols have so many brave men, but all we seem to do is fight and kill each other. If we were united," he said, looking out to the horizon, "we could make all the world's grasslands ours!"

Temujin's words stirred Guo Jing's heart and he felt his admiration for him grow. "Great Khan, we will never be defeated by a coward like Senggum!"

"Exactly. Remember those words," Temujin said with a smile. "If we survive this, you will forever be a son to me." He leaned down and embraced the young man.

The sun was starting to climb in the sky and enemy horns began echoing around the plain.

"It doesn't look like help will be coming," Temujin said eventually. "I don't expect to make it down from here alive." Among the blasts of horns, sounds of weapons clanging and neighing horses drifted up on the wind. A dawn attack.

"Great Khan, my horse is swift. Why don't you ride it back and get help? We will hold them off. We won't surrender."

Temujin smiled and stroked the young man's neck. "If I, Temujin, were capable of abandoning my friends and generals in order to save myself, I would not be the Khan you see before you."

"You are right, Great Khan. I was wrong."

Temujin, his three sons, and his officers and soldiers all took their positions behind the mounds of earth they had piled up the previous day. Bows were aimed and ready.

Before long, three men broke free of the enemy ranks and ap-proached under Senggum's yellow banner, followed by four sol-diers on foot, dressed in black. Senggum on the left, Jamuka on the right, and there in the middle, the Sixth Prince of the Jin, Wanyan Honglie. He wore a suit of armor made of gold and carried an equally resplendent shield on his arm. "Temujin, how dare you betray the Jin Empire?"

Temujin's eldest son, Jochi, shot an arrow at the Prince but one of their retinue leaped up and caught it.

"Bring me Temujin!" Wanyan Honglie shouted. The black-clad foot soldiers began running up the hill at an unusual speed.

Guo Jing watched in amazement. They were using *qinggong* lightness kung fu; these were no ordinary fighters from the steppe. Jebe, Bogurchi, and the others began firing arrows but the men skipped between them. Our men are brave and strong to be sure, Guo Jing said to himself, but they cannot compete with such accomplished masters of the martial arts. What are we going to do?

One of the men made it to the top. Ogedai tried to block him with his saber, but just as the man in black raised his arm, Guo Jing struck out at his wrist. He stumbled back three steps and looked up at the young, sturdy man shielding Ogedai.

"Who are you?" he said in Chinese, unable to conceal his surprise at finding such an excellent swordsman among Temujin's men. "Tell me your name."

"My name is Guo Jing!"

"I've never heard of you. Surrender!"

Guo Jing glanced around him and saw the other three men in black had also reached the top and were engaged in hand-to-hand combat with Tchila'un, Bogurchi, and the others. Again, he thrust his sword at the first man, who blocked and returned with all his weight.

Just as Senggum's soldiers were preparing to follow behind up the hill, Muqali placed the point of his blade on the back of Tusakha's neck. "Come any closer and I'll kill him!"

"Your Highness," Senggum said, turning toward Wanyan Honglie, "instruct your men to retreat. We will find another way. My son must not be hurt."

"Don't worry, he will be fine," Wanyan Honglie said with a smile. In fact, he was hoping Temujin would kill the young man and thereby cement a lasting hatred between the tribes, thus preventing them from ever uniting.

Senggum's soldiers froze but the Prince's men in black kept fighting.

Guo Jing made use of the techniques of the Yue Maiden Sword Jade Han had taught him. His opponent possessed considerable internal strength, but Guo Jing's sword was swift and it swooped and flicked around the man's body. He was visibly flustered.

Having seen off several of Temujin's men, the man in black's three companions ran over. One rushed forward with a spear. "Elder Brother, let me help!"

"Stay where you are and admire your brother's technique instead!" the first man countered.

Guo Jing dropped his knee and raised his elbow in a Soaring Phoenix Rising Dragon, flicking his blade upward as he did so. The man lurched back but the blade tore through his sleeve.

"Who is your Master?" the man shouted, breaking away from immediate danger. "What brings you here, to the northern steppe?"

Guo Jing maintained a defensive stance and answered in the dialect of the rivers and lakes as his Masters had taught him. "I am a disciple of the Seven Heroes of the South. And may I ask it is with whom I am conversing?" he managed to stutter. He had been practicing such polite phrases for some time now, but this was his first chance to make use of them and his nerves had garbled them.

The man with the saber glanced at his martial brothers. "What would be the point of telling you who we are? Your ancestors will never know!" At this, he thrust his blade forward.

Guo Jing knew the extent of their power, having already engaged them in combat, but the sophistication of the moves Jade Han, his Seventh *Shifu,* had taught him was such that he was not merely on the defensive. The man with the saber struck at Guo Jing's lower body in a Search the Sea, Behead the Dragon. Thirty thrusts of their weapons passed in quick succession. He was growing nervous and his moves were becoming more erratic. He made a lunge at Guo Jing's middle. Guo Jing twisted and flexed his blade in a Pick the Fruit, rolling on the ground before aiming at his arm.

The young man isn't defending himself, the man in black thought. This is my chance! Before your sword can reach me, I will have cut you in two!

But Guo Jing knew what he was doing. Using his *neigong* inner strength, he dodged the blade with only the slightest movement of his wrist. He then thrust his sword toward the man's heart.

The man screamed, dropped his saber and knocked Guo Jing's sword away with his hand. He was just in time; the tip only penetrated his flesh half an inch. More devastating was the cut to his hand, which was gushing blood. He jumped back.

As Guo Jing bent down to pick up the man's weapon he heard a rush of air behind him. Without turning, Guo Jing kicked back, knocked the spear away and followed with the saber. The second man in black shrank back and Guo Jing stepped forward, performing a Seize the Basket by the Handle. The moment his palm touched the spear, he could sense that this opponent was much slower than the first. He easily twisted and grabbed hold of it with his left hand, before sliding his blade down the shaft with his right. The man let go as the saber swept to within inches of his fingers.

Guo Jing was buoyed. He cast the saber down the slope below and took hold of the spear. The third man howled and came running at him with two short axes. Guo Jing had studied spear technique with his Sixth *Shifu,* and in that moment all the eccentric moves he had been taught flashed before him. He feigned a moment of weakness, to his opponent's delight. The man cried out and lurched forward. But moments later, he was doubled over in pain as Guo Jing's foot jabbed into his stomach. The force sent him hurtling back and the axes he was holding ricocheted toward his head.

The axe was knocked away just in time. An iron whip. The last remaining man in black. Sparks flashed, the axe flew one way and the man landed with a thump on the ground. It took him some time to realize what had just happened.

Then, with a roar, he reached for the axe head and leaped up again.

Three clashes later and Guo Jing's weapon was in two pieces. He had no choice now but to use Bare Hand Seizes Blade kung fu to defend himself.

Shouts came from further down the hill. The soldiers were watching in indignation; for two men to fight a lone unarmed opponent was an insult to any basic code of combat. Guo Jing may have been their enemy, but somehow they found themselves cheering him on.

Bogurchi and Jebe had been watching and could stand it no longer. They drew their sabers and hurled themselves into the fray, as did the other man in black. Temujin's men were formidable on the battlefield, where their bravery knew no bounds, but they were not practiced in the intricacies of one-on-one combat with members of the *wulin*. After a minute or so, their weapons had been knocked away and they were forced to retreat. Guo Jing leaped to defend Bogurchi, striking his palm against the spine of one of the men. He answered by slicing his blade at Guo Jing's wrist. Guo Jing retracted his hand and jabbed his elbow into another who was attacking Jebe.

The men in black were now focused on one goal only: to kill Guo Jing. They were not interested in the two Mongolian generals and closed in on the boy. Below, the soldiers cheered louder and their insults grew even uglier, but the men in black paid them no heed. One picked up his spear. Saber, spear, whip, and axe; Guo Jing's eyes darted between them. His only weapon was his lightness kung fu as he danced between the blades.

Guo Jing held them off for at least twenty moves, before the saber sliced his arm. Blood was now pumping onto his clothes. Just then a tumult broke out below and six of Senggum's men broke free from their ranks and began running up the hill. Assuming they were yet more of Wanyan Honglie's men coming to join the attack against Guo Jing, the soldiers jeered and cursed.

Temujin's men at the top aimed their arrows.

"Wait! It's the Freaks of the South!" Jebe called out. "Your *shifus* have come, Guo Jing!"

So exhausted he could barely see, Guo Jing was overcome with relief and rallied his spirits.

Zhu Cong and Gilden Quan were the first to arrive and the danger their student was in was instantly apparent. Gilden Quan launched himself forward and blocked all four weapons with his scales. "Shameless dogs!"

Their hands trembled from the force and the men in black knew at once they were dealing with a more accomplished fighter. They backed away, allowing Zhu Cong to check Guo Jing's wounds. Within moments, the other Freaks had joined them.

The man with the saber understood the situation had changed and they would most likely be defeated. But it would be a considerable loss of face if they retreated back down the hill. How could they continue to serve the Sixth Prince?

"The Six Freaks of the South?"

"That is correct." Zhu Cong smiled. "And who may I ask are you?"

"We are disciples of the Dragon King, Master of the Daemon Sect."

The Freaks had not been expecting this. These men in black had been willing to fight four against one; such a violation of the code of the *wulin* had led them to assume they were rogue bandits without a master. But contrary to appearances, their *shifu* was one of the most well-respected fighters of the south, Dragon King Hector Sha.

"How dare you abuse the Dragon King's good name? How could such a patriotic and brave master have disciples as low-down and contemptible as you?" Ke Zhen'e's voice was as icy as the northern wind.

"Abuse his good name?" the man with the axe said, holding his free hand against his stomach where Guo Jing had kicked him. "That man you dare to chastise is Shen the Strong. This is my second brother, Wu the Bold, and my third brother, Ma the Valiant. And I am Qian the Hardy."

"It appears you are telling the truth," Ke Zhen'e said. "The Four

Daemons of the Yellow River. With such a reputation in the *wulin*, why lower yourselves to fight four against one?"

"Four against one? Your student fights with the Mongols, it is we who are outnumbered." This was Wu the Bold.

"Third Brother," Qian whispered, turning to Ma. "Who is this pompous blind fool?"

But Ke Zhen'e had heard him and he was enraged by the insult. He tapped his staff on the ground and launched himself forward, grabbing Qian by the collar and throwing him back down the hill. The other Daemons of the Yellow River were momentarily paralyzed with fear and within seconds they had been similarly discharged.

The soldiers above and below were cheering now. Covered in sand and flushed with embarrassment, the four men staggered to their feet. They had been lucky; had the ground been harder they would have broken many bones.

At that moment, shouts rose up as plumes of dirt clouded the horizon. A murmur spread through Senggum's ranks as the front line made ready.

These were Temujin's reinforcements! The Great Khan was much relieved and their arrival gave him the confidence to proceed with the fight. Temujin pointed in the direction of Senggum's left flank. "Take that side first!"

Jebe, Bogurchi, Jochi, and Chagatai led the charge. Shouts came up on the wind from the relief troops. Muqali held Tusakha in his arms and placed his blade against the young man's neck: "Let me through! Let me through!"

Senggum was about to send men to intercept the attack when he caught sight of his son in the general's grip. This moment of hesitation allowed Temujin's best men to descend the hill. Jebe aimed an arrow at Senggum's head and released. Senggum ducked but the arrow caught him in the cheek and he fell from his horse. With their commander in chief injured, Senggum's men scattered.

Temujin began the next charge, and thousands of Jamuka's soldiers

rode forward to meet it, their ranks thinned by the arrows that followed the Khan. Temujin knew Jamuka to be a skilled commander with an army to match. Senggum was mediocre in comparison and was merely protected by a powerful father.

Some miles in the distance, Tolui was approaching, riding a large globe of dust. Tolui had in fact struggled to get the Generals to come with him after being left alone by his father and three older brothers back at the camp—he was young and did not carry his father's seal— so had come with only a few thousand younger soldiers. Concerned that his return would not have the desired impact, Tolui conceived of a most ingenious idea: they would tie branches to the tails of their horses, therefore creating a mighty display on the horizon. It worked.

Ong Khan's army had always revered Temujin and now they saw he had yet more reinforcements on the way. His men, Jamuka's, and the remnants of Senggum's turned and fled.

With the enemy forces now scattered, Temujin's army could return to their camp, encountering Khojin and a small company of soldiers on the way.

3

THAT EVENING, TEMUJIN HELD A BANQUET TO REWARD HIS men. But to the party's indignation, Tusakha was placed in the seat of honor. "Three toasts to Tusakha," the Great Khan called out.

"I owe a debt of gratitude as mighty as any mountain to my father Ong Khan and my brother Senggum, who have always treated me with such kindness. There is no reason for hate to spread between our families. I now beg for forgiveness for my wrongs and present my father and brother with the finest gifts I possess. I bear no grudge in my heart for all that you have done and in return I will prepare my daughter for marriage. Together we will host a sumptuous feast for all the tribal chiefs. Tusakha, you will be my son-in-law and thus my son. From this day forward, our families must be united and never let ourselves be divided by plots and discord."

Tusakha, relieved just to still be alive, nodded his agreement. But throughout his speech, Temujin had been clutching at his chest and coughing. Could Temujin Khan be injured? he wondered.

"Today," the Khan began, as if hearing his question, "I was hit by an arrow. It may take me many weeks to recover, otherwise I would accompany you back myself." He pulled out his hand from under his robes and it was smeared with bright red blood. "Do not wait to get married. I fear it will take too long."

Temujin's officers had watched the scene unfold with increasing outrage. Why was he in such a hurry to marry Khojin to Tusakha? It made him look scared and weak before Ong Khan. One of his commanders had lost a son in the defense of the hill. Enraged by what he was hearing, he drew his saber and ran at Tusakha. Temujin stepped in, dragged him outside and, with the crowd as his witness, beat him thirty times with his club until the commander fainted from the loss of blood.

"Lock him up. On the third day, he and his family will be beheaded." Temujin then fell to the ground in pain.

THE NEXT day, Temujin sent Tusakha home with two carts of gold and furs, one thousand plump sheep, one hundred of the finest battle horses, and an escort of fifty soldiers. He also included in the retinue one of his most eloquent men, who would beg forgiveness of Ong Khan and Senggum. When the time came for them to leave, Temujin was too weak to ride his horse and so bid a frail farewell from his stretcher.

Eight days after Tusakha's departure, Temujin called his officers together. "Gather your men and make ready. We are going to attack Ong Khan."

Temujin's commanders were shocked.

"Ong Khan's army is larger than ours," Temujin continued. "The only way for us to beat them is to take them by surprise. The gifts and the wound were all a ruse to throw them off guard."

They were impressed by the Khan's cunning. Temujin then ordered the commander he had beaten and imprisoned be set free, and bestowed on him a handsome reward. The commander was delighted to hear of the Great Khan's plan and knelt to express his gratitude and beg for the honor of leading the attack. His request was granted.

Temujin divided his army into three columns and together they set off under the cover of darkness, using little known trails through mountain valleys. Shepherds they met along the way were forced to join them so that no word of the attack could precede them.

Ong Khan and Senggum had indeed feared retribution by Temujin and had maintained vigilance at first. But when Tusakha returned with so many great treasures, a simpering ambassador, and news of Temujin's wound, they were reassured. Guards were recalled and time was given over to feasting with the Sixth Prince of the Jin and Jamuka. How were they to know that a force was coming that would shatter the ground beneath them?

Temujin's army arrived while the sky was dark and the raid sent panic through the camp. Such was their surprise that Ong Khan's men barely put up a fight. Ong Khan fled west, as did Senggum, where they were later killed by the Naiman and Liao respectively. Tusakha was trampled in the confusion. Wanyan Honglie escaped under the protection of the Four Daemons of the Yellow River and made for the Jin capital.

Abandoned by his soldiers, Jamuka took five bodyguards and made his way to Tangnu Mountain. But they set upon him while he was eating his mutton and delivered him straight to Temujin.

Temujin, however, was furious. "You betrayed your commander? How can I let you live?" They were then decapitated with Jamuka as witness. "Brother, should we make peace?"

"I cannot face you or the world after what I have done," Jamuka replied, tears soaking his cheeks. "I can only ask my sworn brother that you let me die without bleeding, so that my soul will stay with my body."

Temujin was quiet. "I will grant your request," he said at length, "and you will be buried where we used to play as children." Jamuka knelt before the Khan, who turned and left. He ordered his men crush his brother with something heavy and be sure not to let him bleed.

Now there was no one left among the Mongols who could match Temujin's power. He called the tribes together on the banks of the Onon River and brought the various armies under his command. Most of the men gathered that day submitted to his authority and he was given the title of Great Khan of all Mongolia, Genghis Khan, to rule with the strength of all the seas.

The Great Khan rewarded his most deserving men, the Four Great Generals, Muqali, Bogurchi, Boroqul, and Tchila'un, while his officers Jebe, Jelme, and Subotai were promoted to the same rank.

Guo Jing's outstanding bravery during battle did not go unnoticed and he too was made general. Not yet twenty, he was to stand among such excellent men and call them his equal.

As they drank and ate, the Great Khan's soldiers came in turn to toast and drink with him. Once merry, Temujin turned to Guo Jing and said, "Boy, I have one more gift for you. It is my most precious possession."

Guo Jing knelt down as a gesture of gratitude.

"To you I give my eldest daughter, Khojin. When the sun rises tomorrow, you shall be known as the Prince of the Golden Blade!"

The generals and soldiers whooped and cheered and began chanting, "Hail the Great Khan's son! Prince of the Golden Blade!"

Tolui was overjoyed as he locked his sworn brother in a tight embrace.

But Guo Jing was in a daze. To him, Khojin had always been like a little sister, he felt no other kind of love toward her. His youth had been devoted to the study of the martial arts, he had given no thought to romance. Panic rose within him at the Khan's words.

Everyone saw his dumbstruck expression and laughed.

Once the banquet was over, Guo Jing went to report the news to his mother. Lily Li was silent for some time before instructing her son to invite the Six Freaks to speak with her.

The Freaks congratulated Lily Li on her son being thus honored. But she said nothing in reply and instead fell to her knees and kowtowed.

"Auntie, please, get up," they said. "Why so formal?"

Jade Han helped her to her feet.

"I must thank the Six Heroes; it is due to your training that my son has become a man," Lily Li said. "Words cannot do justice to my gratitude. But now I have a problem and I need your advice." She then told the Freaks about the marriage agreed by her late husband and his sworn brother, Ironheart Yang. "It is an honor to my family that the Great Khan wants my son to be united with his," she said. "But if Brother Yang's wife gave birth to a daughter and I don't keep my husband's promise, I will not be able to face them in the next world."

"Don't worry about that, Auntie," Zhu Cong said with a smile. "Ironheart Yang's wife gave birth to a boy!"

"How do you know that, Master Zhu?" she said in astonishment.

"A friend of ours in the Central Plains wrote us a letter. He wishes us to take Guo Jing south to meet Yang's son, to compare their kung fu."

All these years, the Six Freaks had never told Lily Li or Guo Jing about their bet with Qiu Chuji, avoiding Guo Jing's questions about the Taoist Harmony Yin. They had realized that Guo Jing would be unable to fight Yang Kang to the best of his abilities if he knew the whole story.

Zhu Cong's words excited Lily Li. She asked after Ironheart's wife, Charity Bao, and for any news they had about the boy. But the Freaks could give her no answer. They would take Guo Jing south to meet the young man. If they could find Justice Duan along the way, so much the better. Then Guo Jing would come back and marry Khojin.

Guo Jing went to report their decision to Genghis Khan.

"While you're there, bring me back the head of the Sixth Prince of the Jin, Wanyan Honglie," Temujin said. "It is all his fault that my sworn brother Jamuka betrayed me and lost his life. How many men do you need?"

Having unified the Mongols, Genghis Khan was now a serious threat to the Jin Empire. Confrontation was inevitable. Having met Wanyan Honglie on several occasions, Temujin knew that he was intelligent and must be dealt with as soon as possible. Of course, the true reasons for his rift with Jamuka were not so simple. Temujin had overturned centuries of tradition and actively appealed to Jamuka's men to join him. Their oath of loyalty was already broken, even if he preferred to place the blame on outside forces.

Guo Jing had grown up on his mother's stories of the evil deeds of the Jin, and his battle with the Four Daemons of the Yellow River had only reinforced his hatred.

If I take my six *shifus,* I'm sure we can succeed, he mused. But soldiers with no knowledge of the martial arts would only be a hindrance. He looked up to the Khan and answered, "I will travel with my *shifus,* I don't need any more men."

"As you wish. We are still weak and cannot yet take on the Jin directly. You mustn't let them know of our intentions."

Guo Jing nodded. The Khan then gave him ten ingots of gold for the journey and offered the Six Freaks some of the treasure recovered during the defeat of Ong Khan. Guo Jing's Mongolian friends also offered him gifts.

"Brother," Tolui said. "People in the south are clever and not to be trusted. Be careful."

THREE DAYS later, Guo Jing and the Freaks went to visit the grave of Zhang Asheng and pay their respects. They then returned to say goodbye to Lily Li, before heading out on the road south. Lily Li watched the silhouette of her son on his horse disappear over the horizon. She recalled his birth on that snowy battlefield and felt a twinge in her heart.

After some ten *li,* Guo Jing spotted two white condors high above them, and moments later Tolui and Khojin came riding up to bid them farewell. Tolui gave Guo Jing a fine black fur coat taken from Ong Khan's treasure store.

Khojin knew of her father's decision and she looked on in silence, her cheeks flushed.

"Say something, Sister!" Tolui urged. "I'm not listening." He laughed and moved away.

Khojin bowed her head and paused. "Come back soon!" She looked up at him again.

Guo Jing nodded. "Was there anything else?"

She shook her head.

"Then I have to go."

She did not move. Guo Jing approached and took her awkwardly in his arms. He rode over to Tolui and embraced him too. With a kick to his horse, he then rode off to catch up with the Freaks, who by this time were some way ahead.

Khojin was much vexed by Guo Jing's stiff and cold goodbye. He had shown not even the slightest tenderness or sign of love. She cracked her whip hard, staining her horse's beautiful white coat with specks of fresh blood, and sped back to the camp.

CHAPTER SEVEN

FOR THE MAIDEN

I

THE SIX FREAKS OF THE SOUTH AND GUO JING KEPT MOVING AS long as there was light, making their way in a southeasterly direction out of the grasslands.

They were heading for the fortress town of Kalgan, some four hundred *li* north of the Jin capital. It was the first time Guo Jing had laid his feet on Chinese soil and there was a lightness in his heart. Everything was new to him. He squeezed his thighs and felt the wind whistle in his ears as his horse bolted along coppiced roads and past small brick houses, until Ulaan stopped by an inky stream of flowing water next to an inn. Guo Jing dismounted to wait for his *shifus*.

Taking pity on the tired horse, Guo Jing took out a piece of cloth and proceeded to wipe the sweat from its coat. Quickly he pulled back in astonishment; the material had turned a crimson red. He wiped the young horse's right shoulder and found still yet more blood. Tears of self-reproach collected in his eyes. Why had he not stopped earlier to let the animal rest? Had his neglect caused permanent damage? He threw his arms around its neck. But Ulaan seemed to be in fine spirits and not in the least bit of pain.

Guo Jing surveyed the road to see if Ryder Han was approaching so that he might tend to the colt. Just then he heard the sweet tinkle of bells followed by the sound of four camels plodding toward him from the main roadway. Two were snowy in complexion and all four were straddled by men also dressed in white. They approached the inn and the riders drew their mounts to a halt. Guo Jing noticed the finely embroidered cushions padding the saddles.

Guo Jing was a child of the steppe's deserts, but white camels were rare and he had never seen such fine animals. He could not take his eyes off them. The riders were only a few years older than him, in their early twenties he guessed, each one as delicately handsome as the last. They leaped from the camels and made for the inn. Guo Jing was enraptured by their expensive robes, fringed at the neck by the finest fox fur. One of the young men glanced across at Guo Jing, blushed, and lowered his head. Another glared at him and growled, "What are you staring at, little boy?"

Flustered, Guo Jing looked away. He heard them laugh. "Congratulations," one of them mocked in a girlish voice. "He likes you!"

Guo Jing's ears burned and he was just deciding whether he should leave when Ryder Han came clattering toward him on his horse, Wind Chaser. Guo Jing quickly explained that Ulaan was bleeding.

"How could that be?" Ryder Han approached the animal and stroked its shoulder, before lifting his hand up to the light and breaking into laugher. "That's not blood, it's sweat!"

"Sweat?" Guo Jing stammered. "Red sweat?"

"Young man, this is a most valuable horse, I thought you knew that."

Guo Jing was just relieved he had not injured it. "But, Third *Shifu,* how can sweat look like blood?"

"My own late *shifu* once told me that, long ago, way out west in the Kingdom of Fergana, they kept celestial horses whose sweat was red as blood, and who could run as if possessed of wings. Of course, no one has ever seen one and I assumed it was just a legend. I certainly never imagined you would end up riding one!"

The other Freaks had arrived in time to hear Ryder Han's story. Together they went inside and found a table, and Zhu Cong, who was well-read in the classics, began to explain. "The story appears in the *Records of the Grand Historian,* as well as the *Book of Han.* Imperial envoy Zhang Qian returned from his expedition to the western lands and reported to Emperor Han Wudi that he had seen just such a heavenly horse in the Kingdom of Fergana. The Emperor ordered a life-sized version to be cast from one thousand *jin* of gold and sent it back to the west in exchange for one of the animals. The King sent back word: 'The Fergana Celestial Horses are treasures of the Kingdom and cannot be gifted to Han Chinese.' The envoy, considering himself able to speak on behalf of his Emperor and the mighty dynasty of the Han, replied in anger and with words most uncouth, striking the golden horse right there in the King's Great Hall. Incensed by such rudeness, the King ordered the envoy's decapitation and confiscated the Han Emperor's gift."

"What happened next?" Guo Jing sat wide-eyed and watched as Zhu Cong paused to sip some tea. The four young men in white were similarly mesmerized by the story from where they sat at a nearby table.

"Third Brother," Zhu Cong said as he lowered his teacup, "you are the horseman among us. Do you know where the Celestial Horses came from?"

"My late *shifu* told me they were a cross between domesticated and wild horses."

"Correct. According to the historical records, wild horses were known to gallop all over the mountains outside the capital, Ershi, but they were impossible to catch. The people of Fergana, however, came up with a most ingenious idea. One spring evening, they led some of their female horses to the foot of the mountains and let them free. They were later rounded up and brought back to the city, where they gave birth to these most precious beasts. Guo Jing, young man, your horse might have traveled thousands of miles from the Fergana valley."

"What did the Emperor do?" Jade Han asked, eager to hear the rest of the story. "Did he give up?"

"Give up? A Chinese Emperor? No, he sent tens of thousands of troops to Ershi under the command of General Li Guangli, giving him the title of Commander of Ershi. But once they passed through the treacherous Jiayu pass, they had to travel through desert. Supplies soon ran out and they lost most of their men before being forced to retreat back to Dunhuang, where they could send to the Emperor for help. In his anger, the Emperor sent envoys to the pass with swords and ordered them to chop off the heads of any soldiers who dared to retreat back into Chinese land. General Li was stuck in Dunhuang."

At that moment, a faint sound of bells interrupted Zhu Cong's story as more camel riders arrived at the inn. This time only one of the animals was white. Guo Jing watched as four more handsome young men in white robes fringed with fox fur entered. They joined the others at their table and ordered more food.

"Of course, the Emperor felt the humiliation most acutely, so he ordered another two hundred thousand men to be dispatched, this time with adequate supplies. But even in such numbers, the Emperor feared they were too few, so he ordered all criminals, petty officials, merchants, and sons-in-law who lived with the families of their wives to report for service. He then chose two of the Empire's finest horsemen, investing one with the title Legate of the Whip and another Legate of the Rein, and provided them with only the best horses. The Han Emperor despised merchants; Sixth Brother Quan, it wouldn't have been a good time for you. But, Third Brother Han, you would have been most in demand." Zhu Cong chuckled.

"Why were sons-in-law who lived with their wives' families to be punished?" Jade Han asked.

"In those days, men who married into a woman's family did so only out of poverty. In fact, they were bought by the families as slaves. Recruiting these men into the army was a way of punishing the poor. General Li and his men besieged Ershi for forty days, killing thousands until the nobles of Fergana beheaded their king in fright and surrendered. They presented the Celestial Horses to the Han as a gift. The Emperor was delighted and General Li and his men were rewarded with gold and titles. So many perished, and for what exactly? Emperor Wudi gathered his highest officials in a banquet and wrote a song, declaring only the dragon fit to befriend such a fine beast."

The camel riders listened silently to Zhu Cong's story, casting envious glances every now and again at the wine-colored horse outside.

"But it's hard to believe that such a wonderful animal could come from cross-breeding with wild horses alone. And since they only obtained a few, they were cross-bred again with our local horses, meaning that, within a few generations, their sweat was no longer red like blood."

The Freaks and Guo Jing continued chatting as they ate their noodles.

Whispering together, the camel riders on the other table started to form a plan. But what they did not know was that Ke Zhen'e could hear every word, despite the distance between their tables and the general hubbub of the inn.

"We have to do it before he gets on the horse, otherwise we'll have no chance of catching him."

"But it's too crowded. And he's not alone."

"If the others get involved, we'll kill them all!"

Why were these young girls so vicious? Ke Zhen'e thought to himself as he continued to slurp his noodles, never giving any sign that he could hear them.

"We shall offer this magnificent horse to the young Master and he can ride it north to the capital," one of them said. "He will be even more admired and no one will even think of the Ginseng Codger or Lama Supreme Wisdom again!"

Ke Zhen'e had heard of Lama Supreme Wisdom Lobsang Choden Rinpoche, of course, a man of great learning from an esoteric school of Buddhism in the northern plains of Kokonor, known across the south and west for his Five Finger Blade kung fu. The Ginseng Codger came from beyond the Great Wall, far up in the north.

"Master doesn't need this horse to strike fear into the people!" another of the company said.

"Of course not, crowds form like chickens admiring a crane wherever he goes. His prowess is clear for all to see."

"We have encountered many outlaws out on the roads these past few days," said another, "all men under Butcher of a Thousand Hands, Tiger Peng. Perhaps they too are heading for the capital? Will we have another chance if we don't take the horse now? What if they capture it?"

Ke Zhen'e froze. Tiger Peng was a terrible outlaw who controlled much of the mountainous area surrounding the Jin capital in Yanjing. He commanded many thousands of men, all as ruthless as him. Why would they be heading for Yanjing? Was that where these eight young women were from?

Their hushed whispers continued. They decided to wait by the side of the road outside the village, where they could capture Guo Jing's horse. Their plan confirmed, the conversation turned to gossip.

"You are the one the young Master prefers."

"He's thinking of you right this very moment!"

Ke Zhen'e scrunched his brow; he could barely endure such senseless girlish chit-chat, but still he kept listening.

"What reward do you think awaits us if we present the Master with such a wonderful horse?"

"For you? A few more nights in his bed, I should imagine," giggled another.

The young girl protested and rose to her feet, but was only met with more laughter.

"Control yourselves, don't give us away. I don't think it's going to be that easy."

"The woman who sits with him, she has a sword. She must know how to fight too. She's rather attractive. If she was ten years younger, I'm sure the Master would fall madly in love with her."

Ke Zhen'e grew angry. This "Master" could not be an honorable man. He listened as they finished their noodles and went outside to mount their camels.

Ke Zhen'e turned to Guo Jing. "Boy, what did you make of those young women? Do they look like fighters?"

"What women?" Guo Jing replied.

Ke Zhen'e looked confused.

"They were dressed as young men," Zhu Cong explained to Ke Zhen'e. "Guo Jing, you didn't notice that they were women in disguise?"

"Have any of you heard of the Master of White Camel Mount?" asked Ke Zhen'e.

None of them had. Ke related the discussion that had just taken place at the neighboring table. The Freaks were stunned to hear of such audacity, but could not help finding it funny.

"I noticed that two of them had particularly big noses and blue eyes," Jade Han said. "I don't think they were Chinese."

"Indeed, those white camels are native only to the deserts of the west," added Ryder Han.

"They spoke of outlaws gathering in the north. It must be a plot to attack the Song. This could be a calamity for our people. We must stop them."

"But the competition in Jiaxing is drawing close," Gilden Quan replied.

It was indeed a conundrum.

"Let the boy go on ahead by himself!" Nan the Merciful said, breaking the silence.

"Let Guo Jing go to Jiaxing alone and we join him once we have sorted this business in the north?"

Nan nodded.

"Not a bad idea," Zhu Cong said. "The time has come for Guo Jing to be more independent . . ."

But Guo Jing did not look happy at the thought of parting with his teachers.

"You are a grown man now," Ke Zhen'e scolded. "Don't act like a child!"

"Go ahead and wait for us in Jiaxing," Jade said gently. "We will be there before the new moon comes into view."

"We never explained to you what exactly is to take place at Jiaxing," Zhu Cong began. "But the most important thing is that, at midday on the twenty-fourth day of the third lunar month, you must go to the Garden of the Eight Drunken Immortals. Whatever happens, you must be there."

Guo Jing nodded.

"These women won't be a problem on such a fast horse," Ke Zhen'e said. "Don't bother fighting them; you have more important things to do, so don't waste your time on such trifles."

"And if they really are so bold as to try to cause you trouble, the Seven Freaks of the South will stop them!" Ryder Han exclaimed.

It had been more than ten years since Zhang Asheng's death, but still they could not get used to referring to themselves as six. Their brother was always with them.

"I'm not sure where this White Camel Mount is, but it sounds like a formidable place," Zhu Cong said. "It's best to avoid any confrontation with them."

Guo Jing took leave of his *shifus*. Having witnessed their protégé single-handedly take on the Four Daemons of the Yellow River, the Freaks were confident that he had absorbed the lessons they had taught him. And while they did have to deal with this gathering of outlaws in the Jin capital, it was also part of a young man's training in the *jianghu* to travel alone. Only then would he learn the things a teacher could not pass on.

The Freaks imparted their last piece of advice.

"If all else fails, run!" said Nan the Merciful. But he knew very well that Guo Jing was not one to give ground, even if his opponent was a master of superior skill.

"The martial arts are without limit," Zhu Cong added next. "Every peak sits under the shadow of another, so every man may meet one stronger than himself. This is true for even the most accomplished masters. When faced with an opponent of considerable skill, the real fighter knows to retreat, practice, and wait for another opportunity to prevail. Never strip the mountain bare and you will not want for firewood. These are not the actions of a coward. And indeed, they are especially pertinent when faced with many foes, rather than just one. Remember your Fourth *Shifu*'s words, young man!"

Guo Jing nodded and kowtowed, before mounting his horse and heading south. He felt a great sadness to be parted from them; they had spent every day together for the past twelve years. Tears gathered in his eyes and began to wet his cheeks. His thoughts also turned to his mother, alone in the desert. She did not want for clothes or food, as she was being looked after by the Khan and his sworn brother Tolui, but he knew she too must be feeling lonely.

HE RODE for ten *li* before the road cut between high mountains. Above him, craggy rock formations hung ominously. It was the first time he had traveled alone in such a strange and foreign landscape. He placed his hand on the hilt of his sword and gazed ahead down the road. His Third *Shifu,* Ryder Han, would be most angry if he knew how scared he was.

The road began to ascend, becoming ever more narrow and precipitous, before disappearing behind a large rock. As Guo Jing turned the corner, four white shapes appeared on the road before him. Four of the young women in white, dressed as boys, riding camels. They were blocking the road.

Guo Jing pulled sharply on his reins. Keeping his distance, he called to them: "Hello there! Please let me pass!"

They laughed. "Little boy, why are you scared? Come closer. We won't eat you."

Guo Jing's cheeks turned hot. What should he do? Approach slowly and talk, or rush at them and start fighting?

"Nice horse you have there!" called another. "Come closer, let us take a proper look."

She spoke as if he were a little child, which angered him, but the road was perilous; to the right the rock face was like a wall and the drop to his left was sheer and absolute. Mist cloaked the way ahead. My *shifus* told me not to go looking for a fight, he thought. If I charge at them with my horse, they will have to let me pass.

He lifted his sword, squeezed his thighs and his trusty Ulaan shot forward.

"Move aside!" Guo Jing cried. "Or I will knock you into the valley!"

What happened next took only seconds. One of the women jumped from her camel and threw herself at Ulaan's bridle. With a loud whinny, Guo Jing's horse flew into the air, through the high mountain clouds, and up over their heads, before landing safely on the other side. They could only watch in amazement.

Behind him, he heard them curse. He turned, just in time to catch sight of two objects flashing in the sunlight as they approached. He knew better than to try and catch them, for fear that they were poisoned, so he whipped the leather cap from his head and caught them before he could be hit.

"Very nice!"

"Impressive kung fu!" called another.

Guo Jing looked into the cap: two silver darts. These are deadly! We are not sworn enemies, Guo Jing thought in alarm, and yet they are willing to kill me for a horse!

He carefully stored the darts in his pouch and spurred his prize colt on, for fear of meeting the next four women.

He rode like this, high up in the clouds, for nearly two hours, covering some eighty *li* without coming across a trace of them. He allowed himself a brief rest before pressing on, arriving in Kalgan before night fell. It would take them three days to cover the same distance on their camels, so he reckoned he was safe now.

2

KALGAN SITS AT THE MEETING POINT BETWEEN NORTH AND south China, a lively trading center specializing in furs. Guo Jing rode through the city gates and looked around in amazement. He had never seen such a large city. Everything was new to him. He stopped before an inn, hunger gnawing at his stomach. He tied his horse to the post in front and went inside, where he ordered a plate of beef and a kilo of the local flatbread. He ate in the manner of the steppes, rolling the meat in the bread and tearing chunks out of it.

But his meal was interrupted by the sound of shouting outside. Fearing that someone might be stealing his precious horse, he ran to the door. But Ulaan was quietly munching on his fodder. The noise came from two men who worked at the inn. They were taunting a young, gaunt boy dressed in rags. He must have been only a few years younger than Guo Jing, his leather cap full of holes and his cheeks so smudged with dirt that he would have been hard to recognize had they been the best of friends. The boy was clutching a piece of steamed bread and all he could do was laugh, revealing a row of bright white teeth completely at odds with his overall appearance. There was a remarkable intensity to his big, black eyes.

"Go on! Get out of here!"

"I'm going," the boy replied. He turned, but before he could leave the other man who worked at the inn called back at him.

"Leave the bread!"

The boy placed it on the ground by his feet: a white, round steamed bun blemished by five round, black fingerprints. There was no way they could sell it now. Enraged, one of the men launched a fist at the boy, who ducked.

Guo Jing watched, feeling pity for the hungry beggar. "Come now, there's no need to fight! I'll pay for the bun." He picked up the bread and handed it back to the boy.

But instead the boy turned to a nearby dog and said, "Disgusting!

Here, you have it," and threw it at the mutt. The dog pounced on it with gratitude.

"Shameful, giving a perfectly good bun to a dog!" one of the inn men cried.

Guo Jing did not know what to say. Was the boy not hungry? He returned inside to finish his food, but the dirty young boy followed, took a seat nearby and proceeded to stare at him as he ate, greatly embarrassing Guo Jing.

"Do you want some?" Guo Jing said finally.

"Yes please." He smiled. "I've been alone so long, I was looking for someone to talk to." He spoke in the dialect of the rivers and lakes of the south.

Guo Jing was delighted to have someone speak to him in his mother's tongue. The young boy took a seat at the table and Guo Jing asked the waiter for some tableware. But the waiter was displeased at this new guest's filthy appearance, so it took a few requests before he reluctantly brought over a bowl and set of chopsticks.

"You consider me too poor to eat here?" the boy said directly to the waiter. "You mistake me. I fear even your best dishes would not satisfy my palate."

"Is that so?" the waiter replied. "We would be happy to serve them to you, but my real concern is, can you pay?"

"Will you treat me to whatever I order?" the boy said, turning to Guo Jing.

"Of course!" Guo Jing said, and then turned to the waiter. "Another pound of roast beef and half a pound of mutton liver!" These were the finest delicacies he could imagine. "Do you drink wine?" he asked the boy.

"Wait," the boy said to the waiter. "First we will eat some fruit and nuts, four dried, four fresh, two sour-salted and four preserved in honey."

The waiter looked surprised. "Which fruits would you like?"

"I doubt you serve anything of note in a poor little inn like this," he said, "so we'll have to make do with dried lychees, longans,

271

steamed jujube, and ginkgo nuts. As for the fresh, give us whatever's in season. And we want sliced, perfumed sour cherries and sour plums with ginger. Can you get them here? And the honeyed? Hmm. Rose-scented kumquats, grapes, sugar-coated peach, and some pear, done in the style of Lord my Master." His Mandarin was far from perfect, but it was passable.

The waiter was impressed and was no longer haughty with the boy.

"I take it you don't have any fresh fish or seafood to have with our wine," the young man continued. "So we will have to be content with eight dishes of whatever you've got."

"What do the sirs like in particular?"

"Of course, they need everything to be explained down to the last detail." The boy sighed. "Petal-dressed quail, fried duck's feet, chicken-tongue soup, drunken deer tripe, pan-fried beef done two ways, rabbit slivers in chrysanthemum, flame-cooked venison and . . . pig's trotter in ginger vinegar. We'll take these simple dishes, I don't anticipate you have anything more refined."

The waiter's mouth was by now agape.

"Those are all rather expensive dishes, sir," he replied. "The chicken-tongue soup and duck's feet alone will be most costly as they require the slaughter of many animals."

"This gentleman is paying," he replied, pointing at Guo Jing. "Are you questioning whether he has the means?"

The waiter glanced at Guo Jing's fine sable coat. I will take that in lieu of payment if he doesn't have enough, he said to himself. "Is that all?"

"We will also have another twelve dishes to accompany the rice, and eight sweets. That is all for now."

The waiter did not dare to ask what exactly these should consist of, fearing that the urchin might name dishes the inn could not supply. Instead he returned to the kitchen and told them to prepare their best.

"And what can I get you to drink?" he said upon his return. "We have Bamboo Leaf, a sorghum wine, aged for ten years. How about that to start?"

"Fine. We can take that to begin with."

The waiter came with the fruit and nuts. Guo Jing marveled at each plate. Never had he eaten such delicious food. The boy spoke continuously, telling stories of the south, their local customs and the deeds of famous men. Guo Jing was captivated by his incredible knowledge, which clearly went beyond the culinary. Guo Jing had learned to recognize only a few basic characters in between his martial arts lessons. But this young man appeared every bit as cultivated as his Second *Shifu,* Zhu Cong. *And here I was taking him for just a poor beggar,* he thought to himself. *Chinese men are very different from those on the northern steppe.*

Not an hour later the dishes had all arrived—enough to cover two tables pushed together. Guo Jing's companion merely picked at the plates, however, and hesitantly sipped at the wine. Suddenly he called the waiter over.

"This wine is only five years old! How dare you try to cheat us?"

"Please, sir"—the manager came rushing over—"your palate is most exquisite. Our little inn did not have sir's requested wine in stock, so we had to procure some from a nearby establishment, the Eternal Celebration. It's not easy to get vintage wine in Kalgan."

The boy waved for them to take it back. Having just learned that Guo Jing had come from Mongolia, he resumed their conversation, asking Guo Jing all about the desert wilds of the north. The Freaks had told Guo Jing not to reveal his identity while on the road, so he related only anecdotes about hunting hares and wolves, shooting eagles and racing horses. The boy listened with fascination, clapping his hands and laughing like a little child.

Guo Jing felt an instant ease with him, the likes of which he had never known before. This was only strengthened by the fact that the boy spoke his mother's dialect. He had grown up in the desert alongside his good friends Tolui and Khojin, but the Great Khan kept his beloved son close and Tolui had had less and less time to spend with Guo Jing of late. He often bickered with Khojin, who was headstrong and usually wanted him to do as she wished. Theirs was not the easiest of relationships. Guo Jing was taciturn and found it difficult to express himself. Most people found it necessary to probe him with questions to get him to speak. Jade Han teased him for taking after Nan the Merciful, as if words spoken out loud cost their weight in gold. But now, sitting with this young man he had only just met, he talked nonstop, sharing everything save for his martial arts training and his connection to the Great Khan Temujin.

Guo Jing lost himself in the moment while relating a particularly exciting encounter with a wild animal, and without any thought to propriety, grabbed the boy's hand. To his astonishment, it was soft and smooth and somehow almost boneless. The boy blushed and looked away, revealing the alabaster skin of his neck. It was perfectly clean, not at all smudged in dirt like his cheeks, Guo Jing noticed.

"The dishes have gone cold," the boy said, gently pulling his hand back.

"Yes, but they're still delicious," Guo Jing said.

The boy disagreed.

"Then let's have them warm them up," Guo Jing suggested.

"No, that spoils the food." He called over the waiter and ordered him to throw away the cold food and prepare the same dishes anew. The innkeeper, cooks, and staff were puzzled, but did as the boy requested. Guo Jing wanted to please his guest, and having never been entrusted with money before, he was not sure of its worth. The boy's company alone was enough to warrant such extravagance.

The new dishes arrived, but again, the boy ate only a few mouthfuls before declaring himself full.

"This street child is playing you for a fool," the waiter muttered to himself as he glanced over at Guo Jing, before bringing him the bill. Nineteen *taels,* seven *mace,* and four *candareens.* Guo Jing handed the waiter an ingot of gold and told him to change it into silver and settle the account.

A northerly wind was blowing fierce as they left the inn. The boy shivered. "My sincerest gratitude. Farewell."

But Guo Jing could not stand to see the boy head into such a cold night wearing such scant clothing. He placed his black sable coat on the boy's shoulders. "Brother, I feel as if I've known you my whole life. Take this against the wind."

He slipped four ingots of gold into one of the pockets, leaving himself four more for his journey. The boy left without even saying thank you, and began to trudge against the weather, before turning around for one last look.

Guo Jing was standing beside his bridled horse, watching him. The young man waved and Guo Jing ran over to him. "Does my brother need anything?"

"I didn't ask you your name," he said and smiled.

"Yes, we forgot. My family name is Guo, my given name Jing. And you?"

"My family name is Huang, my given name Lotus." His companion looked at him meaningfully, but Guo Jing did not know what a lotus was and thus could not understand the significance of the revelation.

"Where are you going? I am heading south; if you are going the same way we could go together."

"I'm not going that way," Lotus said. Then, after a pause, "But I'm still a bit hungry."

"Then let's get something to eat!" Guo Jing said, despite being very full from their first meal.

Lotus led Guo Jing to Kalgan's premier eating establishment, the Eternal Celebration, a richly adorned inn decorated in the southern style favored by the courtiers of the Song. This time, Lotus ordered four plates of pastries and buns and a large pot of Dragon Well tea. Though it was considered a delicacy from his ancestral homelands, Guo Jing had never before tasted such a weak and tasteless drink. But conversation picked up where they had left off.

"I'm not sure where to go next, but I think I should go north and find myself a pair of white condors just like yours!" Lotus declared.

"They're pretty rare," Guo Jing said.

"Then how did you come across them?"

Guo Jing smiled but did not answer the question. How is such a delicate young boy going to survive the harsh northern winds? Guo Jing asked himself. "Why not go home? Where do you live?"

"My father doesn't want me back," Lotus replied, her eyes moist.

"Why?"

"He was keeping a man hostage and I took pity on him, bringing him food and chatting to him. My father was furious, he shouted at me. So I ran away in the night."

"I'm sure he's worried and wondering where you are. What about your mother?"

"She died many years ago. When I was very little."

"I think you should go home."

Lotus started to cry.

"I'm sure he wants you back."

"So why hasn't he come looking for me?"

"How do you know he hasn't? Maybe he hasn't been able to find you?"

"Maybe you're right," Lotus said, smiling through the tears. "I'll go home once I've finished with my adventures. I have two white condors to tame first."

Guo Jing related his encounter with the eight women dressed in white and disguised as men who wanted to steal his horse. Lotus was intrigued.

"Big Brother," Lotus began, "I want to ask you for something. But I fear it is something you value highly and you won't want to part with it."

"Anything."

"Would you give me your horse?"

"Gladly," Guo Jing replied without hesitation.

In fact, Lotus was teasing him. It was clear that Guo Jing felt a great attachment to the animal, and they had only just met. But his reply took her by surprise and she buried her face in her sleeve.

Guo Jing watched awkwardly. "What's the matter, Brother, are you unwell?"

Lotus looked up. The tears had cleaned her cheeks, revealing a jadeite glow beneath. "Let's go," she said.

Guo Jing paid and together they went outside. Guo Jing took his horse by the reins and spoke to it, caressing its mane.

"You will now go with my friend here. Be good and do as he says, and no more of your foul temper!" He then turned to Lotus. "Brother, up you get!"

The horse was not usually given to allowing other people to mount it, but it had grown calmer over the passing days and now it had special instructions from its master. Lotus jumped up into the saddle. Guo Jing let go of the reins, gave the horse a light clap and watched as they disappeared into a cloud of dust.

Guo Jing stood watching until they had faded on the horizon before turning back to the inn. It was late, and he settled into a room. But just as he was about to blow out the candle, a scratching started at his door. Was it the boy? The thought made him feel giddy.

"Brother, is that you?"

But the reply came in a voice considerably older and croakier: "Yes, it's me. What are you so excited about?"

Guo Jing opened the door cautiously and, to his surprise, there in the flicker of the candlelight, he saw five men. He peered closer and felt a shiver go up his spine. The Four Daemons of the Yellow River, one with a saber, one with a spear, another carrying a whip, and there, the twin axes. The fifth man was thin, with a long face. He looked to be around forty. Guo Jing made out three large lumps on his forehead. He was one of the ugliest men Guo Jing had ever seen.

This last man pushed Guo Jing aside with a sneer, and entered the room. He sat himself down on the hard bed and turned to look at Guo Jing. The light from the candle fell upon the three bumps on his forehead, casting his whole face in shadow.

But it was the eldest of the Four Daemons who spoke, Shen the

Strong, wielder of the Spirit Cleaver: "This is our martial uncle Browbeater Hou, the Three-Horned Dragon. Show your respect."

Guo Jing was surrounded; there was no way he could overcome all four Daemons and Browbeater Hou all by himself.

"What do you want?" Guo Jing said, cupping his fist. But there was an edge to his voice.

"Where are your Masters?" Browbeater Hou asked.

"My *shifus* aren't here."

"Ha, then you shall live another day at least. I couldn't kill you now, people would say the Three-Horned Dragon took unfair advantage of a weak opponent. But tomorrow, at noon. I will be waiting for you and your *shifus* in the forest of black pines, ten *li* west of here."

He left before Guo Jing could reply. Wu the Bold, carrier of the Soul Snatcher whip, pulled the door shut behind them and pulled across the latch.

Guo Jing blew out the candle, sat on the bed and watched their shadows move across the paper window as they kept watch outside. Just then he heard a noise on the roof, a weapon striking tiles and then a voice: "Don't even think about trying to run away, young man. I'm watching you!"

Escape was impossible. Guo Jing lay down on the bed, his eyes fixed on the ceiling. How was he going to get out of the fight tomorrow? But he was asleep before he could think of a plan.

The next morning, one of the inn boys brought noodles for breakfast and hot water so that Guo Jing could wash. Qian the Hardy was visible outside, clutching his pair of axes known as the Great Reapers and keeping guard.

His *shifus* were who knew where, and could not help him now. He had no choice but to fight and die like a man. "If all else fails, run!" His Fourth *Shifu's* words rang in his ears. But he had to at least try to fight first. The fact of the matter was, he could have easily escaped, as Qian was alone at that moment, but he wasn't known for his quick-wittedness. Browbeater Hou was convinced the Freaks could not be far away, and they would have to show up when presented with a challenge.

Guo Jing sat on his bed, practicing the breathing techniques Ma Yu had taught him. Qian had entered and was standing before him, spinning his axes and barking suggestions for how he could improve. But Guo Jing ignored him, until the sun approached its highest point, when he rose to his feet.

"It's time," he said to Qian.

Guo Jing settled his bill with the innkeeper and the two of them made their way to the forest of black pines to the west. Qian ran on ahead, leaving Guo Jing to enter alone.

Guo Jing gripped his whip and crept through the undergrowth. He moved slowly, his breath tight and alert, but after almost one *li*, he was still yet to see another soul. Only the occasional squawk of a bird broke the silence. He grew ever more nervous as he went.

Why not hide? Guo Jing thought to himself. Hiding's not running away!

But just as he was preparing to slip into a nearby bush, a voice came from above: "You bastard! You toad! Coward!"

Startled, Guo Jing jumped back. He looked up and then burst into laughter; there, in the branches above him, the Four Daemons of the Yellow River were tied up and hanging by their feet. They wriggled like caterpillars caught in a spider's web; there was no way they could get free. The sight of Guo Jing only made them more furious.

"Are you having fun?" Guo Jing shouted up, not bothering to conceal his delight. "I won't disturb you." He started to walk away but turned back. "Wait, how did you end up like that?"

"Damn you, we were taken by surprise. Hardly an honorable way to fight!" Qian shouted back down at Guo Jing.

"Young man." Shen spoke next. "Let us down if you're brave enough and we will decide this honorably. One on one, of course."

Guo Jing could not be called intelligent, but he wasn't that stupid. "I am perfectly happy to acknowledge your superior bravery without fighting you." He smiled. He was well aware, of course, that Browbeater Hou was not among them, and he had no desire to wait for his arrival.

Guo Jing made a quick departure and headed back to the city, where he bought a new horse. But he could not help wondering who it was who had helped him. The Daemons of the Yellow River had most excellent kung fu; tying them up like that was no small feat. And what happened to Browbeater Hou? My *shifus* have always said, you must never decline an invitation to fight. I showed up; it's not my fault he didn't.

3

THE JOURNEY CONTINUED WITHOUT INCIDENT AND HE ARRIVED at the capital of the Jin Empire before nightfall. Known to the Chinese as Yanjing, Zhongdu's riches dwarfed even those of the former Song capital at Kaifeng and the new capital of Lin'an. For Guo Jing, a boy of the desert, it was a marvel. Home to more than a million inhabitants, the streets were lined with decorative redbrick buildings with painted doors, and crowded with ornate carriages. Merchants stacked their storefronts with a multitude of goods, the likes of which Guo Jing had never seen before, as the fragrance of tea leaves wafted into the street. Music hung in the air; colors, sounds, and smells overwhelmed him. Guo Jing did not know which way to look.

He was hungry, but he was too intimidated to enter one of the more luxurious-looking restaurants, so he chose an unassuming stall, where he gulped down a bowl of rice before continuing to explore. Suddenly cheers broke out and he saw a crowd gathered up ahead.

He approached and slipped between the spectators to get a better look. In the middle of the circle of people he saw the words DUEL FOR A MAIDEN embroidered in red upon a large white banner. Beneath it, two people were fighting, a rotund man in yellow and a young girl dressed in red. She had considerable skill, Guo Jing could tell right away. Her movements were balanced and well thought out. The man was no match for her. The girl lowered her guard and the man advanced with a Double Dragon Flies the Cave, launching his two meaty fists at her shoulders. She leaned to the side and then planted her left shoulder into his flank. The crowd cheered. He looked up from where he had landed, embarrassed and covered in dust, before slinking away.

She neatened a stray strand of hair and took her place beneath the banner. Guo Jing looked at her more carefully: she looked to be around eighteen years of age and had a most elegant figure. The shadow of the fluttering banner flickered across her pretty features. On either side of her an iron spear and two short halberds had been planted into the dirt.

The girl turned and whispered something to a nearby middle-aged man. He nodded and stepped forward. He clasped his hands in a gesture of respect and addressed the crowd:

"I, your humble servant Mu Yi, have traveled from Shandong to your great city. I seek neither fame nor fortune, but my daughter has reached the age at which she may put comb to her hair and yet she is still without a betrothed. She has declared that she desires neither wealth nor nobility in a future husband, merely a man expert in the martial arts. It is for this reason we stand so boldly before you and propose this challenge. All unmarried men below the age of thirty are eligible, and I promise my daughter's hand as long as they can over-come her in one single move. We have come from the south because all masters in the land of the rivers and lakes are already engaged, or else have been too cowardly to take up the challenge. But we have heard much of the bravery of the men in the north, home to many valiant warriors. Do please forgive my boldness!"

He looked to be a sturdy man, but Guo Jing could not help but notice the slight hunch in his back. White flecks had turned his hair a speckled silver and wrinkles marked his face. He had a melancholy air and his dress was coarse and patched—a contrast to the vibrant colors of his daughter's outfit.

Mu Yi fell silent and waited. No one stepped forward. The crowd dared only lob vulgar insults about his daughter's ripening beauty. He looked up at the black clouds gathering above. The wind from the north was picking up speed.

"A blizzard threatens," he said darkly. "It was stormy that day, too . . ."

He turned and had begun to fold away the banner when two voices called out at the same time, "Wait!"

Two men jumped forward and the crowd whooped in delight. One was pudgy and far older than thirty years. The other was an even less appropriate match: a shaven monk.

"Why are you laughing?" the older, fat man cried to the crowd. "I am still single, why can't I give it a try?"

"Dear sir," the monk replied with a smile, "you wouldn't want the poor girl to become a widow before she had even turned twenty, would you?"

"And what about you?" he snarled in reply.

"If I were to win the hand of such a pretty girl, I would cast off my religious robes."

This delighted the crowd even more.

The girl frowned, clearly displeased, but she removed her cape and prepared to fight. Mu Yi gripped her arm and urged her to stay calm. He then turned, unfurled the banner and once more planted it into the ground. The monk and the heavyset man continued their bickering, each wanting to fight first.

"Why not start by fighting each other?" a wit from the crowd called out. "The winner fights the girl!"

"Fine by me," the monk replied. "Let's put on a show for the crowd, old man." He launched himself fist first at the man's head but the old man ducked before returning the blow.

Guo Jing recognized their moves; the monk was using Shaolin Arhat style, and the older, rotund man practiced Five Style Fists. Both were forms of external kung fu. The monk was agile, but his opponent possessed considerable power.

Just then the monk struck three blows at the older man's stomach. The older man brought his fist down heavy on the monk's head, who landed on his rear. After a moment of confusion, the monk staggered to his feet and, removing a blade from his robes, lunged at the man. The crowd gasped, while the old man leaped back and removed an iron whip from his belt. They had both come armed! The fight had taken a desperate and dangerous turn.

The spectators clapped but edged back.

"Stop!" Mu Yi edged toward the two men. "It is forbidden to fight with weapons."

But the men paid him no heed. Mu Yi leaped into the air, kicking the blade from the monk's hand and seizing the end of the whip. He pulled hard and the old man had no choice but to let go. Mu Yi threw the whip to the dirt and stood defiantly. The two men stooped to pick up their weapons and, accompanied by the jeers of the crowd, slipped shamefully back into anonymity.

Just then came the tinkling of bells. The crowd turned toward the sound and there they saw a throng of servants accompanying an expensively dressed young man sitting astride a handsome horse. His eyes went from the banner to the girl and a smile crept across his face. He jumped down from his saddle and stepped forward.

"Is this the maiden?" he asked.

The girl's cheeks flushed bright crimson and she turned without answering. Mu Yi approached him and bowed. "Sir, our family's name is Mu. How may I help the Master?"

"What are the rules?"

Mu Yi explained.

"Then I will take my turn." He looked to be around the same age as the young girl, handsome and evidently from a good family.

Finally, a young man suitable for the maiden, Guo Jing thought. Much better than the monk and the old fat man.

"Your Lordship must be teasing," Mu Yi replied.

"What do you mean?"

"We are a wandering family without fixed abode, we are not

suitable for a man such as yourself. This is no ordinary duel; it concerns the hand of my daughter," he said, pointing to the young girl.

"How long have you been holding this contest?"

"We have been more than six months on the road, sir."

"And still nobody has won your daughter's hand?" The young Master sounded incredulous.

"It is most certainly because the Empire's masters of kung fu are all already married," Mu Yi replied with a smile. "Or they believe a duel with my daughter to be beneath them."

"Very well, let me try!"

He is a most refined young man, Mu Yi thought to himself. Were he from a more humble family he would make a very worthy son-in-law. But he is of noble birth and could be related to someone important at court. In any case, he is rich and powerful. If my daughter wins, it will bring trouble. If she loses, how could I allow our families to be joined forever?

"We are mere wanderers of the south, we are no match for a man of your standing. Please forgive us, we will leave."

"Your challenge is an honorable one," the young man replied. "I will not harm your daughter, I assure you." He turned to the girl and said, "All the lady has to do is make contact during combat and she wins, is that agreeable?"

"There are strict rules in a contest such as this," the girl contended.

"Get on with it!" came a cry from the crowd.

"The faster he wins, the faster you can be married and show us an heir!"

Laughter echoed around the square.

The young woman scowled, removed her cape once again and bowed to the young man.

He too lowered his head. "Young lady."

Can he really know any martial arts, having grown up with such wealth? Better defeat him quickly and leave the city at once, Mu Yi reflected.

"Very well, sir," he said. "Perhaps I may take the Master's coat?"

"That will be unnecessary," the young man replied.

He's in trouble, the crowd thought, aware of the girl's considerable talents. And yet, maybe he, too, has experience of fighting in the south? Father and daughter both knew the danger of letting the son of a nobleman lose face before so many people.

"Do you think the contest is real?" some in the crowd whispered to each other. "Maybe that old Mu Yi is just trying to cheat vain fools like this young man out of money?"

"He'd better watch his purse!"

"My lord," the young girl said, and lowered her head. The fight was on.

The young nobleman turned to the right and whipped his left sleeve at the girl. Surprised, she bent to avoid the move. His right sleeve came with equal speed at her head and she could only leap upward to avoid being pincered between them.

"Nice!" the young man exclaimed, advancing before she could land on her feet. The girl twirled in the air and kicked at his nose. He lurched back and they both landed at the same time. They regarded each other with mutual respect. The girl's cheeks blushed again, but she moved first into attack, the man a flicker of brocade, and she a cloud of red mist.

Guo Jing was amazed. They're no older than me, he said to himself, and yet they are such skilled fighters. They would make the perfect couple. They could keep replaying the circumstances of their first meeting. He smiled to himself.

He traced each move with anticipation, until the girl tugged at the young man's sleeve and ripped it from his coat. She landed back and held her trophy high in the air.

"My lord, we apologize most humbly!" Mu Yi ran forward, bowing, and grabbed hold of his daughter. "We will leave."

"Not so fast," the young man replied, his displeasure evident. "We haven't found a winner yet."

Grabbing at the front of his coat, he pulled hard, causing the jade buttons to burst in all directions. Servants ran to collect them, while one of his men rushed forward to help the young man remove his outer robe, revealing a tunic of lake-green satin tied at the waist with a sash the color of spring onions. It was a fine outfit designed to accentuate his delicate, handsome features.

He swung his left palm high and brought it down swiftly, sending a powerful gust of air at the girl's cheeks. He looked to be focused now, the fight was no longer just a bit of fun. The girl retreated.

Marriage looks to be in sight, Guo Jing said to himself. My *shifus* were right: there are many fighters of exceptional talent in the Central Plains. I would never win against such sophisticated palm technique.

"My girl," Mu Yi called to his daughter, sensing the outcome was inevitable, "it's time to give up. This fine gentleman is much more skilled than you." He was clearly not one of those idle youths who adored nothing but gambling and women, Mu Yi reflected. He would ask about the family and, provided he was not related to the Jin nobility, he would approve the marriage. His daughter's future would be secure.

He called for a halt to the fight, but the young man had no intention of stopping now.

If I wanted to hurt this girl, I could, he thought to himself. But he didn't have the heart. Instead, he grabbed at her wrist. Alarmed, she tried to wrestle free. He pushed and she lost balance and he swept her into his arms. The crowd burst into cheers and clapped.

"Let go of me," the girl hissed, her cheeks hot with shame.

"Call me your beloved, and I will release you at once."

The young girl was incensed, but despite her struggles, she could not break free.

"You have won her hand," Mu Yi said, approaching them. "Please let go of my daughter."

The young man began to laugh, but still he clutched the girl's wrist.

Her patience now sorely tested, the girl kicked at the pressure point on his temple. But he caught her foot with his other hand. She panicked and pulled back, losing her red embroidered shoe.

There she sat on the ground, her head lowered, nursing her white stockinged foot. The young man smiled and, to the crowd's delight, lifted the cloth shoe to his nose and sniffed.

"Bet that smells delicious!" someone cried.

"Sir, may I ask your name?" Mu Yi interrupted.

"There's no need!" he answered with a smile.

He took back his brocade coat, glanced at the girl and slipped her shoe into his pocket. Just then the wind picked up and large petals of snow began to fall.

"We are staying at the Prosperity Inn," Mu Yi called after the man, "in the west. Shall we go together and settle everything?"

"Settle what? I'm going home, the weather is turning."

Mu Yi's cheeks turned a snowy white. "But you won the contest, I promised you my girl's hand in marriage. This is a serious matter, young sir!"

The young man laughed even louder. "It was just a little fun. A rather interesting game, I must admit. But as for marriage? I'm afraid I must decline your generous offer."

Anger caught in Mu Yi's throat. "You . . . sir . . ."

"What did you expect?" one of the servants called back. "That our master would marry a wretched girl of the *wulin*? You're living in dreamland!"

Incensed, Mu Yi reached out and slapped the servant on the cheek. The young man, in fact a prince of the Jin court, said nothing, but motioned to the others to carry his man away. He went to his horse and was about to mount when Mu Yi shouted again after him, "Why do you mock us?"

The Prince made no reply, at which point Mu Yi ran forward and grasped the young man's arm. "I would never let my daughter marry such an indolent and hateful young man as you! But at least give us back the shoe."

"She gave it to me. I have declined the first prize; I am keeping it as my consolation." And with a quick flick of his wrist, he was free from the old man's grip.

"I'll fight you!" Mu Yi was getting desperate in his rage.

He leaped up and aimed at the Great Sun pressure point on the Prince's temples with both fists, in a move known as the Bell and Drum. But the Prince jumped up into his stirrup and called out, "And if I beat you, I won't have to marry your daughter?"

The crowd were just as enraged by the Prince's arrogance as the old man, but they remained quiet save for a few lone guffaws from some of the rougher men in their midst.

Mu Yi adjusted his sash and leaped into a Seagull Skims the Sea. The young man responded with a blow to the old man's belly, in a Poison Snake Seeks the Cave. Mu Yi dodged this attack and struck with his left palm at the young man's shoulder. The young man turned, advancing his right palm under Mu Yi's arm in a Steal the Clouds, before bringing his other hand up toward the old man's face. Mu Yi blocked with his elbow before slapping the Prince across both cheeks in a Protector Skanda Defends Evil.

His cheeks throbbing, the Prince was furious. He dug his fingers into the backs of Mu Yi's hands and pulled away, revealing nails red with blood.

The crowd cried out. Mu Yi's daughter ran forward, tore a strip of cloth from Mu Yi's clothing and bandaged her father's bleeding hands.

"Move," Mu Yi said, pushing aside his daughter. "It's either him or me!"

"Father, let him go, he's too nasty!"

The onlookers were disgusted that the rich young man's actions should result in the spilling of blood and even the rougher elements of the crowd were indignant. By now, everyone was in agreement that he was a most disagreeable young man.

The Prince rubbed at a spot of blood that had been splattered on his clothes and turned once again to mount his horse. Guo Jing could no longer stand by and do nothing. He pushed through the crowd, and out into the open space before the crowd. "You! Your behavior is a disgrace!"

The Prince was momentarily affected by these words, but then brushed them off. "A disgrace?"

His servants were much amused by their master's mocking version of this peasant boy's southern accent, but Guo Jing did not understand their joke. "Yes. You should marry this young lady!"

"And if I don't?"

"Why did you take part in the contest if you had no intention of marrying her? It's written clearly on the banner."

"Why are you sticking your nose in where it isn't wanted?"

"This fair maiden is not only beautiful, but is in possession of the most excellent kung fu. Why won't you marry her? Don't you see how you have offended her?"

"You're too dull to understand. I'm not wasting my breath on the likes of you." The Prince turned, but Guo Jing stopped him.

"You can't just leave."

"What do you want?"

"You must marry this young lady."

The Prince laughed and turned again.

What a nice, if rather naïve young man, Mu Yi thought. "Young sir, don't worry. As long as there is still breath in these lungs, I will have my revenge for this insult." Then, turning to the Prince, he said, "At least tell me your name!"

"I told you, I am never going to call you Father, so why do you need to know?"

Furious, Guo Jing rushed forward. "Give her back her shoe!"

"Mind your own business. Have you taken a liking to the young girl?"

"No! I just think you should give it back."

The Prince punched Guo Jing on the ear. Stunned, Guo Jing crossed his hands and seized the Prince's wrists.

"Do you want a beating too?" the Prince shouted as he leaped up and kicked Guo Jing in the abdomen.

Guo Jing pushed at him while still in midair, but the Prince had good lightness technique, and instead of falling, corrected himself and landed on his feet.

"Come on then, little peasant boy, let me see what you can do!" The Prince removed his brocade coat.

"Why would I want to fight you?" Guo Jing said. "I just think you should give the lady back her shoe!"

But the crowd wanted the show to continue, so they goaded from the sidelines:

"He's all talk!"

"A hero fights!"

The Prince could see that Guo Jing too was accomplished in the martial arts, and, in particular, possessed considerable internal strength. He would rather not fight, but neither could he return the shoe without losing face. So he picked up his coat and made for his horse, laughing. But Guo Jing grabbed at his clothes. "Are you just going to leave?"

The young man had a sudden thought. He threw his coat over Guo Jing's head. Blackness descended, and Guo Jing felt a heavy blow to his chest. He tried to suck in air and shrink back, but two fists cracked against his ribs. Luckily the years of training with Ma Yu ensured that, as hard as the Prince's punches were, they did him no injury. Guo Jing kicked out nine times in rapid succession in a Mandarin Duck Drill, a move Ryder Han had taught him. It had served his *shifu* well over the years. Having not practiced hard enough, however, and being unable to see, Guo Jing's aim was not quite true and the Prince avoided all but the last two blows.

The two young men leaped back. Guo Jing threw away the coat. It had been a treacherous move. His Masters had warned him about such fighters, but he had never come across one himself. He was rather too innocent and trusting to believe they could exist. Sometimes his *shifus'* warnings came across as amusing fireside stories. Having been so isolated from the *wulin,* he had not been able to appreciate the truth behind their words.

Enraged by the two kicks he had received, the Prince advanced with his fists raised in an Angled Whip. Guo Jing tried to block the punches aimed at his head, but felt another pain in his chest. He tried to fight back but was beaten once more to the ground. The Prince's retinue burst into laugher, and their master puffed his chest in pride. "You think your three-legged cat technique can beat me? Go back to your *shifu*'s wife and ask for another twenty years of instruction, maybe then you can fight me!"

Guo Jing scrambled to his feet, panting. He was circulating the *qi* around his body to relieve the pain.

"My *shifu* isn't married," he retorted.

"Then tell him it's about time."

"In fact, I have six *shifus*," Guo Jing called as the Prince turned to leave. He ran at him with his fist high.

The Prince ducked, Guo Jing's left hook missed, and his right was then blocked. They stood facing each other, their arms locked, each marshalling the best of his internal energy to overpower the other. Guo Jing's was just a little stronger, but his opponent's technique was more advanced. There was little to choose between them.

Guo Jing reached deeper and pressed just as the other young man relaxed the pressure, causing Guo Jing to stumble forward. A punch to the back followed. Guo Jing landed on his elbow and bounced back up, spinning in the air and kicking with his left.

This remarkable recovery was met with delighted whoops and shouts from the crowd.

The Prince launched forward with both palms, the first in a false move designed to distract. Guo Jing replied with a Split Muscles Lock Bones move, striking rapidly at various points across the Prince's body. The Prince echoed the same technique back.

But Guo Jing's was an unorthodox version invented by Zhu Cong. At first glance it looked the same as the technique practiced in the Central Plains, but in actual fact he was aiming all along for the Tend the Aged pressure point on the wrist, whereas the Prince was trying to clutch at Guo Jing's knuckles. They continued like this for at least forty moves, but neither triumphed over the other.

Large flakes of snow continued to fall, forming a thin white blanket over the heads and shoulders of the gathered crowd.

Just then Guo Jing realized the Prince had left his chest exposed. He reached for the pressure point in its center, known as the Turtledove Tail, but at the last moment he hesitated. There is no real emnity between us, it would be wrong to use such a deadly move on him, he said to himself. Instead, he pressed to the side of it, a move that had no effect at all. The Prince grabbed his wrist, hooked his foot, and in a flash, Guo Jing was once more in the dirt.

Mu Yi, his hand now bandaged by his daughter, was still watching the fight. This was the third time Guo Jing had fallen. He ran over to the kind young boy and tried to pull him to his feet. "Young man, forget it. We mustn't waste our energy on such scoundrels."

But Guo Jing was too furious to listen and made another rush on the Prince, his hands a blur.

The Prince was surprised at the young man's persistence. "Don't you know when you're beaten?"

But Guo Jing did not answer and merely continued his attack.

"If you don't stop, I am going to be forced to kill you," the Prince snarled.

"And I will kill you if you don't return the shoe."

"Why are you acting like an overprotective older brother?"

This was in fact a standard insult in the area and the onlookers burst into laughter, but Guo Jing did not understand what he meant.

"I don't even know her," Guo Jing said.

The Prince did not know if he should laugh or cry. "All right, idiot, watch this!"

The fight resumed. Guo Jing was now more cautious of his opponent's tricks. He knew that the rich young man's kung fu was more accomplished, but Guo Jing had a persistence honed in the harsh environment of the northern steppe. Tusakha's gang had given him his first lesson in this regard. His Fourth *Shifu* may have told him it was better to run in the face of an enemy he could not defeat, but Guo Jing, in his heart, preferred to stand firm.

The spectacle was drawing an ever-greater crowd and people were crammed into every corner of the market square, despite the intensity of the wind and snow.

Mu Yi knew well that, if the fight continued, the crowds would alert the authorities. The last thing he wanted was to get into trouble, but how could they walk away when this young man was trying to help them? He looked out nervously at the crowd and noticed a group of men who looked like they, too, might be wandering martial arts men of the rivers and lakes.

Mu Yi edged closer to where the rich young man's servants were gathered. Three of them also looked like they might practice kung fu. Among them was an exceptionally tall lama dressed in scarlet robes and a yellow hat. Another was shorter, rounder, his head crested with a mane of silver hair; his skin was smooth and his face dressed in a wide smile. He too was in robes, but Mu Yi was not sure if his outfit indicated he belonged to a Taoist sect. The third man was short, with a neat mustache and piercing, bloodshot eyes.

Mu Yi listened to their conversation.

"Your Eminent Holiness," one of the young servants in the Prince's retinue said to the lama, "you must put a stop to this stupidity. Go in and take the young boy. If the Prince gets injured, we'll all be for the gallows."

He is a prince! Mu Yi said to himself in astonishment. These people are servants of the court, sent to assist the young man.

The lama only smiled.

"Supreme Wisdom Lobsang Choden Rinpoche is an eminent lama of Kokonor," the old man with silver hair said with a smile. "How could he lower himself to intervene in a fight with a young hooligan?" Turning to the servant, he continued, "At most the Prince will have your legs broken. He can't exactly have you killed."

"The Prince is a better fighter than this peasant boy," the short man with the bloodshot eyes added. "What have you got to be scared about?"

Everyone heard this and a chill ran through the crowd. They averted their eyes back to the fight, afraid to catch the short man's lightning gaze.

"The Prince has been training for so long," the man with the silver hair continued, "he wishes to let the people see his skills. He would not be happy for us to intervene."

"Elder Liang," the short man said, "what palm technique is it the Prince practices?"

"Brother Peng, are you testing me?" The silver-haired man smiled. "He fights with speed and agility, indeed the moves show great complexity. Unless I am much mistaken, he has learned his kung fu with a Taoist of the Quanzhen Sect."

A disciple of the Quanzhen? Mu Yi almost jumped. And could this "Brother Peng" be Tiger Peng, Butcher of a Thousand Hands, one of China's most famous bandits?

"Elder Liang, you have a good eye. You have lived as a recluse at the foot of the Mountain of Eternal Snow, dedicating yourself to the art of alchemy. You rarely grace us with your presence here in the Central Plains, and yet you are so well acquainted with all the different schools of martial arts."

"You flatter me, Brother Peng," the old man said with a smile.

"And yet, while the Taoists of the Quanzhen Sect are an eccentric bunch, they are known for their loyalty to the Song. Why would they take a prince of the Jin as their disciple?"

"You think the Prince is unable to persuade those he wishes to engage in service? You, for instance. You command the mountains east and west of the Yellow River, and yet are you not also part of the Prince's household?"

The short man nodded, and they turned their attention to the fight. Guo Jing was now fighting with slower, more deliberate moves which allowed him to maintain a strong defense. The Prince was unable to land any blows.

"And what about the peasant boy?" the silver-haired man said to the short man.

"His kung fu is mixed in style. I would guess he has more than one *shifu*."

"Master Peng is correct," a voice interrupted. "He is a student of the Seven Heroes of the South."

Mu Yi examined this new character. He was thin, his cheeks darkened by the sun, and on his head three large cysts protruded. The Seven Heroes of the South? It had been so long since Mu Yi had heard them mentioned, he had assumed they were all dead.

"You little rascal—found you at last!" The man with the cysts suddenly roared as he charged toward the two young men, clutching an iron club.

Guo Jing turned and found the strange-looking man inches from his face. Browbeater Hou, close friend of the Four Daemons of the Yellow River. Guo Jing hesitated, not sure what to do, and the Prince struck him on the shoulder.

The crowd began booing at what they felt to be an ignoble intervention.

Mu Yi moved closer, ready to help Guo Jing. But the Prince appeared to have a great many fighters at his disposal.

And yet Browbeater Hou did not stop to join the fight, and instead continued past Guo Jing and the Prince, and on to the other side of the crowd, where a young boy in rags turned and pushed his way back through the wall of people. Browbeater Hou ran after him, followed by another four men.

Guo Jing saw that the boy was his friend Lotus.

"One moment, please," he said to the Prince. "I must attend to something before we can continue."

The Prince was in fact tired of fighting and was hoping for a way out. "If you admit defeat, we can stop."

But at that moment Lotus Huang danced back into view again, this time laughing and clutching an old broken shoe above her head. Behind her, Browbeater Hou was trying to strike her with his club. Lotus dodged the man's attacks with ease and was already threading her way through the gathered onlookers.

Browbeater Hou stumbled into the center of the crowd, two large blue-black bruises visible on his cheeks. He stopped, panting.

"I will slice you up, as these people are my witness!" he cried out with rage.

Lotus paused and waited for Hou to catch up, before running off again. The crowd howled with laughter just as three of the Daemons of the Yellow River came gasping into the arena. Only Qian the Hardy was missing.

Guo Jing smiled. So my friend Lotus is also trained in kung fu? He must have been the one to lure this man away and hang the others in the trees.

But Guo Jing was not the only one watching in surprise. "Master Liang, what about the young beggar?" the lama said. "To which school does he belong? He's running rings around Browbeater Hou."

Old Liang was an alchemist of great fame, known across the south as the Ginseng Immortal, the white-haired Master of the Mountain of Eternal Snow. Since his youth, he had consumed great quantities of ginseng and other natural remedies, protecting him from the ravages of old age. But he did not recognize the beggar boy's kung fu. He shook his head. "The Three-Horned Dragon outrun by a mere beggar boy? I thought his skills were better than that, but perhaps I have been away from the *wulin* for too long."

Tiger Peng could not explain it either. Browbeater Hou joined him often on raids; he knew full well the extent of his friend's considerable fighting skill.

The Prince, meanwhile, was thankful for the diversion, for all that he had the upper hand over his opponent. He untied the scarf he wore as a sash and mopped the sweat off his brow.

Mu Yi approached Guo Jing and shook the young man's hand, before going to pick up his banner. Just then Lotus broke through the crowd again, this time clutching two pieces of cloth torn from Browbeater Hou's shirt. He was not far behind, his hairy chest exposed to the winter chill. Behind them, Wu and Ma ran heavily, stopping every few meters to catch their breath. Shen had been lost along the way. The spectacle brought yet more laughter from the crowd.

Just then shouting echoed from the western side of the square. A squad of soldiers, carrying wicker canes, marched in, striking passersby as they went. All to make way for a large red and gold sedan chair carried by six more of their men.

"The Consort!" the servants cried.

"Who had the impudence to tell my mother?" The Prince scowled. The servants did not dare reply and instead hastened to the sedan.

"Fighting again?" A soft voice came from inside. "It's snowing and you're not wearing a coat. You'll be sure to catch a cold."

The voice was like a bolt of lightning striking down on Mu Yi. *How is this possible? She sounds just like . . . No, it's impossible, she is a member of the Jin house. I miss my wife so much I've gone mad . . .* But he could not stop himself from trying to get closer to the chair. A dainty hand holding a handkerchief appeared from inside to wipe the last of the sweat from the young Prince's brow. Mu Yi continued to listen to their conversation.

"But Ma, I'm having fun. I'm in no danger," the young Prince said.

"Put on your coat, we're going home," the Consort said.

How could her voice sound so familiar? Mu Yi was still astonished. He watched her white hand disappear behind a silk curtain embroidered with golden peonies. He tried to peer in but he could not see past the colorful cloth.

One of the servants picked up his master's brocade coat. "Look what you've done to His Lordship's coat! You animal!"

One of the Consort's guard raised his wicker cane and aimed it at Guo Jing's head. Guo Jing jumped aside, seized the man's wrist, and wrestled the cane from him before tripping him up. Guo Jing then dealt him two steady blows as he lay on the ground.

"Who gave you the right to harass innocent men?" Guo Jing cried, and his words were met with cheers from the crowd. More soldiers charged in support, but Guo Jing began fighting them off in pairs.

"How dare you assault my men?" the young Prince cried as he

leaped at Guo Jing and they resumed their fight. The Consort shouted for her son to stop, but she instilled no fear in the young man. In fact, he still craved his mother's praise and attention despite being old enough to know better, so he redoubled his efforts. Guo Jing stumbled twice under the force of the Prince's attack.

"Ma! This peasant boy is causing trouble. I've got to teach him a lesson in respect."

Mu Yi, meanwhile, could not take his eyes off the sedan. A corner of the curtain had been drawn aside, and he caught a glimpse of a pair of the most delicate eyes and the finest strands of black silken hair. The face of a frightened mother.

Guo Jing was confronted with an adversary of renewed vigor. The young Prince sought to cause serious injury now, in order to put a definitive end to their combat.

But Guo Jing had thick skin and considerable inner strength, so a few blows would not hurt him. And while the Prince's technique was sophisticated, he was still lacking in experience. Several times he tried to replicate a move that had been successful against Mu Yi, but every time he tried to make a claw and seize hold of Guo Jing, Guo Jing defended himself with another move from his Split Muscles repertoire.

Meanwhile, Browbeater Hou was still chasing after Lotus Huang. The old Three-Horned Dragon had in his hair two heads of corn, a practice of the marketplace to indicate an item was to be sold. Lotus must have put them there, but Hou was blissfully unaware that she had put his head up for sale. The remaining Daemons of the Yellow River were nowhere to be seen.

Old Graybeard Liang and his friends were puzzled. Who was this ragged young peasant boy? Why could Browbeater Hou not catch up with him?

"Is he a member of the Beggar Clan?" Tiger Peng asked.

The Beggar Clan was the most powerful secret society of the south at the time. The question made Old Graybeard Liang twitch, but he did not answer.

Meanwhile, the fight between the young men was growing faster and more intense. Guo Jing received a blow to the shoulder, the Prince a kick to his thigh. The merest distraction could result in a fatal blow. Tiger Peng and Graybeard Liang prepared themselves to jump in at any moment.

Guo Jing's upbringing on the steppe may have been poor in worldly luxuries, but it had provided him with exceptional mental strength. The Prince, however, had only known a life of gold and silks, and it showed. He was growing tired and his movements were at times clumsy. Guo Jing cried out, took the Prince by the collar and lifted him high. The Prince felt himself sail through the air and winced as the ground approached. This was no move from the *jianghu*, but one Guo Jing had learned from his Mongolian Master, Jebe.

The Prince's reactions were sharp; he tapped the ground and flew up again, and grabbing hold of Guo Jing's legs, he brought them both back down. The Prince then seized a lance from a nearby soldier on horseback and aimed for Guo Jing's stomach. Guo Jing rolled away, trying to take hold of the weapon, but it evaded him.

"Dearest son! Don't be vengeful; it is enough to defeat him. Don't hurt him!"

But the Prince was determined to have his victory in the bloodiest manner possible.

The tip of the lance was only inches from his nose, but Guo Jing deflected it with his arm. Just then he heard a clatter behind him. The banner! Launching into a perfect Part the Clouds to Reveal the Sun, Guo Jing grabbed the pole.

Now they were both armed. Guo Jing used the Exorcist's Staff technique developed by his First *Shifu* for the purposes of defeating Cyclone Mei. The banner pole was a bit too long, but he managed to make good use of the many variations and subtlety of the repertoire, forcing the Prince back into a defensive position. Yet the Prince's moves were also impressive. Mu Yi watched in astonishment; they were consistent with those of the Yang Family Spear, a technique handed down only from father to son, and rare indeed, even in the south. Yet his style was not entirely orthodox and somehow lacking in a core understanding, as if it had been copied through observation rather than passed down through personal instruction.

The lance and banner poles crossed and clashed as the snow continued to fall.

"Stop! Stop fighting!" The Consort, seeing her son sweating and covered in blood, could hold back no longer.

Tiger Peng strode into the middle of the crowd and struck with all his might at the banner pole in Guo Jing's hands. A sharp pain shot through Guo Jing's hands and he let go; the large embroidered characters flapping in the wind were barely visible through the dense snow: DUEL FOR A MAIDEN.

Guo Jing had no time to make out the man's face; all he could do was leap back to safety, but not before Tiger Peng had managed to tap his arm, sending him tumbling to the ground.

"Young Prince, let me take care of the boy. He won't bother you again."

He held his palm up, took a deep breath, and went to give Guo Jing a rude punch to the head. Guo Jing raised his arms to block it, but he knew such an attempt at defense was futile. Lama Supreme Wisdom and Old Liang exchanged a meaningful glance; Tiger Peng could snap those arms with one blow.

Just then a cry rose from the crowd: "Stop!"

A gray shadow leaped into view and grabbed hold of Tiger Peng's wrist. In his other hand, he was carrying a strange weapon. Tiger Peng hit out with his left palm and broke the weapon at once. The man in gray ducked, took Guo Jing by the hand and leaped beyond reach. Only then did the likeness of this strange intruder become clear: a Taoist monk, at least thirty or forty years of age and dressed in gray robes. His weapon appeared to be a horsetail whip, the head of which had become detached from the handle and was now wrapped around Tiger Peng's wrist.

The two men took each other in. In one exchange, the extent of their respective martial skills had been made apparent.

"You must be the famed Master Peng? What an honor to meet you at last," the Taoist said.

"You are too kind. May I ask the monk's name?"

All eyes turned to the Taoist, but he did not answer. Instead, he pushed his foot through the snow and pulled back. There, on the ground, was revealed a hole at least ten inches deep! Such was the power of his kung fu.

This startled Tiger Peng. "The Iron Foot Immortal, Jade Sun Wang Chuyi?"

"Master Peng flatters me. I am indeed Wang Chuyi, but I am undeserving of the name Immortal."

They all knew very well who Wang Chuyi was: a Taoist monk of the Quanzhen Sect whose fame was second only to Eternal Spring Qiu Chuji. But they had never seen him in the flesh before. He was handsome, his chin capped with a wisp of the blackest beard. His socks were a brilliant white, his cloth shoes gray. This was a man who took great care in his appearance. Had they not seen his brilliant display of kung fu for themselves, they would never have guessed that he was in fact the Iron Foot Immortal who had once balanced on one leg on the edge of a precipice, swaying like a lotus leaf in the wind. Word of his skill had spread all through the south and even up north into the hinterlands of the Jin capital itself.

"I am not personally acquainted with this young man, but I admire very much his bravery in intervening in such a way. Therefore, I beseech Master Peng to let him live."

"A most courteous request," Tiger Peng was forced to admit. "And who would dare refuse an Elder of the Quanzhen Sect?"

"In which case, I am most grateful," Wang Chuyi said, cupping his hand in a gesture of respect.

Wang Chuyi turned to the Prince and at once his expression darkened and he was severe. "Who are you? And who is your *shifu*?"

The young Prince had turned pale upon hearing Wang Chuyi's name, and he would have liked nothing more than to slip away unnoticed. But he had also felt the monk's attention during his exchange with Tiger Peng.

"I am Wanyan Kang, but I cannot reveal the identity of my *shifu*."

"He has a red mole on his left cheek. Am I right?"

Wanyan had wanted to reply with something witty, but the sight of the monk's fierce gaze silenced him, and he merely nodded.

"I thought as much," Wang Chuyi said. A student of his brother, Eternal Spring Qiu Chuji. "And did your *shifu* not teach you certain principles of how to fight nobly before you began your training?"

Wanyan Kang understood the gravity of the situation. His *shifu* would be furious if he learned of his behavior today.

"Seeing as the Master is acquainted with my *shifu*, perhaps he might come with me to my humble abode, so that I might benefit from his wisdom?" He then turned to Guo Jing and bowed. "Perhaps a friendship might grow between us, since we have already been acquainted in combat? Your kung fu is most impressive. May I extend the invitation to you as well?"

"What about the young girl? Will you marry her?" Guo Jing replied.

"This matter . . . is not so easily resolved," Wanyan Kang answered, embarrassed.

"My friend," Mu Yi said, tugging at Guo Jing's arm. "Let's go. We needn't take up any more of the sir's time."

Wanyan Kang bowed to Wang Chuyi. "Elder Wang, I shall await you at my home. Ask for Prince Zhao's residence. The day is cold; we shall sit by the fire and admire the snow from inside. There will be wine waiting to celebrate our meeting."

Wanyan Kang climbed up onto his horse and spurred it straight at the crowd, which scattered before him like ants.

Such arrogance merely irritated Wang Chuyi even more. "Young man," he said, turning to Guo Jing. "Follow me."

"But I must wait for a friend," Guo Jing said.

At which point, Lotus Huang jumped out of the crowd and called to him. "Don't worry, I will find you. You go ahead!" Then she disappeared back into the throng of the dispersing crowd. In the distance, they saw Browbeater Hou running toward them.

Guo Jing kneeled down in the snow and bowed before the Taoist monk as a mark of gratitude for saving his life. The Taoist leaned down and lifted Guo Jing up to his feet.

Together they left the square, threading their way through the crowd, and on to the outskirts of the city.

CHAPTER EIGHT

EVERY MAN A MYTHICAL SKILL

I

WANG CHUYI MOVED QUICKLY, EAGER TO ASSESS THE EXTENT OF Guo Jing's martial arts, and in no time they were clear of the city. They continued on for some miles as their path led them into the shadow of a mountain and began to rise steeply.

Ma Yu had taught him to ascend a vertical cliff face, so Guo Jing had no trouble keeping up, despite having just taken part in a long duel. The wind and snow blew in their faces. Wang Chuyi began the climb, undeterred by the slippery ground beneath his feet, pulling Guo Jing behind him. As the path became ever steeper, Wang Chuyi wondered at the boy's steady breathing, which was just as if he were running on flat ground.

"You have considerable inner kung fu," the Taoist said, releasing Guo Jing's arm. "Why were you unable to beat the young man?"

Guo Jing did not know how to answer and just smiled.

"Who is your *shifu*?"

Guo Jing now knew that this man was martial brother to Scarlet Sun Ma Yu. This gave him confidence to answer truthfully.

305

"Elder Ma Yu and the Seven Heroes of the South!"

Guo Jing's answer delighted the Taoist. "Then I shouldn't worry about angering Brother Qiu."

Guo Jing's eyes widened. He did not understand what he meant.

"Prince Wanyan Kang, the young man you were fighting just now, is a disciple of Qiu Chuji. Didn't you realize?"

"No, I didn't . . ." Guo Jing was surprised indeed.

Ma Yu's teachings had focused on inner strength breathing techniques as well as a branch of lightness kung fu known as Flight of the Golden Eagle. But he had never given him instruction in the art of combat or the use of weapons, which is why Guo Jing was wholly unfamiliar with the Quanzhen-school style. Now that he thought about it, the Prince's moves were reminiscent of those he had encountered in his fight with Harmony Yin.

"I was unaware that the Prince was a disciple of Elder Qiu," Guo Jing said, bowing, believing he had offended the Taoist. "Please forgive my mistake."

Wang Chuyi responded with a hearty burst of laughter.

"You are a courteous and humble young man, just to my liking! Why would I be angry? The Quanzhen Sect is most clear about this—disciples are punished when they are in the wrong. This young man is arrogant and unworthy of our school, and I will instruct Brother Qiu to deal with him."

"But he must be forgiven if he agrees to marry the maiden."

Wang Chuyi shook his head. Guo Jing had a good heart which forgave readily, making him only more agreeable to the Taoist. But Brother Qiu has always been an enemy of injustice, especially any committed by the Jin, Wang thought. Why did he agree to take on a Jin prince as his disciple? The young man shows a deep under-standing of our kung fu, which means Brother Qiu has devoted considerable energy to teaching him. And yet there is also a hint of unorthodox and pernicious technique in his fighting. He could not understand it!

"Brother Qiu told me to meet him in the Jin capital," Wang said to Guo Jing. "He should arrive in the next few days and we will have our explanation then. I heard that he has taken on a young student by the name of Yang whom you are to fight in Jiaxing. I don't know how sophisticated his skills are, but don't worry, I will be there to help."

Guo Jing had been told by the Freaks to make his way to Jiaxing before noon on the twenty-fourth day of the third lunar month, but they had not told him why.

"Please Master, why am I to fight this Yang?"

"If your teachers did not explain the reason to you, it would be improper for me to say."

Qiu Chuji had given him only the barest details, but from what he had heard, he could not help feeling admiration for the Freaks. Like his martial brother Ma Yu, he too hoped Guo Jing would prevail. Yet Brother Qiu was his senior and he could hardly tell him to concede the fight. Now that he could see what a good young man Guo Jing was, he decided he must find a way to help him without damaging his Brother Qiu's reputation. Exactly how he would do this he would have to see once they arrived in Jiaxing.

"Let's go back and visit Mu Yi," Wang said. "His daughter is a fiery character, don't upset her."

These words startled Guo Jing.

Together they made their way to the Prosperity Inn, located in the western part of the city. A dozen or so servants dressed in finest brocade were waiting by the entrance. They made their way closer and one of them spoke: "The Prince invites Master Wang and Guo Esquire to join him at his residence for a banquet."

One of the men handed them a red card with the characters "A Humble Invitation from your Disciple Wanyan Kang."

"Well, well," Wang Chuyi said, shaking his head. "We will be along soon."

"Please accept these cakes and fruits as a present from the Prince," the head servant declared. "If the Master would instruct me where they are to be placed, I will organize it."

The servants presented Wang with twelve large boxes filled with all kinds of colorful fresh fruits and delicate pastries.

Brother Lotus is fond of cakes, Guo Jing said to himself, I will save some for him.

Wang Chuyi had intended to refuse the present, but seeing Guo's pleasure at receiving it, he told the servants to leave them at the inn. Young people are always a little gluttonous, he thought, smiling.

They went to knock on Mu Yi's door. He was laid out on the bed, his cheeks pale. His daughter was perched on the bed beside him, tears moistening her eyes. Both father and daughter were surprised to see Wang Chuyi and Guo Jing at the door. The girl rose to her feet and Mu Yi struggled to sit up.

Wang Chuyi examined the old man's wounds. The scratches on his swollen hands had cut to the bone. They looked as if they had been made by a weapon, not the Prince's fingers as was the case. His daughter had applied a balsam to soothe her father's pain, but fearing infection, had yet to bandage them.

Who had taught Wanyan Kang such a cruel and brutal technique? Wang thought to himself. It would have taken time to develop such power. How could Brother Qiu not have noticed? And if he knew, why didn't he stop it?

"May I ask the young lady's name?" Wang said, turning to Mu Yi's daughter.

"My name is Mercy, after my mother," she said, glancing at Guo Jing before making a quick bow of her head.

Guo Jing spotted the banner pole at the end of the bed. The banner itself had been torn to pieces. "Have you stopped your search for a husband?"

"Your father's wounds are grave, they need to be treated properly," Wang said.

Wang looked around the room. Father and daughter were of slender means, that was obvious. They would struggle to pay for medicine. He removed two ingots of silver and placed them on the table. "I will return tomorrow to see how you are feeling."

Wang took Guo Jing by the arm and left before father and daughter could give their thanks.

Four servants in brocade were waiting for them as they emerged from the inn.

"Our master is waiting, please come with us."

Wang Chuyi consented, but Guo Jing stopped him. "Master, please wait one moment."

He ran back into the inn, opened one of the boxes and picked out four pastries, wrapped them in a handkerchief and tucked them into his pocket. He then went back out and followed Wang and the servants.

2

FLAGS FLUTTERED HIGH ABOVE THE IMPOSING ENTRANCE. Two fierce jade lions stood guard. A flight of white jade steps carried them up to the vast red door that opened onto the main hall. Above the large door was written an inscription in the finest golden calligraphy: RESIDENCE OF THE PRINCE OF ZHAO.

Prince of Zhao: the title given to the Sixth Prince of the Jin Empire, Wanyan Honglie. Guo Jing knew this already.

The young Prince is the son of Wanyan Honglie? Guo Jing said to himself. I can't go in! What if his father sees me?

He hesitated. Just then drums started beating and horns echoed around them. The Prince emerged in person, dressed in red robes and a golden crown, his hair swept back in a bun. Around his waist was tied a gold belt. He rushed down the steps to greet them.

The young men caught sight of each other's swollen and bruised faces and smiled.

Wang Chuyi was less impressed by the Prince's luxurious dress. He frowned and followed them into the Great Hall.

"It is my great honor to have the pleasure of Elder Wang and Guo Esquire's company," the Prince said, gesturing for Wang Chuyi to take the best seat.

The young man neither kowtowed nor addressed him as a fellow member of the Quanzhen, which angered the Taoist. "How long have you been receiving instruction from your Master?"

"I am unfamiliar with the martial arts," the Prince replied with a smile. "My *shifu's* lessons only lasted a few years and what he taught me was nothing more than three-legged cat skills. You would laugh at them."

"While the skills passed down in the Quanzhen are certainly nothing exceptional," Wang said through gritted teeth, "it seems a little unfair to call them three-legged cat skills. Did you know your Master will be arriving in a few days?"

"My *shifu* is already here," Wanyan Kang said, the smile not leaving his lips. "Do you wish to meet him, sir?"

"He is? Where?"

Wanyan Kang clapped his hands. "We're ready for the food!"

He then led his two guests along several corridors and past many decorated pavilions, until they came to the banqueting hall. Guo Jing was overcome with the sight of such riches. But he was ever anxious that they might run into the Prince's father. The Great Khan wanted him dead, and yet he was also the father of Elder Qiu's disciple! Should Guo consider him an enemy or a friend?

Half a dozen people were already waiting for them. One man had three distinct protrusions on his forehead; this was of course Browbeater Hou, the Three-Horned Dragon. He watched them enter, dressed in a look of displeasure. Guo Jing was not sure if they were welcome here, but the presence of the Prince reassured him. He averted his gaze as the memory of how his friend Lotus Huang had teased and taunted Browbeater Hou only that afternoon came to him. He felt a giggle rise that was fed into his sleeve.

"Elder Wang, these people are your great admirers. They have long desired to be acquainted with you," Wanyan Kang said in his most charming tone. "Master Peng, you have already met."

The two men nodded.

"And this is Master Liang, also known as the Ginseng Immortal," the Prince continued. "He comes from the Mountain of Eternal Snow." Graybeard Liang extended his hand in greeting.

"Such an honor to meet Elder Wang, the Iron Foot Immortal. My trip was not in vain! This is the most distinguished Lama Supreme Wisdom with the Five Finger Blade. I am from the northeast originally and he has come all the way from Kokonor. We have both traveled thousands of miles. We were all fated to meet here, I believe."

He had a way with words, this Old Liang. Wang Chuyi cupped his hands and nodded to the lama.

Just then a loud noise came echoing from out in the corridor: "You mean to say, the Seven Freaks of the South are so bigheaded because they think they have the support of the Quanzhen?"

Wang Chuyi turned and saw a shiny-headed bald man with bulging eyes enter. "Hector Sha, the Dragon King?"

"Yes?" the man growled. "Who speaks my name?"

How could I have offended him? Wang thought. We've never even met.

"I've heard so many speak in admiration of you, it is my honor," he said in a soothing tone.

Hector Sha's martial skills far surpassed those of his brother-in-arms, Browbeater Hou. But he was ill-tempered and was always shouting at his disciples, the Four Daemons of the Yellow River, which meant none of them had managed to learn anything but the most rudimentary skills. They had been out of favor with the Sixth Prince since that debacle of a fight between the Four Daemons and Guo Jing out on the Mongolian steppe, and Hector Sha had been ruthless in his punishment of the four young men. He had also ordered Browbeater Hou to capture Guo Jing as revenge, but humiliation had once again followed, not only in Guo Jing's escape the day before, but now at the hands of a rather slim and feminine-looking young beggar.

Hector Sha had now lost patience and he saw no reason to hide his anger from the two guests. Guo Jing stumbled back and Wang Chuyi stepped in front of the young man to shield him.

"You would dare to protect the little vandal?" Hector Sha cried, striking out at Wang. Wang defended the attack, but at that moment, someone grabbed at their wrists and separated them. Both Sha and Wang had engaged their internal energy against each other, so it was a most remarkable feat to pull them apart.

The man was dressed in white and wore a thin fur coat tied with a wide belt. He must have been in his midthirties. He was handsome and moved with poise. Descended from a noble family, perhaps.

"May I present Master of White Camel Mount in the Kunlun Range, Gallant Ouyang!" Wanyan Kang exclaimed. "Master Ouyang has never been to the Central Plains before, so I believe none of you will have met."

The young man's appearance surprised not only Wang Chuyi and Guo Jing, but also Tiger Peng and Graybeard Liang. His skill was apparent to all, but apart from Guo Jing days before, they had never heard of White Camel Mount. He must have come from the western borderlands of the Chinese Empire.

"Brothers, I should have arrived days ago, but I encountered a small problem along the way. My apologies."

He must know the women dressed in white that had tried to steal his horse, Guo Jing realized. I wonder if my *shifus* have met him already? Are they injured?

Wang Chuyi realized that he might not be able to defeat this man in a fight. "What about your *shifu*?" he asked, turning to the Prince. "Why don't you ask for him?"

"Yes, good idea," the Prince replied, and turning to his servants, "Ask my *shifu* to come and greet my guests."

If Brother Qiu is here, Wang Chuyi thought, we might stand a chance.

Before long the sound of boots against stone came echoing down the hall. A hefty officer of around forty, dressed in brocade, appeared at the main door. His chin was adorned with a thick beard. Wanyan Kang approached him.

"Sir," he said with a nod of his head. "Elder Wang insisted that he be allowed to meet you. He asked several times."

A pulse of anger rose in Wang Chuyi. How dare this arrogant young rascal mock him? There was no way this plodding officer had taught him those moves.

"What do you want?" the man said, looking at Wang Chuyi. "I prefer not to associate with Taoists."

Wang Chuyi was furious. "I've come to collect alms. One thousand *taels* of silver."

Officer Tang was the head of the Sixth Prince's personal guard. He had given the young Prince some basic lessons in martial arts when he was a boy, hence why Wanyan Kang addressed him as *Shifu.*

"What impudence!"

"One thousand *taels* of silver is a trifle." Wanyan Kang stepped in. "Prepare the alms for the esteemed Taoist."

Officer Tang was incensed and could not take his eyes off the monk. Nor could he understand why the Prince should be showing him such reverence.

"Please be seated," Wanyan Kang continued. "Elder Wang, this is your first visit with us. You must take the best seat."

Wang Chuyi refused, but after some jostling, he ended up settling at the head of the table. Three rounds of wine were served in quick succession.

"You are all the finest men of the martial world," Wang Chuyi began. "Let us decide the matter of Mr. Mu Yi and his daughter together."

All eyes turned to the Prince. He took his time pouring himself a glass of wine, stood up and raised his cup to Wang Chuyi. "Your Reverence, do me the honor of drinking with me. The matter shall be dealt with as Elder Wang sees fit. I dare not presume to go against your word."

Wang Chuyi had not been expecting this. He raised his cup and drank with the boy.

"Then let us bring Mu Yi here and we shall speak with him."

"Why not send brother Guo to fetch him?" the Prince suggested.

Wang Chuyi nodded.

Guo Jing was dispatched immediately to the Prosperity Inn, but upon his arrival he found Mu Yi's room empty. Father and daughter had left, taking all their belongings with them. The inn boy said someone had come to visit and paid for the room, but he did not know who. Guo Jing hurried back to the Prince of Zhao's residence.

"My sincerest thanks, brother," the Prince said on Guo Jing's return. "Where is Mr. Mu?"

Guo Jing told them he had gone.

"This is my fault," the Prince said. "Gather five men and look for them," he ordered one of his servants. "You must find Mr. Mu!"

The servant ran out the door. But Wang Chuyi's head was swirling with suspicions. Two servants would be enough; why send so many? And why insist Guo Jing go himself in the first place? "The truth will always out," he said out loud, a cold smile on his face.

"Exactly! Who can say what that Mr. Mu is up to. A most odd fellow."

"Elder Wang, to which temple do you belong?" Officer Tang asked coldly. "What are you doing here demanding money?"

"And may one ask to which country you belong, Officer? What are you doing here holding rank in the Jin army?" Wang Chuyi could see the man was Chinese. The thought that he had assumed a position in the Jin court to abuse his fellow countrymen disgusted the monk.

But Officer Tang hated nothing more than being reminded of his ethnicity, since it barred him from advancing further within the Jin ranks, despite his skill and loyalty to the regime. He had served the Prince of Zhao for two decades, and yet he was there for nothing more than show. Before the others knew what was happening, Officer Tang had barged past Graybeard Liang and Gallant Ouyang and was launching his fist at Wang Chuyi's nose.

But Wang Chuyi caught his wrist with his chopsticks. "No need to resort to violence!"

Officer Tang was unable to struggle free of the Taoist's grip. "Sorcery!"

"Come now, sir, sit down and join us for some wine." Graybeard Liang laughed, patting Officer Tang on the shoulder.

Wang Chuyi was aware that he would be unable to use the same trick with the chopsticks on Old Liang, who was still gripping Officer Tang's shoulder, so he let go of Tang's wrist and aimed them instead at his other shoulder. Such a lowly, insignificant fighter as Officer Tang should be proud to have the attention of two such masters of the *wulin* at the same time. With a couple of short exhalations, Tang lurched forward, his hands plunging into a plate of fish bones and a bowl of hot and sour soup. Pottery fragments tore the skin on Tang's hands and a few drops of blood tinged the spilled soup a pinky red.

The guests burst into laughter as they pulled back and out of the way of the hot liquid. Flushed with shame, Officer Tang fled from the hall. The servants, just as amused as the visitors, suppressed smiles as they cleaned up.

"The Quanzhen's reputation is well deserved," Hector Sha said. "I wonder if Elder Wang might care to enlighten me on something."

"It would be my pleasure."

"The Daemons of the Yellow River and the Quanzhen Sect have long been at peace now. Why does Elder Wang stir trouble by supporting the Seven Freaks of the South? The Quanzhen may command many disciples, but we are not afraid to resume old enmities on equal ground."

"There has been a misunderstanding," Wang Chuyi replied. "While I have heard of the Seven Freaks of the South, I do not know them personally. My martial brother has a bet with them, that is true, but I have no intention of helping them against the Daemons of the Yellow River."

"Excellent. Then you will let me have this boy," Hector Sha said, making a grab for Guo Jing's throat.

Wang Chuyi gently pushed Guo Jing from his chair, just as Hector Sha's hand cracked the back of it as easily as if it were made of rotten wood. It was a rare technique, executed perfectly.

"And still you protect the boy?" Hector Sha cried out.

"I brought him here, so I will see that he leaves in one piece. Why not settle this another day?"

"The boy has offended Brother Sha?" Gallant Ouyang interrupted. "Why not tell us how, and let us all decide what is to be done."

Unsure of where Gallant Ouyang's loyalties would fall, Hector Sha was reluctant to be drawn into a fight against him and the Taoist. "My four good-for-nothing disciples followed the Prince of Zhao north to Mongolia as part of his household. Just as we were about to succeed in our mission, this young scoundrel ruined everything and angered the Prince. If we don't deal with him, what right do we have to stay here enjoying the Prince's hospitality?"

Hector Sha was ill-tempered by nature, to be sure, but he was no fool. Attention now turned to Guo Jing. This young man and the Taoist were the only ones present who were not guests of the elder Prince Wanyan Honglie. Wanyan Kang was most displeased upon hearing Hector Sha's account. He decided he would go along with the others and present the young man to his father.

Wang Chuyi was growing nervous, desperate for an escape plan, but fighting so many men at once was not an option. Had Wanyan Kang planned the entire affair? Had he been too naïve to think the young Prince would refrain from acting against his *shifu*'s martial brother? He should not have brought the boy here, but it would be difficult to get out now with both of them unhurt.

I must play along, that's my only option, Wang Chuyi said to himself. Test the extent of their skills. "Men, you are all excellent fighters, famed throughout the *wulin*. It has been my honor to meet you all today. But this boy"—he pointed at Guo Jing—"is unaware of the offense he has committed, especially against you, Brother Sha. If you will not let him go, I am powerless to change your mind, even if I cannot agree with the way you are handling the situation. Perhaps it would be better if you all let the boy know the extent of your skills. That way he will know it is not that I don't want to help him, but that I can't."

Browbeater Hou had been finding the whole exchange extremely boring, but this last sentence pulled him out of his stupor. "I'll go first!" he cried, jumping up and standing before Wang.

"I, sir, am no match for your superior skills. No, rather than fight me, I suggest you give us a display to open my eyes to some new techniques, as well as teach the boy a lesson. That way he will never be so arrogant again."

Browbeater Hou could sense a note of sarcasm in the Taoist's words, but he could not quite be sure what meaning lay behind them, nor how to answer him.

Just as well, Hector Sha was thinking. I'm not exactly keen to fight a member of the Quanzhen. "Brother," he said, turning to Browbeater Hou, "why don't you show Elder Wang your Buried Under an Avalanche?"

Snow was still falling outside. Browbeater Hou rushed to the entrance and swept his arms up around his head, bringing the snow in until he had gathered a pile four feet high, kicking it into shape. He then retreated three steps and vaulted head first into the middle, where it reached up to his chest. Guo Jing looked on in puzzlement. He had never seen anything like it. Why should he choose to be upside down, motionless, in a mound of icy snowflakes?

Hector Sha turned to the others. "Please, everyone, bury him deeper."

The others found the whole thing most amusing, if not a little strange, but together they kicked more snow into the pile. What they had not realized was that, being from the Yellow River, Hector Sha and Browbeater Hou were well-versed in water kung fu, and could hold their breath in water, snow, and even soil for as long as a whole afternoon. This was just an everyday exercise for the two men.

The other men raised their cups and toasted the display. It was not until some time later that Browbeater Hou at last flipped out and back onto his feet in a display of Jumping Carp.

Guo Jing clapped the loudest. Browbeater Hou resumed his place at the table and shot him a fierce look.

"Third Uncle, you still have snow on your forehead," Guo Jing said, unable to stop himself.

"My name is the Three-Horned Dragon, not Third Uncle, thank you! Do you think I don't know I have snow on my head? But now that you've mentioned it, I'm not going to brush it away." The heat from the fire was melting the flakes so that they now ran in three rivulets down his face, but he was playing the stubborn wife who will not heed her husband's advice.

"My martial brother's technique is a little clumsy, but quite amusing," Hector Sha said, stretching his meaty fingers into a bowl of melon seeds, before flicking the empty shells into the pile of snow. The others were surprised to see the seeds were forming the shape of the Chinese character for "yellow."

No wonder the Dragon King and his Four Daemons control the Yellow River; their skills are considerable indeed, Wang Chuyi said to himself. Turning back to the snow, he saw another character emerge, this time "river." Next came "nine." The Nine Bends of the Yellow River.

"Such accuracy, Brother Sha!" This time it was Tiger Peng the Outlaw who spoke. "Now it's my turn to show Elder Wang what I can do!" At that he jumped up, and landed near the pile of snow, proceeding to catch the seeds Hector Sha was flicking to form his last character. Tiger Peng missed not one, despite the fact that they were small and traveling at speed.

The gathering erupted in applause and Tiger Peng returned to his seat with a smile spread across his face. Hector Sha stubbornly finished his phrase. His friend had stolen his thunder somewhat, but he did not seem to mind too much. He turned to Gallant Ouyang and said, "And what about Master Ouyang? What do you have to teach us rough and ignorant men of the east?"

Gallant Ouyang sensed the displeasure in Hector Sha's voice. The Dragon King was a man to hold a grudge. He would have to do something to impress him. At that moment, the servants entered, bringing four types of sweets, and replaced the used chopsticks with clean ones. Gallant Ouyang snatched up the dirty chopsticks, and with a flick of his wrist, ten pairs flew through the air and landed in the snow, poking out like incense sticks in a temple censer. Four plum blossoms appeared beside Hector Sha's melon-seed writing. Guo Jing, Wanyan Kang, and the others were puzzled by the display but clapped in delight. Only Wang Chuyi and Hector Sha understood the significance of such skill.

Wang Chuyi began to turn his thoughts to why the men were gathered in Yanjing. Master Ouyang, Lama Supreme Wisdom, and the Ginseng Codger had traveled great distances. There must be something suspicious afoot.

Old Liang laughed and nodded to the men, before walking into the center of the banqueting hall. There, he leaped up and landed so lightly on top of the chopsticks that they did not sink any further into the snow. There, he performed a series of Yanqing Sparrow boxing moves, such as Embracing the Moon, Gentleman's Cape, Shoot the Arrow, and Remove the Boot, his feet dancing across the still-vertical chopsticks. He finished with a Jump the Tiger and a Retreat to Advance, before skipping back to his seat. The hall echoed with cheers. Guo Jing's were the loudest.

The banquet was over by now and the servants brought up golden bowls of warm water for the guests to wash their hands.

Now for Lama Supreme Wisdom, Wang Chuyi thought. He glanced at the lama. He was sipping the water in his bowl, seemingly oblivious to all else. The others had finished, but he seemed lost in thought. Everyone watched as steam started rising from the golden bowl, followed shortly after by the sound of bubbles popping on the surface.

With such powerful internal energy, I must make the first move! Wang Chuyi realized in alarm.

He flew up and grabbed at the Prince, pressing at his pressure points. The others looked on in shock.

Wang Chuyi reached for a bottle of wine and said, "A toast, to my new friends. It is an honor!"

He sucked in a mouthful of the wine and then spat it out into everyone's cups, some half empty, some nearly full, each one filled without spillage.

With the Prince in one hand and the wine in another, the Taoist's internal kung fu was plain to see. Were the Taoist to press a little harder, he could turn the young man's internal organs into pulp. No one dared approach them.

Wang Chuyi served Guo Jing and himself last and, raising his cup, spoke in a calm and steady manner. "I bear no one present any ill will, and neither do I call the young Guo Jing my particular friend. But he is a good boy, compassionate and well-intentioned, not to mention brave, when required. All I ask you men present is that you let him go, for my sake."

No one spoke. Wang Chuyi continued: "If everyone agrees, I will release the Prince in exchange for the boy. A good deal, I think: a commoner for a royal?"

"As it pleases Elder Wang, let's call it a deal!" Old Liang laughed.

Wang Chuyi released Wanyan Kang, confident that none among them would wish to show themselves so dishonorable in front of the others, despite what people said about their predilections for cruelty.

"We bid you men farewell, and may we meet again soon!" Wang Chuyi grabbed Guo Jing's hand, bowed, and made hastily for the exit.

Just as Wang had thought, the men made no move to stop them, despite being frustrated that the fish was escaping their net.

"Elder Wang is most welcome," Wanyan Kang called after them, having recovered from the force of the Taoist's grip. "Come again whenever you please so that I might learn from you!"

"Our problem is as yet unresolved," Wang snorted. "We shall be sure to see to it another day!"

"Elder Wang is skilled indeed," Lama Supreme Wisdom said just as they reached the door, and he bowed, his hands held in prayer.

Then he charged.

Wang Chuyi defended himself with both palms and all his inner strength. But the lama grabbed instead at Wang's wrist, exchanging internal *qi* for external kung fu. Wang blocked with a twist, meeting force with force. The color drained from the lama's cheeks as they pulled apart. "Most impressive," he breathed.

"The lama is known for his righteousness throughout the *wulin,* and yet he does not keep a promise?"

This made the lama spit with anger. "I was trying to stop you from leaving, not the boy . . ."

It was his pride that was wounded, but just as he finished speaking he started coughing blood.

Wang Chuyi knew they had to leave that very moment, so taking hold of Guo Jing's hand, he quickly ran out.

The others stood and watched, not daring to stop them.

3

IT WAS SOME TIME BEFORE WANG CHUYI DARED TURN AND LOOK behind them.

"Carry me back to the inn," he breathed, once he was sure no one was following them.

Guo Jing was shocked to hear how weak he sounded. But indeed, Elder Wang's cheeks were pale and he looked to be very sick. Nothing like the vigorous man of a few hours before.

"Elder Wang, are you hurt?"

Wang Chuyi nodded and lost balance. Guo Jing stooped to prop him up, then took the Taoist onto his back and began to hurry back in the direction of the inn. Just as they reached the door, Wang Chuyi whispered to him, "Not here, find somewhere more remote . . ."

Guo Jing paused and then realized Wang was afraid the men would come looking for them. His skills were not enough to make up for his *shifu*'s injuries. Guo Jing began to run down the quieter alleys in search of another place to spend the night. The farther he went, the fewer people he encountered. Wang's breathing was getting fainter all the time.

At last he found somewhere suitable. It was small and dirty, but he entered, procured a room and placed Wang down on the bed.

"Water . . . A tub of clean water," the Taoist sighed. "Quick."

"Anything else?"

Wang waved the boy away.

Guo Jing hurried out of the room and gave some silver to the inn boy to fetch some water. Guo Jing had come to realize the importance of these little tokens for getting what one wanted. Before long, a few boys arrived with a large tub and placed it in the courtyard. Then they came with buckets of water and filled it to the brim.

"You are a good child," Wang said. "Now put me in the tub. And don't let anyone near."

Guo Jing did as he was told, even though he wasn't sure why. When Wang was submerged up to the neck Guo Jing instructed the inn boy that no one was to disturb them.

Wang Chuyi sat in the water, his eyes closed, his breath a rapid panting. Guo Jing watched in amazement as the water turned black and color returned to the Taoist's cheeks. Then Wang emerged.

"Help me out," Wang said to the young man. "Change the water."

Guo Jing called the inn boy back for fresh water and helped Wang Chuyi back into the tub. Wang was forcing poison from his body with just the power of his internal energy. They repeated the process three times before the water stayed clear.

"All is well," Wang Chuyi said with a smile. "That Lama's kung fu is vicious."

"He had poison on his hands?" Guo Jing asked, just relieved Elder Wang was out of danger.

"Yes. We call it Poisoned Sand Palms. I've seen it many times before, but I've never known any as powerful as the lama's. I nearly didn't survive it."

"I'm just happy you're well! Are you hungry? I can ask the inn boy to make something."

But all Wang wanted was a brush, ink, and paper. He then proceeded to write down a prescription. "I am out of danger for the moment, but my internal organs are still infected. If I don't take this herbal remedy within the next twelve hours, the poison may yet be fatal."

Early the next morning, Guo Jing took the paper and ran out. He found an apothecary nearby and asked the owner to make up the recipe as Wang had written it.

The owner checked the shelves, but returned empty-handed. "I'm sorry, my boy, I've sold out of these herbs."

Guo Jing grabbed back the piece of paper and ran out the door before the owner could say any more. Yet the second shop was also out. Eight tries later, and he was still having no luck. Guo Jing was getting anxious. And angry. He ran to every herbal medicine shop in the city, but the answer was always the same. They had all sold out.

Those scoundrels! Guo Jing realized Wanyan Kang and his men must have sent someone out to buy up the entire supply of the herbs in Yanjing.

Guo Jing returned to the inn and told Wang Chuyi what had happened. The two men were in despair. Guo Jing flopped onto the table and began sobbing.

"Dear boy, everyone must go at some point," Wang said with a smile. "The heavens decide it, it's not up to us. Don't cry." He patted the edge of the bed and then began to sing:

> "In peacock there is peahen,
> Just as in color there is gray.
> For a Taoist fame is ruin,
> In permanent replay."

Guo Jing wiped his cheeks and looked up at the Taoist, who was grinning and sitting up in bed.

A thought suddenly struck Guo Jing: what if he tried another city nearby? He was sliding quietly out of the room when the inn boy came running up to him with a letter addressed to "Master Guo."

Who can this be from? Guo asked himself. He tore open the letter and began reading: *I have something urgent to tell you. I will be waiting for you by the lake ten* li *west of the city.* Beneath the characters was the picture of a smiling face: Lotus! It was an exact likeness.

How does he know I'm staying here? Guo Jing turned to the inn boy. "Who came with this letter?"

"A beggar," the inn boy replied simply.

Guo Jing hurried back into the room. Wang Chuyi was stretching. "Elder Wang, I'm going to try to find the herbs in a nearby city."

"I'm sure they've already thought of that. Don't trouble yourself, boy."

But Guo Jing was not going to give up yet. Brother Huang would know what to do!

"A good friend of mine wants to meet me. I will be back as soon as I've spoken to him." Guo Jing passed the piece of paper to Wang.

"How do you know him?" Wang asked after a brief pause.

Guo Jing related the story to Wang Chuyi: the young boy who had run circles around Browbeater Hou. "Some most unusual skills. I remember him." He thought for a little longer and then continued, "But you must be careful. Your skills are no match for his, and there's something untrustworthy about him. I can't put my finger on it."

"We are sworn friends, he won't do me any harm," Guo Jing replied.

"You haven't known him long." Wang sighed. "How can you be sure of his character? You would be unable to defend yourself."

But no matter what the Taoist said, Guo Jing was not in the least bit suspicious of Lotus. It's only because he doesn't know him, Guo Jing said to himself. He reassured Elder Wang again of the young man's good character.

"Fine," Wang said, smiling. "You young people must make your own mistakes in order to learn. But there's something a little odd about his appearance and voice. Haven't you noticed?"

Guo Jing said nothing, and Wang Chuyi realized there was no point going on and just shook his head. Guo Jing tucked the prescription into his shirt front and left.

ONCE OUT of the western city gates, Guo Jing began running. The snowflakes were falling in even larger formations as they swirled around his head and landed on his cheeks. The landscape was a vast, empty expanse of white. He kept going ten *li* due west until, up ahead, he could make out the glimmer of water. The lake had not yet frozen over and the banks were dressed in plum blossoms, the petals creating the illusion of snow settling on the water's surface.

Guo Jing could not see anyone. What if he had left already?

"Brother Huang! Brother Huang!"

Just then a sound startled him. He turned quickly, but it was just birds. He called out again. Maybe Lotus was yet to arrive? Guo Jing decided to wait a little.

He sat down by the side of the lake and his mind began to wander. First to Lotus, then to Wang Chuyi. He was in no mood to take in the beautiful scenery. Snow was nothing special, he had seen it many times in Mongolia, and he was not so sentimental as to marvel at the poetry of nature and plum blossoms in winter.

After a long wait, he heard noises coming from a knot of trees farther along. He approached carefully, pausing when a rough voice broke through the quiet.

"What makes you any better? We're all stuck here together, aren't we?"

"If you hadn't been such a coward and run away, we would have been four against one. How could we have lost?"

"Unless I'm mistaken, you fell over while running away yourself. Doesn't make you much of a hero," said a third.

It sounded like the Four Daemons of the Yellow River.

Gathering his courage, Guo Jing entered the thicket, but he could not see anyone.

"We should have taken him together. Who knew the little beggar had so many tricks?"

Guo Jing looked up and saw four men hanging in the canopy above. It was them. His heart fluttered. Lotus had to be nearby!

"Are you practicing your lightness kung fu again?" he called up, grinning widely.

"Lightness kung fu?" Qian the Hardy snarled. "Can't you see we're stuck?"

Guo Jing laughed and Qian kicked out, but he was not even close to hitting Guo Jing.

"Go away, or I'll pee all over you!" Ma the Valiant cried out.

Guo Jing was doubled over by now. "Go on, I bet it won't reach me."

Laughter sounded suddenly behind him. Guo Jing turned to see ripples on the water and a boat suddenly appear from behind the tree line.

A young maiden was rowing toward them, her black hair tumbling down over her shoulders and white robes. Her golden hairpins twinkled in the winter sunlight. She looked like a celestial goddess and Guo Jing was struck dumb. As she came closer, he realized she could not be more than fifteen or sixteen. Her skin was as white as the surrounding fields and her beauty was like none he had ever seen before. She approached with a broad smile.

Guo Jing turned, unable to look straight at her, and blushed.

The young girl steered the boat to the bank. "Brother Guo, step on board!"

Guo Jing was surprised that she should know his name. He turned and glanced up at her smile and fluttering robes. At first he said nothing, as if caught in a dream.

"Don't you recognize me?" The young girl laughed.

She did sound like Brother Huang, but how could a dirty beggar boy have turned into such a radiant fairy? He could not believe his eyes.

"Miss! Cut us down, if you please."

"We will give you a hundred *taels* of gold for your trouble!"

"Each! One hundred each, that's four hundred *taels*!"

"Eight hundred *taels*!"

But the young girl ignored them. "It's me, Lotus. Brother Guo, have you lost all affection for me now?"

She did bear a resemblance to his friend, it was true. "But . . . you . . ."

"Yes, I'm a girl. I never actually told you to call me Brother Huang. Come now, we've got to hurry."

Guo Jing stumbled forward and tripped into the canoe. The Daemons were still shouting behind them, offering more and more money.

Lotus rowed into the middle of the lake, where she brought out some dishes from a basket and a small jug of wine. "Let's eat and enjoy the scenery." They were far enough from the shore that they could no longer hear the Daemons shouting.

"I'm just so confused," Guo Jing stuttered. "I thought you were a boy. Now I can't call you Brother Huang anymore."

"And no calling me Sister Huang either! Just call me by the name my father gave me: Lotus."

"I brought you cakes," Guo Jing remembered suddenly, and pulled out the sweets Wanyan Kang had given Elder Wang from inside his shirt. By now they were nothing but a bag of crumbs.

Lotus giggled. Guo Jing blushed. "Ruined," he said. But just as he was about to throw them overboard, Lotus reached out and took the bag.

She fished out a piece of broken cake and placed it in her mouth. "Delicious." He looked at her; her eyes were red and had begun to moisten. Why was she crying?

"My mother died when I was very young. No one has ever cared enough to notice what I like and dislike before. Until I met you." A few tears started running down her cheeks. She took out a handkerchief, but instead of using it to dry her eyes, she wrapped the remaining cakes in it and placed them inside her robe. She looked up at him, this time with a smile. "I'm saving them for later."

Guo Jing was not experienced when it came to romance, but he could sense there was a special meaning behind her actions. "You said you had something urgent to tell me, in your letter."

"This is what I wanted to tell you. That I am not Brother Huang, but Lotus. Doesn't this count as urgent?" She smiled.

"Why did you disguise yourself as a dirty beggar boy when you are so pretty?"

"You think I'm pretty?" Lotus turned away, her cheeks flushed.

"Yes, very. Just like a fairy that lives at the top of a snowy mountain."

"Have you seen a fairy before?"

"Of course not, I wouldn't be here if I had!"

"What do you mean?"

"In Mongolia, our elders told us that if you see a fairy you will never return to the grasslands again. You will be dazed and freeze to death."

Lotus giggled. "And is that how you feel now? Dazed?"

"We're friends, it's different," Guo Jing said. Now it was his turn to blush.

"I know that you are true of heart. It wouldn't matter to you if I were a boy or a girl, beautiful or ugly." She paused before continuing. "Everyone is nice to me when I'm dressed like this, but you took care of me even when I was dressed as a beggar boy." Lotus smiled, and then said, "Shall I sing for you?"

"Could you sing for me tomorrow? We need to find medicine for Elder Wang first." He went on to tell Lotus all that had happened the previous day, and how Wanyan Kang's men had bought up all the herbs essential to curing the Taoist in the city.

"No wonder I saw you running between apothecaries today," Lotus said.

So she was following me; that's how she knew where I was staying, Guo Jing thought.

"Brother Huang, may I ride your horse Ulaan to find the herbs?"

"For one thing, I am not your brother. And the horse is yours.

Did you think I was going to keep it? I was just testing you. But I worry you won't find the herbs in the neighboring towns."

This made Guo Jing even more anxious.

"Let me sing this song first. Listen carefully," Lotus replied, turning around and continuing to row the boat through the lake. Her voice was as clear and crisp as the water itself:

> "*Wild goose weather,*
> *Winter frost seeps through window screen.*
> *Veiled in protective clouds is the moon,*
> *Tender is the ice unweaned.*
> *The stream her mirror, she combs her hair,*
> *Perfume and powder*
> *all brushed away.*
> *Jade complexion*
> *layered silk outweighs.*
> *Leaning against the east wind,*
> *One moment of her smile*
> *Turns ten thousand blossoms away,*
> *Blushed and beguiled.*
> *Oh, loneliness!*
> *Where is home?*
> *A garden after snow?*
> *A lakeside pagoda?*
> *To Jade Lake, a ne'er forgotten beau.*
> *But which messenger can she trust?*
> *Butterflies only know to search for peach and willow,*
> *Of southern blossom they do not care.*
> *And so with sorrow she sheds her petals*
> *Into sunsets*
> *Accompanied by bugle blare.*"

Guo Jing listened carefully. The meaning of the lyrics was hard to grasp, but Lotus's voice was so sweet and the surroundings so beautiful that it lulled him into a warm daze. Only thoughts of the Elder Wang popped on the surface of his consciousness every now and again.

"This song was written by an official of the court, His Excellency Mr. Xin," Lotus almost whispered once she had finished, "and it describes the winter plum blossom. It's very beautiful, isn't it?"

"I didn't understand it, but it was lovely. Who is Mr. Xin?"

"His name is Xin Qiji. My father says he was a good and just official who takes care of the people. He was the only patriot left defending our lands when the Jin captured the north and tortured General Yue."

Guo Jing's mother, Lily Li, had often told him of the cruel deeds carried out by the terrible Jin, how they had brutally killed many of his people, but the injustice had burned only faintly up on the Mongolian steppe. He had never been able to muster a strong hatred toward the invading Empire.

"It is my first time here, in the Central Plains. You will have to tell me more stories later. Right now, I must save Elder Wang."

"Just a little longer, there's no hurry," Lotus said.

"But if he doesn't get the antidote within twelve hours, he will be forever crippled. He is most sick!"

"Then let him be crippled, it doesn't much concern us!"

Guo Jing leaped to his feet. "But . . . but . . ." His cheeks burned.

"Don't worry. I will make sure you get the medicine," Lotus said, smiling.

She is certainly cleverer than me, and I don't have any more ideas, Guo Jing said to himself. She sounds confident. So he relented and listened, laughing and clapping, as she related the story of how she had run circles around the Four Daemons of the Yellow River and Browbeater Hou.

The snow twinkled in the sun and the ice crystals and plum blossoms together painted the most perfect and romantic scene. Lotus slowly reached for Guo Jing's hand. "Nothing scares me now."

"Why's that?"

"Even if my father has rejected me, you will stay by my side, won't you?"

"Of course, Lotus. I . . . like . . . being in your company."

Lotus laid her head against his chest. A sweet perfume filled the air. The lake seemed to stretch around the earth. Was it the blossoms? Or was it Lotus? They held hands and did not speak.

After what seemed like hours, Lotus let out a sigh. "This place is so beautiful, what a shame we have to go."

"We do?"

"Didn't you want to get the herbs for Elder Wang?"

"Yes, of course! But where can we find them?"

"How come the shops in Yanjing couldn't supply them?"

"Wanyan Kang's men got there first."

"In that case, we'll go to the Prince's residence and take them back."

"To the Prince's residence?" Guo Jing was stunned at this suggestion.

"Indeed!"

"We can't do that! It's too dangerous."

"Then you are prepared to let Elder Wang become a cripple? Or perhaps even die?"

Blood pumped into his cheeks. "You're right. But I must go by myself."

"Why?"

Guo Jing could not think of an answer. "Just promise."

"But what if something happens to you? I will be all alone."

Guo Jing's heart leaped and a flush of love flooded his brain. Suddenly he felt much braver. Why should he be scared of Hector Sha or Tiger Peng? He could do anything. "Fine, we'll go together."

They rowed the boat to the edge of the lake and started back toward the city gates. Halfway along the road, Guo Jing suddenly remembered the Four Daemons were still hanging in the trees. "Should we release them?" he asked Lotus.

"They call themselves the Iron Heroes," Lotus said with a smile.

"A little bit of wind and snow won't hurt them. Though I suppose they might starve to death. But the Four Daemons of the Plum Blossom Forest sounds much better than the Four Daemons of the Yellow River, don't you think?"

CHAPTER NINE

SPEAR SPLITS
PLOW

I

GUO JING AND LOTUS SNEAKED ROUND TO THE BACK OF THE palace and climbed over the wall into the courtyard.

"You have excellent lightness kung fu," Lotus whispered to Guo Jing.

Guo Jing beamed with pleasure from where he was crouching, looking out for movement inside.

Just then they heard footsteps and then laughter. Two men were walking toward them.

"What do you think the Prince is going to do with her, now that he's got her locked up?"

"Do you have to ask! Have you ever seen a girl as luscious as that since the day you were born?"

"Watch that the Prince doesn't hear your dirty talk, or he'll cut your head off! She may be pretty, but she's got nothing on the Consort."

"That lowly country girl? Of course she's got nothing on the Consort."

334

"But I thought you said the Consort came from—" He suddenly stopped and coughed. "The Prince took a beating today from that old Taoist. You'd better not upset him, or he'll take it out on you."

"If he tries, I'll duck to the left, kick to the right."

"Sure." The first man laughed.

So Wanyan Kang has a sweetheart, Guo Jing said to himself. No wonder he refused to marry Mu Yi's daughter. But then he should never have joined the competition, let alone taken her embroidered shoe. But what was that about keeping his lover locked up? Was he forcing her to stay against her will?

The two simply dressed servant boys came closer, one carrying a lantern and the other a basket of food.

"First he locks them up," the one with the food basket said, "then he worries that they'll go hungry. This late at night!"

"Winning over a lady takes charm and a gentle touch, don't you know?"

They laughed as they passed by and disappeared around a corner.

"Let's go and see how pretty she is," Lotus said in hushed tones, her curiosity getting the better of her.

"But Elder Wang's herbs!" Guo Jing replied.

"I want to see the young lady first!" Lotus scuttled off after the two servants.

What's so interesting about a young lady? Guo Jing said to himself. I can't understand it. He knew that if a woman heard another described as beautiful she would have to see it with her own eyes, especially if she was herself considered pretty. And Lotus was the type of girl who had to get what she wanted. So he set off after her.

They followed the two servant boys through the vast Zhao Palace until they came to a large stand-alone house guarded by an officer armed with a saber. Lotus and Guo Jing hid and listened as the servant boys exchanged a few words with the guard. He then opened the door and the young men went inside.

Before they could close the door again, Lotus picked up a stone and threw it at the lantern, extinguishing the flame with one *poof!*

She then grabbed Guo Jing's hand and slipped through the door. The guard did not think it too strange; rocks were known to fall sometimes from the roofs. The servants cursed and went to fetch tinder and a flint to relight it. They then carried the lantern across a small inner courtyard and in through another small door.

Lotus and Guo Jing crept behind them and saw a large cage with iron bars. Inside sat two prisoners: a man and a young woman.

One of the servants lit a candle, which he fed between the bars and placed on a table. Guo Jing peered closer. The man had a large gray beard. He looked angry. It was Mu Yi! And the young maiden sitting beside him, her eyes firmly set on the floor, was his daughter Mercy. But what were they doing here? Wanyan Kang had taken them hostage. But why? Had he fallen in love with her, after all?

The servants proceeded to pass some snacks and dishes through the bars.

"Kill us already, if that's what you're planning! I'm fed up with being pampered like a pet. Hypocrites!" With that, Mu Yi took one of the plates and smashed it on the ground.

Just then a voice came from outside. "Your Highness!" It was the guard.

Lotus and Guo Jing exchanged glances and slipped behind the door, just as Wanyan Kang entered.

"Who has angered the valiant Mu Yi?" he announced. "Be careful or I'll break your stinking legs!"

The servants dropped to their knees.

"Please, sir."

"Go, get out of here."

"Yes, sir."

They stood up and scurried away, but as they got to the door, they turned and poked out their tongues and made faces at each other.

Wanyan Kang waited for them to close the door before speaking. "Please don't be alarmed. I invited you and your daughter here to the palace for a special reason."

"Then why lock us up like common thieves?" Mu Yi snarled in response. "How dare you call it an invitation?"

"My apologies, please be patient. I truly am very sorry."

"Such excuses are good for convincing a three-year-old, but don't try them on me. It's just typical of you greedy officials—always feeding off us common folk. I've seen enough of it to know."

Wanyan Kang tried several times to reply, but each time Mu Yi cut him off with another flood of angry retorts. Somehow, the Jin Prince managed to keep a smile on his face.

"Father, let him speak," Mercy pleaded quietly.

Mu Yi snorted, but at last fell silent.

"Your daughter possesses rare talent, and is of course extremely beautiful. I have eyes that can see, how could I not acknowledge it?"

Mercy's cheeks flushed crimson and she lowered her gaze even further.

"But you see, I am the eldest son of the Prince of Zhao. My father is strict. If he found out I had agreed to marry a young girl of no family, a wandering performer from the rivers and lakes, he would be furious and the people would despise him for it."

"What are you saying?"

"I would like you to stay a few days, rest, recover from your injuries, and then go back to your village. Wait until two summers have passed and talk has died down, and then either I will go south to ask for your daughter's hand in marriage, or you can send her here. Wouldn't that be better?"

Mu Yi made no reply. He was thinking about something else.

"My father has had to suffer enough from my mischief. Not three months ago he reprimanded me severely for my conduct. If he were to find out about this, there could never be a wedding. I beg you, sir, to keep it a secret."

"You mean my daughter is forever to be your secret wife? Your marriage will never be out in the open?"

"No, of course not. I will make proper arrangements when the

337

time is right. I will have some men of the court act as matchmakers and we will have a proper celebration."

Mu Yi's expression changed suddenly. "Bring your mother here, we can discuss it with her."

"How could I let my mother know?" Wanyan Kang laughed.

"There will be no agreement if your mother does not come!" He grabbed the carafe of wine and threw it through the bars.

Mercy had taken a shine to the young man ever since their duel. To her, the plan sounded perfect. She was both surprised and aggrieved by her father's reaction.

Wanyan Kang flicked aside his sleeve to reveal the wine jug in his hand; he had caught it before it smashed to the ground. "I'm going now!" he announced with a smile, turning to leave.

Guo Jing, too, thought the plan sounded a good one; who would have guessed Mu Yi would turn it down in such a rage? I will try to convince him of his error, Guo Jing said to himself. But just as he was about to stand up and reveal himself, he felt a tug at his sleeve and he was pulled back down.

Outside, more voices.

"Did you bring it?" Wanyan Kang said.

"Yes, sir," the servant replied.

They peeked out through the window. He had in his hand a small rabbit. The Prince coughed, and then snapped the animal's hind legs, before placing it inside his robe and striding away.

How odd! Guo Jing and Lotus glanced at each other before slipping out again and scurrying after the Prince.

They circled a bamboo fence and came to a cottage with white walls and black tiles on the roof. It had been built to look exactly like the peasant homes of the south. To Guo Jing, everything in the palace complex was new, so he saw nothing odd in the design, but to Lotus it looked most out of place. They watched as the Prince opened the front door and disappeared inside.

They crept to the back of the cottage and peered in through a window. What was the Prince doing in such an unassuming place? He had to be up to no good. But just then they heard him speak:

"Ma!"

A woman murmured an indistinct reply.

Wanyan Kang went through to another room. Lotus and Guo Jing shuffled along to the next window. There they spotted a middle-aged woman sitting by a rustic wooden table, her head held in her hands as she stared into space. She could not have been more than forty, and was possessed of such natural beauty that there was no reason to smother it in makeup. She wore the simplest of cotton garments.

The Consort is many times more beautiful than Mu's daughter, Lotus thought, but why is she dressed like a peasant woman? And why does she live in such a shabby cottage? Did she do something to offend the Sixth Prince?

Guo Jing was thinking the same thing, but put it down to some strange custom he did not understand. Had Lotus not done the same, pretending to be a beggar boy? It must be a game women here liked to play, pretending to be poor.

Wanyan Kang walked up to his mother and touched her on the arm. "Ma, are you feeling unwell again?"

The woman sighed. "I worry about you so," she said.

Wanyan Kang leaned in closer and smiled. "But look, your son is here now. And he's all in one piece, isn't he?" His behavior struck the two onlookers as most arrogant and unfilial.

"Except your eyes are puffy and your nose has been bleeding. All this messing around. It would be one thing if your father were to find out, but if your *shifu* were to hear . . . you'd be in big trouble."

"Ma, do you know who that Taoist was who appeared yesterday?"

"Who?" she said, looking up at her son.

"My *shifu*'s martial brother. Which would make him my martial uncle, I suppose. I pretended not to recognize him, just called him Elder this, Elder that. I could see it made him angry, but he couldn't do anything about it." He laughed.

"Oh dear." The Consort looked worried now. "I've seen your *shifu* angry. He has killed people before. He is very frightening."

"You've seen my *shifu* kill? When? Why?"

The Consort looked up at the light as if gazing far into the past. "It was a long time ago, I can barely remember."

But the young Prince was too impatient to listen to his mother's story. "The old Taoist, my martial uncle, asked what I was going to do about the young girl today, and I told him I'd do whatever he said as long as he brought her to me."

"Have you asked your father's permission?" the Consort said, brought back to more urgent concerns than reminiscences of days past. "He said yes?"

"Ma, you're too naïve. I got my men to trick them into coming here. I've got them locked up. That way the old Taoist won't be able to find them."

Outside, Guo Jing was fuming. To think I believed that he had good intentions! The valiant Mu Yi is too wise to fall for such a dirty trick.

"How can you mock his daughter like that, and lock them up?" His mother too was displeased at her son's conduct. "Go back to them and apologize. And give them some silver as recompense."

This was a good idea, Guo Jing thought.

"Ma! You don't understand. The men of the rivers and lakes don't care for money. A man's reputation is more precious than gold. If I release them, he will tell everyone what happened and my *shifu* will find out."

"So you plan to keep them locked up forever?"

"I told them to go back to their village and wait for my return. Ten, twenty years, it's up to them—a lifetime, if it pleases them." The young Prince was really laughing now.

Guo Jing was about to bang on the door and let the Prince know what he thought of him when a soft, smooth palm covered his lips and another hand seized his wrist. "Be calm."

Guo Jing turned to Lotus and smiled faintly before turning back to the window.

"That old Mu is smarter than I thought, though," the Prince was saying. "He hasn't fallen for it yet. But we'll see how long he'll hold out."

"Miss Mu is beautiful. I like her. Why don't I tell your father that you could do worse than take her for a wife? Then all will be well."

"Ma, do I have to keep reminding you? We are a royal family. How can I marry some wandering peasant girl from the rivers and lakes? Father says he will find me a suitable wife. It's just a shame we are Wanyans."

"Why?"

"Because otherwise I could marry the Princess and become the heir to the whole Jin Empire!"

His mother sighed. "Peasant girls aren't good enough for you," she said under her breath. "If only you knew . . ."

"Ma, let me tell you something funny. Old Mu says he will only say yes if he gets to meet you!"

"I'm not going to help you cheat and lie! It's not right."

Wanyan Kang walked around the room, laughing. "I wouldn't have let you see him anyway. You're such a bad liar. You would have given it all away within seconds."

Guo Jing and Lotus looked around the room, with its simple wooden furniture and farm tools. A rusty spear and a broken plow hung on the wall; in the corner sat a broken spinning wheel. Why did the Consort live in a house like this?

Wanyan Kang tapped his chest and the rabbit inside his robes yelped.

"What's that?"

"I almost forgot. I came across an injured rabbit just now, so I picked it up. Why don't you look after it?"

He removed the rabbit from his robes and placed it on the table. Its hind legs were broken and it could not move.

"You're such a good boy." She got up and went to a cabinet, from where she fetched some herbs and other medicines to tend to the animal's injuries.

This only made Guo Jing even more furious. Hurting an animal on purpose to gain his mother's affection? To distract her? How could someone stoop so low as to trick their own mother like that?

Lotus could feel him shaking, and fearing that he might explode, she started pulling at his sleeve. "Come, never mind them. Let's go and find the herbs for Elder Wang."

"Do you know where they keep them?"

"No," she said, shaking her head. "We'll have to look around."

How could they possibly find the medicine store in such a vast complex? And what if Hector Sha and the others found out they were back? But just as he was about to discuss it with Lotus, a lantern flickered into view up ahead.

My dear, my love, who is it you hold dear? Why not love me instead . . . ?" a man was singing as he approached.

Guo Jing was going to duck behind a nearby tree when Lotus stood up and rushed toward the stranger. He froze in alarm, and before he could react, she had already raised a pair of glinting Emei Needles to his throat.

"Who are you?" she demanded.

"The . . . I'm . . . the housekeeper," the man managed to stammer. "What are you doing?"

"What am I doing? I'm about to kill you, that's what. The housekeeper? Excellent. The younger Prince ordered people of the household to buy herbs. Where did you put them?"

"The younger Prince took them. I . . . I don't know!"

Lotus gripped his arm and twisted, while pressing the tips of the blades deeper into his throat. A sharp pain surged in his neck and wrist, but he was too scared to call out. "Are you sure about that?"

"Yes. I really don't know!"

Lotus removed his cap and stuffed it into his mouth, before twisting harder on his wrist. A loud crack. She had broken a bone in his right shoulder. The housekeeper screamed and fainted, but no one else heard his muffled cry.

Guo Jing was stunned by Lotus's vicious actions. He continued to watch as she jabbed the housekeeper twice in the shoulder and he came to with a groan. "Do you want me to do the other one?" she said as she put the cap back on his head.

Tears gathered in his eyes and he knelt before her. "Miss, I really don't know. Killing me won't change that."

She seemed to believe him, albeit grudgingly. "Go to the young Prince and tell him you broke your shoulder in a fall. Say that the doctor told you to take cinnabar, resina draconis, notoginseng, bear's gall bladder, and myrrh for the pain, but you can't find any anywhere in the city. Beg him to give you some."

The housekeeper nodded. He dared not refuse her.

"He's with the Consort. Go! I'll be right behind you. If you fail to get the herbs, or reveal in any way what actually happened, I will break your neck and scoop out your eyeballs. Do you remember which herbs I asked for?" She scratched her fingernail across his cheek as she spoke. He trembled, but struggled to his feet. Clenching his jaw against the pain, he stumbled to the Consort's house.

Wanyan Kang was still talking to his mother when the housekeeper's sweaty, tear-soaked face appeared in the doorway. Snot bubbled in his nose. He repeated Lotus's list. The Consort noticed his arm dangling from the shoulder socket and the scars of pain etched across his face. Before her son could answer, she was urging him to go and fetch the herbs for him.

"Old Liang's got them, go and get it yourself," the Prince replied with a frown.

"May I beg the Prince to write me a note?"

The Consort placed paper, a brush, and ink before her son, and he scribbled a few characters. The housekeeper bowed in gratitude.

"Go, take the medicine as quickly as possible and rest," the Consort said.

The housekeeper was only a few steps out of the door when he felt the cold blade against his neck again. "I'm coming with you to see Old Liang."

But the housekeeper could barely stand the pain, and after a few steps he staggered and collapsed.

"If you don't get the medicine, I'm going to cut your neck in two," she snarled, grabbing him by the back of the neck and twisting his head.

Cold sweat ran from every pore, but somehow the housekeeper found his last reserves of strength and he pressed on. They passed at least half a dozen other servants, but though they clearly saw Lotus and Guo Jing, no one said anything.

2

THEY REACHED OLD LIANG'S QUARTERS AND THE HOUSEKEEPER went to check the door. Locked. He asked a passing servant boy, who replied that the Sixth Prince was holding a banquet in the Hall of Perfumed Snow. Guo Jing propped up the hobbling housekeeper and together they made for the hall.

Just as they were approaching the entrance, two guards with lanterns and sabers called out, "Stop! Who goes there?"

The housekeeper passed them the note he had been given by Wanyan Kang. They stood aside, but just as they were about to stop Guo Jing and Lotus, the housekeeper intervened. "They belong to the household too."

"The Prince is hosting some very important guests, he mustn't be disturbed. You can come back tomorrow."

The guards felt a numbing sensation in their ribs and they could not move. Lotus had her fingers on their pressure points.

Having dumped the guards in a nearby bush, Lotus took Guo Jing's hand and followed the housekeeper to the door of the Hall of Perfumed Snow. She gave the man a nudge and then flew up onto the large window frame above with Guo Jing. From there they could see what was happening inside.

The hall was lit with hundreds of candles, and at its center guests sat around a large wooden table. Guo Jing's heart was thumping. There they were, from last night: the Master of White Camel Mount, Gallant Ouyang; the Dragon King, Hector Sha; the Three-Horned Dragon, Browbeater Hou; Old Liang the Ginseng Codger; the Butcher of a Thousand Hands, Tiger Peng; and, in the seat of honor, the Sixth Prince of the Jin, Wanyan Honglie. A large armchair was placed beside the table, piled up with sumptuous cushions, upon which sat the Lama Supreme Wisdom, his eyes barely open and his face puffy and jaundiced. He was clearly in great pain. Serves him right for plotting against Elder Wang, Guo Jing thought with a smile.

The housekeeper entered and approached Old Liang with a bow. He then passed him the note he had received from the young Prince. Old Liang read it, glanced at the housekeeper and then gave the note to the elder Prince Wanyan Honglie. "Your Highness, does this look like your son's handwriting?"

"Yes, do as he requests, Liang," the Prince replied.

Old Liang turned to a servant boy who was standing behind him and said, "Go and fetch half a *tael* of each of the herbs the young Prince gave me today, and give them to the housekeeper here."

The boy nodded, and followed the housekeeper outside.

"Let's get out of here before they see us," Guo Jing whispered in Lotus's ear. But she just smiled and shook her head. He felt the soft silken strands of her hair brush against his cheek and the tickle throbbed through his whole body. Instead of arguing with her he made to jump down from the sill, but she grabbed his hand and leaped up, hooking her feet in the eaves. She then placed him down on the ground softly.

If I'd just jumped, they would have heard me thudding against the ground, Guo Jing realized. He was yet to learn the subtler tricks of the *jianghu*.

The housekeeper and the servant boy emerged from the hall and Guo Jing followed. After fifty feet or so, he turned back and saw Lotus perform a Roll Down the Bead Curtain somersault from the eaves. She then turned back to the window and glanced in, her robes flapping in the breeze like a blooming white lily in the night.

No one had noticed her, so she turned to Guo Jing and watched him disappear into the darkness, before turning back to the action in the banqueting hall.

Just then Tiger Peng started looking around the room. Lotus ducked out of the way of the window and listened intently.

"Did Wang Chuyi turn up yesterday by coincidence, or is something going on?" a husky voice asked.

"Never mind his intentions," another voice boomed. "If he doesn't die from the Lama's attack, he'll surely be crippled." Lotus peeked inside. This was Tiger Peng, a stocky man with eyes like lightning.

A clear and crisp voice replied: "Quanzhen kung fu is famous even out in the far west where I come from. If it weren't for the Lama Supreme Wisdom's Five Finger Blade technique, we would have all been killed."

"No need to flatter me, Master Ouyang, we were both hurt. There was no winner in that fight." The Lama's voice was thick and deep.

"His injuries were graver than yours. Your Reverence will be fine after some rest," Gallant Ouyang replied.

Silence descended, before a toast was proposed. "My esteemed guests, you have traveled thousands of *li* between you to be here today. I am most honored. The Jin Empire is humbled by your presence." This must be the Sixth Prince Wanyan Honglie, Lotus thought. The others replied with polite protestations, which the Sixth Prince waved away before continuing. "The Venerable Supreme Wisdom is Kokonor's most celebrated lama, Master Liang controls the region beyond the passes of the northeast, Master Ouyang's fame extends farther than the Empire, Tiger Peng controls the Central Plains, and the Dragon King Sha is Master of the mighty Yellow River. If just one of you heroes gathered here today were to come to the aid of the Jin, we would surely prevail. But if all of you were to join us, well . . ." He paused to chuckle. "It would be like a lion fighting a rabbit."

Old Liang smiled. "Your Highness need only say the word, and we would be happy to. But my kung fu is nothing to boast about, so I am perhaps not fit to bear such a heavy responsibility as aiding the Great Jin Empire represents."

Tiger Peng added some similar comments of his own.

These men were all used to being the chieftains of their own domains, and in reality they spoke with as much arrogance as the Prince.

Wanyan Honglie made another toast: "And now it comes to me to explain why I invited you all here. The matter in hand is too important for me not to address it directly. All I ask is that, once we have spoken of it here, you do not share what I have said with any-one outside this hall. I don't want our enemies to have time to pre-pare. But I trust that you all have the Jin's best interests at heart."

This had the men's attention. "Fear not, Your Highness," they all reassured the Prince. "We will not speak of it."

They were to be entrusted with a most important and difficult task, that much was evident. He had sent them gold, silver, and other treasures before their arrival, and he was at last going to reveal the reason for the special attention. Anticipation filled the room.

"In the third year of the reign of our great Emperor Taizong," the Prince began, "that is, almost one hundred years ago, when the Huizong Emperor ruled the Song, two of our great generals led a mission south against the Chinese Empire, taking first the Emperor and then his successor captive. It was a victory without parallel in the history of our people."

The men cheered.

Shameless! Lotus fumed. Apart from the Lama and Master Ouyang, they were all Chinese, born and bred. How could they applaud the capture of two Song Emperors, especially after the Jin had betrayed an alliance agreed to only four years before?

"The Jin army in those days was strong and disciplined. We should have been able to take the entire Chinese Empire. But now, almost one hundred years later, the Song still holds court in Lin'an. Do you know why this is?"

"Please, let Your Highness explain," Old Liang said.

Wanyan Honglie sighed. "The following year we were defeated by General Yue Fei—of this everyone is aware. I need not repeat it. Our great Commander Wu was a most brilliant strategist, but in all his days he never once defeated Yue Fei. And though we brought Chancellor Qin Hui onto our side and he helped us kill General Yue, our momentum had been stalled and we did not continue our attack south. But this is where my ambition comes in. I want to make a great contribution to my people, to take my place in history. But you see, it is a mighty task and I cannot do it on my own. That is why I need the help of you heroes gathered here today."

The guests exchanged glances, unsure what the Prince meant. Charging enemy lines, laying siege to cities, that was all very well. But was he asking them to kill the southern Song's great commander?

Wanyan Honglie smiled, pride written across his face. He continued, with a slight quiver in his voice. "A few months ago, I happened upon some poems in the palace. In fact, they came from the brush of General Yue himself. But the phrasing was most strange. It took me days to decipher their meaning. Yue Fei was in prison when he wrote them, with no hope of escape. People are not exaggerating when they call him China's greatest patriot. He was in fact recording a campaign strategy, the sum of his many years of learning and practice, in the hope that it could be sent out of the palace without our knowledge. But Qin Hui had anticipated that Yue Fei might attempt to communicate with the outside world. He selected the guards watching over the General for their unwavering loyalty, so that no such letters would get out. Had Yue Fei's instructions got out, there would have been no stopping such a rebellion against Qin Hui's corrupted court. Yet, ever the patriot, Yue Fei was reluctant to move against a Chinese Emperor, even if the heart of the court was working on our behalf. What Qin Hui did not realize, however, was that Yue Fei was concerned more with saving the rivers and mountains of his home-land than himself. Fortunately, the poems never left the palace, even after his execution."

Everyone was so enthralled by the story, they forgot to drink their wine. Lotus was just as riveted from where she was listening outside the window.

"He wrote four poems, to be exact," the Prince continued. "To the tunes 'The Bodhisattva of the Barbarian South,' 'The Ugly Slave Boy,' 'All Hail the Emperor!' and 'The Heavens are Joyful.' But they are incomplete and do not follow the proper rules of prosody. Sentences are jumbled to the point of nonsense. Even Qin Hui, famed for his learning and intellect, could not make them out. So he sent them to the Jin, which is how they ended up here, in the palace. Everyone assumed they were nothing but the ravings of an angry and frustrated man. Nobody realized the secret hidden within the lines. But after rereading them many times, I realized that if you take every third character and then read them in reverse, the message is revealed. He was setting down a plan for a renewed offensive against our Jin army. But no one ever got to read it!"

The guests were astonished that the Prince should be the one to decode Yue Fei's writing.

"I think there must be more poems buried with him, in his tomb. Yue Fei's military prowess is without equal, no one was able to beat him while he was alive. So imagine if we had his secret strategies. The entire Song Empire would be ours!"

The Prince wants us to dig up his grave and steal Yue Fei's poetry!

The Prince paused, and then continued. "You are all the bravest men for thousands of *li*. You must be wondering, how could I be asking you to rob his grave? And while Yue Fei may have been an enemy of the Jin, he is admired everywhere for his determination and loyalty to his country. To disturb his last place of rest would be most disrespectful. I've been reading through the papers my men have obtained from the Song court and it appears that, after he was executed at Storm Pavilion and buried at the nearby Peace Bridge, his body was then moved to his current resting place by the West Lake, where the court built a memorial hall for him. But his clothes and personal effects were taken and buried elsewhere. This is where I believe the rest of his poetry will be found."

He examined his guests intently. They were waiting for the exact location of the tomb.

"For a while, I feared that the poems might have been lost in the move. But after extensive research, I no longer believe this to be the case. The people of the Song hold the General in such high esteem that they could not possibly disturb his tomb. I am certain this is where they are, in Lin'an. But it is of vital importance that word of this does not spread. Others may go looking first. This is a very serious matter that concerns two great nations. I could not begin to undertake it without the help of the greatest heroes of the *wulin*."

The men nodded in agreement.

Just as Wanyan Honglie was about to give the precise location of the tomb, the main door to the hall burst open and a young boy, his face swollen and his cheeks as white as the snow outside, came rushing in. He ran straight for Old Liang. "Master!"

Everyone recognized the servant that Old Liang had sent to fetch the medicine.

3

GUO JING WENT WITH THE HOUSEKEEPER AND THE SERVANT boy to fetch the medicine, to make sure the housekeeper had no opportunity to explain to the young boy what they had done to him. They hobbled down a long corridor, passing many doors before arriving at Old Liang's storeroom. The boy unlocked the door, entered and lit a candle.

Guo Jing stepped inside. His nose was assaulted by the aromas of hundreds of different medicines. The table, bench, and floor were all covered with bottles of strange dried plants, seeds, tree bark, and insects, jars big and small, bowls, vats, and barrels. Old Liang may have only been a guest at the palace, but he had built up a considerable collection with which he could concoct all kinds of tinctures to treat every ailment. The boy knew exactly what he was looking for. He measured the herbs and divided them into packets wrapped in rice paper. He then gave them to the housekeeper.

The housekeeper reached out and took them, before turning to leave. Now he had the medicine, he wanted to get out. Guo Jing made to follow, but suddenly the housekeeper pushed the door shut, locked it and started shouting, "Thief! Thief!" Guo Jing threw his weight against the door, but it would not budge. The housekeeper then threw the medicine packets out of a small window and into a pool of water outside.

Guo Jing was panicking now. He placed both palms against the door and, using his internal energy, pressed against it. The bolt cracked and the door flung open. Guo Jing rushed out and jabbed at the housekeeper's jaw, splitting it. Luckily the storeroom was so far out of the way no one in the palace could hear what was going on.

The boy had followed Guo Jing out into the corridor and was making for the banqueting hall. Guo Jing gave chase and caught the boy by the neck. The boy aimed a low sweeping kick. Clearly he had experienced many a fight while traveling with Old Liang.

Not only had Guo Jing lost the medicine, but he was now in danger of alerting the palace to his presence. Lotus, too, would be in mortal danger. He used a move from his Split Muscles technique in an effort to control the boy.

Within moments he had managed to render the servant unconscious. He hid him in some nearby bushes and then hurried back to the storeroom, lit a candle and looked inside. The housekeeper was still lying on the floor.

Which jars had the boy taken the medicine from? Guo Jing cursed himself for not having paid more attention. The bottles were marked with strange symbols, but no Chinese characters that he could decipher. Perhaps he should just grab a small amount from as many as he could. That way, Elder Wang could choose for himself. The boy had been standing here when he made his selection. Guo Jing grabbed a pile of paper packets and began filling them with handfuls of herbs.

But just as he finished folding a wrap, he turned and knocked a large bamboo basket over. The lid rolled clear and a loud hissing sound filled the storeroom.

A bloodred snake launched itself at Guo Jing's face.

Guo Jing jumped back.

Most of the snake's body was still curled up inside the basket and there was no knowing how big it was. It flicked its tongue at him. Guo Jing had never seen such a large snake before; the ones in Mongolia had been stunted by year after year of cold winters. He stepped back and banged into the table. The candle went out with a *poof!* The darkness was instant and absolute.

He turned to the door, but just as he reached the handle he felt something wrap itself around his leg. He tried to jump clear, but at that moment, a cold sensation went through his arm. He could not move it!

With his free hand he fumbled for the little dagger Temujin had given him. A bitter stench filled his nostrils and something cold moved across his cheek. The snake's tongue! He grabbed it by the neck, but it pulled closer. Guo Jing squeezed as hard as he could, amazed at the animal's power.

Guo Jing was growing weaker and he was having difficulty breathing. The snake was now wrapped around his chest and pulling tighter all the time. He pushed back with what he had left of his internal energy, gaining a moment of relief before the snake tightened again around his lungs. He had barely any strength left in his good arm now. The snake's breath was making him feel nauseous. He would not be able to hold on much longer.

Meanwhile, the servant boy awoke in the bushes. Where was the intruder? He ran back to the storeroom, but all looked dark and silent. The young man must have fled. He ran back toward the Hall of Perfumed Snow to report to his master.

4

LOTUS LISTENED IN SHOCK AS THE BOY RELATED WHAT HAD just happened. She dropped back to the ground silently in a Goose Lands on the Sandy Bank. Everyone had been too enraptured with the Prince's story to pay attention to what had been going on outside the hall, but now they were on the alert.

Old Liang had heard her. Seconds later, he was standing before her, blocking her way. "Who are you?"

Lotus could see Old Liang's kung fu was more accomplished than her own, and he had a room full of companions also famed for their martial arts. "Isn't this plum tree beautiful? Could you break off a small branch for me?"

Old Liang had not expected to be confronted by such a pretty young girl. Her smile was radiant, like a string of pearls. He reasoned that she must be a lady of the palace, perhaps even the Prince's young betrothed, and so he did as she requested.

"Thank you, sir," Lotus replied with a shy smile.

The others were already standing at the entrance to the banqueting hall, watching the exchange.

"Your Highness, is she a lady of the palace?" Tiger Peng asked the Prince.

"No indeed," Wanyan Honglie replied.

"But she must have heard the Prince's story just now."

Tiger Peng rushed forward. "Wait! Young lady! Please let me break off a branch for you too." He reached out, but made a grab for her wrist instead. Then he formed a claw and lunged at her throat.

Lotus had intended not to reveal her kung fu skills, but Tiger Peng had already seen through the pretense. She had no time to duck the move and instead blocked him with her right hand, which she shaped like a flower in bloom, her thumb and index finger touching and the remaining fingers splayed. It was a beautiful move.

Tiger Peng's elbow went numb, followed by his whole arm. But he had barely felt any contact. How did this pretty young girl know about such an obscure pressure point? And how was she able to hit it so quickly and precisely? He had never, in all his years in the *wulin*, seen anything like this Orchid Touch kung fu, a technique that emphasized speed, accuracy, surprise, and clarity. It was this last aspect, clarity, which really distinguished the accomplished practitioner, as it principally required a stillness of the heart, graceful movement born of an unhurried mind. Too urgent, too brutal, and the move would be clumsy and unbefitting of Orchid Touch style. Clarity: that was the hardest part to master.

Everyone had noticed it and all were watching in amazement.

"Young lady, may I ask your name?" Tiger Peng said. "Who is your *shifu*?"

"This plum blossom is most beautiful. I'm going to put it in some water," came her reply.

This made the men even more suspicious.

"Didn't you hear Brother Peng's question?" Browbeater Hou snarled.

"What question?" she replied with a smile.

That smile, that laugh. She was the dirty little beggar boy that had so tormented Browbeater Hou the day before! Tiger Peng realized.

"Old Hou, don't you see who this is?"

This startled Browbeater Hou, and he looked her up and down.

"You played hide-and-seek together for most of yesterday. Have you forgotten?"

Browbeater Hou looked even more shocked. "It's you, you stinky little rascal!" He charged forward, but Lotus dodged his clumsy hands, and all he managed to grab was a fistful of air.

At that moment, Dragon King Hector Sha rushed at her, seized her wrist and snarled, "Where do you think you're going?"

Lotus scratched at his eyes with her free hand, but Hector Sha caught the move in time.

"Shameless brute!" she spat in his face.

"Shameless? Who are you calling shameless?"

"Bullying a child. A young girl!"

This hit right at Hector Sha's sense of pride; it did seem like an uneven fight for someone of his reputation. He relaxed his grip somewhat. "Let's go inside and talk instead."

Lotus realized she had no choice and followed them inside.

"Let me give the stinky little rascal a good beating first," Browbeater Hou said, preparing to strike again.

"Let's find out who her Master is, who sent her," Tiger Peng said. Her level of kung fu and rich clothing were enough to tell him it had to be someone very influential. They had to know who they were dealing with before making any rash decisions.

But Browbeater Hou could not contain himself, and launched his fist at Lotus. She dodged again. "You really want to fight?" she asked.

"You think I'm joking? You won't get away this time." He did not want to have to chase her again, knowing he would be unable to keep up.

"Fine, let's fight to see who has the better skills." She picked up a bowl filled with wine and placed it on her head, then took two more, one for each hand. "Want to try?"

"What is this nonsense?"

Lotus turned to the others and smiled. "This old uncle with the horns and I have no long-standing grudge to speak of. Surely it would cause the rest of you gentlemen great offense, were I to beat him in a fight?"

"Beat me?" Browbeater stepped forward in anger. "How dare you? And these are not horns, they're cysts! See?"

Lotus ignored him and continued to address the other men. "We each take three bowls of wine, and whoever spills the first drop loses. How does that sound?"

Old Liang, Tiger Peng, and Hector Sha were all much better fighters than her, she knew that, but this old man with the horns on his head was slow. She only needed to rely on her lightness kung fu, and her wits, and she was confident she could humiliate him. But what if she were overestimating her own abilities? Her best tactic was to continue playing the fool. That way they would not take her seriously.

"I'm not here to play parlor games!" exclaimed Browbeater Hou angrily, and he ran at her with his fists raised.

Again, Lotus dodged out of his way. "Fine, we'll do it like this. I'll have the three bowls of wine, you fight empty-handed."

Browbeater Hou had never been able to claim a reputation equal to his martial brother Hector Sha, but he was a well-regarded fighter, nevertheless. He did not take kindly to being humiliated like this, so, without pausing for thought, he placed a bowl of wine on his head and grabbed two more, one for each hand. He then bent his left leg and kicked with his right.

"That's more like it!" Lotus called out, before flying across the room in a graceful display of lightness kung fu. Browbeater Hou followed, kicking wildly, but he was never even close to hitting her. The hall erupted in laughter. Lotus kept her focus steady and her body balanced, her robes fluttering after her. She looked as if she were floating on clouds, or had wheels attached to her feet. Browbeater Hou's strides were clumsy where hers were delicate and smooth. He puffed and clattered. She danced around him, aiming at his wine bowls with her elbows, forcing him to lurch out of her way.

The girl has skill, Old Liang thought to himself. But I still fancy Browbeater Hou the better fighter. But Graybeard Liang's main concern was protecting his store of medicines, so while the others remained transfixed by the fight, he slipped toward the door. If I'm missing cinnabar, resina draconis, notoginseng, bear's gall bladder, and myrrh, then I'll know Wang Chuyi sent her. The medicines Wang Chuyi needed weren't expensive, but Old Liang had many valuable ingredients in the storeroom that had taken him years to collect.

5

THE SNAKE WAS PRESSING TIGHTER AROUND GUO JING'S chest and he was about to faint. The strange smell attacked his nostrils again. The snake was getting closer to his face. If it were to bite him, would he survive? He could feel its body brushing up close to his mouth, nose, and brow.

He strained to reach for the snake's neck, and using the last of his strength, he bit into its taut flesh just below its head. The snake hissed and writhed in pain, pulling tighter around him. Guo Jing kept biting, until he felt a burst of bitter blood flood his mouth. It tasted disgusting. Was it poisonous? But he did not want to let go either, in case the snake got free and attacked him again. If he could make it lose enough blood, it just might loosen its grip. He kept clamping his teeth down harder, until he found it easier to breathe. A few spasms, and the snake dropped to the floor. Dead.

Guo Jing was exhausted, his body ached. He grabbed hold of the table, but his feet were too numb for him to make his escape just yet. He took a moment to rest like this while a warm sensation flowed through him. He was a piece of meat roasting by the fire. He began to panic. To his surprise, he found movement returning to his arms and legs, but his body temperature did not seem to be going down. He placed the back of his hand against his cheek: scalding hot.

He felt for the herbs tucked inside his robes. I've got the medicine, I can still save Elder Wang, he said to himself. But Mu Yi and his daughter need my help first. Who knows what the Prince will do with them?

He stumbled out of the storeroom and looked around him. He then hobbled in the direction of the cage where father and daughter were being held captive.

6

JUST AS BEFORE, THERE WERE GUARDS KEEPING WATCH OVER MU Yi and his daughter Mercy. Guo Jing waited, but could sense no opportunity presenting itself as it had last time. He moved round to the back and waited for the patrol guards to walk past, before jumping silently onto the roof and down into the courtyard. He leaned against the wall and listened. Once he was sure there were no guards inside, he slipped through the door and hissed, "Mr. Mu, I've come to help you escape."

"Sir, who are you?" Mu Yi was shocked to see the young man.

"My name is Guo Jing," he replied.

Guo Jing? When the name had been spoken the day before, exhaustion and injury had prevented him from making the connection, but now the name struck at his eardrums. A sharp jolt shot through his body.

"What? Guo Jing? Your . . . family name is Guo?"

"Yes, I was the one who fought with the Prince yesterday."

"What is your father's name?"

"My father was Skyfury Guo. But he's dead now." Guo Jing had learned his father's name from Zhu Cong, not his mother.

Tears flooded Mu Yi's eyes. He looked up and sighed. "Heavens above!" He then reached though the bars and grabbed at Guo Jing's hands. Guo Jing could feel the old man shaking, and a few drops of hot, salty tears fell on his skin.

"I have a small dagger. We can use it to pick the lock, then sir will be able to escape. Pay no attention to what the Prince was telling you before. I overheard him, it's all lies."

"Your mother," Mu Yi continued. "Is her family name Li? Is she still alive?"

"Oh, you know my mother? She's in Mongolia."

Mu Yi was even more excited now. He clutched even tighter at Guo Jing's hands.

"Sir, please, I should break the lock."

But Mu Yi gripped on to the young man's hands as if they were the most precious treasure he had ever had the pleasure to hold. "You're . . . I only have to close my eyes and I can still picture your father."

"Sir knew my father?"

"We were brothers-in-arms, we took an oath together. A bond closer than blood. We are not really looking for a husband for my daughter; we came looking for you, dear boy. This silly competition was just a ruse." At this point, Mu Yi started choking on his sobs and was unable to continue.

Guo Jing's eyes were blurred with tears.

Mu Yi was, in fact, none other than Ironheart Yang. That fateful day, eighteen years previously, in Ox Village, he had taken a spear to the back, but the horse had carried him many *li* until he fell into some long grass. When he awoke by the first light of the following day, he managed to crawl to a nearby farm, where they fed and nursed him for a month until he was well enough to get out of bed and move around with the aid of a walking stick. He had ended up in Lotus Pond Village, fifteen *li* from Ox Village, and had been most fortunate to encounter such a kind family, whose young daughter had been particularly doting. Once strong enough, Ironheart was keen to go back to Ox Village to look for his wife, but dared only return by cover of darkness for fear that it was under watch. As he approached their old house, he saw the door was ajar. His heart clenched tight as if seized by a cold hand. He pushed open the door and entered. He saw, laid out on the bed, the clothes his wife Charity had been sewing for him the night Justice Duan's men had arrived. He looked up at the spot where the two spears had hung on the wall. One had been lost in battle, but the other remained, lonely and abandoned just like Yang himself. Everything else was as it had been that night. His wife had not been back. And neither had the Guos.

Perhaps she had returned to her parents in Plum Blossom Village? On his way, he passed Qu San's inn, but it was locked, with no one in sight. He arrived at his parents-in-law, only to discover Charity's mother alone with Qu San's daughter. They had heard nothing from Charity and her father had died from the shock. With Qu San also missing, Charity's mother had taken the young girl in.

In despair, Ironheart turned back to the family that had been looking after him in Lotus Pond Village. But misfortune never strikes just once, and by the time he had returned, an epidemic of the plague had broken out. Within days it had taken three members of the family, leaving only the little girl. Yang decided he would raise her as his own daughter. Wherever he went, so did she, following him on his searches for Skyfury's wife and his beloved Charity. But one had ended up on the steppes and the other was lost somewhere in the north, and despite years of searching, he had been unable to locate either.

Until now.

In all these years, Ironheart had dared not use his real name, adopting instead the name Mu Yi, whose meaning in Chinese was "Change," an oblique reference to his previous identity. For more than ten years, father and adopted daughter had traveled around the rivers and lakes of the south, during which time Mercy Mu had blossomed into the young woman and capable fighter she was today. He had come to accept that his wife had probably not survived, but still hoped that the heavens had been good enough to bestow their mercy on the Guo family at least. It had always been his dearest wish that their little competition would uncover his sworn brother's son and that he might be able to join the families in marriage, finally fulfilling the promise he had made Skyfury Guo that day as they drank by the fire. But over the years, many men had taken up the challenge, and Mu Yi's hopes had begun to fade. He had had no indication that Lily had survived, let alone borne a son all those years ago. He would have been content with any decent man of the *wulin,* so long had they searched in vain. And yet the young fighter who had come to his daughter's rescue the day before was just the man he had been looking for all these years. It was almost too much for the old man to take in.

Mercy, meanwhile, had been listening impatiently. Guo Jing had come to rescue them, she wanted to remind her father—there would be time later to talk. And yet, it struck her suddenly, if they were to leave now, she would never see the Prince again. She shrank back and decided not to interrupt.

Guo Jing was all too aware that time was precious and he must act now if he was going to get them out of the palace alive. He reached back inside the bars and was about to strike at the lock with his dagger. Just at that moment, a light flickered beneath the crack in the door and he heard the sound of footsteps approaching.

Guo Jing slipped back behind the door just as it was thrown open. He watched what was happening through a small crack in the wood. The first to enter was a guard carrying a lantern, followed by Wanyan Kang's mother, the Consort.

"Are these the prisoners my son took into custody yesterday?" she asked the guard.

"Yes, ma'am," he answered.

"Release them at once."

The guard hesitated, but the Consort continued, "If my son asks, you may tell him that I gave the order. Now!"

The guard slid the key into the lock and let the prisoners free. The Consort approached Ironheart Yang with two silver ingots. "Hurry now," she said.

But Ironheart merely stood there staring at the Consort.

He must be angry, she thought, noticing the strange look the old man was giving her. "Please forgive my son," she said quietly, feeling deeply how they must have suffered. "He has wronged you most gravely."

But Ironheart could not take his eyes off her. He reached out, took the silver and placed it inside his robes. He then took his daughter's hand and led her out.

"Don't you have any manners?" the guard said gruffly. "Won't you thank the Consort?"

But Ironheart gave no sign that he had heard him.

Guo Jing waited until everyone had left. Once he was sure the

Consort had gone, he opened the door and peered around in the darkness. There was no sign of Mu Yi or his daughter. They must have left the palace, he thought, so he decided to go to the Hall of Perfumed Snow to drag Lotus away from her eavesdropping. He still needed to get the medicine to Elder Wang, after all.

But before he was even halfway there, he spotted two figures carrying lanterns, rounding a corner up ahead. He ducked behind a small rockery covered in plants. But he had been seen.

"Who's there?" The man was running at him, seemingly ready to fight. A palm struck at him. Guo Jing blocked the attack. By the flickering light he saw that it was none other than the young Prince Wanyan Kang.

The guard had gone straight to the Prince to tell him of the Consort's orders.

My mother has always been too kind, she doesn't see the bigger picture, Wanyan Kang had said to himself. What if they go to my *shifu*? I won't be able to deny what I've done.

He had run out at once to try to find father and daughter before they could escape. Guo Jing was the last person he expected to encounter on the way.

And now they would have to fight—again. Guo Jing tried to run a few times, eager to get the medicines to Elder Wang, but Wanyan Kang blocked his path. He caught sight of the guard drawing his sword, ready to assist the Prince. There was no way out now.

7

JUST AS BROWBEATER HOU THOUGHT HE HAD THE YOUNG GIRL, a cry went up from the onlookers. Lotus jumped up and threw the three bowls of wine straight up above her. She then launched two fists at him in a move known in the *wulin* as Eight Steps to Catch the Toad. With his hands occupied by his own wine bowls, Browbeater Hou was unable to defend himself, so he lurched to the left. Lotus went in again with her right palm, Browbeater Hou blocked. Wine spilled onto his hands and the bowl balanced on his head fell and broke against the stone floor.

Lotus leaped and caught two of her bowls; the third landed on her head as if cushioned by a cloud. She had not spilled a single drop. The crowd gasped in wonder, and Gallant Ouyang exclaimed out loud: "Wonderful!"

Hector Sha shot him an icy glance, but he took no notice. "Most wonderful indeed!"

"Try again!" Browbeater Hou snarled.

"Haven't you had enough?" she said sweetly, tapping him on the cheek.

"You are a tricky young thing," Hector Sha said, furious on his martial brother's behalf. "Who is your *shifu*?"

"Let's save that for another time. Right now, I have to go."

But Hector Sha was already in the doorway, blocking Lotus's exit. She was perfectly aware of the extent of his kung fu, but she did not let her concern show. Instead, she frowned and spoke in a tone of frustration rather than fear. "Why do you stand in my way?"

"I want to know which school you belong to and why you're here."

"And what if I don't want to tell you?" she replied, arching her brow.

"When the Dragon King asks a question, he gets an answer!"

She was not going to get out easily with all these fighters in the hall. But she saw Old Liang was also making for the door. "Uncle, this horrible man won't let me go home!"

Old Liang could not help but be amused by her flirtatious manner. "The Dragon King asked you a question. Be a good girl and tell him what he wants to know? I'm sure he'll let you go after that."

"But I don't feel like it," she said, giving him her sweetest smile. She then turned to Hector Sha. "If you won't step aside, I'll just have to run past you."

"Ha! See if you can," he sneered.

"But you mustn't hit me," she said.

"The Dragon King doesn't go around hitting young ladies."

"Good. A gentleman never goes back on his word. Look, over there!" She pointed up into a corner of the room. Despite himself, Hector Sha glanced in the direction she was pointing and Lotus dashed at him.

She moved like lightning, but he was even faster. He held out two fingers at the same height as her eyes. If she didn't stop she would be blinded. Lotus jumped back just in time. She kept trying, each time from a different angle, but still she could find no way past the bulky man. When one last attempt nearly resulted in her nose breaking against Hector Sha's shiny bald head, she squealed with frustration.

"You can't beat the Dragon King at this game." Old Liang laughed. "Why not give up?" He slipped past Sha and hurried for his storeroom.

8

THE SMELL OF FRESH BLOOD ASSAILED HIS NOSTRILS. ALL WAS not well. He raised his torch. There, on the ground, was his red snake, its body already shriveled. Its blood had been sucked dry. Everywhere, medicine jars had been knocked over and opened. More than ten years of collecting, now in ruins. And his precious snake. He could not help the tears from gathering in his eyes.

Graybeard Liang had started out as a hermit in the Mountain of Eternal Snow, until one day, an injured old traveler came by. When the hermit realized the man was carrying a manual full of secrets of the martial world, he decided to kill him. There, in the man's bag, he also found a dozen or so assorted herbs and medicinal potions. From that day forward, Old Liang devoted himself to studying the book and its many prescriptions, the most potent of which required the venom of a specific species of deadly snake. He had searched deep in the mountains and forests to find just one specimen, which he then raised on a strict diet of marten flesh and medicinal remedies such as cinnabar, ginseng, and deer antler. Gradually, over many years, the snake began to turn from grayish black to scarlet red. It had been only a few days away from completing its final transformation when Old Liang was called to the Jin capital by the elder Prince Wanyan Honglie. Once the snake was ready, he would only need to drink its blood to become immortal, and one of the most powerful fighters of the *wulin*.

But now it lay dead on the stone floor, all his hard work lost for good. The thought that someone else might have drunk the blood and gained the benefit of all those years of careful nurturing was almost too much for him to bear.

He managed to regain his composure and studied the scene before him. The spots of blood had yet to congeal. The thief must have just left. He ran out and found a nearby tree from where he could get a better view. That's when he saw the Prince and Guo Jing fighting.

By the time he had drawn close, he could smell the stench of the snake's blood on Guo Jing's clothes. He burned with fury.

9

GUO JING HAD STARTED THIS FIGHT AT A DISADVANTAGE, AND now he was distracted by a fiery sensation in his stomach, as if his blood had become a pot of boiling water. His mouth was dry, his skin was itchy and felt like it was going to split open.

I'm dying, he thought. The snake poison is taking hold.

Wanyan Kang continued to beat and punch at his back, but he could no longer feel it.

Old Liang was sure the young man did not know to drink the blood himself; it was a most guarded secret in the *wulin*. Someone must have sent him to collect it on their behalf. And he was almost certain it was Wang Chuyi. "You little thief!" he snarled from the fringes of the fight. "Who sent you to steal my precious snake?"

Guo Jing looked up and saw Graybeard Liang. "So the snake was yours? It attacked and poisoned me!" He ran at the old man with his fists at the ready.

Old Liang could smell the herbs on the boy's body. A thought struck him. If he killed the boy and drank his blood, perhaps he could still gain the effects of the potion? Perhaps they might even be enhanced? Buoyed by this thought, Old Liang fought back, and within seconds he had Guo Jing in a powerful lock and pinned to the ground. Now he would at last harvest the fruits of his labors.

10

LOTUS WAS TRAPPED. WHAT IF HECTOR SHA DECIDED TO STOP toying with her? She needed a new tactic.

"If I get past you," she said to Sha, "and through the door, do you promise not to come after me?"

"Then I will admit defeat, yes," he replied.

"But my father only taught me how to enter, not how to leave." She sighed.

"How to enter but not to leave? What good is that?" Hector Sha said, unsure what she meant.

"Your Shape Changing kung fu is good, but not as good as my father's. Not even close. At least a hundred thousand *li* behind, in fact."

"Stop talking nonsense, you silly little girl. Who is your father?"

"If I told you that, it would scare you senseless. So I won't. He taught me how to enter a room using kung fu. He stood blocking the doorway just like you are now. He knew all the tricks. Made it very difficult. But if it were you trying to block me, I'd have no problem."

"What difference does it make whether you're going in or going out of the room?" Hector Sha sneered. "Come on then, show me." He moved aside so that she might demonstrate these great skills of "entering."

"Ha!" Lotus cried out as she ran outside then turned to face them. "Tricked you! Now I'm through, you must admit defeat—you said so yourself. I got out, didn't I? You are an honorable man, Dragon King, I'm sure you will keep your word. And so, goodbye to you, sir."

He scratched his head. She was right, he could not go back on his promise. His cheeks flushed red. There was nothing he could do.

But Tiger Peng was not about to let her get away so easily.

He raised both arms and threw two copper coins, which flew just over her head. Lotus watched as they passed her, but just as she was wondering how a master of the martial arts could be so hopelessly inaccurate, she heard a *pang!* as they hit the marble pillar out in the corridor and came bouncing right toward the back of her head. As she could not block them, she leaped forward. Tiger Peng threw a dozen more, each one forcing her forward a little more, until she found herself standing back in the banqueting hall.

This had been exactly Tiger Peng's intention, and the others howled in delight. "Come back to join us?" He laughed.

"What exactly is honorable about using weapons to bully an unarmed young girl?"

"Bully you? I never laid a finger on you."

"Then let me go!"

"First tell us who your *shifu* is."

"I taught myself while still in my mother's womb!"

"In that case, I will find out another way," Tiger Peng retorted, and launched himself at her shoulder.

Lotus neither dodged nor attempted to block the attack. He could not possibly be as dishonorable as to hit a girl who had no wish to fight.

He noticed her reluctance to engage and pulled back at the last moment. "Come on, silly little girl! I bet I can determine your *shifu* within ten moves."

"And what if you can't tell after ten moves?"

"Then you may leave here in peace." And without waiting for her response, he launched into a Triple Chain Penetration.

Lotus turned and touched her first finger and thumb as she had done before, creating a fork with the remaining three fingers, in a move known as Trident Searches the Sea by Night.

"Brother, that's one of ours!" Browbeater Hou called out.

"Nonsense!" Hector Sha said, reasoning that she must have observed Browbeater Hou performing the move in one of their earlier encounters.

Tiger Peng laughed and swirled round to attack again. This time Lotus turned left and suddenly jumped to the side without so much as bending a knee or taking a step.

"A Shape Changing move!" Browbeater Hou called out again. "Did you teach her that, Brother?"

"Hold your tongue! Stop talking such hogwash." But Hector Sha was secretly impressed that she could execute these skills after only observing them once. Perfect they weren't, but good enough to avoid Tiger Peng's attacks.

Lotus followed up with moves from Shen's Spirit Cleaver blade technique and Ma's Soul Snatcher whip.

"Brother! Brother! She has studied with the Daemon Se!" Browbeater Hou caught sight of Hector Sha's furious expression just in time to stop himself from blurting out any more.

Tiger Peng was growing more and more furious. I've been gentle so far, he thought, but she is a crafty little witch. I must use fiercer skills on her if I'm going to get her to reveal the identity of her *shifu*.

It was common for fighters of the *wulin* to adopt and experiment with certain moves from rival styles, but when it came to life and death moments, they always reverted to the repertoire they had first learned and were most comfortable with.

His fifth move came like a hurricane. The others were concerned for the girl. She may have been crafty, irritating even, but they bore her no real grudge. They could not say they wanted such a pretty young girl to actually come to harm.

Except for Browbeater Hou, of course, who felt the sooner the little vixen was dead the better.

Lotus defended herself with some of Wanyan Kang's Quanzhen

kung fu to force back the attack, and then a bit of Guo Jing's Southern Mountain Fists style. She had learned them only the previous day while watching the Prince and Guo Jing fight in the marketplace. Her seventh move was Tiger Peng's Triple Chain Penetration, which she had seen for only the first time at the start of this very fight!

The fighting was growing more furious and more dangerous, however, and she would most probably struggle to hold him off using her own kung fu, let alone with borrowed moves she had only seen and never tried. She was taking a risk, based on the assumption that he would not actually try to kill her.

"Clever girl, using Outlaw Peng's moves against him. Oh, wait— careful, go left!" Gallant Ouyang found he was now giving her advice.

Tiger Peng's style was to mix feigned and real moves, switching between the two at great speed. His eighth was just such a false strike to the left as he lunged to the right. Lotus had expected him to do just the opposite, and come in on his left despite faking a right. She had meant to dodge to her left, Tiger Peng's right, but after Gallant Ouyang's cry, she dipped low and sailed right. It was a most elegant move, everyone could see that.

Tiger Peng was furious. Who was this Gallant Ouyang to interfere? And who said he wouldn't kill her? He wasn't known as the Butcher of a Thousand Hands for nothing, after all. He had a terrible cruel streak when he was angry, and with only two moves left and still none the wiser as to the identity of her *shifu,* his scruples were fast dissolving. He moved into an Open the Window to Gaze at the Moon, his left hand yin, his right hand yang, and with all his strength, pushed both out at once.

Lotus knew she was in grave danger. She stepped back as his fists came at her face. All she could do was duck, bend both her arms and strike at his chest with the points of her elbows.

Tiger Peng had expected her to try to block him, and was going to follow with his tenth move. He was halfway through a Falling Star when she made her surprise attack, so all he could do was gather his internal energy to stop himself from falling over from the momentum of his own forward thrust. But it was like pulling on the reins of a horse at the edge of a cliff.

"You must have studied kung fu under Twice Foul Dark Wind!" he cried out as a shiver shot through him and into his voice.

Lotus jumped back several feet. Fear grasped the room. Everyone present, apart from the Sixth Prince of Zhao, Wanyan Honglie, knew about the fearsome might of Twice Foul Dark Wind. Even Tiger Peng, who had killed hundreds without the merest pang of remorse, was scared to touch her now.

Lotus pushed him away and steadied herself. Every part of her ached and her arms were numb. But before she could say anything, a cry pierced the night sky. Guo Jing! He sounded like he was in danger. The blood drained from her cheeks.

I I

OLD LIANG HAD GUO JING PINNED TO THE GROUND SO THAT he was unable to move a muscle. The young man watched as his opponent strained toward his throat, teeth bared.

But just at that moment, a strange surge of power pulsed through his body, and he performed a Jumping Carp, flipping the old man off him and landing on his feet. But Old Liang responded immediately with another attack, and despite Guo Jing's attempts to get away, he felt a heavy thump to his back.

It felt like the old man's meaty fist had penetrated his flesh and had entered his spine. Wanyan Kang's punches had been nothing compared to this. Guo Jing pressed forward, mobilizing what he could of his lightness technique, as he dodged and threaded through the palace gardens. Old Liang could not keep up.

After a while, Guo Jing gasped and came to a halt. He inspected the back of his robe. A large hole had been torn through it. He felt for the large, bloody wound where a chunk of flesh had been torn from his back.

He needed somewhere to hide. The Consort's cottage! It was just up ahead. He ran round the back, hoping they would not think to look there, allowing him to escape later. He found a spot by the wall at the rear, and there he lay, waiting.

Soon, he heard Old Liang and Wanyan Kang calling to each other. They were drawing near. He could hear the anger in Old Liang's voice.

They'll find me if I stay here, Guo Jing thought. If the Consort finds me, however, she may take pity on me.

Given the gravity of the situation, he had no time to stop and really consider the merits of this plan, and instead slipped inside the small house. He saw only a lit candle placed in the middle of a table. The Consort must be in another room. He looked around and spotted a wooden cupboard in the corner. He ran over and slid inside. He pulled the door shut, leaving just a crack so that he could keep watch. He removed his golden dagger and let himself relax a little.

At that moment, he heard footsteps as the Consort entered the room. She sat down at the table and seemed to stare at the candle. Not long after that, Wanyan Kang appeared at the door. "Mother, did a young man come past here?"

The Consort shook her head, and Wanyan Kang left to continue his search with Old Liang.

The Consort closed the door and started to prepare for bed.

I'll slip out through the window just as soon as she's blown out the candle, Guo Jing thought. No, I'd better wait, in case I meet the Prince and Old Liang. Guo Jing's thoughts began to turn back to the fight, and his opponent's strange kung fu. He tried to bite me! I must ask my *shifus* about that when I see them next; I've never heard them mention biting as an appropriate way to fight. And what about Lotus? She must be gone by now. I'd better make my escape soon, or she'll be wondering what's happened to me.

Just then the window opened and a man leaped in. Guo Jing and the Consort froze in shock. To his even greater surprise, Guo Jing realized almost at once that it was Mu Yi. He had assumed the old man and his daughter had already fled the palace.

The Consort too recognized him. "Quick, please. Before they find you."

"I must express my gratitude for the Consort's concern. Had I not come here in person to thank you myself, I would have regretted it until my dying day." Yet a hint of bitterness and sarcasm could be heard in his voice.

"Never mind that. My son wronged you and your daughter."

Ironheart Yang cast his eyes around the room. A cupboard, lamp, and bed—that was it. The furniture was worn, but familiar. A well of sadness grew inside him, and a tear gathered in one eye and spilled down his cheek. He wiped it away with his sleeve and walked over to where a spear was fastened to the wall. He unhooked it and saw that the iron tip was russet in color from lack of care. He could still make out the characters carved on the shaft: *Ironheart Yang*.

He caressed it and sighed. "The tip is rusty. It hasn't been used in a while."

"Please don't touch that," the Consort said softly.

"Why?"

"Because it is my most precious possession."

A pulse of anger surged within him. "Is that so?" Ironheart Yang paused, and then continued, "This spear used to be one of a pair."

Surprise was evident on the Consort's face, but Ironheart did not explain and instead placed it back on the wall. "The tip is worn," he murmured, still staring at it. "Someone should go to see Carpenter Zhang tomorrow to see if he can fix it."

The Consort felt a bolt of lightning flash through her. "Who are you?" she managed eventually.

"Someone should go to see Carpenter Zhang tomorrow to see if he can fix it," Ironheart repeated, looking the Consort in the eyes.

The Consort felt her knees going weak. "Who are you?" she stammered again. "Why are you saying that? My husband said exactly the same words the night he died."

The Consort was none other than Charity Bao, Ironheart Yang's wife. She had saved Wanyan Honglie's life, all those years ago, in

Ox Village. The Prince of Zhao had been unable to forget her, and so had bribed Justice Duan and his men to fake an attack on the village so that he might go back and "save" the young woman and bring her back to his palace. With her friends and family dead, she would have no one else to turn to, and he would be her hero. He had been sure that she would agree to marry him eventually, at least once she had given up hope of ever being able to return south.

She had barely aged at all, having lived these eighteen years in luxury in the palace. His face was scarred by hardship and his travels across China looking for her, so much so that she had not recognized him. And now they were reunited, but under such dangerous circumstances that it did not seem real.

Ironheart made no reply, but walked over to the table and pulled open a drawer. There they were: two blue cotton shirts, just like the ones he used to wear. "You shouldn't have wasted your energy sewing them. You were pregnant," he said, lifting one up to examine it.

Charity Bao ran to him and tugged at his sleeve. There it was: the scar! For eighteen years she had thought him dead, and here he was, her husband, standing before her, like a spirit reincarnated. She fell into his arms and clutched him tightly. "Quickly, you must take me with you. I will show you how to get out, no one will see us. I am not afraid."

Ironheart held his wife in his arms and tears cleaned his cheeks. "Afraid? Why would you be afraid of me?" he said.

"Even if you are a ghost, I will never leave your arms again," she managed to say through her heavy sobs. "But how? All these years, you were still alive? Where were you?"

Ironheart was about to reply when they heard Wanyan Kang's voice from outside the window, startling them both. "Mother! Are you crying? Who are you talking to?"

"No one, it's nothing!" Charity called back. "I was sleeping."

But Wanyan Kang had heard the sound of a man's voice coming from inside the room. He walked round to the door and knocked gently. "Mother, I want to talk to you."

"Tomorrow, my boy," she replied. "We can talk tomorrow. I'm very tired and I want to go back to sleep."

His suspicions only increased. "I will be quick and then I'll go."

Ironheart Yang moved toward the window he had come through and pushed at the wooden shutter, but he could not open it. It had been locked from the outside! Charity continued talking to her son outside the door as she scoured the room for somewhere for her husband to hide. She pointed at a cupboard, but when Ironheart opened the door, he found tucked inside it none other than Guo Jing.

Charity yelped.

Concerned for his mother's safety, Wanyan Kang began bashing at the door with his shoulder. Guo Jing grabbed Ironheart and tugged him in, only just managing to pull the door shut as the iron bolt creaked and the door burst open.

Wanyan Kang rushed in to find his mother crouched in the middle of the room, her pale cheeks wet with tears. "Mother, what's the matter? What's happened?"

Charity paused and looked up at her son, trying to steady herself. "Nothing, son. I am just feeling a bit unwell."

"Please, Mother," he said, coming to her side. "I promise I won't do anything like that ever again. I know I have been a bad son to make you worry so."

"Don't worry, child. I'm just a little tired. I think I will go to bed; I need to sleep."

But Wanyan Kang could detect a slight quiver in her voice. "No one has been in here, have they?"

"What do you mean?"

"Two bandits entered the palace tonight."

"Is that so? You should really be going to bed yourself. Let the servants deal with it. It's not for you to worry about."

"Yes, Mother, I'm sure the guards have taken care of it, incompetent as they are. You must get some rest."

But just as he was about to leave, he spotted a piece of clothing sticking out from under the cupboard door. His suspicions were alerted again, but instead of saying anything, he went to the table, poured himself some tea and sat down. He sipped at the tea, contemplating the scene. Perhaps his mother was unaware that someone was hiding in the cupboard?

After a few more sips, he got to his feet and sauntered over to where the spear had been fastened to the wall. "Mother, what did you think of my spear technique today?"

"I've told you before, I don't like you bullying people like that," Charity chastised him.

"Bullying? It was a competition, we were fighting fair and square." Wanyan Kang's tone was a little aggrieved. He reached for the spear and traced a Rising Phoenix Soaring Dragon through the air, the red tassel dancing behind him, until the point thrust forward, straight at the cupboard. Charity fainted, fully aware that Ironheart Yang and Guo Jing were in grave danger in their shared hiding place.

So she knew! He leaned the spear against the wall and went to pick up his mother, his eyes fixed on the cupboard door all the while.

Charity was only unconscious for a few seconds. Her eyes opened and searched immediately for the cupboard; the door was still intact. Her body flopped in relief. The events of the last hour or so had drained her to the point of collapse.

"Mother, am I not your son?" Wanyan Kang demanded.

"Of course, my dearest. Why would you ask?"

"Then why do you keep so many secrets?"

Charity knew she should tell him about the day's events and let him be reunited with his real father. But this would also mean he would lose his mother, as she had not been loyal and chaste as widows were supposed to be. She had betrayed her husband by living with a Jin prince and lying to his son about who his real father was. She was not destined to be reunited with Ironheart Yang after all. Tears cascaded down her cheeks.

Wanyan Kang was unsure what to make of his mother's behavior. He waited for her to speak.

"You must take a seat and listen to me."

Wanyan Kang sat his mother down and took a seat beside the spear. But he did not take his eyes off the cupboard.

"Do you see those characters written on the spear?" she said.

"I asked you about them when I was a boy, but you wouldn't tell me what they meant. *Ironheart Yang,*" he read aloud.

"Now you shall know."

Ironheart could hear every word from where he was crouching in the darkness. But Charity was used to life in a Jin palace; how could she possibly return to him and live in a dirty hut? Go from Prince's Consort to farmer's wife again? Could she be about to reveal his identity? His son might kill him.

He listened intently as she began.

"This spear comes from Ox Village, a small hamlet on the outskirts of the Song capital, Lin'an. I sent some men many *li* to fetch it for me. The plow, the table, lamp, bed, and cupboard," she said, pointing around the room, "all of it came from Ox Village."

"I've never understood your affection for these dingy farmhouse furnishings. You could have the finest comforts money can buy, but you won't take them!"

"To you they are dingy, but to me this is the most beautifully decorated room I could hope for. I pity you sometimes, my son, that you have never lived with your real mother and father in a place just as dingy as this."

Ironheart Yang could feel tears bubbling up inside him as he listened.

But Wanyan Kang's response was laughter. "Ma, you really are getting stranger and stranger. Why would Pa agree to live in a place like this?"

"It is a shame indeed that he has not had the chance. He has spent the last eighteen years wandering the rivers and lakes of the south. A room such as this would have been more than enough for him."

"Mother, what are you saying?" There was a tremor in his voice now.

"What do you think I'm saying? Do you know who your real father is?" Charity's tone was sharper than she had intended.

"My father is the Sixth Prince of Zhao, Wanyan Honglie. Mother, why are you asking me these questions?"

Charity rose to her feet and took the spear in her hands. She cradled it to her bosom, and with the tears once again in full flow, she turned to her son. "My child, it is not your fault. I should have told you long ago. This spear . . . it belongs to your father. Your real father." She traced her fingers along the characters carved into the shaft of the spear. "Ironheart Yang."

"Nonsense! Stop it, Ma! You've gone mad!" The young Prince's body was shaking violently. "I shall call for the doctor."

"Nonsense is it? Son, you are no Jin prince, you are Chinese. Your real name is Yang Kang."

"I will ask my father!" He turned to leave the room.

"He's here," Charity cried. "Your father is here." She opened the cupboard door, reached for her husband's hand and pulled him out of the darkness and into the room.

"You!" Wanyan Kang grabbed the spear and aimed it at Ironheart's throat.

"But he's your father, don't you understand?" Charity ran toward her husband and then fell to the floor.

Wanyan Kang froze, lurched a few steps and pulled the spear back. She was covered in blood. Had he killed his own mother? He stood watching, helpless.

Ironheart Yang scooped his wife into his arms and ran for the door.

"Put her down!" the young Prince cried out, launching into a Wild Goose Leaves the Flock, thrusting his spear at Ironheart's back.

Ironheart heard the rush of air and reached back, seizing the spear five inches from the tip with his left hand. His Yang Family Spear technique was unrivaled. He thrust backward in a Returning Horse, a move unique to the Yang family. Usually he would have spun round

and grabbed with his right too, but he was still holding Charity in his arms. "This is a move we Yang men teach our sons, but your *shifu* won't have taught it to you."

The force pushing from both ends snapped the old spear in half.

"He's your own flesh and blood! Your father!" Guo Jing, who could bear to watch no longer, rushed forward. "Why do you disrespect him in this manner?"

The Prince hesitated.

Ironheart Yang dropped his end of the spear, and holding his beloved wife tight to his chest, stumbled out of the room. Following her directions, he supported her as they ran through the complex to where Mercy was waiting outside the palace walls. She helped them climb down the other side, and together they fled.

APPENDIX I

A NOTE ON THE USE OF THE TERMS "MARTIAL ARTS," "KUNG FU" ETC.

"MARTIAL ARTS," AS A TERM IN ENGLISH, WAS FIRST USED TO describe the combat systems of Europe during the Renaissance, "martial" being derived from the Roman god of war, Mars. Nowadays, the phrase in English instantly evokes the combat practices of east Asia, which according to legend are said to have their origins in the Xia Dynasty, over four thousand years ago. Some contend that Chinese martial arts were not military in origin or purpose, but the Chinese word *wushu* suggests that they were, as it literally means "military" or "martial" and "art" or "skill," and has been in common use for nearly two millennia. Over the course of these two thousand or so years, the Chinese martial arts have incorporated influences from Indian combat styles and have in turn spread out all over eastern Asia, developing into the distinctive fighting traditions that can be found across Japan, Korea, etc.

The Chinese word *gong fu,* of which "kung fu" is a Romanization, actually refers to any practice or achievement that takes time and dedicated study. This could be playing the violin just as much as learning how to perform a Lazy Donkey Roll.

There are hundreds of styles of Chinese combat, all with their own distinctive moves, ideas, and names. Categorization of these styles can be geographical—northern versus southern, for example, or even down to the province or town. In this volume, if you remember, Jade Han's Yue Sword technique is identified as local to Jiaxing, where many centuries previously the two kingdoms of Wu and Yue had fought a bitter war. Fighting styles are often also divided into either "external" (*waigong*) or "internal" (*neigong*) forms, that is, concentrating on physiological technique or on mental strength and the movement of *qi* around the body through breathing or other meditative practices. In reality, however, this distinction is often blurred and styles frequently contain elements of both.

Chinese martial arts have a strong connection to the various ancient philosophies and religions of the region, primarily through the idea of self-cultivation. In the popular mind in both the east and west, the most famous example would be the "kung fu monks" of the Shaolin temple in Henan Province, established in the late fifth century. The temple's first preacher was an Indian monk by the name of Buddhabhadra, and along with another fellow Indian monk, Bodhidharma, and their first Chinese disciples, he was said to have given birth to a new Buddhism that, by the Tang dynasty (A.D. 618–907), would develop into Zen. Given its emphasis on the breath and the mind, the links to martial arts fighting is not at once obvious. But, as monasteries and temples both Buddhist and Taoist owned land and other wealth, they came frequently under attack, which has led some historians to postulate that monks practiced martial arts as a form of self-defense.

That there is a deep relationship between Zen, Taoism, and Chinese martial arts is undeniable, and the emphasis on discipline and lifelong study in the pursuit of enlightenment was incorporated into the latter. Cultivating oneself through the martial arts is less about prevailing against an enemy and more about finessing movements and turning attention to the workings of the body as well as the heart-mind. Fighting is an actualization of these philosophies; the physical, a manifestation of the spiritual.

The association between these ancient Chinese philosophies and the martial arts is all the more pronounced in fiction and film, where history and legend, fact and make-believe intertwine in a cocktail of breathtaking set pieces performed by strange and wonderful men and women in robes, fighting for righteousness and the moral code of the *jianghu*. This code reinforces the idea that fighting, in the futherance of good and noble ends, could coexist with the core Buddhist teaching of pacifism and Taoism's "non-doing," *wu wei*.

Many fight scenes in the novel focus around characters trying to strike or press on their opponent's "vital points," also translated here as acupressure points or pressure points. This is built on the theory of the meridian system found in traditional Chinese and Indian medicines, which maps the flow of life-energy, *qi* in Chinese, around the body. Pressing or striking certain spots on the body is thought to create or relieve pain, and in the case of martial arts fiction, even kill. Scientific research into the theory has proved inconclusive, but certainly this kind of "Death Touch" fighting has become a significant feature of martial arts literature and film, especially in the twentieth century.

Chinese martial arts literature has been around almost as long as the combat practices themselves. The earliest examples date from around 200 B.C., and by the Tang dynasty they had become increasingly popular, and they were developed into something approaching the contemporary novel form by the Ming (A.D. 1368–1644). Jin Yong's stories first appeared in serial form in newspapers in late 1950s Hong Kong and were key to revitalizing the genre in the second half of the twentieth century. To this day, Jin Yong remains the most widely read contemporary author writing in Chinese.

THE "CONDOR CONTROVERSY"

A WORD ON THE TITLE OF THE SERIES: *Legends of the Condor Heroes.* The character in the original Chinese title, "diao" 雕, is usually translated as "eagle." The word eagle does not refer to a natural group but to any bird of prey capable of hunting large vertebrates. However, the birds described in this volume are in fact much larger than the species of eagle found in Asia, and some are white in color. As we will discover in future volumes in the series, these are fantastical creatures that practice martial arts and are even capable of teaching humans their skills. The Chinese character used, "diao," provides no more specific information beyond the genus, *Aquila,* true eagles. Therefore, there is much to merit "eagle" as a translation.

Since the novel's first publication, however, the title has been translated into English many different ways. The one that has gained traction in various forums, on YouTube and online discussion sites, translates the bird as "condor." The earliest concrete example I could find was the 1983 Hong Kong T.V.B. adaptation for television, and all the television adaptations since seem to have adopted this translation. Condors are native to the Americas, not to Asia. They are considerably larger than all the Asian species of eagle, but still appear to be smaller than the mythical birds in *Legends of the Condor Heroes*. I decided to continue with "condor" as a translation for the simple fact that many English-speaking fans already know the series by this name, and as the bird is fictional and clearly described in fantastical terms, there is no scientifically accurate translation to be found in any meaningful sense. This is fiction, after all. And Jin Yong's work already belongs to a collective imagination, even in English. I want my translation to interact with these existing fans and the considerable time and passion that they have already invested in the series under this title, as well as to attract new readers.

APPENDIX III

NOTES ON THE TEXT

PAGE NUMBERS DENOTE THE FIRST TIME THESE CONCEPTS OR names are mentioned in the book.

P. 2   WOLF-FANG CLUB

A weapon that consists of a long wooden pole of varying lengths with one end covered in sharp spikes, reminiscent of the sixteenth-century English weapon known as the holy water sprinkler. The other end can be fitted with an additional point.

P. 9   STEEL TAOIST EIGHT TRIGRAM DISK

Qu San's secret weapon, not otherwise in common use in martial arts fighting or in battle.

P. 10   *THE MARSHES OF MOUNT LIANG,* ATTRIBUTED TO SHU NAI'AN

Also known in English as *Water Margin* and *Outlaws of the Marsh* among other titles, *The Marshes of Mount Liang* is considered one of the four great classical Chinese novels. Published in the sixteenth century during the Ming dynasty and written in the vernacular, the story is based on a real band of outlaws who fought against the Song until the gang's surrender in A.D. 1121, when they started fighting with the Song against foreign invasion.

P. 10 GENERAL YUE FEI

General Yue Fei is one of China's most beloved patriots and has appeared frequently in Chinese novels, poems, and films throughout the centuries since his death in 1142. General Yue fought to regain the north after the Song capital in Kaifeng was sacked by the Jurchen Jin Empire and the Emperor Qinzong was captured, but he met a tragic end when he was imprisoned and later executed by the Song government itself when the new emperor realized General Yue's success would likely dethrone him. Yue Fei's name has become synonymous in China with righteous loyalty and he was quickly rehabilitated only some twenty years after his death.

P. 18 QIU CHUJI

A real historical figure and disciple of Wang Chogyang's Taoist Quanzhen Sect. Jin Yong has taken creative license to deviate somewhat from the historical record, including making him only around thirty years old at the start of this book, when in fact he would have been fifty-seven in the year 1205.

P. 18 QUANZHEN SECT

The Quanzhen School is a branch of Taoism that was founded by Wang Chogyang under the rule of the Jin. According to the school's own legend, Wang met two immortals in the summer of A.D. 1159, who trained him in secret immortality rituals. Upon a second meeting, he was given a set of five instructions which led him to set up residence in a grave in the Zhongnan Mountains and dedicate himself to his training for three years. After seven years on the mountain, Wang met the first of his seven disciples. Each established their own branch, ensuring the school's thinking would survive to this day.

P. 23 JINGKANG INCIDENT

In the year 1127, the Jurchen were on the march southward and sacked the Song capital of Kaifeng. During the raid, they captured the Song emperor, Qinzong, along with his father, Emperor Huizong, and several of the imperial family, effectively bringing the period of the Northern Song to an end. Having lost large parts of the Chinese hinterland, what was left of the Chinese Empire fled south and settled in Lin'an, but the psychological damage caused by the incident was to send ripples throughout the centuries and still looms large in the Chinese cultural mind.

It should be noted here that references to years in the western Dionysian system are merely for the convenience of the reader. In Chinese tradition, years were counted according to the lunar calendar from when an emperor declared a new "era name." The name was designed to act like a motto or statement of intent for the emperor who chose it. Before the Ming and Qing dynasties, emperors often declared several different era names over the course of their time in power. The Jingkang incident is therefore named after the particular era name in which the event occurred, the meaning being "Serenity and Vitality," reflecting a desire for peace and prosperity in such a tumultuous time politically.

P. 41 THE NINE SPRINGS OF THE UNDERWORLD

This is one of the many names given to the Chinese concept of the realm of the dead, or "hell." It draws influence from the Buddhist *nakara,* but also folk ideas about the afterlife, and it serves as a kind of purgatory before reincarnation. The significance of the number nine in Chinese is complex, and it is often associated with the emperor and imperial system of government. Hell was thought to be presided over by a system of courts, ten in number, as laid out by the Jade Emperor, the first god in Chinese culture. More importantly, the number nine also sounds like the character for "lasting" or "abiding" and therefore likely means "eternity."

P. 57 *SYCEE* INGOT

The *sycee* was a shaped gold or silver ingot used as currency over the course of two millennia. Made by individual silversmiths, the designs and sizes varied and their value was determined by specialized money handlers.

P. 78 GE HONG'S IMMORTALITY PILLS

Ge Hong (A.D. 238–343) was a philosopher who dedicated his life to the search for immortality through alchemy.

P. 81 IMMORTAL CLOUD SECT AND SOUTHERN SHAOLIN CONTROVERSY

The Immortal Cloud Sect in *Legends of the Condor Heroes* is most definitely a Jin Yong invention, but it does appear to have at least a loose imaginative connection to the so-called southern Shaolin temple, built during the Tang dynasty in Fujian Province. The connection between the Shaolin temple in Henan and the southern Shaolin temple, long-since destroyed, is controversial. The current Abbot of Shaolin in Henan denies the legitimacy of the association and many believe it to be merely the stuff of folklore.

P. 89 POINTS OF THE WHEEL FROM THE I'CHING

The I'Ching, or *Book of Changes* as it is commonly translated, is one of the oldest Chinese classics and has its origins in the Western Zhou (1000–750 B.C.) as a divination text. Central to the text are the hexagrams, which are made up of two trigrams, that is, two sets of three lines, each either solid or broken. These are then arranged into the King Wen sequence and can also be laid out as a wheel. When done so, this wheel can operate a bit like a compass, the named points providing direction. In this sequence, Zhu Cong is calling out the names of hexagrams in order to give instruction to the blind Ke Zhen'e as to where he should throw his devilnuts. With sixty-four hexagrams in total, this system would provide very accurate guidance to within an angle of six degrees.

P. 102   JING KE OR NIE ZHENG

Jing Ke and Nie Zheng were ancient assassins who in the popular mind are known for their righteous self-sacrifice and loyalty because they carried out their work though it meant certain death for themselves. Nie Zheng was known for his filial piety, taking care of his mother until her death, before following through on his promise to assassinate the political enemy of his patron and kill himself in turn. Their stories were collected by the ancient historian Sima Qian in his *Biographies of the Assassins.*

P. 107   *GER*

Literally "home" in Mongolian, *ger* also refers to the characteristically round, portable tents covered in felts and animal skins that housed nomads across the steppes of Central Asia. More commonly known in English by the Turkic name "yurt," a reference to the round imprint left in the grass when the tent is moved.

P. 109   BANNER OF WHITE HORSEHAIR

In this instance, "banner" does not refer to a flag made from cloth but rather a long pole with a crown of horse hair hanging from its top. The white banner was used to announce peace, the black in battle to declare war. Later, the banners were to become administrative and military divisions under the Manchu Qing dynasty.

P. 112   TAYICHI'UD

The Tayichi'ud were rivals of the Naiman and described as bitter enemies of Genghis Khan in *The Secret History of the Mongols,* a text written for the royal household. There are people who bear the clan name to this day in Mongolia, Inner Mongolia, and the Republic of Kalmykia.

P. 127 *KOUMISS*

Koumiss is a mildly alcoholic fermented drink traditional to the Central Asian steppes, made from sheep's milk.

P. 128 WHISTLING ARROW

Whistling arrows have a hollow bulbous head which creates a shrill sound when the arrow is fired. They were primarily used to relay messages and warnings in battle.

P. 131 THE NAIMAN

The Naiman were a tribe from western Mongolia. It is claimed that many Naiman were Nestorian Christians descended from the biblical Magi, but there is no archaeological evidence to support the idea that they were in fact Christian in this period. The Naiman later converted to Buddhism and Islam. Their khanate was destroyed by the Mongols and the people fled and spread across the Mongol Empire.

P. 185 TOMB-SWEEPING DAY

Tomb-Sweeping Day is an annual festival that falls on the fifteenth day of the spring equinox. Families take this day to remember their ancestors and recently deceased loved ones, whom they honor by cleaning their graves and praying to them.

P. 211 ULAAN

Mongolian for "red."

P. 256 LET ME DIE WITHOUT BLEEDING

This story, and specifically Jamuka's request, comes from *The Secret History of the Mongols,* the oldest known literary work in Mongolian, written after Genghis Khan's death in 1227. The oldest surviving examples of the text are all transcribed into Chinese, however, and date from the fourteenth century as part of a history of the Mongol Yuan dynasty.

P. 262 KINGDOM OF FERGANA

Located in the Fergana Valley of modern-day eastern Uzbekistan, this ancient kingdom is thought to have had contact with the city of Alexandria Eschate, founded by Alexander the Great in 329 B.C. in the Jaxartes Valley. Greek statues have been found in the region. Chinese sources identify the kingdom as Indian or perhaps Greek in origin, and record that contact was made by a Chinese envoy in 128 B.C. This is the story given in this book.

P. 275 MY GIVEN NAME IS LOTUS

Lotus Huang is known to many fans by the pinyin transliteration of her name, Huang Rong. I wanted to translate her name as Lotus, however, as at this point in the story we the readers are let in on a secret that Guo Jing is not party to. As soon as we see her name written down, we know at once this "beggar boy" is, in fact, a girl—the character for "lotus," "rong" 蓉, is far too girly to be used for a boy's name. But due to the fact that there are several Chinese characters that could be pronounced the same way or similar, Guo Jing doesn't pick up on this. We know that Guo Jing is barely literate in Chinese, so he can be forgiven for his mistake. He is an honest young man, but clearly not the most perceptive, and this moment in the novel is an important way in which Jin Yong develops Guo Jing's character, while letting Chinese readers in on the joke. If I had kept Lotus's name in the pinyin, we English readers would be left feeling just as dim as poor Guo Jing.

P. 280 ZHONGDU

The Jin capital is referred to by two names in this book. Zhongdu was the new name given by the Jurchen when they seized the old Chinese city of Yanjing and made it the center of their expanding Empire. The Chinese patriots in the book, such as Wang Chuyi, still call the city Yanjing, as an act of symbolic resistance or perhaps out of habit. The city first became an imperial capital in the State of Yan during the Zhou, established during the eleventh century B.C., and was later conquered by the first united Chinese Empire, the Qin, in 222 B.C. The name "China" comes from this first "united" Qin Empire. Yanjing and its environs was to continue to be an important sight of imperial power when the Mongols razed the city and built the capital of their Yuan Dynasty nearby. Yanjing was later to become Beijing, China's current capital.

P. 281   MEANING OF MU YI'S NAME

While the "yi" in Mu Yi's name means "change," there is in fact another layer to the word game here. The Chinese character for the surname Yang is 楊, which itself is composed of two "radicals"—that is, small components that themselves have meaning. These two radicals are "mu" 木, meaning "tree" and the very same "yi" 易, meaning "change." Mu Yi's new surname "mu" 穆 is therefore a homonym of the first radical, tree.

P. 299   BEGGAR CLAN

The Beggar Clan or Beggars' Sect is an entirely fictional martial arts sect that appears in the fiction of several writers, Jin Yong among them, and in a number of films. This patriotic band of martial artists was established during the Han dynasty (206 B.C.–A.D. 220) and survived into the Mongol Yuan dynasty.

P. 331   HIS EXCELLENCY MR. XIN

Xin Qiji led his first military campaign against the Jurchen at the age of twenty-two, and he later went on to capture notorious traitor Zhang Anguo. In addition to his military exploits, Xin Qiji was known as one of the period's best poets. Great Chinese statesmen were often cultivated in other arts such as literature, music, and calligraphy, as befitted their status as intellectuals.

This song is called "Plum Blossom," written to the tune of "Auspicious Immortal Crane." This type of poetry was written to specific rules of prosody, and was always arranged as a tune. The music itself has long since been lost. Although such poetry was written over many centuries, the Song dynasty is synonymous with the genre, as poets found it particularly suited to expressing their sorrow over the crumbling of the Chinese Empire and the tragic and unsettling effects of war.

P. 342 EMEI NEEDLES

Emei Needles are a traditional weapon in the Chinese martial arts that originated on Mount Emei and consist of two metal rods with points, attached to a ring that is worn on the middle finger. They are designed to confuse an adversary so that the attacker can get close enough to punch.

P. 347 VICTORY WITHOUT PARALLEL

Wangyan Honglie is referring to the Jingkang incident of 1127. (See note to p. 23, above.)

P. 349 THE TUNES

These song titles are all examples of standard tunes to which poets wrote lyrics. As noted above in the entry for Xin Qiji on p. 331, the music has long since been lost, but the underlying rhyming scheme and rhythm can be re-created from reading examples of lyrics written to the same tune. Yue Fei's most famous lyric poem, written to the tune of "River Runs Red," was supposedly composed when his military campaigns against the Jurchen were halted by the Song government. Many modern literary historians dispute the fact that it actually came from Yue's brush, however, believing instead that it was written some three hundred years later.

JIN YONG (pen name of Louis Cha) is a true phenomenon in the Chinese-speaking world. Born in Mainland China, he has spent most of his life writing novels and editing newspapers in Hong Kong. His enormously popular martial arts novels, written between the late 1950s and 1972, have become modern classics and remain a must-read for young readers looking for danger and adventure. They have also inspired countless TV and video game adaptions.

Estimated sales of his books worldwide stand at 300 million, and if bootleg copies are taken into consideration, that figure rises to a staggering one billion. International recognition has come in the form of an O.B.E. in 1981, a Chevalier de la Légion d'Honneur (1992), a Chevalier de la Légion d'Honneur (2004), an honorary fellowship at St. Antony's College, Oxford, and honorary doctorates from Hong Kong University and Cambridge University, among others. Jin Yong died on Oct. 30, 2018, at age ninety-four.

ANNA HOLMWOOD translates from Chinese and Swedish into English. She was awarded one of the first British Center for Literary Translation mentorship awards in 2010 and has since translated novels and short stories for publication and samples for agents and rights sellers. In 2011 she co-founded the Emerging Translators' Network to support early career translators, and served on the UK Translators Association committee in 2012. Anna was editor-in-chief for Books from Taiwan 2014–2015, and has previously worked as a literary agent, representing some of China's top writing talent. She is now a producer alongside her translation work.

THE NEXT THREE VOLUMES OF
LEGENDS OF THE CONDOR HEROES

VOLUME II: A BOND UNDONE

Yang Kang denies his Chinese roots, while Guo Jing grapples with the ramifications of breaking his betrothal to the daughter of Genghis Khan in order to pursue his love for Lotus Huang.

VOLUME III: A SNAKE LIES WAITING

Guo Jing is faced with the evil plotting of Venom of the West Viper Ouyang, who is determined to become the most powerful Master of the *wulin* and win Lotus Huang for his nephew Gallant Ouyang. The full extent of Yang Kang's treachery is also revealed.

VOLUME IV: A HEART DIVIDED

Guo Jing's love for Lotus Huang is tested when he becomes convinced that her father has murdered someone dear to him. Upon his return to Mongolia, he discovers Genghis Khan wants to enlist him to help conquer the Chinese. Guo Jing must prove his loyalty to the country of his birth if he is to be worthy of bearing the name of his patriot father, Skyfury Guo.